Author's photo: Vanessa Correira/Menina and May

Ina Brink was born on September 3, 1972 in Kimberley, South Africa.

She graduated from La Rochelle Girls High school 1990 and went on to study clothing design and production. She served for four years in the Police Force.

She has been married for 25 years and has three daughters. She also ran a small dressmaking business from home for nine years and has been actively writing for 14 years.

Her hobbies include painting and dressmaking.

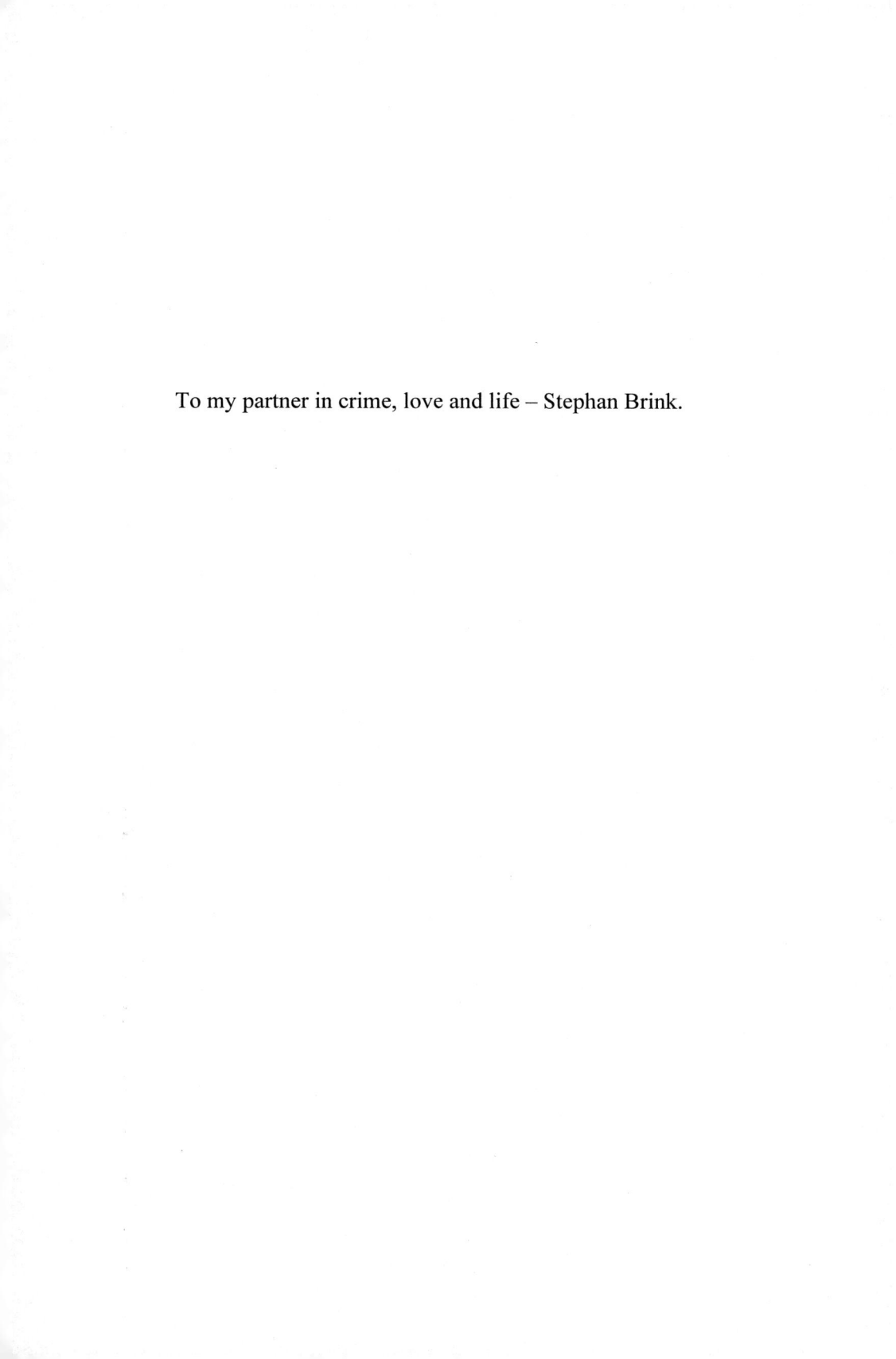

To my partner in crime, love and life – Stephan Brink.

Ina Brink

Defeated by Justice

AUSTIN MACAULEY PUBLISHERS™
LONDON * CAMBRIDGE * NEW YORK * SHARJAH

Copyright © Ina Brink 2022

The right of Ina Brink to be identified as author of this work has been asserted by the author in accordance with section 77 and 78 of the Copyright, Designs and Patents Act 1988.

All rights reserved. No part of this publication may be reproduced, stored in a retrieval system, or transmitted in any form or by any means, electronic, mechanical, photocopying, recording, or otherwise, without the prior permission of the publishers.

Any person who commits any unauthorised act in relation to this publication may be liable to criminal prosecution and civil claims for damages.

This is a work of fiction. Names, characters, businesses, places, events, locales, and incidents are either the products of the author's imagination or used in a fictitious manner. Any resemblance to actual persons, living or dead, or actual events is purely coincidental.

A CIP catalogue record for this title is available from the British Library.

ISBN 9781398447561 (Paperback)
ISBN 9781398447578 (ePub e-book)

www.austinmacauley.com

First Published 2022
Austin Macauley Publishers Ltd®
1 Canada Square
Canary Wharf
London
E14 5AA

Chapter 1

Nicole's heart started racing again as she heard her name sounding in her ears: "Nicole Burger?" It had taken her more than an hour, since she had been waiting for her name to be called out, to calm the wild beating of her heart in her chest. It frustrated her immensely that she did not have control over her body and as she needed to feel in control at all times, her body's weakness frustrated her. At this point in time, there was a lot she was unable to control in her life, but she was determined to change this, hence the decision that placed her here today.

This was the first step in regaining control. Over the last few days, her world as she knew it had been disintegrating at a dizzying speed and she could hardly keep up with the daily discoveries she had to deal with. Everything that she knew and cherished as a child seemed to have been a distortion of the truth and now that she had finally finished school, it felt as if her parents regarded their duty towards her as something that had come to an end. Even if this was not the case, it sure as hell felt like it. They did not even try to spare her feelings as they started arranging their new separate lives. Their marriage of almost twenty-five years had fallen apart long before this, but in order to give Nicole, their only daughter, the best chance to develop into a well-balanced young individual, they stuck to their vows until she had finished her final exams.

Now, her parents had too much to deal with and everything they had bottled up for so long came bursting out. The trauma of them admitting defeat and being able to let their true feelings show, meant that it came out unedited and emotionally raw, something Nicole was not used to. Up until this point, her life had been an illusion of harmonious order, planned to the finest detail by two parents who believed that it was their duty to provide her with a safe and stable environment for her to develop in.

They never argued or discussed politics, finances or adult life in front of her. They wanted to protect her from unnecessary worry. Although they were right in doing so when she was a young girl, they failed to gradually let her experience the reality of life as she became ready to do so. This made the discovery that they had a failing marriage and that they were actually living a lie, that more confusing for Nicole.

Nicole had to discover that both her parents had very different ideals of how they wanted to live their lives, as opposed to what she had been led to believe. Only two weeks after being told that they were divorcing, her father had packed his belongings and moved to another province and she was left in a house with her mother, who was distant and interested only in chasing the life she had missed out on while she was trapped in the marriage.

Nicole felt that she was to blame for their years of obvious torment and she felt disillusioned and confused as to what to make of the values and morals her parents had tried to instil in her over the years. At a time when she was supposed to think of what career path she would follow and which tertiary institution to join to succeed in her goal, she was now faced with no certain future at all. Her parents were so caught up in their own pain that they completely lost track of her and since they were both fighting for the best financial gain from the divorce, there was no mention of her being able to study.

For the first time in her life, she had to make decisions regarding her future without guidance. She felt desperate; she had no siblings to share the load of her guilt and no close relatives that offered their support. It seemed as if the few loving relatives that she had were too scared to come too close to them. It felt as if they feared that they might catch whatever madness came over the Burger household.

Desperate people do desperate things and when her best friend announced that she had decided to join the police force, it all suddenly made sense. The more Jacqueline explained her reasoning for doing so, the more Nicole became convinced that it was the answer she was waiting for. If she joined the Force, it would mean financial security, even while she was in training. She would have medical aid, pension, a place to board and a whole new family of police members that fought an honourable cause of protecting and serving the public. As a bonus, she could also stay in contact with her closest friend.

Nicole thought that she would be able to let her disappointments take a backseat by joining and be forced to rather concentrate on serving her community in a place of order and discipline, where they had very clear guidelines as to how their members were to act and where she hoped to find unconditional support. Or so she believed.

Nicole's parents were relieved when she announced her decision. It took care of a pressing problem with which they could not deal at this stage. Where they would normally not have encouraged her to make such a choice, they now reasoned that their daughter would at least be taken care of while they were trying to sort out their own mess and it would mean that they would not have to deal with any further financial strain.

Nicole's mother even offered to accompany her to the recruitment office, but Nicole refused. She knew that the mother she knew before the news of the divorce became known would never have wanted this for her daughter and the betrayal she felt by her mother settling for second best, for her own selfish reasons, made her doubt her mother's authority even more. This was something she was going to do on her own, so that she could be responsible for her own actions. She would never again let anyone determine her future. She felt determined to do this alone, but she was frightened by the prospect of facing her future alone though. She had never done anything remotely as brave in her life before.

Although she was a strong leader among her peers and confident of her academic and physical abilities, she had never been challenged in the real world and she had nothing to measure her abilities by. The only thing she knew was that, if Jacqueline, who was physically and mentally not as blessed as she was, could join the Force without any problems, she would surely be accepted as well.

"Nicole Burger!" The voice impatiently sounded in her ears again and she looked around as if she too was searching for this stubborn soul who would not answer. Only when she realised that she was the only female in the room and everyone was looking directly at her, did she come to her feet.

"I'm sorry," she said and stuck her hand out, in the most confident manner her body would let her, to greet the man that had been calling her name.

"I am Nicole Burger." Nicole could see how the older man's expression relaxed as she flashed her beautifully arranged teeth at him.

"Come," he invited, "we do not have all day," and as she followed him into his office, she could see that, although he sounded stern, his eyes smiled at her. Nicole knew, in that moment of his weakness, that he would become her ally in being chosen out of the thousands of applicants to join the police force that year. Nicole was not your typical applicant. Unlike some of the men that applied, women seldom joined the Force to make a career out of it when they possessed the level of intelligence that Nicole had; the few that did, usually did so as graduates to join the police as officers in the field of psychology, forensics or other specialised fields. Although there were beautiful girls in the Force, Nicole was blessed with the genes of an Amazon.

Nicole was almost six feet tall, she had long auburn hair with a natural curl and her skin was flawlessly creamy. She had a natural blush to her cheeks that most women could only accomplish by applying blusher, which in turn enhanced the intensity of her startling emerald green eyes. Nicole's lips were full and plump and she could see how the man seated opposite her stared at her mouth while she spoke. She meticulously planned her outfit for the day, as she knew that the simplest of garments could make her stand out even more.

She knew that she was not going to be able to hide her obvious beauty, but she wanted to be taken seriously and therefore she chose to wear an understated, almost conservative floral skirt that she had borrowed from her mother's closet. She finished the outfit off with a cream-coloured silk blouse, as it was the only formal piece of clothing that she could find that would match the skirt. In her mind, she looked prim and proper and definitely decent enough to help keep law and order in a very conservative country such as South Africa, which was still dwelling in the midst of Apartheid.

I have to make a good impression, she naively encouraged herself. In reality, the innocent eighteen-year-old girl in front of him had already charmed Lieutenant Visagie. Nicole was dressed appropriately for the interview, but she could just as well have walked in naked, as the sheerness of the material that she wore hugged her body in such a manner that it might as well not have been there. Not only was she so beautiful that he found it difficult to take his eyes off her, but she had the most pleasant and charming demeanour about her.

I must make a note of this one, he reminded himself, but it would, as with most men, be difficult for him to forget her in any event. It seldom happened that people did not like Nicole, except for the odd girls who felt jealous when their partners afforded her too much attention, but even then her likable personality confused and frustrated them. Although confident in the knowledge that she was exceptionally beautiful, she was by no means arrogant and although she had become accustomed to the power that it held over the opposite sex, she was still not mature enough to know how to deal with it or how to use it to its full extent.

"So why have you decided to join us?" the Lieutenant asked while he rearranged the applications in front of him in an attempt to avoid staring at her any further. The truth was that he had already made up his mind that, even if she was the most mentally and physically challenged person he knew, he was going to do all in his power to ensure her acceptance into the police force.

"I want to do something worthwhile with my life," she answered with a serious face in an attempt to convince him that she had given the matter a great deal of thought. Lieutenant Visagie gave a faint smile and then continued to ask her about her academic accomplishments, interests and her take on life in general, as he would normally do with all the other applicants.

Nicole found it easy to make conversation about most topics, as she had grown up mainly around adults and as a skilled conversationalist, she soon turned the conversation around to suit her. She cunningly managed to gather information about the Force, what to expect and what they were looking for in their members, in order to give her a better chance at being selected. She also got the man in front of her to give her a glimpse of who he was, without him even realising it.

She knew that from now on she was on her own and her survival instincts were kicking in. She saw every new person that she met as a possible ally on her journey. She needed to create a safety net and she was going to make sure that it consisted of people that she felt she could trust. She liked the Lieutenant and could sense that he was a decent person. The fact that he was working at the head office in Cape Town was a perk, because if she ever needed to have strings pulled in the future, he would be able to help her. They were busy for over an hour when the Lieutenant suddenly looked at his watch.

"Shit!" he said, alarmed and then apologised quickly for his language.

"You will have to excuse me, I did not realise what time it is," he explained.

Nicole realised that they had been chatting for too long and that the Lieutenant was not supposed to have kept her so long.

"The secretary will give you the necessary forms for your medical examination and she will explain to you what to do from there," he said gently, as if he was an old friend that wanted to help her on her journey. When she reached the door, she gave him a knowing smile and took his hand while she looked him straight in the eye. "Thank you."

"It's been a pleasure, Nicole," he returned her smile.

Nicole felt relieved that her interview had gone so well. She knew that she had passed the first elimination phase, as in the hour that she had to wait before she was called, she had witnessed many disappointed faces disappearing down the hallway, without an invitation to a medical examination. She took a seat, as the secretary ordered her to do and wondered how such a young girl was able to work as a secretary.

She cannot be much older than me? she thought.

The girl looked as if she took her work very seriously. She hardly smiled and frowned as she worked through the paperwork in front of her. Nicole was fascinated. She could not understand how people could take worldly tasks so seriously. She knew that, in order for the world to function properly, it was imperative for people to complete certain tasks, but she failed to see why people took it all so seriously. In her mind, you could take care of what needed to be done and still enjoy life around it as well.

Nicole could not resist her mischievous nature: "How old are you?"

The girl looked up, clearly confused by the question.

"I said how old are you?" Nicole repeated her question, as if the girl had not heard her, although she knew that the girl had heard her clearly the first time.

"I am eighteen," she answered before she could stop herself and she looked surprised by her compliance. Nicole smiled at her; her suspicions were right, as was usually the case.

"So am I. My name is—" she tried to make small talk, but she was rudely interrupted.

"Nicole Burger, yes I know," the girl said seriously as she looked down at Nicole's file.

"Are you a student?" Nicole persisted.

"Yes," the girl gave in. The two started chatting about the Police College and about when they would be attending, if Nicole was selected.

"You will only be going to the Police College at the end of the year, as all applicants that are selected now will start in September. I will be going in June," the girl informed her.

"That's too bad," Nicole said, honestly disappointed that she would have to face the dreaded college on her own, as Jacqueline was also going to the college in June.

"Listen, I really have to get through this," the girl said, and she picked the stack of files up to show Nicole.

"Take these forms and go to the big white building across the street. There you hand in your forms at the desk on the first floor. Doctor Manning will give you your medical examination. I will let them know that you are coming and maybe you will not have to wait that long," the girl offered as she handed Nicole the necessary forms.

"Thank you. What's the examination like?" Nicole wondered out aloud.

"Don't worry, it's no worse than your boyfriend's fumbling," and she burst out laughing.

"Oh, so now you're being funny?" Nicole teased back, and they shared the laughter of newfound friendship. Nicole took the forms from the secretary and headed down the hallway to the lift.

That wasn't so bad, she thought to herself. *I can do this.*

Nicole walked out of the building and there, in front of her, was an impressive white five-level building. Nicole's body was still on an adrenaline rush from the interview and her hands were shaking a little. As she was not comfortable with undressing in front of strangers, the medical examination was a challenge in itself, so she braced herself before she took the first step in the direction of the building.

Chapter 2

As if the first few hours of the morning were not strenuous enough, Nicole's heartrate quickened again.

Will you stop already? she scolded herself. This always happened; the willpower of her logical brain was once again overpowered by the reaction of her body when faced with unknown territory.

Can the two of you work together? she appealed to her senses, but she knew that no matter how hard she tried to convince her body that there was nothing to worry about, her pulse would continue to quicken and she realised that her palms were sweaty when she opened the door of the building.

Nicole found her way to the lift, which was crowded with young men on the same quest as she was. She noticed that they all had athletic physiques and that they were all neatly dressed. They made space for her, as if she was someone of importance. She had not noticed any other women in the recruitment office, except for the secretary and came to the conclusion that she was outnumbered.

This should have been a sign that the police force was not necessarily the right place for a young innocent woman, but instead she chose to see it as a challenge. She viewed it as an incentive that only the strongest women were able to get selected for the job. Especially now, she had to prove to herself that she was one of those strong women and she vowed that she would persist even if it meant pushing her body to breaking point. When the door of the lift opened, the men waited for her to exit and then they followed her through the glass doors that faced them.

A fat middle-aged woman placed a sandwich that she was busy devouring on a piece of paper in front of her and with her mouth still filled with the remains of a monstrous bite, ordered them all to take a seat. Nicole's body hardly touched the seat when she heard the woman calling her name.

"Nicole Burger?"

"Yes?" she answered quickly and she came to her feet.

"You will be first. Come, I don't have all day!" and she impatiently held a file with Nicole's name on it out for her to collect.

"Must I go in?" Nicole asked cautiously, not sure if she was only supposed to take the file and wait, or if she should take it and enter the only visible door in the room.

"No, the doctor will call you," the woman spat the words out. If she could just have entered immediately, Nicole would not have had time to fear the unknown embarrassment she was about to face, but now she had to patiently take a seat and await her fate.

It took a further ten minutes of watching how the young men in the room were called in one by one to collect their individual files and sent back to take a seat, before the stained door, of which the white paint had started to peal, opened.

"Nicole Burger?" the grey-haired man inquired.

"That's me," Nicole said in a chirpy voice in an attempt to lighten the mood in the room, but the seemingly grumpy old man did not even look up. The doctor did not even wait for her response; he only turned and disappeared into the hole he came from.

"At least someone had thought of me so I can get this over with," she encouraged herself as she remembered the secretary's words that she would let them know in advance that Nicole was coming.

The man stood with his back turned to Nicole while he looked at some papers on his desk. He did not remotely resemble the well-groomed doctors she had been accustomed to as a girl growing up in a privileged neighbourhood. This man was overweight, his hair was a mess and he hunched over as if he carried the world on his two broad shoulders. He wore a white overcoat, which made him look more like a lab assistant than a doctor and Nicole could imagine him doing experiments on his young unsuspecting victims.

"Put your file on the bed!" he ordered in a deep crackling voice, before clearing his throat. Nicole did as he asked.

"Undress, but you may keep your panties on," he said in the same smoker's voice as before and once again, he tried to clear his throat. Nicole felt stripped of all her dignity; for the first time in her life, she felt like a number and nothing else. The doctor kept fiddling with the papers in front of him. For a moment, Nicole contemplated fleeing the room, but her feet remained glued to the floor. She could not understand why she had to rid herself of her bra as well, but convinced herself that the doctor must have a good reason.

Nicole stripped to her panties as fast as she could, in the hope that it would set the pace for the rest of the examination. As if the doctor had eyes in the back of his head, he turned as soon as she let her bra fall onto her blouse, which she had already placed on the chair next to the examination bed. Now, for the first time, he lifted his head to face her, but instead of searching for her eyes, he looked at every other inch of her body.

"We need to measure you, come," he said and indicated the measuring stick against one of the walls. Nicole walked over to it, so annoyed by the fact that she had to do this dressed in only her panties that she did not even feel self-conscious anymore. With her shoulders pulled back and her backbone straight, she proudly stood still so that the doctor could measure her. He took much longer than he needed to, first to adjust the metal pin that indicated her length and then to adjust his thick spectacles to take the reading.

"Hmm, hmm," he cleared his croaky throat, "one seven six," and he bent over his desk to write her length down.

"Climb on the scale," he ordered, and she did this as proudly as she could, while biting her tongue. The doctor then came closer, peering over his spectacles, with his head bent forward at the near naked body in front of him. When he reached her, he took a stance next to her and bent forward with his head nearly touching Nicole's one breast. Nicole jerked away.

"No, you must stand still!" he reprimanded her and with his one huge hand placed in the small of her back, he roughly pushed forward, while countering the movement with his other hand placed just above her breasts. This action, with one hand pushing forward and one pressing back, forced her spine into such a position that it seemed as if she was pushing her chest out. The coarseness of the skin on his hands made her skin crawl and gave her goose pimples. As a result, Nicole's nipples jumped to attention and she felt like screaming at the doctor, but she decided to swallow the little pride she had left to get the medical examination over with.

"Sixty-two," the doctor said softly, and he went back to the desk to write it down.

"Can I get dressed now?" Nicole asked, desperate to cover her body.

"No, you can get onto the bed," he said without turning to look at her. Nicole gave a sigh and did as she was told. Her body felt rigid and she lay on the narrow metal framed bed with her arms tucked in tightly next to her torso.

"Okay," the doctor said as he came to stand next to the bed and looked down at Nicole's body, "let's see."

Haven't you seen enough? Nicole silently asked herself. The doctor did not touch her and instead only questioned her about previous injuries, operations and other illnesses that she might have had. While he was doing this, he kept his gaze on her delicate, exposed body. Not once did he look her in the eyes and Nicole wished that she knew in advance that she would be subjected to this, as she would at least have dressed in panties that were less revealing.

Instead, she was only wearing a small white cotton bikini panty and as she glanced down at the small mound that it covered, she could see that it did not leave much to the imagination. Then, as she placed her head back on the cushion, she saw the doctor's face for a split second and she could see his face was pulled in concentration as the sight before him fixated him. She sighed again and closed her eyes, hoping that if she did not witness what was happening, it would not haunt her later.

"So, you say you had a mole removed under your arm when you were thirteen?" he echoed her answer to one of his previous questions.

"Let's see here…" he said as the warm rough tips of his fingers touched the skin on her one breast.

Nicole was so shocked at the touch that she gave a little gasp and opened her eyes to see if she was not imagining it, but to her amazement his hand was hovering over her breast. To her, something just did not seem right with the situation. Up until then no one except herself had ever touched her breast, as she was still very innocent. His hands were much too big for the small firm breast he was fondling. He slowly messaged her breast in a circular movement, taking his time, and when he finally reached her nipple, he pressed on it with his index finger, which nearly covered it entirely, and moved it in a circular motion.

"No, nothing there…" he said and then he continued to feel her other breast in the same fashion.

Obviously, there wouldn't be anything there, you stupid old man, I am only eighteen, she cursed him silently.

"Now," his voice boomed in her ears and she opened her eyes in bewilderment.

What now? she thought, panicking about what his fingers might do to her next. As she feared, he moved down towards her lower body and stretched his hand out to touch the rim of her panties.

"No!" Nicole nearly screamed and they both looked straight into each other's eyes, bewildered by the shrieking sound that came out of her mouth.

Nicole had to think fast.

"I...I need to go to the toilet," she quickly explained her reaction.

"Oh, okay," he said and relaxed. "I think I have seen enough anyway. You may go," he said while still staring at her. Nicole was amazed at the intensity of the blue eyes that hid behind his glasses and for an instant, she saw something there that made her feel pity for him, but it was not enough to keep her attention, as she wanted to get dressed and get out of the office. Doctor Manning turned his back on Nicole while she dressed and hunched over as if he had a new burden to carry. Nicole did not even bother to greet him and when she finally exited the room, she felt free and able to breathe again.

"Miss," the receptionist called after Nicole as she reached the lift, "you have to go back to the recruitment office for another interview."

So quickly? she thought to herself. After what she had just been through, she did not feel like going back, but she was sure the worst was over, so she encouraged herself to do as she had been asked.

"So, how was the medical?" a knowing face greeted Nicole.

"I thought you were joking about the boyfriend thing," Nicole accused the secretary, who seemed to take pleasure from the fact that she was not the only one who had experienced the infamous Doctor Manning.

"At least it is over," the girl took pity on Nicole as she could see that it had been more traumatic for Nicole than it had been for her. Nicole was not amused and she took a seat in a corner, while grabbing one of the magazines that lay on the coffee table in front of her so that she could bury her nose in it.

"We all went through it, it isn't that bad, Nicole," the secretary persisted.

"Well, maybe that's the best you can do, but if I want someone's hands all over me, I prefer them to be much younger and attractive," Nicole answered tartly.

"Can I make you some coffee?" the girl offered. "I am Nicky Vos, by the way."

"Yes, that would be nice," Nicole capitulated, not really upset that Nicky had not warned her, but feeling very humiliated by the fact that she had to endure the sort of treatment that applicants were subjected to. Nicole was accustomed to the best and expected to be treated accordingly, but in this one morning she had discovered that life outside her safe haven was something completely different to what she had imagined. Then the phone rang, and Nicky answered it. When she finished the call, she looked at Nicole.

"Nicole, I am sorry, but they forgot to tell you that you have to have blood tests done. It is in the same building where you had your medical examination, but this time on the ground floor," she sighed.

"Ag, that's okay, the morning cannot get any worse," she tried to set Nicky at ease.

"I am really sorry," Nicky sympathised with her.

Another hour elapsed before Nicole arrived back at the headquarters.

"Okay, now I refuse to run around anymore. I have been questioned, fiddled with and had blood drained from my body, so what's next?" Nicole teased as she fell back into the same chair that she had previously occupied. "It baffles me that the police force even gets people to apply for positions!"

"Well, don't run away now, I enjoy seeing other people suffer," Nicky teased her back.

Before long, Nicole was ushered into a Captain's office. She could see that the woman behind the desk was small and that she looked stylish in her police uniform: a blue pencil skirt and matching princess style jacket. The three stars on her shoulders made her look decorated and important and Nicole could imagine herself in one of these uniforms. The Captain wore practical navy-blue heels and blackmail stockings.

Not bad, but the shoes I don't like, Nicole thought to herself.

"Good morning, I am Captain Meiring," the woman introduced herself and offered a tiny hand for Nicole to shake. Nicole felt huge in comparison when the woman rose to her feet. She reached to Nicole's nose, with heels on, while Nicole wore flat slip-on shoes. Nicole could not imagine how they had accepted such a small woman into the police force, as she perceived it to be a place for strong woman and she looked around for evidence of a degree or other qualifications. She found what she was looking for on the walls of the office. The woman she was looking at had a doctor's degree in psychology.

So, this is a pencil pusher? she thought to herself, but answered, "Good morning, I am Nicole Burger," and then her mouth erupted into a spontaneous smile as she immediately felt at ease with this woman. The interview did not last long, as the Captain was quickly taken with the witty and well-mannered young girl in front of her. They spoke about Nicole's interests, the reason for her joining the police force and Nicole's take on life. Nicole answered comfortably, in true beauty queen fashion, while drawing from the ideals she was groomed on as a child. Nicole did not see them as her ideals anymore, however, as she was busy discovering a whole new take on life and was not too sure how she, Nicole Burger, felt about it.

"Well Nicole, it was nice meeting you. I will see you next week then," the Captain confirmed her safe passage.

"How did it go?" Nicky asked before Nicole could speak.

"I think it went well," she said, "but where do I have to be next week?"

"So you made it, that's great!" Nicky said, obviously relieved. "You must be at the Wynberg police station on Wednesday at 09:00 for tests."

"What tests?" Nicole demanded.

"Nothing to worry about, it's a physiological and intellectual evaluation," Nicky said, "but the good news is that it's the final step in joining the police force."

"Can I go now?" Nicole asked, tired out by the events of the morning.

"Yes, and good luck," Nicky greeted.

"Yes, and good luck with your training," Nicole greeted back.

As she stepped out into the sun, Nicole was suddenly filled with excitement. She felt confident that she was going to be accepted, as the interviews had gone well and she knew that she had passed the medical examination. The tests the following week was of no concern to her either, as she knew she would pass them with flying colours as well. When she reached home though, she found her mother sulking over yet another one of her parents' fights and she quickly fled to her room to ponder the events of the day.

Chapter 3

The week that followed flew by and within a few days, she found herself seated in a passage at the Wynberg police station, which was situated next to the Wynberg Magistrate's Court. Nicole had never been in a police station before and this was one of the bigger ones that she would have the privilege to see. It was a three-level building that consisted of red clay bricks and huge windows. The ground level was allocated for the police station, the second level housed the detectives and administrative personnel and the third level was where the barracks were situated. Only male members were allowed to reside here. There were also a couple of out buildings at the back.

One served as the prison cells and the other was the mess hall where the police officers ate. The dining hall was converted into an examination room to accommodate the day's tests. There was very little talking amongst the aspirant recruits, as they all looked nervous. There were three other girls in the group of thirty and as her direct competition, Nicole immediately sized them up.

One girl looked shy and timid and Nicole predicted that she would not be able to last long if she had to be selected. The other two girls looked hardened by life and were much more comfortable between the men than she was. Nicole was not quite sure where she fitted into the picture, as she was not as spoilt as the one and not as worldly wise as the other two.

After half an hour's wait, the applicants were called into the examination room and they were seated at desks. Each one was supplied with a pencil and the silence reminded Nicole of her final school exam, which made her stomach turn with nervous excitement. *I have nothing to lose*, she tried to set her mind at ease. Nicole could hardly concentrate on what was being explained to them by Captain Meiring, who was dressed casually in jeans and a blouse and instead, she opted to scan her surroundings. Some of the applicants looked constipated and a few were chewing their nails and the pencils that had been handed to them.

There were a few confident young men though that sat back relaxed in their chairs as if they had done this many times before. One of these young men was a very attractive dark-haired individual, with a wide jaw line and dimple cheekily hiding in the middle of it. He turned to Nicole as her eyes ran over his muscular body. He returned her evaluating gaze and smiled in appreciation.

Yes, you too, Nicole thought to herself.

"You may start," Captain Meiring's voice startled Nicole back to reality.

Shit, what? Nicole panicked, not sure what exactly she had to do, but thanks to her skilful mathematical brain, she quickly followed the others' lead and turned the papers in front of her over and started with the questionnaire. The questions resembled the IQ tests that she had done as a child in primary school, only this time there were also secret codes to decipher, but the answers still came easily.

After they had finished and handed in the first questionnaire, they had to complete a psychological questionnaire. This was easy; as she instinctively knew exactly what they wanted to hear and she answered accordingly. Nicole was able to place herself in anyone's shoes, as she had a natural ability to understand people and it afforded her the skill to assess and manipulate people and situations as she pleased.

"You may hand your papers in at the front desk," the Captain said when all the applicants were finished, "and we will let you know if you had been selected as soon as possible."

Nicole immediately rose to her feet to leave. She walked behind a group of applicants that frustrated her as they were walking at a snail's pace. When they reached the back door of the front building, through which they had to pass to exit the complex, they filed into the building one after the other and she followed them. She was walking head down, mesmerised by the rhythm of her feet, but when she reached the door, she suddenly saw a huge pair of black leather shoes in front of her small slender feet.

She looked up, recognising the pair of muscular legs, torso and shoulders of the young man she had appreciated earlier in the examination room, finally settling her gaze on the strong face in front of her. He was much taller and broader than she had anticipated and the smell of his deodorant was intoxicating to her. She froze for a second, taking time to take all of him in and then she gave a soft and gentle smile and his mouth mirrored hers.

"Thank you," she said as he held the door for her.

He did not speak, only acknowledging her with a gracious nod and then she willed her body through the door.

Nicole walked through the corridors and then passed through the Charge Office and although she could feel him towering over her as he followed her through the police station, she did not dare to turn and start a conversation. When they finally exited the building, she felt relieved to open a gap between them, as the mere size of his powerful body intimidated her, although not enough to prevent a last appreciative glance before she opened the door of her mother's car, which she had borrowed for the morning.

Within two weeks, Nicole received the much-anticipated news. Nicky telephoned her to confirm and congratulate her on her acceptance into the police force and informed her that she had to report for duty at the Table View police station the following Monday morning, as she lived in Table View and it was the closest to her house. She was told that she would be a student and that she had to learn as much as possible in the time that she was stationed there, until she had to report at the Police Training College in September. Head Office would let her know of her travelling arrangements well in advance and the rest of the information that she required would be given to her during her first day at work.

Nicole was also informed that she would be paid a basic salary during her term as a student and that she would receive a salary adjustment after she had graduated as a Police Constable. In addition, she would have medical insurance from the first day that she started working and she would also join the police's pension fund immediately.

"Aaaaaa!" Nicole screamed as she put the phone down.

She could not believe how easy it had been to get accepted into the police force and gain financial independence. Things looked rosy and she felt that her future looked bright again.

Chapter 4

Monday morning could not have come sooner than it did, as Nicole now hated being at home. Her mother did not cook anymore; she seldom left their house and hardly came out of her room. Where they normally had daily conversations, their conversations were now limited to the most necessary. Although Nicole was worried about her mother's emotional state, she could do nothing about it, as her mother would not let Nicole near her. Nicole chose to walk to the police station, as it was situated only three blocks from where they lived.

Nicole was dressed in a black ankle-length pencil skirt and grey polo neck short sleeved t-shirt, which highlighted her long athletic physique. Her long layered auburn hair was tied into a ponytail at the back of her head and her long fringe was tucked behind one ear. She looked very stylish and the dull colours accentuated the red colour in her hair, making her look more beautiful than usual. When she entered the building, she felt apprehensive as the five middle-aged men in their uniforms all turned their heads to face her. Table View police station was one of the less busy stations as its crime rate was low and therefore there was no one else in the room she entered, except for five policemen on duty.

As they could not perceive the young beauty in front of them as being one of them, they all jumped to their feet to help her, mistaking her for one of the civilians who had come to report something. The first to reach the counter was a long sinewy man in his late thirties, and although he looked much too young for it, his hair was nearly completely grey.

"Can I help?" he offered.

"Yes, I am looking for the Station Commander."

"Well, follow me," he invited. Nicole followed Sergeant Muller down the corridor of the face brick building, past three doors and stopped behind him as he came to a standstill in front of the Captain in charge of the station's office door. This police station was small in comparison to the one in Wynberg and as such did not have a high-ranking officer in charge.

"Captain?" the Sergeant inquired as he peered around the door.

"Yes?" she heard the distinctive sound of a mature and gentle voice.

"Captain, there is someone to see you." he informed the man hiding behind the wall.

"You may let them in." Nicole braced herself for the introduction, as this would be her boss over the next few months and when she entered the office, she smiled as friendly as possible and took his hand in a firm grip as he offered it to her.

"Good morning, I am Nicole Burger. I am the new student." she explained her presence and she could see that he had been informed of her coming as he nodded in acknowledgement.

"Good morning, Nicole, I have been waiting for you." the Captain said and nodded to the Sergeant, "Thank you, you may go." Nicole turned to look at the Sergeant that had just delivered her to the Captain and could see the shock on his face at discovering that she was one of them. He stood there frozen for a second as the information struck him and he looked at her in a totally different way than he did when she had entered the building. She was family. A smile appeared on his face as he turned to join the rest of his shift in the Charge Office.

During the next hour, Nicole was informed that she would work shifts of eight hours, for five days, after which she would have two days off, the day that the night shift ended excluded. So, although technically you only had the next two days off, it felt like three as the day your shift ended you had to yourself as well. She would have to work two afternoon shifts from two in the afternoon until ten in the evening, for two consecutive days, and then she would work two morning shifts from six in the morning until two in the afternoon. On the fourth day, when she was to work her last afternoon shift, she would have to work double shifts, which meant that she would have to report for duty on that same day for night shift, which started at ten and ended at six the following morning. The last day of her cycle would end with a night shift.

At first, when she heard this, she thought it sounded like torture, but as the possibilities of such a work schedule sank in, she realised that she would have a lot of free time during the day and the fact that she would be off during the week at times would afford her the time to visit shops at times when they are least active due to normal office hours for civilians.

The Captain then proceeded to walk Nicole through the station, explaining what the offices were for and what each one of the people inside of them were responsible for. There were too many people to remember and Nicole did not even try to do so.

"You will remember everything in time," the Captain said as if he knew exactly what she was thinking, and it dawned on her that he too once was a student and probably remembered what it felt like to be in her shoes.

"This is why I am going to place you with a shift. That is where you will learn to understand the working of the station best," he continued. Nicole did not speak; she was in awe of her surroundings and kept an arm's length behind him. When they reached the door that separated the offices and the Charge Office, the Captain turned to face Nicole.

"Since you are here and the morning shift has already started, I think you can just as well fall in with them, I will introduce you." he said. Nicole was nervous. The men she had previously seen looked like hardened men and there was no one of her age she would be able to relate to. The Captain opened the door and came to a standstill in the doorway.

"Guys, I want to introduce you to Nicole Burger, she will be joining you on your shift," and then he stepped out of the way for the men to look at their newest member.

One by one, the men stood closer to introduce themselves.

"Hi, I am Muller," the Sergeant that had led her to the Captain's office introduced himself.

"Hello, I am Vos," a younger and attractive tall and dark-haired man said while shaking her hand enthusiastically.

"Hi, Baardenhorst," an enormous bearded man introduced himself and although he looked reserved and serious, she sensed an underlying mischievousness. She immediately took a liking to him and knew they would become friends.

"Burger," she responded as she picked up that they used their surnames and not their first names, when referring to themselves.

"Bergie," Sergeant Baardenhorst proclaimed aloud and the room fell apart as they doubled over with laughter. (Bergie is also a name used for a destitute person in South Africa.) Nicole knew that she would not escape the new nickname as they found it too funny.

"It looks like you are going to fit in quite well," the Captain said as he turned to return to his work, trying his utmost not to let her see that he too enjoyed the joke.

"Don't forget about me," a grey old man said from behind the Charge Office desk, where he was busy writing in a large book. Nicole came closer and took his hand as he offered it.

"I am Sergeant Mostert," he smiled at Nicole and could see that this man was gentle and could not figure out why he had joined the Force. She liked him, so she smiled accordingly.

"Nicole," a deep voice made her swing around and she looked into a bloated sweaty face, which was uncomfortably close to hers. Nicole took a step back so she could size up the man standing in front of her.

"Yes?" she answered, immediately annoyed by his intrusion of her personal space.

"I am Sergeant Swart," he introduced himself, "but you can call me Eugene." Nicole reluctantly took his hand and tried to make the contact with the soft, sweaty sausages covering her hands as short as possible and pulled away nearly as soon as her hand touched his. She made a mental note to stay clear from this man as his presence made her skin crawl.

She had mastered the art of ignoring a person's existence without them even realising it, as she was taught this by example from an early age, by two parents who wanted only the best for their daughter. They would not allow her to mix with people of a lesser social background as her, out of their own ignorance, from growing up in similar advantaged homes as they had created for themselves. By ignoring the existence of people and circumstances that they did not understand or know how to deal with, they thought that it would not affect them. In truth, it only allowed circumstances and feelings to boil to such a point that the damage in the end sometimes was nearly impossible to rectify.

The Burgers' were not mean-spirited in the least, but like most white South African young people in the Apartheid era, they were groomed into a passive ignorant culture of adults who chose to ignore the absurdity of their government at the time in order to enjoy the security, wealth and stability that it offered, at a price they would only in future discover and have to pay dearly for.

"Is this the whole shift?" she directed her question to Sergeant Mostert as she thought he, as the oldest, would be in charge.

"No, we have a female member as well, but she is off sick today. She is also a Sergeant and her name is Ava Brighton," he said and went on with his work.

Contrary to what she perceived, Sergeant Mostert was not the shift commander, this she was informed of by the shift commander himself, namely

Sergeant Baardenhorst. He continued to explain that they took turns doing duty in the Charge Office and outside. They were posted two per vehicle and they had two vehicles at their disposal in which they had to patrol the whole of Table View and Bloubergstrand. Although this was a large area, it was not very populated yet.

In the mid-eighties, most of the area consisted of farms with the exception of the town itself and the oil refinery on the outskirts of Table View. The refinery was heavily guarded, as this was a prime target for the Resistance Movement to Apartheid, and they seldom needed to patrol there. For the time being, Sergeant Baardenhorst felt that it would be better for Nicole to stay in the Charge Office to learn how to do the administration involved in their work, as this would give her a clear view of what they did. This meant that she would sit with the Charge Office commander, who was also rotated, but Sergeant Brighton mostly performed the duty, as she did not like working on one of the patrol vehicles.

Here, the Charge Office commander would teach her how to take a statement from a complainant and how to open a docket for investigation, how to book prisoners into their cells, until they could be transferred to court and all the other logistics of keeping book of the contents of the safe and the fire arms which the officers had to book in and out on each shift. She would also be taught how to give the Charge Office over to the next Charge Office commander and how to take meticulous notes in the Incidence Register so that if anything happened, which needed to be questioned, she would know exactly when and how it happened.

This was to protect the Charge Office commander and the officers on duty, as sometimes things get lost or stolen on shifts, people are hurt, prisoners are locked up, prisoners escape and so forth. For this reason, every little detail had to be written in this holy book. Nicole would only later learn the true meaning of how important the book was to the workings of the Charge Office and how it could be used or abused to safeguard police officers from prosecution for criminal behaviour. Although she was not immediately informed of the silent oath that existed between policemen, she could sense that there was a deep understanding and silent language that existed, which she had to tune into if she wanted to survive.

"Well, we have to start the day; I hope you enjoy it on our shift. Sergeant Mostert will take care of you until Ava comes back," Sergeant Baardenhorst said and turned in unison with the other men and disappeared into the cold sea air outside.

"Come, pull up a chair," Sergeant Mostert invited with a genuinely caring smile. Nicole sensed that he took a liking to her as much as she had him and that he felt protective of her. Nicole took the chair next to Sergeant Mostert and he offered her coffee from a flask he had brought from home.

"That would be lovely," she said and gratefully took the steaming cup from him as he handed it to her.

"I will be with you in a moment," the Sergeant said as he started writing in the Incidence Register, "I need to finish this first." In silence, Nicole sat back in her chair and started sipping the hot brew of cheap instant coffee that was handed to her and strangely, it tasted surprisingly pleasant. She could for the first time since she had entered the station take in her surroundings and she saw that the police station was impeccably clean. The tiled grey floor had obviously just been mopped and she wondered who was responsible, as she did not notice any servants in the station, except for the tea lady that was there to cater to the needs of the office personnel.

The charge office counter was made of solid wood and varnished to a glistening sheen. She suspected that this had to be done regularly as she could see how, over the years; it has taken its fair share of abuse as the dents and scratches on it attested. In the middle of the counter, there was a partitioning structured on top of it that separated the counter, and the partitioning extended to the entrance, where the civilians entered. The Charge Office could be entered from two single doors. On the left side, there were wooden benches and the other side was empty. You could enter the floor space, where the policeman sat, from either side through the counter, which was cut and attached by hinges and could lift up.

She would later see that the open space was where complainants came to give their statements and the other section was for use by police officers from other stations who came to fill their vehicles, at the petrol pump the station housed on its grounds. Here they would come to fill in the petrol register, make small talk or have a cup of coffee. This space was also used for taking statements in rape cases, child abuse cases or any other sensitive case where the officer in charge of taking the statement required some privacy.

There was a hallway leading from the entrance to the station, behind the Charge Office, to the offices, with a seating area for visitors to wait until they would be called to the respective offices where they needed to be. There was also direct entry to this hallway from the inner Charge Office. The door opened into a small corridor, which led into the main hallway. Out of this smaller corridor the door to the small kitchen was housed. On the left of where Nicole sat, and opposite the door to the offices, there was an opening which led to a temporary holding cell, where prisoners were held until they were registered in the Charge Office books.

Nicole would only be shown what was hidden here on her first night shift, where she would discover the proper prison cells, behind this cell, all consisting of heavy iron doors and small barred windows, a single open toilet, a few grey blankets, bare cement floors and blue painted walls with graffiti of all sorts bearing testimony to the hordes of criminals that had passed through them. The cells had a distinctive urine smell to them and due to the small windows, the cells were dark and a person's eyes had to adjust from the light in the office to be able to see inside. They were also lice-ridden and not a place where any dignified human being would want to spend a night.

Nicole looked at the walls in the Charge Office, which were decorated with maps of the area and posters informing the public of their rights, safety tips and all sorts of notifications of importance. Then a young black man clothed in neatly pressed green overalls entered the Charge Office from the temporary holding cell and Nicole, immediately sensing that it was a detainee, jerked as his presence startled her. Nicole's heart pounded so hard against her chest that she did not even feel the hot fluid in her hand spilling onto her lap.

Sergeant Mostert lazily looked up as Nicole's body jerked and in that instance, he realised what Nicole must have thought. He looked at the young man and they both started laughing, with the young man's grin emphasised by the contrast of his brilliant white teeth to his dark skin. This only annoyed Nicole as she realised her mistake in believing the prisoner was trying to escape and it was obvious that the Sergeant was well aware of the young man's presence in the station and that they knew each other.

"It's okay, John, you can go to the kitchen," Sergeant Mostert said to the young man who came to a halt as a result of Nicole's reaction. In that instance, Nicole could sense the mutual respect between the two men. The young man hung his head to disguise his amusement with the silly white girl's reaction towards him and he unknowingly shook his head. Nicole felt embarrassed and angry for making such a mistake.

Until now, the only people of colour she had ever had to deal with was her nanny, Maria, who had taken care of her from an early age. Maria was a big coloured woman, with four upper front teeth missing. Nicole was very fond of her and although she knew that she was not white, she never even considered the colour difference, as Maria became a mother figure, which she freely hugged and kissed as she would her own mother. As a raised Christian, she saw people of colour as human beings and she believed that all things living were created by God and needed to be treated with respect.

Her religion, which was supposed to instil these values in her, was also the downfall of many old white Afrikaners (a Afrikaans word for a South African who spoke Afrikaans), as it made them haughty in believing that anyone not serving God was an untrustworthy infidel who became a threat to their way of life. Therefore the "Wise Men" at head of state found it their duty to protect this at any means necessary. The sad thing though, was that since she like many other young people, was fed the propaganda and misconceptions of the reining "Christian" government at the time, that people of different races than whites, was criminals and out to destroy the peaceful existence of what they perceived as order and stability, she was as a result subconsciously judgmental and weary of men of colour, as the only images she saw of them was on television.

Here, they were portrayed as barbaric, by a government ruled media which manipulated the ANC's protest marches by not showing the desperation of a nation not being allowed the right to freedom, but chose to use the anger of the masses to frighten the privileged minority into wanting to protect their children from the savages. The image of black men and woman being set alight by their fellowmen, with fuel-filled tires around their upper torsos, burning the skin from their naked bodies, still haunts many young South Africans today. Thus, her naïve assumption that poor John, who was serving time for petty theft, was trying to escape, or worse, going to harm them.

Sergeant Mostert, wise beyond his years, which was a substantial number already, placed a hand on Nicole's shoulder as John disappeared into the hallway.

"Don't stress, John is a decent guy," he said softly so that no one else could hear. He understood the wariness Nicole experienced as a result of her secluded upbringing, but also recognised her empathetic soul. He knew that as time would pass, she would come to understand, as he has, that people of colour were just as human and barbaric as the souls fortunate enough to be born to pale skins.

Sergeant Mostert went on to explain that although they only had temporary holding cells at police stations, convicts like John were placed at police stations, where they worked as hard labourers.

They were responsible for keeping the station clean, gardening, washing the police vehicles, cooking for the other prisoners being held there and in return they were allowed more freedom and more space to sleep in than they would be afforded in the overcrowded prisons of South Africa. They were hardly ever dangerous and were mostly locked up for petty crimes. Nicole relaxed when he explained this to her and felt thankful for having such a gentle, kind man looking out for her. This relationship would become one of her most cherished she would develop on her journey in the Force. The feeling was mutual and Mostert smiled at her as he fondly took her under his wing.

The rest of the day went by faster than she could concentrate on and when she finally picked up her handbag to leave the station, she felt drained by all the new information. She wondered how she was going to remember all the registers and the finer details of keeping them up to date, when she would finally be put in charge of doing so.

The rest of the shift slowly returned to book their firearms into safekeeping and to log off so that they could have a well-deserved rest. The whole day was mostly spent alone with Mostert, with the odd visit from one of the shift members, when they had to book a prisoner into the cells or had to hand a docket in for processing.

If work is going to be like this every day, I am going to love it! Nicole thought to herself, happy to find not only that she felt confident that she would master her new work, but for making a new friend.

(A docket consisted of a cardboard file containing the statement of a complainant opening a case for investigation. These files get registered in the Charge Office by the Charge Office commander and will be collected by the detectives on duty for investigation. At the end of an investigation, these dockets can be as thick as a novel, consisting of statements of the complainant, witnesses, the accused, evidence, photos, medical files and so forth. Then it is presented to the state prosecutor for evaluation and if it is deemed a watertight and worthy case, a court date is set.

If not, it is sent back for further investigation and if the prosecutor sees it as a waste of the government's time and money, it is thrown out. There are no copies, and if it gets misplaced or lost, it can lead to a criminal avoiding being prosecuted, and therefore it must be monitored carefully and the only way it can be handled is by booking it out in a register to keep track of its whereabouts.)

Chapter 5

The next day flew by as she and Sergeant Mostert tried to keep up with the work in the Charge Office. They were particularly busy that week and Sergeant Mostert commented on it, trying not to discourage Nicole about the amount of work awaiting her, but unbeknownst to him, she did not care to work hard; she loved a challenge and the harder she had to work for something the more she appreciated the end result on its completion. Minor tasks usually bored her and up until now, the work she witnessed was by no means difficult or overwhelming.

Nicole actually got a little frustrated by the sergeant as he did not have the time to train her at a pace she could cope with. She was used to processing huge amounts of information in a short period of time and possessed the ability to retain and implement it in an efficient and accurate manner. She did not flaunt this capability of hers though, as she had discovered, from a young age, the power of letting people assume that she was of average intelligence, since they then unknowingly revealed more about their true nature, as they relaxed in her company, not intimidated by the power of her brain.

Especially with men, she kept her intelligence understated, as men, or the boys up until then she had to deal with in particular felt threatened by her and tried to dominate conversations or put her down in order to feel in control, as young men were brought up in a society that frowned upon any sign of weakness. Boys had to be rough and tough and in charge of their woman and men who were not, nor had a preference to love their own gender, were shunned by the men who believed that it was the right way.

Once again, a way of habit, enforced by years of ignorance and unwillingness to change, but slowly and surely a new breed of young people was starting to develop into adults, who questioned the ways of the past, as these rules they were taught failed to keep them or the parents, who taught it to them, happy.

"You must remember to take an afternoon nap," Sergeant Mostert reminded Nicole as she readied herself to return home.

"Why?" Nicole frowned and for an instant she thought the old man was taking this fatherly figure thing a bit too far.

"You have to be back here at ten, and there is no way you are going to survive the night if you don't," he knowingly challenged her.

"Oh, that's right, I totally forgot," she replied.

Nicole was still energised by the buzz of the morning's activities and found that first afternoon nap difficult. This would be the only time though as this was the start of a bizarre skill she was beginning to master. When you serve in the police force, you quickly learn to sleep at all times of day and at will, as your body bypasses its natural rhythms to ensure that it receives enough rest. What Nicole did not know just yet was how she would also master the skill to stay awake for three days straight, especially when she discovered partying up a storm with her fellow officers, while still working shifts in between. A dangerous feat if you take into consideration that you need your wits about you when in charge of a firearm or worse still, driving a police vehicle at high speed in peak traffic.

Since she was still young and in an environment that created a false sense of invincibility, she fell into the same trap as most police officers, not acknowledging the reality and seriousness of the work she chose to do. This was a time when police officers were respected and obeyed, as they still enforced fear into the public. The death penalty was still enforced, and police officers still got away with beating arrestees, while the law did not favour criminals and therefore the country was a safe place to live in.

Children could play in the streets, walk to school or travel into town on their own, without any harm befalling them. There was a heavy price to pay for this privileged life in the police force though, which Nicole would discover in the nearing future, but for now things could not look more promising.

That evening, Nicole walked the short distance to the police office in the well-lit main road. She could smell the sea on the cool night breeze and she became aware of the change in her surroundings. The streets were lit by the streetlamps into an orange haze and the sea breeze made little droplets appear on everything, which in return made the surrounding surfaces sparkle in the light. The road she had so many times paced now looked unfamiliar. Before she could give it thought, she heard the "Special" in charge of guarding the gate's voice;

"Good evening, the Charge Office is through there…" he smiled a friendly smile at her.

She could hardly make out his black face in the dark unlit cubicle situated in the middle of the big cast iron gate that protected the police station, and the smaller one for pedestrian use. The only thing she could make out was the man's brilliantly white teeth grinning at her.

"Don't worry, I know my way, I am a student," she replied before he could finish.

From the darkness, his face came peering out: "Then good evening, miss," he smiled even wider and the size of his mouth surprised and amused her. "I am Moses," and before Nicole could think about what she was doing, she offered him a hand and he hesitated only for a second before taking it into his rough and warm black hand, cupping it on top with his other hand, as was their custom, and shook it with vengeance. Nicole liked Moses and from the face she saw, she could see that he was a warm and honourable man with huge kind eyes.

"I am Nicole, Moses," she introduced herself, before she continued on her way down the paved walkway that led her into the police station.

("Specials", as they were known in the police force, were men of colour that were employed and trained in the handling of firearms and self-defence skills by the police force to assist them in keeping guard and other security tasks, which did not merit the time of a well-trained officer. As only white males and females were allowed to join the Force in the Apartheid era, the only way men of colour could join the police force was as one of these special attendants.)

When Nicole entered the office, she could see her whole shift, to which she had become accustomed to, prepare for the night ahead. Somehow she felt more excited about her night shift than she did about her daily shifts; maybe it had something to do with the feeling of excitement she had experienced as a child when she would stay up late with her friend when they had a sleepover. She knew that she would come to love her night shifts as, it was a welcome change to the monotonous rhythm of live and the night and early morning hours, held promise of adventure as this was the time serious crimes were committed.

There was no one sitting at the Charge Office commander's post though and she found it strange that Sergeant Mostert was putting on his police-issue overcoat and pack his flashlight in his backpack. He was obviously preparing for a night on the road and she felt disappointed. She had not really had the opportunity to get to know the rest of the shift as they were too busy during the day and she was now wondering how her first night's shift would be like in the company of some stranger.

"Good evening," the members of the shift said in near unison.

"Hi," she said in a disappointed tone. She made her way around the counter and placed her handbag on a counter behind a partitioning, to the left of the Charge Office, so that it would be out of sight from the public. Here, the other members of her shift had already placed their snacks and drinks for the evening. There was more than enough space, as the surface was about 2 metres in length and 1 metre in width.

Without a word, she took a seat on the chair next to the Charge Office commander's seat, as she usually did. She did not dare ask who would be placed in the charge office with her, in fear of Sergeant Swart being the lucky one. She absolutely dreaded the thought of spending the night in his creepy presence. During that first week, she noticed that the rest of the shift's members kept to themselves, only occasionally staring at her as if they were trying to figure out what to make of her. She did not mind it though, as she too was trying to size them up.

It was only when Sergeant Swart looked at her that she hated it, because she instinctively knew that he was probably having filthy thoughts while doing so, as the slyest smile always appeared on his face when he looked at her, his eyes became hazy and she could swear that she once or twice saw a droplet escape the corner of his mouth, but he licked at it before she could be sure. This always seemed to pull him back to reality and then he would continue with what he was doing.

"Please don't let it be him, please don't let it be him, I won't..." she was pleading for some intervention while her head was turned down to the table in front of her and while her eyes were tightly shut.

"Hi Nicole," a most harmoniously pleasant sound sung in her ears. Nicole did not know the voice, but since her eyes were closed, she could concentrate on the sound and the vibrations of the woman's vocal cords, and from this she gathered that this was a confident and pleasant human being and somebody she immediately felt attracted to, without even looking up.

Nicole's eyes followed suit and there in front of her stood her mentor and absolute confidant for the future. She did not know this at the time though, but what she did know was that the attractive fair-haired woman in front of her was someone she felt a connection with.

"I am Ava Brighton, you will be working with me tonight," she continued in the same hypnotic tone as before.

"Hi, I am Nicole," Nicole said while she nearly tripped over the leg of her chair when she tried to come to her feet as her body jerked into a stance of respect. Nicole smiled like a young child in awe of an adult they admire, while Ava, confidently and unaffected by the young girl's obvious adoration, took a seat and started with her tasks for signing on as Charge Office commander.

Only after the men left the station in their respective vehicles for their nightly patrols did the two women get a chance to converse. Nicole waited patiently as she watched Ava contently, taking in all she could of what Ava was doing. When Ava finally had nothing else to do, she offered to make Nicole a coffee and invited her to walk her to the kitchen.

The conversation that followed came naturally and easily and they talked as if they were old friends. Ava immediately took a liking to the open-minded and eager to learn innocence of Nicole. During the conversation, the two women established that they saw eye to eye on most of their respective life philosophies. Ava also felt protective of Nicole as Nicole spontaneously offered to share the circumstances she found herself in and the struggle she was facing in knowing the difference between right and wrong, as she questioned a lot of what her parents had taught her.

Ava came from similar circumstances and understood her quest in finding truth all too well and in recognising herself and her fighting spirit in the young girl, they bonded like long lost sisters. Although both women were very private, they could not resist opening up to each other. They were so engrossed in their conversation that they did not even realise how fast the first few hours of the night shift had past. The night was uneventful, as it always was in the middle of the week and so the only time they were reminded of their surroundings was when the men returned to the station for a snack and some coffee.

The men were busy though, with patrolling the area and visiting businesses where burglar alarms were set off and other minor complaints. This did not affect the Charge Office much as most of their tasks that they had to complete were ordered via radio through Radio Control. This was a central station where officers commanded the emergency phone lines of the police force. Most complaints were received here and radioed to the respective stations in the area that had to deal with the specific complaints.

Sometimes people in a specific area would phone their local police station in the hope that the police officers would reach them sooner, when in fact this was not true, as the vehicles on duty were seldom stationary at the police station and the Charge Office commander had to phone Radio Control to give the complaint through to them so that they could radio it through to the vehicles in the area. Radio Control was also equipped with a task team of their own, called the Flying Squad, which consisted of policemen armed with vehicles specifically for high speed chases. They were always on standby to assist any of the police stations when they needed backup.

Nicole was for now placed in care of this duty of phoning complaints through to Radio Control, which did not keep her particularly busy that night. This caused the Charge Office to be quite quiet during the night and only when people were arrested, detainees were booked out by detectives, a complainant came in to lay a charge, or any other emergency took place, did it get busy or noisy in the Charge Office. Nicole was given a list of codes with a descriptive meaning of the complaint she was dealing with next to it and had to give the complaint through in a specific manner; namely, name of complainant, address of complainant, code of crime or complaint, address where it took place and urgency and her name and official police number, which each police officer received when they were accepted into the Force.

Ava also issued Nicole with a pocketbook and showed her how to write it up, to keep record of her every minute on duty. If booked for duty in the Charge Office, it was the least strenuous, as there seldom happened a lot, or for now she thought. She was to discover over the following years just how in the middle of things you were and how vulnerable you could be when you were stationed in the Charge Office if something went wrong, as you are always aware of all that is going on, be it legal or illegal and it was your responsibility as Charge Office commander to explain any irregularities. Unfortunately, police officers are human and as such, they were split into corrupt and clean officers.

These pocketbooks were sometimes used by corrupt officers to cover their tracks when they made mistakes or committed a crime, with false inscriptions. Seeing that the Charge Officer, for the most part, eventually found out what really happened and sometimes unknowingly documented everything in the Incidence Register, the Charge Office Commander was regularly placed in a moral dilemma. As much as fellow officers stood together when one of them needed protection, be it from a dangerous situation or an event that could see them fired, they frowned upon snitches, whom were targeted and bullied, or even worse. So little mishaps were regularly covered up and made way for even bigger cover ups out of fear and intimidation, especially if the corrupt officers outnumber the clean officers on a shift. On the wrong shift, it was easier to ask for a transfer to a new shift, than to report a corrupt cop, especially if the cop in question had influence higher up in the hierarchy.

"Hey, what are you two up to?" Sergeant Baardenhorst said in a light-hearted tone. Nicole had perceived him as a strict and serious man as he was the Shift Commander; six-foot-tall and enormously big-boned and padded with muscle and fat to make him seem even bigger. He had a thick beard and intensely thick eyebrows that framed his mysteriously green eyes. Up until then she had never heard him speak in this tone, as his voice was powerful, and it seemed as he only knew how to bellow out orders.

Now he was waltzing into the Charge Office, with his big body swaying from side to side as if his head was placed on a large ball and Nicole saw his teeth grinning at them from under his moustache. What Nicole did not know is that he had a secret crush on Ava and whenever she was present, he was in a good mood. Not only that, he was mysterious and loved to play pranks on his colleagues. Somewhere in that huge body hid a huge and kind heart, but this did not mean that he took nonsense from anyone.

"Did you bring the meat, Ben?" Ava confronted the Sergeant.

Nicole frowned at this, why would he need to bring meat to the Charge Office?

"We are having a shift barbeque," Ava explained as if she knew what Nicole was thinking.

"Yes, we have to welcome you properly," Sergeant Mostert, who followed Ben into the Charge Office, agreed and he placed plastic containers containing meat and salads on the counter.

"Are we allowed to do this?" Nicole cautiously inquired, as she was not yet accustomed to all the rules of being on duty. They all burst out laughing.

"We do this often and yes, we may have a barbeque on our night shift, as long as we do it in the back where the public cannot see us and as long as the Charge Office is manned at all times," Ben explained. At that point, the rest of the shift entered the office as well and they were all in a festive mood.

"Why hasn't anybody told me about this? I could have brought something as well," Nicole accused them of leaving her in the dark.

"No, this is a surprise, all new students have to be welcomed," Ben said in an ominous manner, while the whole shift of men grinned at her. Nicole suddenly felt nervous because of all the attention and the sudden friendliness. Before that night, the shift had hardly spoken to her and now they were all focussing on her. Nicole searched for Ava's eyes to get some reassurance, but Ava was now looking down at the Incidence Register in front of her, avoiding Nicole's attempt at receiving some assurance that there was nothing sinister about the men's sudden interest in her.

"Come, we are going to light the fire," Sergeant Mostert said and he started in the direction of the kitchen, with Sergeant Vos following him. Nicole followed submissively. She rather preferred staying close to Sergeant Mostert anyway, as she could not see him doing anything degrading to her. Vos, as the rest of the shift called him, was a gentle, shy and soft-spoken lad. Tall and very attractive, but not at all aware of it, Nicole knew he too would not harm her in any way.

Ben made her nervous though and especially after his weird behaviour, she wanted to stay out of his way. The men made small conversation with Nicole and she soon became relaxed and forgot all about her previous worries. After a while Ben, Sergeant Swart, Sergeant Muller and Ava came to join them.

"Somebody needs to be in the Charge Office," Ben said.

"Nicole, as you are the youngest and the newest, you can man the Charge Office," he ordered Nicole. Nicole went into the Charge Office, where it was dead quiet, except for the hand radio that sporadically announced another complaint to one of the station's vehicles. Nicole could hear the rest of her shift laugh and talk, but she could not make out what they were discussing.

After what seemed like an eternity, Ben came into the office.

"Nicole," he said as if he were going to announce something serious, "come with me."

Nicole came to her feet, she did not know what to expect and followed him, she had no choice as he was shift commander and she had to religiously follow all his orders. Even if she disagreed with them, she had to do as she was told and then file a complaint afterwards. Not that anyone ever dared do such a thing, as the whole station and surrounding police stations' officers would shun you if you did such an unthinkable thing. Ben started walking to the front of the station and soon they walked into the darkness of the night. It was past twelve and the air was filled with mist that was blown in on the sea breeze.

"Where are we going?" Nicole nervously asked.

She felt dwarfed by the huge figure next to her.

"We are going to take the flag down," Ben informed her and his warm breath brushed against her cheek as his powerful lungs dispersed the air it contained. Nicole looked up at the flag post at the end of the walkway as they neared it. There was no flag on it and Nicole suddenly felt scared.

"But..." she tried to argue, but Ben interrupted her.

"You need to know how to take the flag down, so I am going to show you how to do it," he said, not looking at her. Nicole thought he was serious. As they reached the flag post, Ben turned to her and with the practiced hand of a professional, he brought forth his handcuffs and before Nicole could register what had happened, she was cuffed to the flag post by her right wrist.

"There Nicole, now you can guard the station for us," Ben said, and he started laughing and before she could protest, he turned his back on her and in an even more exaggerated sway, he disappeared back into the Charge Office. Nicole watched him disappear in disbelief; she did not know if she should find it as hilarious as Ben did or if she had to be furious at him for leaving her in the cold in such a vulnerable position. She decided to stay calm and let them have their fun as they obviously had planned to humiliate her, as the newcomer, in some sort of attempt to bond with her or make her feel welcome.

Although she deemed it unnecessary, she found it strangely charming that they went to this length to include her into their group. While she stood there in the cold, intently listening for one of them to appear and free her from her captivity, she slowly started to realise that she could be there for quite a while as nearly an hour had passed. Nicole's feet were beginning to feel numb and her hands were turning blue.

That is enough, she thought to herself, *I am not staying here all night*. Nicole studied the cuff that encircled her wrist. Luckily, it was not tightened in such a manner as to hug her skin. There was a small space between her wrist and the metal.

I wonder if I would be able to pull my arm free? she pondered.

Well, it's worth a try, she encouraged herself and she started pulling her wrist out of the cuff. Her hand pulled out to where her thumb started parting from her hand.

"Damn!" she cursed as she left her hand in that uncomfortable position. She thought of the countless times she had to free her fingers from rings when on a warm day she would retain water and she was forced to remove her rings by using soap or licking her finger wet as lubricate it, but she did not feel like licking her whole hand.

There must be another way, she thought. It dawned upon her that theoretically, her skin and ligaments should be able to stretch and give way if she pulled hard enough and decided that she was coming out of this situation, even if it meant she had to pull her hand from its socket. Nicole took hold of her fingers with her free hand and she forced the bones of her thumb and pinkie in her trapped hand to meet, in an attempt to make the circumference of her hand as small as possible. She then slowly continued, while holding her hand in that position, with her other hand, to pull her hand in a rocking motion from side to side.

Slowly but surely, her hand started to move from its confinement. It was a painful experience, but she was so determined not to let them determine how long she was to stay there in the cold, that she continued to pull and struggle against the hard and unforgiving metal. Just when she thought of giving up hope and that her hand would be helplessly stuck in its uncomfortable position, it gave way and came free from its restrictions. As the blood came rushing back into it, it started swelling and turned a bright red. Nicole did not care. She was free!

"Having fun?" Nicole sarcastically asked Ben as she entered the station and found the whole shift in the warm space of the charge office, drinking steaming hot coffee and eating the meat they had just finished barbequing. All the men were staring at her in disbelief as Ben swung around to see for himself if he was imagining her presence in the Charge Office.

"But…how?" he stumbled with finding the words to describe his confusion.

"I simply pulled my hand free," she said confidently.

"That's impossible," Ben said, accusing her of lying.

"Look at my hand then," she said, now really frustrated with him and somewhat drowned in self-pity as her hand was throbbing. Ben just shook his head at the sight of it.

"We would have let you free in a few minutes," he said, and she was not sure if she had to take it as an apology or as an accusation of her being rash.

"Well, I couldn't wait for you," she said as she turned her back on them and fled to the bathroom to hold her hand under the cool soothing of running tap water. The men in the office started to smile. They felt appreciation for this strong-willed girl and they all liked her even better for her determination and gutsy will.

"That was too easy for her," Ben said when she left the room.

"No, leave her, you have had your fun," Ava tried to protect Nicole from Ben.

She knew all too well that Ben did not like it when he did not get his way and this girl sure as hell gave him a run for his money. Ava knew that Ben saw the fact that she did not resort to tears as a challenge, and she was not quite sure how far Ben would go in his attempts at initiating Nicole.

"Yes, maybe she had enough," Sergeant Mostert tried to appeal as well.

"No, this is a tough one," Ben said and before anyone could stop him, he grabbed his can of tear-gas and opened Nicole's handbag. Ben sprayed it quickly, guarding against letting some of it escape the inside of the bag, and then he closed it as fast as he opened it.

"Now keep quiet!" he ordered everyone. Ava could not watch and shook her head as she fled outside to have a smoke. Sergeant Mostert followed her, as he too was not prepared to witness the humiliation Nicole was about to endure. Up until then, Nicole did not even know of the existence of such a gas, let alone that someone would use it on her with no good reason whatsoever. When she returned from the bathroom, the men left in the office kept themselves busy with heaven knows what, and although she knew they had something up their sleeves, she would have never guessed that they would go as far as they did. Nicole went to sit at the counter, much to Ben's disappointment.

"Nicole, do you have your Identity Document here?" Ben asked as innocently as possible.

"Yes," she said simply, not at all in the mood to humour him.

"Can I see it?" he said sweetly.

"What have you done to my handbag?" she asked instinctively.

"Nothing!" he said, taken by surprise at her intuitiveness. The other men burst out laughing as they enjoyed this girl's reaction to Ben's attempts at catching her off guard.

"You have done something, I hope you haven't taken something from my bag!" she said in a threatening manner and made her way over to her bag to check its contents.

"I haven't touched your bag," Ben said while pulling his face into the most pathetic attempt at looking innocent. Nicole plucked her bag open and scratched through its contents, checking everything to make sure all was still there. To her surprise, nothing had been touched. This confused her, as she was sure he had taken something. The rest of the men had moved away from her by now as they did not want to come into contact with the tear gas. Nicole was not convinced that nothing had happened.

"What have you done?" she said in a serious voice.

"Nothing," Ben replied, but before she could even concentrate on what he was saying, her hands, face and eyes started burning as if someone had washed it with acid. Nicole looked at her hands and saw red hives appear on her skin.

"What have you done?" she accused him again, but he couldn't answer her as he was doubled over with laughter.

"He sprayed your bag with tear-gas," Vos offered an explanation, as he took pity on her.

"What should I do?" Nicole asked with tears streaming down her face and burning its path down her cheeks, leaving it stained and swollen.

"Wash your face," she heard someone say, but could not figure out whom, nor did she care as she could not open her eyes long enough to focus. Someone grabbed her by her arm and took her to the bathroom where she washed her face and dried it off with the towel the person offered. Only after quite a while could she start to focus on her surroundings again and did she discover her Samaritan to be Ava.

When Nicole finally looked in the mirror, she found a sorry sight. She looked bruised and battered and the evidence of her experience was burnt into her skin in a sickening red. Now tears of frustration covered her cheeks as she turned to Ava.

"Why would he do that to me?" she looked for answers.

"He does things like that. He did not mean you any harm. I think he doesn't always think things through," she tried to cover for him, secretly annoyed at his error in judgment. She was used to covering up for the lack of common sense the men displayed regularly. Ava lit a cigarette and took a deep drag, holding it in and then she let the air out in a loud sigh.

"Here…" she offered it to Nicole.

"I don't smoke," Nicole protested but her hand took it without hesitation and before she could calculate what she was doing, she took her first deep drag of a cigarette and coughed the smoke that burnt the lining of her lungs out in uncontrollable spasms.

"Not so deep, get used to it first," Ava said, placing her hand on Nicole's back, but not really concentrating on the girl in front of her. Her brain was doing damage control and figuring out what they could do to calm the obviously distraught and disillusioned girl in front of her. By the third drag Nicole took, she felt a sudden calmness wash over her and her head started spinning. She felt dizzy, but peaceful.

As the two women sat there in silence sharing a cigarette, Nicole decided that she could not lose face in front of the men and if she was to survive them and be part of their union, she would have to gather herself and make as if she did not care that they had done what they did. This was now part of her make up, the ability to make a quick and rationalised decision, which would enable her to survive and cope with any circumstances that were flung her way.

"Come, I need coffee," Nicole said and Ava looked up in amazement at the young girl's ability to gather herself in a matter of minutes. Ava knew from experience that not a lot of young women would be able to face the onslaught of the men, but this one did, and it made her proud of her fellow female shift member. Nicole had lived up to the "fighter" she saw in her earlier that night. Ava smiled at Nicole as her respect for the girl increased.

"Only if I can make you some?" she offered, this being a great offering, as students normally had to make the coffee for the Charge Office commander and not the other way around.

"Deal," Nicole said and offered her hand to pull Ava to her feet from where she sat.

As they walked to the kitchen, Nicole decided that just because she was not going to lay a complaint of harassment against her shift members, it did not mean that she could not have fun with her position and she was going to have the men worry about the consequences of their actions for a while. So, she put on her serious face, wore her war scars proudly and only acknowledged Ava's presence. They stood in the kitchen and drank coffee.

From there, she could see that one of the men took her bag out and opened it in the fresh air so that the remaining gas could evaporate. Ben and his vehicle partner, Sergeant Vos, were nowhere to be seen and she gathered that they had decided to carry on with their patrols of the area. Later, Ava and Nicole got some food for themselves. After they ate, they manned the Charge Office like they had done earlier that night and they continued their conversing as old friends would. Daylight came sooner than expected and when Ben finally showed his face, Nicole chose not to greet him when they booked off duty, but she did wink at

Ava as to let her know she only wanted him to suffer a bit, for his part in her ordeal.

She knew that Ava would let him know that there were no hard feelings and therefore, she knew she could afford to torment him a little, as she might never get such an opportunity again. What Nicole did not know at the time though was that she had passed the test they had set for her with flying colours and that all the shift members became fond of their newest member and respected her as one of their own. She also now fell under the guardianship of Ava and Ben, two powerful figures at the station, a position in which most young policemen would want to be.

Chapter 6

In the following months, Nicole became part of the Charge Office. She was bright and very efficient and learned quickly to do all the functions of a Charge Office Commander. This meant that she was sometimes left to do the job single-handedly, although as a student she was not supposed to. Ava trusted her so much that she would book in as Charge Office commander and then let Nicole do the job, only signing her signature when it called for. Nicole enjoyed the buzz in the Charge Office and seeing that it became her focus, she totally looked past the drama taking place at home.

Her mother had by now fallen into a deep depression and because of Nicole's weird working hours and her mother's depression, they hardly saw each other or spoke, although they lived in the same house. Nicole's newfound passion made up for this though. And although at first it took some getting used to all the cursing and high testosterone levels in the police station, Nicole now lived for her shifts as it was entertaining and somewhat addictive. She was also young and pretty and therefore got a lot of attention and special treatment that more than made up for the lonely years as an only child and the lack of her parents' support.

The days flew by and she and the men on her shift became friends. It was only Sergeant Swart she could not stomach. Usually, she could find something in anybody to admire enough to feel some sort of connection, but for some strange reason, there was nothing she liked about him and although she had been working with him daily, he still made her skin crawl if he came too close. She therefore chose to stay as far away from him as possible.

She had just become accustomed to her new routine and her privileged position as a student on a shift that spoiled her to bits. She was allowed to leave a few minutes before the rest of the shift as only one of her privileges, on night shifts, when she sometimes found it hard to stay awake. They let her sleep on the sofa in the hallway, covering her with their warm coats they were issued with. She tried not to take too much advantage of their generosity, as she felt compelled to stay awake as they had to suffer, and she did not want to seem unsympathetic. Thus, she only did this when her eyes would not let her do otherwise. On one such night shift, where her eyes refused to stay open, she resorted to a quick nap on the sofa, where she had curled up in a bundle.

That night, Ben was kind enough to lend her his coat. As she was drooling her way into deep sleep, she was peacefully unaware of the young man entering the dark hallway to use the toilet, as he was unaware of her as well. Only when he returned did he make out the frame of a body underneath the huge coat that nearly covered the two-seated sofa. He walked closer to inspect who it was. He wanted to make sure that there had not by chance entered a destitute person who took shelter in the station. When he reached the curled-up body, he could not make out the face as the coat covered it. He slowly pulled it away as not to awake the sleeping person; he immediately saw that the auburn mane that covered the girl's face was well-groomed and therefore not just some destitute person.

Before he could stop himself, his curiosity took over and he slowly wiped the hair back as to see what was hidden underneath it. He was not prepared for what he saw: the girl was beautiful. She had strong features, but they seemed delicate at the same time, her skin appeared even creamier in the dim light. He let her hair fall back on her face and she moved while a groan escaped her full pink lips. He smiled as he appreciated her beauty and then he turned to return to the office to find out who she was.

"Who is the girl sleeping on the sofa?" Mika asked as he entered the Charge Office.

"Oh, that is the new student, Nicole Burger," Ava answered, "but she is off limits," she warned.

"I have no intention…" he tried to deny his interest in her.

"I know exactly what your intentions are, and she is off limits," Ava emphasised again.

"Oh well, then I will see you," he greeted Ava and he disappeared into the night. Mika was a very attractive dark-haired Sergeant working at Milnerton police station. He was only twenty-one and thus only two years Nicole's senior. Milnerton police station, where he worked, was situated only a few kilometres from Table View's station, as Milnerton was the neighbouring town of Table View.

Up until this point, Nicole had never had a serious relationship. Ava sensed as much and therefore explained her protectiveness when it came to Nicole. It wasn't a fact of no interest; she had, in fact, had many suitors from a young age, as she was exceptionally beautiful, but as a result of her protective upbringing, she was too cautious to let anyone too close. She had normal flirtations and fondling in her teenage years, but as soon as it became too serious, she would end the friendship or avoid the person pursuing her. She was taught that a sexual relationship was meant for a married couple and that under no circumstances was it proper for a woman to let any one touch or fondle her genitals, she was tempted though as her body tingled in the most glorious manner when she kissed someone of the opposite sex.

She never really fell in love and only used her young suitors to practice on. Through this role play, her creative mind and her enthusiasm, and the way men's bodies responded to hers, she learned enough about physical contact to know that when the time came she would fulfil any man's desires. And although this theory wasn't tested yet, as her loyalty to her childhood values restricted her from experiencing it, things have changed. She had not even thought about it yet, but her parents' divorce and her confusion about other life issues, would also spill over in her future decisions when faced with such temptations.

She was also in the right environment for this to happen as the high stress levels under which police officers worked made them highly strung and their sexual desires as a result, were the cause of many scandals and improper behaviour. Something else Nicole had to become accustomed to was the foul language that was second nature to the police force. It was as if they had their own language where they needed to swear in order for them to understand each other. At first this was difficult for her to stomach as she hardly heard swear words in the environment she grew up in, but soon she did not even notice her own adoption to her environment and her new vocabulary rolled off her tongue as if it was natural.

When Nicole finally awoke to join Ava in the Charge Office, Ava smiled knowingly at her.

"What?" Nicole demanded to know.

"No, nothing," Ava kept on smiling at her.

"Have I messed up my hair?" Nicole asked while running her hands over her hair to feel if it felt unevenly tied into the ponytail she had tied it up in earlier, but it felt fine.

"Ava," she scolded, "tell me."

Ava was laughing by now at Nicole's distress. "You have an admirer," she finally answered. Nicole was expecting something much more exciting. She did not even want to know who it was as she thought it was someone working at the station and as far as she had seen, there was no one remotely interesting working there. She flopped into the seat next to Ava, looking bored and disappointed.

"Don't you even want to know who it is?" Ava wanted to know; she could not understand how a young girl would not want to know if someone was interested in her, as most young women would love the attention.

"No, not really," Nicole tried to avoid the conversation as she under no circumstances wanted to be emotionally involved with anyone at this point. Her faith in love had been broken and at this point it looked rather like a waste of time and energy. Ava sensed that something had left a scar on her and that it was still healing. She left the subject of the admirer and directed it to the cause of the problem and she cunningly got Nicole to tell her why she did not believe in love or wanted to get involved in any relationships.

After Nicole told her about her parents' divorce and the disillusion she felt now and how they were emotionally unavailable to her, Ava felt even more protective over her as she too came from a broken home and she knew exactly what a divorce entailed as she had once been married herself. Ava was already in her mid-thirties and when she was twenty-two, she had married another police officer, who was verbally and physically abusive. Luckily, there were no children born from the marriage and Ava as a strong woman was not prepared to take the abuse, so she had left him, but she had gone through the same emotions that all go through when dealing with the end of a relationship.

She then explained to Nicole that even though a lot of relationships do not work out, there is no reason why she should not at least enjoy the company of someone who made her feel special. She did not have to commit, nor feel obligated in any way to the person she is dating, she could just enjoy it while it lasted and then move on. This made sense to Nicole as this was actually what she had been doing up until now. The only difference was that when she was younger, she would take care not to hurt the guy she was dating, but somehow, she now felt a bit self-righteous and without her knowing it yet, she would be a bit more reckless when dealing with others' emotions.

"Well, if you really do not want to know who he is then I will let it be, but he is really cute," Ava said mischievously as she finished their philosophical conversation off.

"Who is it then?" Nicole said with a sigh, giving in to her own curiosity and knowing that Ava would not let it go until she had told her who it was. Ava told her about Mika and how handsome he was. Ava really liked the clean honest face Mika portrayed. She knew he had good manners, did not swear nearly as much as the others on his shift and he had a sense of humour that was infectious. Everybody got on with him and he had a reputation as a good-hearted guy.

To Ava, this seemed like a good match for Nicole. Nicole listened intently, although she pretended not to be interested. Nicole felt flattered that someone so highly regarded by her friend was interested in her, but soon after that night forgot about the incident.

The weeks flew by and Nicole's routine fell back on track without her giving the young man another thought. Mika, on the other hand, could not get the beauty of the auburn-haired girl out of his mind. He constantly caught himself wondering about her, wondering how she looked when awake and what she would be like. The little he saw of her that first night was enough to make him realise that he had never before met someone so intriguing and that he probably would not soon thereafter.

He was popular among the female species, as he treated all with the courteous manner of a skilled lover and he was easy on the eye as well. Normally, he did not have to do much hunting to get his way with someone he felt attracted to, but until now the thrill of that first conquer of physical beauty was what made him pursue women in general. He had never really formed a bond with any of his ladies and was not intending in doing so for quite a while to come. At this stage, he thought it was her beauty that intrigued him and refused to admit to himself that there was more to this girl than just that. She was dangerous ground for him and he could feel it when he had stood next to her there in the hallway. He tried to put her out of his mind, but found himself pining for her.

After the third week of torture, he found himself en route to Table View police station. It was the first afternoon shift and he had to deliver a docket to Melkbosstrand police station. There were two ways to get to this station, a back road, which led straight from Milnerton to the Melkbosstrand turn off, or the longer and more scenic road thought Table View and then Bloubergstrand, all along the coastline until you reached Melkbosstrand. Today however he thought it wise to fill up with petrol, although it was not necessary and a task no one really liked doing, before he went to Melkbosstrand. This meant that he would have to enter the Charge Office to fill in the petrol register and hopefully get a chance to see the young woman who had tormented his dreams the past few weeks.

Nicole was in the ladies room when Mika entered the Charge Office and he felt his heart sink as he scanned the room for a glimpse of her, but she was nowhere. Ava was friendly as always and gave him a huge smile. Mika checked himself as he nearly asked her where the new student was.

"Ah…the key?" he enquired instead, referring to the key of the petrol pump.

"Of course," Ava replied, opening the drawer next to her and holding the key out for him to collect, "here you are." Mika took his time coming around the counter and taking the key from Ava, to give him extra time to scan the hallway and in the hope that the young beauty would make her appearance, but there was no sight of her. Mika reluctantly went outside to fill the tank of his police vehicle. He felt disappointed and did not dare to ask about her as Ava was too cunning and would know he was intrigued by her.

He was not even prepared to acknowledge this to himself, let alone let someone else in on it. He finished up and went in to register the amount he had filled his tank with. There was still no sight of her. Mika sighed and then turned his attention to the register in front of him. In this register, you had to write the date, time, kilometre reading of the vehicle, registration, driver of the vehicle and the Force number of the particular driver, as well as signing it. This took some time, but to Mika today it felt longer than usual, he wanted to get out on the road again, he had already wasted enough time on a fruitless quest and was now irritated by his vulnerability in acting in this manner. He silently cursed as his pen suddenly refused to write another letter.

In the meantime, Nicole had come back from the back of the police station and had placed herself next to Ava, not taking notice of the policeman bent over the petrol register, for she had seen many do so before him and from where she sat, she could only see the top of his head. In blue uniform, they all looked the same, with the grey undertone of their uniform milking all the colour out of even the most attractive of them, so she pulled the SAP 13 Register closer, as she and Ava were busy registering some of the evidence one of the detectives was handing in. All evidence, found items, firearms of the public, stolen motor vehicles that were retrieved, drugs recovered in drug busts or arrests had to be registered in this register and the smaller items were then locked in the SAP 13 safe. The vehicles were kept in the SAP 13 camp, which was situated at the back of the police station and guarded by Specials.

"Ava, can I borrow a pen, this damn pen…" and as he looked up, he lost his words as he saw Nicole. Nicole was still focussing on the register in front of her and her long flowing hair veiled one side of her face, but revealed enough of her creamy skin and strong features and plump lips to arouse an uneasy feeling in poor Mika. Ava noticed this and smiled as she found it amusing.

"Nicole," Ava purposefully tried to intervene, "will you be so kind as to lend Mika your pen?"

Nicole looked up at Mika with a frown still marking her forehead, but as soon as she saw him, her frown melted from her face making room for a friendly smile. She felt her face flush and hoped that he would not see it. She did not however answer Ava nor stand up to take the pen to him, nor did she offer it to him. For a few awkward seconds, they stared at each other while Ava stared at them, enjoying every minute of their out-of-character behaviour.

Mika, embarrassed by his lack of control, pulled himself together. "So are you going to lend me your pen or not?" he said in an agitated tone.

"If you ask nicely," Nicole quickly recovered, angered by his rudeness and she stretched forwards to slam the pen she held onto the table in front of her. Mika had no choice but to come to the table where she sat so that he could finish what he was doing. He was used to girls doing things for him and Nicole's stubbornness agitated him further.

With a determined pace, he walked to her table and plucked the pen from where it lay and as he did so, he looked deep into her face wanting to hate her, but finding himself admiring her emerald green eyes and the perfection of her features, which hinted at a deep and caring passionate soul hiding behind the wall she had just lifted. Nicole in return felt like spitting in his light blue eyes that were set off by his tanned olive-toned skin. And although it only took a few seconds for him to retrieve the pen and make his way back to the register, it was enough time for them both to take in the full extent of the other's presence.

When Mika had finished, he slammed the pen down in front of the register on the counter in the same manner as Nicole, saying: "Thank you!"

Mika then turned and left the Charge Office, leaving Nicole to fetch her pen in the same manner she had made him come and fetch it.

Damn arrogant bastard! she cursed to herself, hating the fact that she was not able to charm him the way the men on her shift were charmed by her. Over the following weeks, Mika made a point of regularly showing his face at the police station and slowly Nicole and Mika started a blooming friendship.

Although they both tried their utmost not to flirt or be too obvious about the mutual attraction, they soon found it difficult to be satisfied with their limited visits. Mika had had enough and when one of his shift members and a close friend of his held a barbeque at his house, he saw it as the perfect opportunity to see Nicole out of work-related circumstances.

Nicole was excited when Mika finally phoned her while she was on duty to ask her if she would join him. She thought he would never ask her out and since she was brought up not to make the first move, she was quite frustrated at this stage by his slowness to do so. They arranged that he would come fetch her, seeing that she did not have her own transport yet.

The next evening, when he was to pick her up, she made a point of starting her grooming rituals a little sooner than usual, taking time to apply her make-up as to enhance her beauty without it being obvious that she had even applied any. She was very artistic and had mastered the art of applying make-up subtly. She then continued to blow-dry her long auburn hair into a smooth mass that framed her face so that it would set off her eyes and emphasise her full plump lips. After she had admired her handwork in the mirror, she stood up and studied her athletic body, dressed in only a cotton bra and panty, trying to figure out what clothing would show off her perfectly formed limbs to its fullest whilst making it appear as if she was not trying to do so.

She decided on a pair of figure-hugging jeans of which the one knee had been ripped open on a previous occasion. This would allow Mika to admire her form, but also give him a view of her smooth tanned skin underneath, all this in a pair of jeans that were ripped and therefore created the impression that she did not take as much time picking her outfit as she actually had. After she slipped into her jeans, she picked out a thin white cotton blouse that buttoned up in the front. The blouse was not too loose-fitting but just enough to flow effortlessly as she moved. She buttoned it up to just above where her bra joined at the front, making sure not to reveal her bra, but knowing that Mika, being taller than her, would be able to get glimpses of what was hidden under the material if she moved and he came close enough to her.

Nicole did not have the biggest breasts, but they were not small either. Her breasts were full and firm and she knew they would please any man no matter which size he preferred. While she was consciously running all this through her mind, she did not once contemplate that she had never before taken so much time in trying to seduce anyone, nor what she would do if she succeeded in doing so, as she had never gone further than light fondling and kissing. She did not really care about the consequences, she for the first time in her life she felt carefree and in control, as if she could take on anything life threw at her.

Since the day her parents had told her about their divorce, she was set free to live life one day at a time and even if it made her a little reckless, her newfound confidence made her feel invincible. She sprayed on a dash of perfume before she gave herself a final appreciative smile and then made her way to the lounge, but before she could reach it, she heard a knock on the door and she made her way to it. She was in a light-hearted mood and it showed when she flung the door open and smiled into Mika's face.

"Hello, can I help you, sir?" she playfully asked Mika.

"I don't know, can you?" he teased back.

"I just might be able to." She smiled and turned her back on him, yelling at her mother, who was hidden somewhere in the house: "I am going now, don't wait up for me."

Not that her mother ever did, but she thought it decent to let her mother know that she wasn't intending on coming home soon.

"Shouldn't I have introduced myself to your mother?" Mika asked, confused as he wanted to do the gentlemanly thing, and for an instant, he wondered why she did not want to introduce him to her. Not knowing that it was because she felt embarrassed by the mental state of her mother, he deduced that he wasn't important enough yet for that honour.

"She is busy, maybe next time," she said and walked to his car. He opened the door for her and as she sat and lifted her long legs to pull them in, the slit in her jean exposed her kneecap, sending an unexpected jolt through his body. He closed the door behind her and got into the driver's seat. Before he started the engine, he paused and stared at her, while she was looking at him.

"You really look good tonight."

Nicole's lips parted and revealed her perfect teeth; she had succeeded in pleasing him.

"You do not look too bad yourself!" she replied. They continued their appreciative gazes for a few seconds longer, as if they had more to say, but could not find the words to say it.

"Well, we should probably go," Mika said and bent forwards to start his car. As he was still young and very attractive, Nicole was taken off guard by the type of car he was driving. He was driving a light blue Toyota Corolla, something she would expect an old man to drive. For some reason, she thought that a young guy like him should have been driving something like a Golf GTI, or something sporty. She did not question it though, as she did not want to insult him, but for a second, she thought that something wasn't adding up, but left it there, as he was much too attractive to let something so trivial bother her.

On their way to his friend's house, they made small conversation, with him telling her about his shift members and about his friends she was going to meet. How they grew up together, went to college together and now how they had ended up on the same shift, affording them their off time to spend together. The four of them sounded like a close and pleasant bunch. She told him just enough about herself to impress him and satisfy him into thinking she had a normal and well-balanced life.

They finally arrived at his friend's house and as they turned into the driveway, three young men were standing there, admiring one of their vehicles' new mag wheels. Mika was first out and the guys came closer to greet him, hindering him from making his way to Nicole's door so that he could open it for her. They did not even notice her climbing out and watching them as they took turns to shake Mika's hand and hug him. When they had finished and Mika turned to get Nicole, they all turned to see what Mika was looking at. They were all confused by her presence, but also admired the beauty standing in front of them.

"I hope you don't mind, but I brought a friend," Mika said to Juan who was mischievously smiling at Mika for hiding Nicole from them.

"No, we don't mind at all," he replied.

"Guys, this is Nicole," Mika continued to introduce her to the boys.

"Nice meeting you," she said politely, feeling a little out of place as she thought she was invited by the host, only to find out he had no clue that she was coming. For an instant, she dreaded that she would be the only female at the barbeque and felt like fleeing, but Juan must have picked up on her discomfort as he came to her rescue.

"The girls are inside, come then, I will introduce you to them," and he took her by the elbow gently and guided her into the house, where three girls were preparing salads in the kitchen.

Nicole immediately clicked with Gerda, Juan's girlfriend. She was outspoken, friendly and well groomed. She was also in the police force and a year older than Nicole. Gerda was stationed in Sea Point where there was a female barracks. She also lodged there and seemed to enjoy her independence. She had purposefully asked to be transferred to Cape Town after she completed her college training as she wanted to get away from her hometown Jacobsdal in the Free State. She had had enough of her elderly parents and their strict rules and had joined the police for pretty much the same reason as Nicole did; independence.

She was also a bit more liberal thinking than Nicole was, and Nicole appreciated her candid open-minded opinions about the restrictive morals that had been forced upon them by the society they were brought up in. It was comforting to meet someone with whom she could discuss and question some of these unwritten rules of society and to know that there were other young South Africans who also were disillusioned by their parents' passiveness in regard to what was going on in South Africa at the time. It now seemed to Nicole that there were others among her peers who were moving in the direction of change.

What she did not know was how the young adults from all races would struggle in the future to find balance in the change they were fighting for and how one race's evils would only make room for another's and how similar all races actually were in striving for individual gain and power, regardless of the consequences. Their conversation kept them so busy that they hardly took notice of the time or of the other two girls leaving the kitchen, and by the time Mika and Juan came to fetch them, they had cemented their bond for the following years to come.

"If I knew I was going to have to compete for some attention, I wouldn't have brought you here," Mika said as he placed his hand on Nicole's shoulder to make her aware of his presence.

"Well, I thank you for bringing me," Nicole said, smiling up into his handsome face.

"Yes, I thank you too!" Gerda agreed.

"Well, you can continue your conversation outside," Mika said in a mockingly agitated voice.

"Aaah, are you sulking?" Nicole teased him.

"Will that help?" he teased back, but silently, he was a little annoyed that he did not receive as much of her attention as he had hoped for, although he was pleased by the fact that Gerda and Nicole got on so well.

The rest of the night Nicole made sure that she gave Mika enough attention by including him in all conversations she had. Although he was intelligent he did not seem to enjoy talking as much as she and Gerda did. And while she enjoyed the company of her new group of friends, she was constantly aware of Mika who was sitting next to her by the fire. As it became later, Mika at one stage took his jacket and wrapped it around her shoulders and then placed his arm around her as if to keep her warm.

She thought it sweet, but also arousing as the smell of him and the weight and warmth of his powerful arms reminded her of her longing for his body. Instinctively, she snuggled into the pit of his arm, resting her head on his chest before she looked up into his face. As she did so, his mouth found hers and he placed a warm kiss on hers as if they had known each other for years. She was taken as much by surprise as he was for doing so. Ignoring what he had just done, he tried to disguise his lapse of control by redirecting his attention back to Juan, while he removed his arm from Nicole's shoulders. And when they finally finished eating and said their goodbyes, they silently climbed in to the car. There was not much said on the way home, but as they neared Nicole's house, he slowed the car down.

"Nicole…" he started but he paused so long that she got the impression he was not going to finish his sentence.

"Yes?" she tried to coax him into saying what was on his mind.

"I just wanted to say that I really enjoyed tonight and that I hope we can see more of each other."

"Oh, well, I did too, and I would like to see more of you as well," she said softly as if she did not want others to hear.

"Good, then you wouldn't mind if I phone you tomorrow?" he asked.

"No, I wouldn't mind," she replied, frustrated by his cautiousness. Her first impression of him was that he would be a little more assertive in expressing his feelings towards her and sometimes glimpses of that confident soul came to the fore, but then he turned into this. Mika turned into their driveway and parked under a tree at the one end.

As Nicole wanted to get out of the car, he grabbed her wrist and she thought he was going to kiss her at that point, but instead he spoke: "No, I will walk you to the door."

Damn, what is wrong with you? she cursed silently, but waited patiently for him to get out as well. He took her hand in his warm hands and it occurred to her that his hands were softer than she had anticipated, but did not ponder on it as at least he was touching her. When they reached the door, she faced him and although she was tall, she still had to look up at him. Before he could say another annoying thing or before she could even think about what she was doing, she reached up and softly placed her lips on his and parted his lips with her wet tongue.

Although he was taken off guard by her forwardness, the softness and taste of her full lips pleased him, and he let her suck at his lips for a few seconds before he replied with a passionate kiss, pulling her close to him to such an extent that the hardness of his arousal pressed against her. As she realised he was just trying to be considerate by being cautious, for he was lusting for her as she was for him, and as she did not need to test him further, she pushed him away, leaving him breathless.

"You can phone me tomorrow," she said smilingly before she turned and disappeared into the doorway, leaving him wanting more.

Chapter 7

Mika did not phone the following day or the day thereafter and although it confused and frustrated Nicole, it did not bother her to such an extent that she could not function properly. By day three, she had actually forgotten that he offered to phone her, and she set about her day as she usually would only for Mika to disturb her plans for the day.

"Hi," he replied when she answered the phone, "I am sorry I am only phoning now. I had a small family crisis to sort out," he offered an apology.

"No need to apologise, I hope everything is all right?" she asked, concerned.

"Yes, it's nothing serious. Anyway," he quickly changed the subject, "I wanted to know if you wanted to come visit me after work, I will pick you up," he offered.

"Umm," she hesitated, not knowing if she should rather let him suffer a bit for forgetting about her for two days, but she missed his presence and caved in. "Okay, but you can pick me up at home as I want to change first."

"That's settled then. I will see you later." and just before he put the phone down: "I did miss you!" as if he knew what she was thinking and wanted to reassure her.

The day flew by quickly as Nicole was now well skilled in running the Charge Office and she took statements and kept records up to date as if she had been doing it for years. Only when she finally booked off from her shift did she remember that she had to make her way home so that she could be ready before Mika came to fetch her. At home, she quickly pulled on a pair of jeans, a t-shirt and sneakers. After re-adjusting her ponytail, she heard her mother calling her.

"Nicole, there is someone here for you!" Nicole rushed to the front door, trying to avoid her mother and Mika spending too much time in each other's company. Since her parents' divorce, Nicole did not want anyone to come to close to her and kept even people she was fond of at a safe distance, only revealing that which she though absolutely necessary. Unconsciously, she resorted to this as a means to protect herself from further emotional hurt, living in her own safe space, emotionally unattached to anyone, in an effort to control not only her life but her emotions as well. The problem, which she did not realise at that stage yet, was that she sometimes used people in her quest to find herself. This meant that she could not only be ruthless with others' feelings, but she in future would sometimes act irresponsibly in experiencing what life had to offer.

"Hi, I see you have met my mother?" she said, hoping that they did not have much time to communicate.

"No, I thought this was your sister." Mika winked at Nicole's mother as if they knew each other well. This infuriated Nicole, not only was she still angry with her parents, but she knew her mother was extremely attractive, and she felt a little jealous that he recognised this and gave her such a nice compliment.

"Well, now you have," Nicole said impatiently and pulled him by the arm out into the driveway.

"Nice meeting you, Nicole's mother," Mika raised his voice and he waved over his shoulder at Nicole's mother.

"You too!" she shouted back and closed the door behind them.

"Hey," Mika pulled loose from Nicole's grip, "what's wrong?" he asked as her behaviour was a clear indication that she did not want him to meet her mother.

"Nothing!" Nicole replied seriously. Mika could sense by her tone that he should not pursue the matter and tried to make light-hearted conversation as they drove to his house.

When they pulled into Mika's driveway, Nicole was humbled by the modesty of his family's house. They lived in a neatly painted three-bedroomed home in the centre of Milnerton and although there were areas in Milnerton where the very rich lived, Mika and his family just managed to stay outside the area of the very poor. Somehow, in her naïve young mind, although she knew there were different social and financial classes, she thought everyone she knew would live in the same privileged circumstances that she did.

Now, for the first time she was confronted by the reality that her family was living far above middle class and that she was even more privileged than she had ever suspected. She followed Mika into the back door, where he had parked his car, and into the kitchen. Novilon floors was something she last saw in the late seventies when she was still a young girl, as they had all the Novilon in their house exchanged for tiles in the early eighties.

Nicole was used to her mother having the kitchen and bathrooms renovated as soon as it became outdated, but in Mika's house, things stayed exactly the way it was done since the house was built in the seventies. What impressed her though was how well preserved everything was and it attested to the fact that this family took pride in their belongings and appreciated everything they had.

Mika walked in front and ordered Nicole to take a seat in the kitchen at the table in the middle of it. Nicole did as he asked and waited patiently as he disappeared into the hallway. When he came back, he looked relieved.

"Is something wrong?" Nicole asked.

"No, I was looking for my mother, but it seems she is out," he replied and switched the kettle on to make them some coffee. For some reason, Nicole got the distinct impression that he knew his mother would not be home, that he had planned it that way and that he was just checking that they were alone and when he had confirmed the fact, he had felt relieved. Nicole was the last to question his motives and therefore did not.

"How many of you are staying in this house?" Nicole asked, curious about the makings of his family.

"It's only me, my mother and my older sister. My father passed away when I was sixteen," he said matter-of-factly, but she could sense the hurt of his loss in his voice.

"Oh, I am sorry!" she said, shocked as the reality of losing one's father at such a young age hit her.

"No, don't be," and he continued to pour the warm water into the cups he had taken out of the wooden kitchen cabinet in front of him. Mika came to sit opposite Nicole and he started to tell her about his mother and sister and how he felt responsible for them and although he had desperately wanted to study after school, he decided to join the police force so that he could help his mother financially. He told her that he did not regret his decision as it allowed him to study through the police force and that he was busy studying criminal law.

He had already finished his diploma allowing him to be promoted to Sergeant and that he was now studying to become a Warrant Officer and in future, hopefully even further, allowing him to be promoted to Lieutenant, which would be enough to let him move through the ranks of the officers as far as his career would take him.

"Why are there so many Sergeants in the police force? Have all of them studied only to Sergeant?" This had been bothering her since she joined the police force, as every second member seemed to hold this rank, irrespective of his or her age.

"No, anybody can be promoted to Sergeant without studying. All you need is four years of service to qualify," he explained.

"But then why are some of the Sergeants so old? Why haven't they been promoted further?" she needed to know.

"Well, you can retire as a Sergeant, as you can get stuck there. Every rank has a number of grading levels, which is determined by years' service and influences your salary considerably. When you have enough years of service you need to apply for a promotion and then things like an impeccable record, job availability, your relationship with your Station Commander and other politics come into play, resulting in a lot of Sergeants finishing their service as such. This is how a Sergeant in his highest grading level can earn more than a newly promoted Warrant Officer. This is why I am furthering my studies as it will ensure that I will have to be considered before the members who haven't."

His determination to better his future impressed her and she felt compassion for his feelings of responsibility towards his mother and sister. What she did not realise though was to what lengths he would go to secure a lustrous future for himself.

"I think that's great," Nicole said. Mika looked into her face, searching for sincerity and when he recognised it, he stood up and walked around the table. He pulled her to her feet and hugged her as if he recognised the force driving him, in her. When he finally let her go, he had to clear his throat before he could speak again.

"Come, I will show you my room," Mika invited while taking her hand and pulling her gently after him.

His room was much bigger than she had expected, with a double bed and single bed easily fitting into the room without overcrowding it. Nicole walked over to the single bed, which was situated underneath the window and made her comfortable on it while she scanned his neat room. Everything was decorated in different shades of blue, except for the white lace curtains covering the window. The sun was shining through the glass, enveloping her in a warm embrace and she felt relaxed and content.

Nicole's eyes caught the trophies, which were neatly stacked on a shelf opposite the double bed, and she questioned him about it. He explained that he was quite good at sport in school and had collected them over the years. He continued to show her his other academic accomplishments and she could not help thinking that it was a waste that he ended up in the police force and intended to make a career out of it.

To her, it was merely a stepping-stone enabling her to pursue a future of her choice as soon as she had saved enough to do so. While she was fixated on his mouth as he spoke, for he had a deliciously perfect one, she was rudely frightened by a sudden bang on the window.

"Mika! Mika!" a young woman's voice echoed through the glass behind her.

"Mika, I know you are in there! Open the door, I need to talk to you!" the voice continued and there was no mistaking that this girl was furious.

"Shuuuuut!" Mika whispered as he placed his index finger in front of his lips, indicating to her not to make a sound. Nicole, still trying to recover from the fright she had gotten, was too scared to make a noise anyway and opted to move her body as far away from the window as fast as she could, as it seemed as if the enraged girl was going to break it with her loud banging.

"Don't worry, she will go away, just keep quiet!" he whispered.

"Amy, I told you it's over. I have nothing further to say to you! Please leave, you are making a fool of yourself!" Mika raised his voice loud enough so that she would be able to hear him, without it seeming as if he was yelling at her.

"Aah! I knew you were in there, you bastard! Is she in there with you?" she screamed.

Suddenly, Nicole felt as if she was the cause of this argument and felt guilty beyond belief although she knew she had no part in it.

"Please take me home, then you two can sort this out," Nicole pleaded softly with Mika, as she did not want to find herself in the middle of this.

"No!" Mika said aloud, and then whispered, "It's my ex-girlfriend and she is too stubborn to accept that it is over. I will not let her spoil this day. She will leave, just give a minute," he tried to reason with Nicole. Nicole took a seat on the double bed, seeing that she was trapped.

"Maybe you should at least go and talk to her," Nicole appealed to him.

"Fine," Mika said, "but you stay here."

Nicole had no intention of venturing outside as she did not want to face the mad woman, but she was curious enough to find out what was going on and so, as Mika went outside, locking the door behind him to prevent Amy from entering the house and discover Nicole there, she leapt to her feet and ran to the window to get a look at Amy and to eavesdrop on what was being said.

Nicole watched how Mika took a small-framed dark-haired girl by her arms and gently pulled her further away from the window. This was obviously so that she would not be able to hear what was being said. The girl was beautiful and Nicole felt a little intimidated by her looks, although she had no reason to be. No matter how hard she tried, she could not hear what they were saying, but she could see that the girl was crying as she spoke and then when Mika could not control his frustration anymore, she heard him yell: "There is no-one else! It's just over!"

Nicole did not like the fact that he was lying about her being there and would normally see it as a sign of things to come, but somehow, she wanted to believe that he was just trying to spare the poor girl any further pain and chose to ignore his lie. The girl wiped her tears and hugged Mika, without saying a word, then she climbed back into her car and drove off.

Before Mika could return to the room, Nicole rushed over to the double bed and sat where he had left her, her heart pounding in her chest at the thought of being caught out. Mika did not even realise that she had moved and without saying anything placed his body next to hers, taking her hand in his.

"I am so sorry that you had to see that," he said without looking at her.

"Is she okay?" Nicole could not help herself, as she pitied the girl.

"Yes," Mika said, but Nicole was not sure if he had really heard her, as his mind seemed to wonder elsewhere. Nicole sat with him in silence on the bed, waiting for him to make the next move. Mika slowly turned to Nicole and took her face in his hands, taking his time to study her features.

"You are the most beautiful thing I have ever seen," he said softly. Nicole was too scared to speak. The afternoon was one of the most confusing she ever had to deal with and she was in unclear waters as how to act or what to say, so she kept silent.

"I think I am in love with you," he continued, "would you consider going steady with me?" Nicole was taken by surprise; this was the last thing she was expecting to hear and although she loved his company and felt very attracted to him, she could not decide if she felt anything deeper for him, as she had never loved anyone in this manner before. Nicole felt guilty for not being able to decide if she felt the same, but she was enjoying the attention and she did not want to have this experience end just jet.

"I would love to be your girlfriend," she said as gently as he did and then he bent forward to kiss her gently.

She might not have been in love with him, but she sure as hell lusted for his body, as he smelt wonderful and the warmness of his hands on her skin, and the softness of his lips, melted away all her will to control herself. Spontaneously she pressed forward, forcing him to fall back onto the bed, while they continued to kiss. Mika pulled her body on top of his, while pulling her legs apart so that they were spread to each side of his body. Nicole once again felt the hardness of his arousal pressing against her and it made her want him even more.

Their bodies started moving against each other, while they kept exploring each other's mouths until Nicole could not stand it anymore and as if he sensed this, he glided his one hand down her back, over her buttocks and down the middle of her, rhythmically stimulating her from behind as well as from the front, in an attempt to satisfy the need in her. This only frustrated Nicole more as she needed to satisfy the burning spasms of desire she felt in her loins.

Suddenly, they heard a key turn in the keyhole of the kitchen door and within a second, Mika had skilfully freed himself from under Nicole and stood at the door of his bedroom, adjusting his clothes and penis to hide any sign of his arousal. Instinctively, Nicole followed his lead and sat up as if nothing happened, but she struggled to control her breathing as her heart raced in her chest from wanting Mika and from the fright she had gotten by Mika's reaction towards the sound of someone else entering the house.

"Mika? Are you home?" an old woman's voice carried through to them.

"Come," Mika ordered Nicole silently.

"Yes Mom!" he answered. Nicole followed him to the kitchen where a small little old lady was waiting for them. She looked much too old to be his mother and Nicole deduced that she must have had him in her late thirties or early forties. She looked annoyed by Nicole's presence and did not smile until Mika placed a kiss on her cheek.

"Hallo, my boy, how was your day?" she asked him politely.

"Fine Mom, this is Nicole." He introduced Nicole and Nicole offered a hand for the woman to shake, which was done reluctantly.

"Would you two like some coffee?" she asked as she turned her back on them.

"No, I just came to pick something up, we are on our way out," Mika said. Nicole did not question why he wanted to flee so soon, but felt relieved when they were in the car on their way to her house, as she had felt very awkward in his mother's company. Mika continued as if there was nothing strange about his behaviour, so Nicole did the same. They made small talk and made jokes on their way to Nicole's house and there they said goodbye with another kiss.

"See you tomorrow?" he asked before he started the engine.

"Yes," she replied mechanically as if they had been doing this for years.

They did see each other the next day, and the days that followed. Only now, Mika came to visit her at her home or they would visit with Juan and Gerda at Juan's house, or go out in a group of friends, dating like an ordinary couple would, constantly flirting and making out while doing so. Although Nicole still did not know how she really felt about Mika, he soon became a constant and pleasant presence in her life, which made her feel, wanted and appreciated.

It also entertained her so that she hardly ever spent time pondering the loss of her family life. Soon the weeks had drawn into months and before she knew it the time drew closer for her to leave for College.

Although Nicole had been waiting for this for eight months, she did not realise how nervous she would be when the time came for her to leave. Where once she saw it as an adventure and a challenge, now the reality of it frightened her more than she thought it would. Nicole was to leave the Friday night and although, according to custom, she had to finish her shifts as per normal, her Station Commander took pity on her and gave her the whole week off so that she could pack and ready herself for the months of training ahead.

Unfortunately, Mika did not get off and he had to work his shifts, leaving Nicole on her own, without any distractions, to struggle through the week. Mika also did not visit as often as usual, with excuses ranging from being tired and needing to rest, to having to help his mother with chores around the house. It was only on the Thursday afternoon that he finally phoned to ask if he could pick her up.

Of course, she said yes, as she needed to say goodbye to him before she left for the next few months. They drove down to the beach where he found a secluded spot where they could be alone. They spoke about the week that had passed and other trivial things, avoiding the obvious reason for his presence. When Nicole could not stand the denial any longer, she dared raise the subject.

"Mika, I do not expect you to wait for me until I come back," she tested his feelings.

"What?" he looked shocked by her suggestion that they should probably take a break while she was in training.

"Why would you say such a thing?" he looked truly upset.

"I just thought that you shouldn't put your life on hold while I am away," she tried to explain, but actually she was pleased to see that he had no intention of breaking up with her, as he was the only moral support she had had at that stage.

"No, don't be silly. Nothing has to change," he said, looking away and staring into the distance over the sea.

"Well, I will miss you," Nicole struggled to get the words out, as she suddenly felt very alone. She realised that she was going to miss his attention more than she was going to miss him as a person and the fact that she knew deep down that she was not emotionally connected to anyone saddened her. Mika looked at her and saw the small droplets forming in the corner of her eyes. He pulled her into a bear hug and held her against his chest while she wept.

For the first time since she swore to determine her own future, she could let herself cry under the pretext that her love for him was causing her pain. She cried as she realised that there where she should have been filled with the warmth of love for the people she loved and who loved her back, there was an empty space of confusion and self-pity. What made it worse was that she could not allow herself to share her burden with anyone and although she thought she could handle it, the load suddenly felt too heavy for her to carry.

Mika, who was under the impression he was the cause of her tears, compassionately lifted her chin and kissed her, while holding her tightly against him, and she responded with the passion of a last kiss and as if it enabled her to communicate her worries and fears through her mouth to Mika. She desperately needed him to understand. When they finally pulled away breathlessly, she saw that her smudged eyeliner had stained his shirt.

"Shit, I am sorry about that," and she pointed at the mark on his shirt.

"It's fine; don't worry about it," he replied matter-of-factly as he started the engine to take her home.

And then she knew: *I am on my own.*

Chapter 8

"Good morning, Nicole," a chirpy voice woke Nicole from her sleep and she could not figure out who was so happy to see her so early in the morning. When her eyes finally focussed on her mother standing in front of her bed with a cup of coffee, she frowned.

"Morning," she reluctantly and sceptically groaned while taking the steaming brew from her mother's hands. Up until that moment, she had not even contemplated that she could have posed just as big a problem for her mother as she felt her mother and father were to her. Her mother for the first time in months was friendly and more than willing to communicate. Nicole did not trust her mother's enthusiasm and chose to believe that her mother was happy to finally be rid of her, instead of her mother sincerely trying to connect with her before she left. Hazel took a seat at the end of the bed.

"So? Are you excited about your big day?" she asked Nicole.

"Yes, I suppose so," Nicole grunted.

"Well, if there is anything I can do for you, just give me a shout," she said while placing her hand on Nicole's leg and gently squeezing it, before she stood up to leave the room, but turned at the door. "Maybe we should go for lunch this afternoon."

"Uuuuh, can I get back to you on that one? I still have a few errands to run, I will try to finish before twelve." Nicole quickly kept her options open, as she was not prepared to trust her mother's intentions just yet.

"Okay, let me know. I am keeping my day open for you," she said in a cheerful voice and disappeared into the hallway. Nicole desperately wanted to believe that her mother was finally opening up again and that their relationship was going to return to what it once had been, but struggled within herself to find the nerve to do so.

Nicole did not really have a lot to do, as she was meticulous in preparing long in advance when it concerned her work and associated responsibilities. After she finished dressing she fled to the mall and spent the morning aimlessly wondering in the stores while trying to figure out a good reason not to lunch with her mother. She finally came to the conclusion that it could not harm anyone if she did decide to do so; what she was in actual fact doing was giving into the hope that they were starting a reconciliation process, without admitting it to herself. She made her way back home and found her mother waiting for her.

"I was hoping you would make it," Hazel said as Nicole entered the front door.

"Just give me a minute, then I will be with you," Nicole replied equally polite and quickly went to her room to place the few parcels she had collected on her morning's excursions in her room.

When she returned, her mother was already waiting for her with keys in hand.

"Do you want to drive? We can decide on the way where we feel like eating," Hazel invited. Hazel hardly ever offered her vehicle for Nicole to use as Nicole only had a learners driver's licence. It was only her father who regularly let her drive his car, even if he was not accompanying her. He even did so when she was only sixteen and did not qualify for a licence yet. He grew up in the countryside and could not see why you needed a driver's licence if you were responsible enough and could drive properly and he made it his cause to teach Nicole to drive properly before she was sixteen, so by the time she was eighteen, it came naturally.

"Yes, if you want me to," Nicole replied and took the keys from her.

They drove down to the beachfront, slowly scouting the countless restaurants lining it and finally settled on one that had only opened a few weeks earlier. Nicole was afforded a day with her mother as if nothing had happened and Nicole was left feeling optimistic that things would return to normal in their household. Nicole and Hazel shared a bottle of wine and ate seafood. Conversation came easily, and both avoided any discussions about Hazel's divorce and stuck to everyday matters.

Hazel questioned Nicole on how she felt about her training lying ahead and about her traveling arrangements, as Nicole until now had kept her in the loop as to what was going on in her life. Nicole confided in her mother that she felt a little nervous, but that she felt confident that she would be able to master anything they could throw at her. Her mother gave a few words of encouragement and handed Nicole a little present.

"What is this?" Nicole asked.

"Open it," Hazel encouraged her.

When Nicole opened it, she felt like crying, but bit hard on her lower lip to fight back the tears.

"Are you sure?" Nicole asked her mother and suddenly felt guilty for the months of hatred she fostered in her heart against her parents, for in front of her in a black velvet box was the one thing she had begged her mother for since she was a little girl. It was the antique golden brooch her mother had inherited from her mother and that she was supposed to inherit from her mother when she turned twenty-one, as a few other generations had passed it on before them. Nicole was very sentimental and admired this tradition that made her feel part of a long line of strong woman. Not only was its sentimental value that intrigued her as a little girl, and now as a young woman, but also the brooch was beautiful.

The base was made of white gold and a scene of a little bird, surrounded by a horseshoe, with a frame of small intricate flowers on the edge of the broach, was depicted on top of the base. All of this was masterfully sculpted from red and yellow gold. Nicole looked at it as if it was the first time she had laid eyes on it, as its beauty and what it represented still left her in awe.

"I know it is sooner than when I said I would give it to you, but I felt it was appropriate," Hazel said.

"But..." Nicole wanted to protest.

"Nicole...all I ask of you is to remember where you come from," Hazel said softly and when Nicole looked up at her, she could see the wetness in her eyes threatening to spill over onto her cheeks.

"I promise," Nicole said and hugged her mother.

"Thank you, I will treasure it," Nicole promised as she sat back in her chair.

"Well, enough silliness, do you want another glass of wine?" Hazel offered Nicole, but Nicole reminded her mother that she still had to get ready for her flight ahead and that they should probably start to make their way home. It was the last thing she wanted to do, as she did not want to leave the safe cocoon of this moment, but she had no choice, so they left and when they entered the front door of the house, things went on as usual, but at least she had hope.

The afternoon was spent checking her list of things she needed, which was not much as they were to receive most of what they would be wearing for the next months at the College. Then she took a nap, as she did not know how late they would be able to get to bed that evening. When her mother finally woke her, she had to rush to finish in time for her mother to take her to the airport. They arrived at Cape Town Airport at around five that afternoon and Nicole weighed in her luggage before finally saying goodbye to her mother. They did not drag it out and opted for a quick hug and kiss, as it seemed easier.

"Good luck," Hazel said as she waved over her shoulder before she disappeared into the crowd, leaving Nicole in the queue in front of the check-in point. She was actually relieved to have Nicole on her way as she found it difficult to find enough space in the house to work through her troubles, but also sad that her daughter had finally left the nest and mourning this as much as she did the loss of her marriage. She too felt alone, but now for the first time in years, she felt free to find herself.

Only when Nicole entered the airplane and took her seat next to the window, did she for the first time remember that she was petrified of flying. As a child, she and her parents had done it countless times when visiting family and holidaying in different parts of the country and although she was already frightened of flying as a child, her fear seemed to grow with age, leaving her avoiding it all together.

Now however, she had no choice in the matter as the police had booked a ticket for her and she was to report at the college that same evening. Nicole was so busy trying to master the will to overpower her fear that she did not even realise that the two seats next to her had been filled with two girls of about the same age as her and was startled when one spoke to her.

"So, you also on your way to Pretoria?" a tall dark-haired girl asked.

"Yes," Nicole said, confused at how she knew, as the flight landed in Johannesburg and she might have been destined to travel to any number of places in the Transvaal area.

"Well, then we will join you!" she said cheerfully.

"Where are you going?" Nicole asked.

"We are going to the Police College. Oh, we thought you were going as well?" she said.

"Yes, I am. Sorry, my mind is elsewhere," Nicole apologised for her lapse of clarity.

"Well, look around you, girl, most of us are going," the girl smiled at Nicole and only then when Nicole looked around her, did she realise that there were hopelessly too many young girls of her age surrounding her for it to be coincidence.

"Hi, I am Tanya," the girl said with a smile and took Nicole's hand, shaking it with the confidence of a man.

"I am Nicole, nice to meet you," she said back as she started to relax in finding companionship.

Soon, the whole group was trading names and stories of where they grew up and where they were stationed, who had boyfriends and who did not. Nicole did not even realise that the engines were revving hard as the pilot was readying the engines for take-off. Only when the nose lifted and the tell-tale butterflies of nerves started dancing in her stomach in reaction, did she realise that she did not like this part.

"Nerves?" Tanya laughed as she recognised the fear in Nicole's face. "Don't worry, as soon as we are in the air, I will take care of it for you," she promised and placed her darkly tanned hand on Nicole's, which was clenched to the armrests next to her seat. And as she promised, she beckoned the airhostess to bring them each a small bottle of sparkling wine. Soon, even Nicole was in the same merry mood as the rest of the girls and the flight felt much shorter than the two hours it took to reach their destination.

By the time she got off the plane and went to look for her father, she did not even care that she had not seen her father in a few months, or that things might be awkward between them. It was not. She was relaxed and happy and hugged him spontaneously as the warmth of the liquid in her veins enveloped her.

Her father was just as pleased to see her, but for other reasons and they caught up on the past months as they drove to the college. Nicole could have taken the bus that the police had organised for them, but her father insisted on coming to fetch her and taking her himself as he wanted to see her.

After an hour of driving, they took the turn off to Pretoria and from there it took only a few minutes to reach the police college. The College was situated in the heart of the city and Nicole's father took a steep road behind a few flats, which led to the large grounds of the College. The road led to an entrance with two huge iron gates and fencing on either side, stretching further than Nicole's eyes could see. From where they were, she could not see buildings, as it was dark. There was just a small security building attached to the frame of the gates, where two armed policemen did duty, to see to it that no unwanted guests entered unannounced. One of the officers indicated with his one hand that they should stop their vehicle and Nicole's father did as ordered.

"Good evening," the young man said and looked into the car, smiling at Nicole as he let his eyes wonder over her body appreciatively, "Can we help you?" He obviously thought they had made a wrong turn off as most of the students had already arrived.

"Yes, I came to drop off my daughter, she is supposed to start her training," Johan said politely.

"Oh, are you a student?" the young man directed his question at Nicole.

"Yes," she answered with the sweetest smile.

"Then you better get a move on, they are about to have row call and you do not want to be late on your first day," he said, nervous for her sake. "Just follow the road until you see a parking area underneath the trees in between the buildings ahead. The busses are parked there. You cannot miss it," and he shone his torch in the direction they should drive.

They did as they were told and from out of the dark buildings appeared, first to their left and then one on their right and just behind this one the road opened up and split into a four-way crossing. To their right, there was a parking area like the policeman had said and the three busses that he spoke about were parked there as well. Young woman of all shapes and sizes stood around in small groups with their luggage surrounding them.

"This must be it," her father said.

"Yes, dad, you do not need to get out with me, I will be okay," Nicole said as she recognised Tanya in the distance.

"Alright, I will get your suitcase," Johan said and got out to take her suitcase from the boot. Nicole went to meet him at the back and planted a wet kiss on his cheek before she hugged him as tightly as her arms allowed her.

"Phone me as soon as you are able to," Johan demanded.

"I will," Nicole promised and then made her way to Tanya.

"Evening ladies!" a woman's voice carried over a megaphone. "I know this looks like a party, but I assure you it is not." Nicole was searching where the voice was coming from, as did the others in her group, and then she saw a small woman with short black hair, in uniform, with a megaphone in her hand.

"Now let us see if you know how to form rows. On the double, ladies!" she screamed over the megaphone impatiently. "And don't forget your luggage!" she continued giving her orders.

Nicole smiled. *This is going to be fun!* she thought while she joined the ant nest in their haste to find a row to stand in. Tanya was standing next to her in a neat line and quickly gave her a smile before she looked forwards, just in case her wandering eyes got her into trouble.

"Looks like we will have to teach you what I mean by rows, but we do not have time now. I will read out your names and then you will follow your platoon leader to your barracks."

"I am Sergeant Dietrich. For tonight, there are a few rules to remember and remember them you will! No one is to leave the barracks until ordered to do so. The building behind me and the one behind you are the women's barracks. The other buildings behind the building behind you are for the men. No man is allowed in the woman's barracks and vice versa. There will be no communicating with male students through open windows and if you have any questions, do not bother your platoon leaders until tomorrow morning, as they need their rest.

"Breakfast will be at eight o'clock sharp and you will be ready and your rooms tidy at seven, as we will gather back here at that time for morning row call. Is that understood?" she roared over the megaphone and all the women spontaneously replied with a loud: "Yes Sergeant."

Names were called out and as soon as a group of about thirty women were called, they were handed over to a female Sergeant and disappeared into the darkness. First the building at the back of where they were standing was filled and then the women who were boarding in the smaller building in front of them were called.

This building was situated on the other side of the road and was the one Nicole and her father had passed before they reached the clearing. Nicole was pleased when she was not called into one of the platoons that had to live in the building on the men's side as the thought of being in such close proximity to so many men made her feel nervous. She was one of the last to be called and was relieved that her name was actually on the list.

Sergeant Dietrich was their platoon leader and came to stand in front of her platoon and as if she knew what they were thinking, she said: "Fortunate to have me, aren't we?"

"Yes Sergeant!" they unanimously replied in true military style.

"Then let's put you girls to bed. You may follow me," she yelled so that everyone could hear and then she turned and started to walk to the face brick building called Rosen Hoff. The girls followed her into the entrance, up the stairs to the second floor where she assigned them two by two to their rooms. The building had three levels; each level had a hallway with double rooms on either side of the hallway. At each end, there were the rooms where the two Sergeants, of the two platoons living on that floor, stayed.

Nicole was lucky enough to be roomed at the other end of the hall where the public phone, bathroom and living room were situated. Here, there was also an ironing room were uniforms were to be ironed every single night, as wrinkled clothes were something that would earn you some sort of punishment. Nicole was to board with Melanie, a blond haired, blue-eyed girl four years her senior. She was even taller than Nicole and although blonde hair and blue eyes normally made for a winning recipe, this was no beauty.

Her eyes were protruding as if she had thyroid problems and her painfully pale skin made her already awkward frame appear even limper than it actually was. It took Nicole only the first few seconds into their conversation to realise that this girl was forced by her parents to work hard at her academics in order to achieve "great things". She had a bachelor's degree in criminal law and although she was a student, she would become a Captain as soon as she had finished her basic training, as she could not serve as a police officer if she did not.

It was also obvious to Nicole that she thought herself mentally superior because of this, which Nicole knew would be a sure way for her to make her unpopular with the other girls. Nicole understood that she was just perceiving her own self-worth through the standards with which her parents had valued her and therefore could not dislike her just because of it.

Melanie immediately took the first bed placed against the wall as you entered the room, without asking Nicole if she minded, but Nicole did not care where she slept and placed her belongings on the other bed on the other side of the room. The room was not very big and although both beds were moved against the walls, there was only about a metre and a half between them. In the middle of their beds, a desk and chair were placed and at the foot of Melanie's bed was another one.

At the foot of Nicole's bed was a metal cupboard and against the wall behind it, there was a washbasin and next to it and the door, a built-in cupboard, which Melanie took. Above both of their beds were windows that allowed them a clear view of the men's buildings and the other ladies building, as well as the mess and the tuck shop. The beds were bare and on top of it, a pillow, two white linen sheets, a linen pillow case and a grey warm blanket was placed.

Nicole made her bed and placed her suitcase on top of her cupboard, as she wanted to get to bed as soon as possible, seeing that she had to get up early the next morning. Melanie, on the other hand, took her time carefully planning her cupboard's interior and arranging her belongings until she felt it perfect, much to Nicole's annoyance, as she could not sleep with a light on.

The next morning, Nicole struggled to will herself out of bed and as soon as she did, she ran for the showers, but had to queue for one and after she finally returned, she found Melanie blow-drying her hair.

"You should wake earlier if you do not want to wait in the queue," she said as if Nicole had not figured it out by now.

"Yes, I can see that," Nicole replied and chose to ignore her roommate for the remainder of the morning in order to stay sane. Then she pulled on her jeans, sneakers and t-shirt, brushed her hair into a ponytail and brushed her teeth. She rushed through making her bed and fled the room in the hope of not being faced with Melanie's "perfection". As soon as she appeared into the hallway, Tanya appeared from the opposite room.

"Hey!" she greeted Nicole.

"Hi!" Nicole returned her welcome smile.

"Looks as if we are neighbours!" she said, pleased. Nicole was as pleased and accepted her invitation to drink a quick cup of coffee in her room before they left for row call. Tanya's roommate was equally pleasant and before long, there were a few faces in the room popping in to say hello to their new friend Tanya.

At seven, they stood in rows outside the building like they were ordered to and their platoon leaders checked if they were all present. Then they were rearranged into their different platoons. Each platoon had to line up in three equal rows of ten, with the tallest girls being the markers. Nicole as such was one of them.

Markers were placed on the end of each row's end and then the rest had to find their individual spaces between them. As soon as they were in position the platoon leader showed them how to, on her order, space themselves exactly an arm's length between their neighbour and the one in front of them by sticking their left arm to the front and the right to the side and then they had to shuffle until the tips of their fingers touched the person in front and at their side, leaving them in neat rows.

"This is how you will report to row call from now on. Is that clear?" Sergeant Dietrich asked.

"Yes Sergeant," and from there on, they did.

They were led in their platoons to the mess where they formed two long queues, waiting for the mess doors to open. By now Nicole was hungry and was looking forward to breakfast. Suddenly, they heard the rhythmic motion of a mass of feet nearing them. From behind the women's barracks, platoons of men neatly jogging in unison, with their platoon leaders next to them, slowly neared them. As they had started their training three months before the girls, they had mastered the art of moving together and it looked impressive as they did so in their blue uniforms and boots and their hair were similarly shaven.

For a moment, Nicole thought they were going to dine together, but soon realised that the building opposite the one they were standing at was where they were eating as they formed similar rows in front of the doors there. As soon as their platoon leaders went inside the building, they relaxed and an excited murmur erupted as they were eyeing the new female recruits. Some were trying to communicate softly with the women and others were pushing and shoving one another, as young men would when trying to attract attention from the opposite sex.

They were obviously deprived of close contact with women, or so she concluded from the strict rules laid down the night before. In that instance, it dawned on her why the strict rules were necessary, as she could only imagine what chaos would develop in such a physical environment where young virile men were kept from the fairer sex. Soon a few of the men opposite her tried to get her attention, so she turned away to avoid them and then she decided that she would keep to herself as much as possible, as this was not a natural environment to get involved in with anyone and the intentions of the men opposite them appeared to be nothing honourable at all, and besides, there was already someone waiting for her back home.

As hungry as Nicole was, so disappointing was the sight when the doors to the mess were finally opened. Tables were set alongside each other in long rows, with just enough space for the students to move in between, as to accommodate all the girls in one big hall. On the other side of the entrance, there were two similar doors, which led to the kitchen. Nicole could see young men and woman running around in earnest to fulfil their tasks so that they could feed the masses within an hour and a half time frame.

It looked like madness, the little bit she could see from the parting in the half-closed doors. *I wonder how sterile the kitchen is*, Nicole thought as she took a seat. She was by no means a fussy eater, but she feared that the hygiene may not be up to her standards, because of Ben, who had teased her about how filthy the kitchens were and what nastiness happened in there, in an attempt to frighten her a bit.

This was just part of his way of letting her go through some of the torture he and others before him had been put through as students. In actual fact, the kitchens were spotless and Nicole now found herself reasoning this, as she knew in such a strict environment where the students also had to run the kitchen, it would not only be expected from them, but would be enforced by any means possible.

Make no mistake; an effort was made to make the tables look decent. White tablecloths were spotless in their task of hiding the metal tables underneath and even flowers in small glass jars were neatly placed ever so often in the centre of the tables, with salt and pepper shakers standing invitingly next to it. It was the food in front of her that was really disappointing. Scrambled eggs that looked more like clumps of egg and drifted in some kind of watery liquid were served in square metal pans. Dried out toast was on offer with burnt bacon fried in oil and overdone sausage. To most, this might seem a normal breakfast, but Nicole unfortunately was accustomed to far more distinguished cuisine.

Porridge was also available for those preferring it, but if Nicole had a choice, it would be neither, so she opted for a dry slice of toast and a fruit and she washed it down with the instant coffee that was available on the table. This would become her eating pattern for the three months following, always taking the seemingly safest option and just enough to keep her going or rather surviving.

When they finished, the men too were ordered into their platoons. The men, who had already completed the first three months of their training, set off in their platoons for their morning classes, while the women were taken to be fitted and kitted with their new student uniforms, books, etc. This took the rest of the day, and it tired them more than they thought possible as they were rudely ordered to speed up their pace while running around between buildings and taking notes of what was expected from them during the following months.

The information was overwhelming, and Nicole flopped onto her thin mattress, not even caring that her aching body struck the metal bars underneath it. Finally, some free minutes. The bed was inviting her to close her eyes and rest her body, but her mind reminded her of the ironing she had to do before lights out so that she would be neat and ready for inspection the next morning. The routine had begun, and there was no turning back and that night when the lights finally faded into darkness, she sunk into a deep peaceful sleep, too tired to contemplate, or procrastinate, the way she preferred it.

Chapter 9

Each day started with the girls having breakfast, morning row call and then an inspection, before they were marched off in their platoons to their College. Their day was filled with classes in criminology, first aid and the workings of the SAP's admin initiating system, firearm training and physical training. Nicole, being a natural athlete, found the physical training difficult, but challengingly satisfying. A place where she could rid herself of her frustrations and a place where her energy was tapped to such an extent that she was afforded the sleep of the dead each night.

During the week, classes carried on till late in the afternoon, with them only breaking for lunch. After supper, they had a little free time to relax, phone their families, mingle with the male students at the tuck shop or just catch up on some sleep. Nicole nearly always retired to her dormitory. She had no need to mingle with the young male students as she was committed to Mika.

She did get constant requests from the young men, via her fellow dorm mates, to join them on these get-togethers, but she faithfully declined. Her reasoning was that she would probably not see any of the students again after they had left the College, and therefore did not see the necessity in getting to know her fellow students, except for those in her dormitory. This was a big mistake though, as she did not fully comprehend the inner workings and politics of this far reaching unit of law enforcers.

In any law enforcement entity, whether appointed by the government or a private company, existing of men and women who are trained and groomed to anticipate criminal activity so that they could prevent it, are in affect groomed to be constantly ready to physically defend themselves and the innocent. Although this is in most instances a good thing, it also nurtures a patriotic inner society of people closely depending on each other for survival, which in turn gives them a false sense of superiority over civilians, but also subconsciously makes them stand together in protecting each other in other areas of life as well, even if they shouldn't necessarily be protected from prosecution when they themselves overstep the boundaries.

When you join the police, you for instance sign a confidentiality contract, restricting you from putting the police force in a bad light. This attitude spilled over into the work place, and anyone in the Force knew the worst thing you could do is speak out about a fellow officer's missteps.

This is where Nicole's drive for independence by joining the police was flawed. Here, you were by no means an independent individual, you were part of the Force, and the more people in influential positions you knew, the better. Fellow students will one day become fellow officers, and so you need to mingle and get to know as many people as you can.

Ironically, the more social you were, the easier it was for any young police officer to deal with the inner politics. Unfortunately, being a woman in the police force made you vulnerable to sexual harassment and all other sorts of abuse. Since you were not to speak out, complain or address most of these menial complaints in this male driven force, you would be marked and targeted as a trouble maker if you dared to do so and life would become so unbearable that you would want to resign.

This too was a problem; few men and women could afford to leave the police force as most of them chose to join the Force when their peers went to study and start their careers. The pay was very basic, so you hardly had the opportunity to further your studies later if you chose to leave the Force. Thus, quitting if you ever found yourself in a difficult situation with a male police officer targeting you wasn't an option to most. Having enough male friends of influence in the Force could afford you some sort of protection as things could be sorted out privately, but if not, you were practically left to the wolves, and this she would soon come to learn the hard way.

Unfortunately, the women who were prepared to join in on socialising with the men fell prey to a whirlpool of shameless liaisons. The men were fit, young and mostly single, not that it was at all taken into account, as were the women. It was a very physical environment, and although such liaisons were frowned upon, most cunningly found opportunities to rid them of their sexual frustrations. This wasn't only the trend amongst the students and although it was forbidden, the officers and platoon leaders used their charm and promise of making life easier in College to their full advantage.

Most of these senior figures were married. Nicole chose to ignore this and what she didn't know was that her road down the path of choosing to run with the pack had already started filing away at her soul. With every blind eye you turn, the once ugly seem to merge into a new reality of normality, and being as blind as you choose to be, you later become so desensitised that your judgment is seriously flawed.

The days stretched into weeks and before she knew it, the rhythm of the College life was all too familiar to her and not at all as overwhelming as in those first days when nearly everyone shed a tear of frustration and sheer exhaustion. Within that first few days, nine of the girls in Rosen Hoff resigned and returned home. This was not an option for Nicole and she reminded herself constantly that she only had to stick it out for three months and in return, she would be financially independent. Normally, their training would last six months, but fortunately for her, the police force at that time was short-staffed and needed to put as many students through training as possible, so the training period was shortened to three months.

The physical part of their training was rough, but not impossible to bear. The students quickly adjusted to the screaming and breaking down part of their training. As one Sergeant explained to them: "We break you down so that we can build you up", after he drilled the poor girls so hard that a few emptied the contents of their stomachs onto the grass in front of them. One girl was careless to discuss the weekend's pass with the girl next to her while Sergeant Du Plessis was explaining to them how to dismantle a Berretta pistol.

This was an absolute no-no and for this, the whole platoon was punished, as they were a unit and had to function as one. He ordered them out of the class to the grass patch in front of it, where some male students were relaxing under a shady tree. Here, he made the girls run on the spot with their R1 rifles above their heads, followed by them having to fall to the ground in a stretched-out position as if they were doing a push-up and then putting the rifle in front of them, only to make them jump to their feet again and run on the spot.

These torturous orders kept them busy for near to an hour until one after another, girls started vomiting and when they were finally brought to a halt, one passed out and hardly anyone didn't have tears in their eyes. Nicole bit down hard not to give in to the urge to break down and sob uncontrollably.

Nicole focussed on studying, cleaning and resting, when she got the chance. She found time to socialise with the girls in the barracks though. She chose to go to bed as early as possible so that she could wake up early to shower, as most of the girls did so in the evening, making the bathrooms overcrowded and the warm water supply scarce. The bathroom was outdated with green tiles decorating the walls, but neat and functional.

No baths, a few cubicles with toilets and then four huge showers. The showers only had curtains in front of them, which did not close properly, so the girls did not even bother closing it. Most mornings, she had the showers all to herself and then she could find strength in the tranquillity in order to cope with the madness of the day that followed.

On one such morning, Nicole stood up as usual. She grabbed her towel and toiletries and made her way to the bathrooms in her groggy state. Nicole did not like to walk down the passage alone, as it was dark and only the lights in the bathroom threw a greenish glow into the dark, eerily inviting her to come closer. Nicole had heard terrible roomers of ghosts and spirits haunting these passages and although she did not believe in such things, she did not want to be proven wrong, but this morning her normal anxieties did not even register, as she was still far too tired for it.

Her feet were snuggly wrapped in their fluffy pink slippers and she faintly listened to their soft sweeping of the passage as she willed them forward. It was only when she neared the opening to the bathroom that she realised the bathroom was steamed up. A soft groan escaped her mouth as she rubbed her eyes, annoyed at their apparent lack of their cooperation to focus properly, but more so because of the intruder disturbing her morning routine.

I hope this doesn't mean I will have to wake up earlier! she thought to herself as the idea that others had caught on to her routine crossed her mind.

She was still concentrating on the floor when she heard another groan. In an instant, even though she had never heard such a moan before, her whole body recognised it and a stinging anticipation erupted deep inside of her. Nicole froze, like a deer, listening out of fear of being found out. Suddenly, every sense in her body was on full alert, waiting for the evidence of her being wrong so that she could let her guard down, but no, another even longer, softer, deeper groan followed.

Nicole forced herself to slowly lift her head and look at what was going on. She did not see anybody inside the bathroom as the shower's interior was still shielded by the entrance wall, and it was obvious now that the person making the noise was in it.

Oh God, I hope the curtain is closed, Nicole thought as she was now under the impression that the girl in the shower was pleasuring herself. Nicole too had countless times resorted to this in the middle of the night when Melanie was sleeping, trying not to make a noise, but doing it nonetheless. It was a natural stress reliever after all and this kept her from wandering off her goal to stay true to Mika, as she wanted him to be the first.

Nicole slowly came around the wall, making sure that she was not looking at the showers' entrance directly, so as to give the girl inside time to keep her dignity and not to be caught out, but as she faced the showers, the curtain was pulled closed and from where she stood, she could only see half a buttock and the legs attached to it.

Clearly, the girl was unaware of her and Nicole thought to herself: *Maybe I should cough to warn her of my presence,* but before she could, she realised that something was terribly wrong with the picture in front of her. Instead of two legs carrying a body on top of it, there were three legs of which one was wrapped around the others and only the lower part visible midway between the buttocks and knees of the two on the ground. With the shock of what she realised she saw, she realised that it was two women's legs and to cement the realisation in further, she heard both women groan.

Nicole was now trapped between her urge to give them some privacy and her curiosity. Unable to move a muscle, she stood entranced, watching an elbow appear and disappear behind the curtain in a slow and rhythmic movement. With each movement, the soft sound of wetness became clear, making the motion of it erotic. It was definitely not the sound of water falling on the floor that she heard, and with each slimy sound, the two bodies leant into each other as though they were trying to fuse into one entity.

Nicole was shocked, but strangely aroused by what she saw in front of her. Nicole had never met a lesbian, or so she thought, as although these were times of change in the old South-Africa (before the election which would rid SA of Apartheid and a lot of other ridiculous beliefs), people were still caught up in their Calvinistic upbringings. Homosexual liaisons were still frowned upon, as were sex before marriage, children out of wedlock and relationships, and even friendships between different cultures and races. This didn't mean it didn't happen; it just meant that you took particular care to put up a front, to be sociably acceptable to the pressures of society.

Although she had never before met a person that was openly lesbian, she now not only knew that there was a couple in the shower, but could see how they gave expression to their physical needs as well. Except for the penis involved when a man is with a woman, there was not much difference, as a woman had hands she could use for a substitute. Nicole hadn't even had the privilege of experiencing something remotely close to what she was witnessing, but knew that the process could be that much different. This was just much more visually pleasing she thought, as it was two beautifully sculpted bodies in front of her, toned from hours of hard physical training. Nicole felt guilty as she stood there, but couldn't get herself to move.

Suddenly, the one girl's leg fell to the ground as the one with her back to the curtain pushed her away and in a practiced move pushed the other girl up against the wet wall behind her. A little cry came from the girl's mouth and with the motion, the curtain moved just enough to see the standing girl's face. Her head was thrown back; her long curly black hair clung to her face, neck and body as the water ran down her waiting body. *It is Tanya!* Nicole nearly screamed, but managed to place her hand in front of her mouth to stop her from doing so.

Shit! What should I do, shit! she panicked and made ready to run, but her feet were stuck to the ground. Tanya was blissfully unaware of Nicole, her eyes shut firmly as the girl in front of her went down on her knees. Nicole stared in amazement as the girl lifted her arms and placed them in front of her on Tanya's body. As she did so, Nicole noticed a tiny tattoo, of the Gemini star sign, on her right shoulder. The lower part of Tanya's body was obscured by the short-haired girl's head in front of her, but Nicole could only imagine where she was fiddling and why, and then the unimaginable happened.

The short-haired girl leaned forward and like a ravaging predator attacked Tanya's most intimate parts. Tanya gasped for air while her hands desperately searched for something to grab on to and just then, she flung her head forwards, giving Nicole such a fright that she ran out the bathroom and back to her room.

Shit, shit, shit... was the only word that spun around in her head and before she knew it, she was back in her bed, pretending to sleep and trying to make sense of what she had just seen.

Who was the other girl? she thought. *Why Tanya? I didn't even realise...* but all too soon the alarm bell rang her back to her senses and their day started a usual.

After breakfast, they had inspection of their rooms. Up until that morning, Nicole never had problems passing this. As soon as their platoon sergeant was ready for the inspection, the two platoon leaders of their particular hallway would bring them to attention in front of their respective rooms, both inhabitants of each room on either side of the doorway in the hall.

Nicole took particular care to stand as straight as possible, focussing on the wall in front of her as to not draw attention to her. Their platoon sergeant was short and as Nicole was quite tall, the sergeant only came up to Nicole's chin. Their Sergeant, Sergeant Dietrich, was one feisty little woman, she was strict, and she had mastered the art of sarcasm. Although short, she had an amazing, delicately toned body and she was beautiful, with protruding green eyes and short, dark, chocolate brown hair. Everyone in the two platoons on their floor had a fearful respect for her as she did not tolerate any variation of their given orders.

Nicole listened to how the Sergeant started at the bottom of the hall, inspecting each room, pulling bedding from beds, emptying cupboards on floors and ordering girls to wax their floors so that one could see your reflection in it. Nicole did not dare look in her direction as this could trigger her to find fault with your room, even if your room met all her criteria. This morning, the little Sergeant was in a particularly fault-finding mood. Not one single room was spared. The two Sergeants of the two platoons on the floor took turns to do morning inspection and most mornings, favouritism reared its head in the form of less rooms of the inspecting Sergeant's platoon were pulled than that of the other Sergeant's, but not this morning.

Nicole's room was in the middle of the hall. When Sergeant Dietrich reached their room, she suddenly stopped in front of Nicole. Nicole's heart started racing while she retraced her steps with lightning speed to figure out where and if she had done anything wrong. The Sergeant stood just a breath's length away from her, their bodies nearly touching. Nicole didn't want to look down, in fear of getting scolded.

"So Nicole…" In a teasing tone, the Sergeant started while gently stepping on Nicole's left foot.

"You think you are going to be spared today?" she continued while rhythmically applying pressure with her small foot and then releasing. Nicole's breath was now outpacing her heartbeat.

Shit, what did I do? she thought to herself, but for the life of her she couldn't figure it out, as up until that day the Sergeant had not even spoken to her directly. Nicole couldn't even understand why the Sergeant knew her name. She never took notice of Nicole.

"I said, Nicole, do you think you are going to be spared today?" nearly whispering it now into Nicole's neck. Her breath was warm and fresh; Nicole couldn't resist looking down, while the other platoon members didn't dare do so. They weren't allowed to move until inspection was finished, where they then only had a few minutes to repack and reorganise their beds before classes started.

Nicole looked down into the delicate face in front of her and where she expected to find a very angry-looking face, she found a soft mischievous little girl-like stare. Nicole was confused but spontaneously started to smile at the little person under her chin and then looked up in her normal uninterested stare.

"No Sergeant Dietrich, I don't think I will be spared today," she shouted it out as they were expected to do.

"Then I think you should assist me in inspecting your room, Nicole," Sergeant Dietrich said matter-of-factly, placing all her weight on Nicole's toes and then releasing so that Nicole could follow her into the room. Nicole did so and from where Nicole stood in the doorway, looking over the Sergeant's head, she noticed all the little flaws that would cost her a pulling of bedding, whereas her roommate's bed, floor and cupboard looked military neat.

Oh well, I will just have to clean up again, Nicole thought to herself.

Sergeant Dietrich stood next to her bed and asked: "This is your bed?"

"Yes Sergeant!" Nicole bellowed.

"Mmmmmm…" Sergeant Dietrich lingered. Then she suddenly went about pulling Melanie's bed, throwing out her cupboard and shouting at Melanie from inside the room, "Melanie, I don't know what you think of my intelligence, but this is unacceptable, you insult me by having me inspect such a mess! You WILL have this cleaned and up to standard in five! Do you understand me?"

"Yes Sergeant!" Melanie replied from where she stood, not daring to move. Pausing, Sergeant Dietrich looked Nicole straight in the eye and winked at her as if they were sharing a secret. Nicole was utterly confused at this point.

"I don't hear you!" Sergeant Dietrich shouted.

"YES Sergeant!" Melanie shouted even louder.

"You may return, Nicole," Sergeant Dietrich smiled up at Nicole and Nicole did so, repositioning herself into attention at the door.

That morning, Nicole's bed was the only one in the whole hall that didn't get pulled. It was obvious to Nicole that Sergeant Dietrich wanted to send some sort of message across, but what that would be was beyond Nicole. To Nicole's relief, from that day forward, Nicole was favoured, very subtly. She just never got scolded for anything and Sergeant Dietrich stepping on her toes became a regular, strangely reassuring, occurrence.

Nicole flourished in the environment of strict discipline, as it gave her a sense of belonging, a sense of purpose and a sense of order. She could throw herself into this life and forget about her own emotional confusion. She enjoyed the gatherings in the evenings in the girls' rooms, the gossiping, the cleaning of the grounds, when the girls normally made fun of each other, throwing each other with buckets of water in the sweltering heat, and the camaraderie of always having someone close who understood exactly what punishment your body went through and the frustrations and accomplishments surrounding the College life.

Each evening at about eight, Mika would phone her and tell her how much he missed her and how he couldn't wait to see her again. Nicole was growing accustomed to the thrill of surviving on an adrenaline high during the day and the utter exhaustion that filled her soul during the evenings, leaving no room to dwell on insignificant troubles. She didn't even miss the absence of her mother's concern for her.

Not once did her mother phone her during this time to hear how she was doing. It was only when Nicole had to arrange for her mother to come pick her up at the airport for their midterm leave that she afterwards realised that she hadn't spoken to her mother since the day she had boarded the plane.

She now had a purpose beyond that of her parents' turmoil. She was spreading her wings, and leaving that which caused her so much turmoil, behind. She was focussed on her future and somehow their troubles became insignificant, even to the point that she could look past it and actually looked forward to going back home for a much-needed break and seeing her love again.

Chapter 10

Not soon enough, after a month of intense training, the girls were on leave. Their flight tickets were booked. Nicole's father took her out to lunch before he dropped her off at the airport. Most of the girls had to take the police bus to the airport, but Nicole now thought herself fortunate to have parents in two different provinces. Quite convenient actually, with her dad at times dropping of food supplies at the College when the mess food became too much to bear. Nicole was chirpy, talking about all that happened during the first part of their training to her father, during their lunch. They sat at a little coffee shop in the middle of Pretoria, surrounded by the purple flowers of the Jacaranda trees that lined the street. Her father smiled at her, as he didn't get one word in. When she finally took a breath by taking a sip of her tea, he seized the opportunity.

"What happened to you?" he asked with genuine appreciation for her good mood.

"Ah, I don't know! I am just happy, I guess!" she exclaimed in a chirpy voice.

"I feel on a high," she said more seriously while frowning, as she now was forced to think about the cause of her happiness.

"I am so thankful. I was really worried about you, my girl. I am so sorry for all the things we have put you through…" and he looked down into the depths of the cup of coffee he was holding in his hands, as if the answers were to be found in it.

"Don't worry," Nicole said before she could stop herself, "you don't have to explain yourself to me," her voice uttered, before she could think about it, and it shocked her as she didn't know where it came from, but it rang true in her ears. In that instant, she came to the realisation that her parents in truth didn't have to explain their choices and lives to her, as she was a grown woman, as much as they were adults, responsible for their own destiny and happiness. She turned her head to the side as it hit her and a spontaneous smile lit her face as she too realised that she then in return, as a fully grown and independent woman, didn't have to explain herself to anybody, except if she chose to. It was a liberating feeling, freeing her of her past worries. Her future lay open in front of her and it felt exciting.

"Yes, but I feel we could have prepared you better for the shock of us splitting up," Johan said adamantly as if he was reprimanding himself. "There are so many things I would have wanted to do differently, had I thought it through," he apologised.

"Please stop it!" Nicole protested, she didn't want to discuss this, as she needed to move on. "I still love you!" she said, while jumping up and swiftly moving around the small table and wrapping her arms around her father's neck and planting a kiss on Johan's clammy forehead.

"Come on, let's eat, that is in the past," she said and took her seat opposite Johan. They finished their lunch and he then took Nicole to the airport.

Nicole enjoyed the flight back to Cape Town much more than she did the initial flight to Johannesburg. She just wanted to get home and didn't care that she needed to board a plane to do so. And when she arrived at Cape Town Airport her mother was waiting to take her home. She actually hoped that Mika would also be there, but he probably had to work. Hazel seemed pleased to have Nicole back home. On their way home, Hazel encouraged Nicole to talk about College and her experiences there, hardly saying anything about her own life and what she had been up to since had Nicole left. Nicole did not even notice that Hazel purposefully kept her talking so that she did not have to.

"Oh, that's wonderful," Hazel said matter-of-factly just as Nicole finally took a breath when they turned into their driveway, "I am very happy that things are going so well for you."

"Wait," Nicole suddenly realised she hadn't asked her mother about her past month, "how have you been?"

"Anything exciting to tell?" she teased as she knew her mother most probably just went to work and relaxed at home in the evenings. How could her mother's life be exciting?

"I will tell you all later…" Hazel announced as if she had something important to share with Nicole. "First, let us get you unpacked. I am sure you are tired after the flight?"

This was far from the truth; in fact, Nicole was on such a high, she probably had enough energy for the both of them.

"Yes, I want to see Mika today as well, and seeing that is already five o'clock, I should get going," Nicole uttered out loud her reasoning.

By the time Nicole had showered and gotten ready to go see Mika, she had already forgotten what her mother had said. She was now only focussed on seeing Mika. She had lost about 4 kgs in a month, because of their intense physical training, and her legs were perfectly toned, affording her the opportunity to show it off to Mika in the hopes of seducing him. She pulled a slightly loose-fitting, black tailored dress over her head. She nearly threw her whole underwear drawer out to find the one satin black G-string she owned, and she opted to go bare-breasted underneath her dress.

She felt sexy and daring, all grown up and independent. She had romanticised, many a times in the College, about her reunion with Mika. He was extremely attractive and she longed for him to hold her. When he kissed her, he moved something inside of her, which she didn't want to suppress anymore. Nicole brushed out her long locks and let them dry naturally so that her natural waves could set the way they normally did, framing her face and exaggerating the voluptuousness of her full lips and showing off her big eyes beneath long lashes.

When she was ready, she phoned Milnerton police station to hear if he was working, which he was, but the Sergeant on duty told her that he knew he would be at Eugene, his best friend's house. He continued to explain to her where Eugene lived so that she could go and surprise Mika.

It was custom for shift members to become really good friends, as they worked the same shifts, were off at the same time, and had to stand together in difficult situations. One's shift became like an extended family, except if there was someone on the shift you didn't get along with, but normally the whole shift would gang together to get that one person moved to another shift until all members got along. This resulted in most police stations having one awkward shift with the cast outs.

Mika and Eugene were very popular amongst their peers and therefore, their shift finally ended up with mostly male members aged between 20 and 25. All of them were extremely attractive and fit. The only female member, a slightly plump, blonde haired, blue eyed girl, got engaged to one of the shift members named Brent. Wendy was really pretty, almost doll-like, and pretty girls in the police force didn't stay single for long, as there weren't many. It was also very convenient for policemen to date policewomen, as they understood the routine and lifestyle that accompanied it.

Eugene was having a barbeque at his house. The whole shift was at Eugene's house for that matter, except for Wendy and Brent. Wendy knew all too well what young policemen were like and kept Brent from socialising with the shift too often as she was focussed on getting married and settling down. Nicole hadn't met Mika's shift yet and didn't know that the whole shift would be at Eugene's house. These shift barbeques normally started early afternoon and lasted till early in the morning hours, or until the last person standing had enough.

Instead of asking for Eugene's phone number to ask if she could come see Mika, she decided to just pop in. She wanted to surprise Mika. She was actually a little nervous and excited about seeing him again. He was by far the most attractive young man she had seen so far. Her police station mostly had older men working there as they had enough pull already to wangle a placing at Table View police station. Table View at that stage was one of the biggest areas and the crime rate was still low in relation to Milnerton and other surrounding areas.

Nicole had only once been to Mika's house but now she found herself in her mother's Mazda 323 driving the road leading to his house, as the Sergeant had explained to her. Eugene stayed a street away from Mika's house and finally, she stopped in front of a very humble-looking three-bedroomed house in the middle of Milnerton. Nicole's heart was racing as she killed the engine. She sat there trying to calm her nerves, but for some reason she felt as if she was meeting him for the first time.

"Come on, Nicole!" she softly reprimanded herself, "pull yourself together!" When she opened the door of the car, she could hear loud music from behind the house. Suddenly, she realised how many cars were standing in the street and then she realised they were having a barbeque. The distinctive smell of "boerewors" (Afrikaans word for a specifically seasoned beef sausage) and lamb chops filled the air as the smell rose with the smoke of a fire, from behind the white building.

"I probably shouldn't have come," Nicole started doubting herself. As always the wind was blowing particularly strong this day, as is the case in October, and as she stood there contemplating if she should dare be so forward as to intrude, a gush of wind blew her dress up, lifting it to her face and blocking her vision. Startled at it, still standing next to her mother's car, she turned from the wind, pulling it down in the front, but as she did this, the wind lifted the back of her dress, exposing her perfectly toned buttocks and long gazelle-like limbs for the neighbourhood to see. Her G-string disappeared into the crevasse between the two rounds, and if it wasn't for the lacy elastic holding everything together, it would have looked like she was totally bare underneath.

"Fuck!" she cursed out loud. *I should rather go home*, she thought as she tucked the front part of her dress between her legs in front so that she could free her hands to pull her dress down at the back. When she finally got her dress under control, she turned around to face the house for a final glance, but to her amazement, she had a crowd of young men staring at her in silence. For some reason, the lot of them came to the front of the house with their beers still in hand. Nicole was so bewildered she didn't know what to do and just stood there staring back. She didn't recognise anyone.

Dear God, just swallow me whole! Her mind slowly started to function again. The seconds passed in slow motion and before she could turn and flee, the group spontaneously started cheering and clapping, she even heard a whistle. Before she could control her body, she spontaneously took a dramatic bow. It was the only way she could make fun of the situation and spare herself any further embarrassment. Just then she saw a desperate soul pushing through the bodies in front of him, in an attempt to see what is going on. Frantically looking around to see what had happened.

"What is going on?" Nicole immediately recognised the voice, and then Mika spotted Nicole standing in front of Hazel's car with her black dress tucked in between her legs and her feet crossed. Both her hands were still pressing down on the hem of the dress, and although there was no evidence of what the young men had just witnessed, the wind tauntingly still swept through her trusses. She looked like a supermodel on a photo shoot as she shook her hair from her face to glance at Mika, very relieved to see him. Nobody moved, they were mesmerised by the vision in front of them. Nicole's legs stretched on forever and her creamy skin was sun-kissed, giving it a shiny golden colour.

"What…what are you doing here?" Mika asked; he too was taken aback by her beauty, as he had only seen her in jeans or in her uniform.

"I mean, wow, this is a surprise…" letting the wind swallow the rest of his words, as he himself wasn't sure what he wanted to say.

Unable to let her dress go, she stood frozen till he reached her and swept her up into his arms while spinning her around. She had to let go of her dress and once again afforded the group a small glimpse of the sight from before. Mika had no idea what had happened just a few minutes before or what his actions now caused.

"Hi," Nicole said in a very vulnerable tone, "I wanted to surprise you," she tried to explain.

"Hi, Babe!" Mika said in a very confident voice as he knew his friends approved of Nicole, "I am glad you did." And then he planted a kiss solidly on her lips as if to mark his property.

"I apologise for their behaviour," he laughed, while saying it loud enough for the rest to hear.

"No, it's fine," Nicole said softly.

"Come, let me introduce the guys to you," he invited and Nicole followed him.

Mika's friends didn't move, they just stared at the two approaching them. They were all about a head taller than Nicole as she had flat sandals on and it made her feel small. She shook hands with the first seven and didn't even try to remember their names. Only when Mika introduced her to Eugene, did she take particular notice as this was his best friend. Eugene was quite lean, but attractive, with black hair, a dark skin and dark green eyes. She immediately sensed a genuine and sensitive side to him, although he looked like a party animal. Eugene took her hand much gentler than the others, as if he was afraid to break her and gently lifted her hand to his lips, softly pressing his lips to her hand. It was warm and soft.

"Okay, that's enough, Eugene," Mika teased Eugene.

"I am just being polite, Mika, you should know me by now," Eugene replied and they both laughed.

"So, who was getting CDs?" Eugene asked the group, and they all sprang into motion, dispersing in different directions to collect CDs from their cars.

Eugene guided Nicole and Mika to the back where the fire was inviting them closer. There were chairs packed in a half circle around the fireplace. The wind was still blowing but here it was restricted by the precast cement wall, surrounding the yard. A small swimming pool was centred in the middle of the yard, its water crystal clear and Nicole who loved water, had an impulse to throw caution in the wind and throw her body into the depths of the blue water, as it was such a beautiful summer's evening. The sun was just setting, but she wouldn't dare. She noticed that she was the only girl there.

"Maybe I should rather go," she suggested softly in Mika's ear.

"No, why?" he asked, confused. "You only arrived now."

"I know, but it feels like I am intruding. I am the only girl here," she explained.

"Don't be silly, Eugene's girlfriend is also here, she is tending to the salads in the kitchen. Come, I will introduce you," he said and took her hand, pulling her to the back door and into the kitchen.

A young woman stood at the counter with her back turned to them. She wasn't very tall, she was well built and her brown hair was cut into a short pixy style. When she turned around, as she heard them enter, she smiled. Nicole immediately knew they would become friends as her smile was warm, sincere and welcoming. Nicole looked into her light brown eyes and saw a twinkle of mystery reflected in them.

"Hi, I am Grete," she said while walking over to Nicole and taking her into a welcoming embrace. Nicole instinctively reciprocated the hug.

"And I am Nicole," she replied, while genuinely feeling pleased by the meeting. This girl was stylish, her hair, make-up and nails were perfectly groomed. Her olive skin glistened from moisturisers she religiously treated it with. Nicole could see her appearance was very important to her. Nicole respected that as she too loved pampering herself and followed the newest fashion trends.

"I can see you two are going to get along," Mika said as he placed a kiss on Nicole's head before he aimed for the door, "so I am going to leave you in Grete's capable hands." And he winked at Grete before he disappeared out the door.

The two girls made small talk while Grete prepared the salads and buttered the bread. She offered Nicole champagne, which Nicole appreciatively took.

"Sorry, it's all I drink," Grete confessed. "I cannot stand Black Label," she said while pulling her face. (Black Label is a South African beer and was one of the cheapest brands at that time. This was thus a favourite drink for both men and women in the police force as they could afford it.)

"Me too," Nicole echoed her disgust, but actually Nicole didn't even know what it tasted like, as she hardly ever drank, except for the odd glass of wine with a meal. The champagne was lovely though. It was pink, chilled and semi-sweet and it went down so easily in the heat. By the second glass, Nicole could feel the champagne numbing the lining of her veins and clouding her personality, as it messed with her judgment. She felt relaxed and not at all insecure or worried about what anyone thought of her. Her confidence soared.

She wasn't drunk; she was enjoying herself though and followed Grete outside when she had finished up. When they came outside, darkness had already fallen. The blue swimming pool light made the water dance in the darkness and where it before beckoned Nicole to feel its soothing presence, it now taunted her. Nicole stood in front of it, not noticing the others surrounding the fire. The meat had already been barbequed and was on the table close to them.

The young men turned to look at the two girls coming from the house. Both of them very appealing to the eyes and while Grete made herself comfortable on Eugene's lap, Nicole got stuck in front of the pool. While turning her head to the group, she asked: "Why is nobody swimming?"

Nobody had an answer. It now sounded so obvious that they should have done so, but they were so focussed on their discussions and drinking their beers that they didn't even think of it until now. Nicole didn't even give the repercussions a thought and in one easy swift movement, she pulled her dress over her head, exposing her body and dropped it next to her feet. One by one she stepped out of her sandals and leapt elegantly into the air, landing perfectly in the pool, with only a slight splash. Everyone was watching her, as she had the slightest of material covering her womanhood.

As she stood up, water was dripping from her small pink hard nipples. Her breasts were small and firm. Nicole, relieved from her inhibitions as a result of drinking champagne, totally forgot that she only cared to wear as little as possible underwear for her meeting with Mika. And now it wasn't only for him on display, but his whole shift. Nobody dared say anything though as Mika was their senior. He was very ambitious and studied criminal law, and therefore he was already promoted to Sergeant, where the others were still constables.

"What are you doing?" Mika protested while he came to his feet.

"She is cooling off, leave her," Eugene came to her defence.

"Yes, leave her," the rest of the shift begged.

Grete, not wanting to be outdone, stripped down to her panties, ridding herself of her bra too and exclaiming: "Wait, I will join you," and as she lifted into the air, she shouted: "Whoo-hoo!" splashing the guys closest to the swimming pool.

"Get out of the pool!" Mika ordered Nicole, but she ignored him. The water was soothing against her naked skin and she dived into its volume before he could scold her.

"Come on, Mika!" Eugene took Mika's arm. "Let the girl swim," he pleaded with him. "She is just having a little harmless fun." Mika didn't want to look the stiff, so he sat down on his chair while looking at the two women's bodies moving in the water. All the men stared shamelessly at them now. Nobody even bothered about the food waiting on the table.

"Come on, guys," Grete invited the young men to the coolness of the water.

They weren't going to wait for a second invitation. They exposed their ripped bodies as one by one they took off their shirts. Nicole swam a few laps, as did some of the guys. Eugene also joined them, but he didn't dive in, he chose to walk into the pool. While he was doing this, he brushed past Nicole, softly touching her breast. The shock of his skin touching her nipple brought her back to reality. She looked up at Mika where he still sat motionless in his chair.

Shit! What have I done? she reprimanded herself and she swam to the side of the pool. As she reached it, she pushed herself up with both of her arms. The water streamed down her body and the light playfully bounced around on the wet rounding's of her body. Her skin hit out in goose bumps as the cool air touched her wet body, making her nipples even harder. Painfully aware of her nakedness now, she swooped up her dress and sandals in a swift movement and held the dress in front of her breasts in an attempt to cover them.

"The water is wonderful," she said in a fake confident voice, not wanting to give Mika the satisfaction of discovering her vulnerability in that moment.

"You should have joined us," she tried to hide the fact that she knew he wasn't too happy about the fact that his girlfriend had just exposed her body to all of his friends. Mika shook his head at her, but didn't answer her, so Nicole spared herself any further embarrassment and fled into the house in search of a towel.

From inside the house, she could hear the music and bantering of the men outside and every now and again, she could hear Grete's squeals of pleasure. She found the bathroom and the towels with it. She didn't need to switch the lights on, as the outside light was so bright that it lit the bathroom in a subtle yellow hue. She placed her dress and sandals on the floor and started to dry her body off with the towel that hung on a railing on the wall. She had to take her G-string off in order to dry it a little with the towel and she bent forward with her back to the door, which she left open as everyone except Mika was in the pool. She was still bent over when she heard a whisper: "Nice ass."

In shock, she flung herself around, holding the towel in front of her.

"Mika!" Nicole playfully scolded him, relieved to find that it was him and not someone else, admiring her from behind and somewhat embarrassed by her nakedness, she blushed. Although they had made out many a times, he had never seen her totally naked.

"What? Now I am not allowed to like what I see?" he playfully teased, and he pushed the door to the bathroom closed as he entered it, while still holding her in his view. Nicole's breathing quickened as he came closer. As he slowly moved forward, he lifted his light blue shirt over his head, but his one hand got stuck and he tugged hard at it, causing his muscles on his dark skin to move playfully under his skin.

Nicole bit down on her lip as his masculine torso rippled down in waves of little dips, leading her eyes down to where the elastic of his shorts couldn't hide his arousal. His endowment was impressive and scary at the same time. Mika tossed his shirt to the side and it landed in the bath. Nicole now clenched the towel in front of her to her bosom; she didn't know how to deal with this situation. She was still a virgin and his body sure as hell was in need of satisfaction.

"Uhmmm…Mika?" she said, not knowing what she really wanted to say, but Mika didn't answer her. He had a passion that needed satisfying and he was frustrated and aroused by her flaunting her beautiful assets in front of other men. Mika didn't know that Nicole was still a virgin; for some reason, she hadn't thought it important to discuss it with him. He reached her and took her hand, which still clung to the towel, in his.

"Shhhht, it's alright…" he assured her, and she relaxed her grip enough for him to take the towel from her with one hand and toss it with his shirt in the bath. While doing so, he wrapped his other arm around her small waist, pulling her closer and pressed her firmly against his chest. His skin was warm from his feverish passion and he followed with the second hand, wrapping it around her waist as well. He looked down at her, she seemed so fragile to him.

"You are so beautiful, dear God, if you only knew how beautiful you are," he whispered into her face. She looked up into his face while he said it, and he looked tender and genuinely moved by her. She loved the feeling, it gave her a feeling of power, her ability to arouse such strong feelings in him. She smiled at him, pressing harder against him. His hard, warm body awakened her body juices to flow and she felt a need to satisfy her arousal, so she lifted herself onto her toes and reached out with her mouth and took his bottom lip prisoner between her soft lips, softly biting down.

This caused him to swiftly move both his hands to grab her buttocks in his palms and pressing her womanhood hard against his penis, while he grunted, and then continued to kiss her very passionately. She kissed back, letting him take the lead. Their kiss made her loins ache as he rubbed himself against her rhythmically. He kept his hands on her behind the whole time, keeping her prisoner to his arousal. Nicole didn't care, for the first time she didn't care. She was swept away by the gorgeous body in front of her.

Mika slowed down to a gentle, but passionately blissful pace, allowing his lips to caress her skin. She felt delicate underneath his rough and large hands. Her buttocks were hard and fitted perfectly in his hands and this drove him wild. Every so often he uttered a grunt while biting down on his teeth. He wasn't very experienced as he had only slept with his previous two girlfriends and not once was it satisfying, as it was done in haste in his own house, in fear of his mother catching him whilst doing so.

Tonight, not only was he afforded to take the time to see Nicole in her full nudity, but to do with her as he pleased. He was passionate though, which made up for inexperience, and he moved his mouth down to Nicole's breast, taking one of her nipples prisoner in his mouth. He fondled it with his tongue and it amazed him how hard her small nipple stood erect. He opened his mouth wider and took as much of her breast in his mouth as was physically possible while sucking down hard.

She gave a little gasp and her head fell back as she allowed him to suck on her breast quite hard. He was bent forward to reach her and without thought, Nicole reached down to his pants and started pulling on it. She struggled to pull it down and Mika stopped to take them off and tossed them on the floor. He paused while trying to take in every inch of her perfectly formed body. He left his underpants on. Nicole was first to move, as his gaze made her feel self-conscious. She bent her arms up as to cover her breasts while locking her fingers under her chin in a protective manner, while she pushed her body forwards and against his torso. Her head was now bowed down in a shy manner, and she turned her head to rest it against his chest. Instinctively, Mika took her in his arms in a protective manner, holding her for a while. They stood like that, caught in the moment.

It took all of Mika to speak: "Nicole…" he said softly, "you don't have to…" but she looked up before he could finish, and she placed her index finger on his lips.

"Let's not talk," she whispered and moved away from him. He nodded and let her go. Now they stood opposite each other, taking each other in and eventually, Mika couldn't take it anymore, so he reached out and pulled her against him so hard that he nearly took her wind from her lungs. She smiled, and they kissed, only stopping for him to lift her from her feet in a cradling position to put her down on the bathroom carpet, placing his body next to hers. His one arm he kept under her head while he started kissing her again, but this time very gently.

Nicole was moved by his gentle manner. To her, this was the sexiest thing she had ever experienced, and she didn't want it to end. By now, she had a longing for him in her loins that made her swollen and wet with anticipation. And as if Mika sensed this, he slowly placed his free hand on Nicole's toned stomach gliding it softly over her skin, moving close to her most sacred part, stopping short of touching her trimmed pubic hairs, and then moving his hand away, not only making sure that she wanted him to go further, but to tease her body into wanting him. He had stopped kissing her and he admired where his hand explored.

"God…" he uttered softly to himself whilst looking at her body, but didn't finish.

Then suddenly and without warning, he slipped his hand down her body and slipped his thick middle finger into the soft moist warmth of her. Nicole threw her head and shoulders back from the shock of it, forcing her torso up into an arching position and her hips downwards, trapping his hand between her legs. Mika didn't let this stop him. He lifted himself onto his elbow next to Nicole so that he could reach down between her legs.

His finger was firmly planted in her and he pushed it in as deep as her body would allow her. He didn't move it until her body relaxed back down and then he slowly started to glide his hand in and out of her. She was swollen, and the walls of her softness hugged the skin of his finger invitingly, causing his body to tremble. Once again, he bent down to her breasts and he sucked on it softly while he stroked the outer lips of her, soaking up the wetness between his fingers.

Nicole's body spontaneously moved in unison with his hand. She felt something build up inside of her, an intensity she hadn't felt before.

She had climaxed many a time before when she had satisfied herself, but her body wanted more. Hungry with passion, she looked up at him, grabbing him by his shoulders and pulled him onto her. He had no choice but to free his hand from its warm nest to lift his weight off Nicole in an attempt to not crush her. Both his hands were placed on either side of her.

"No, the floor is uncomfortable," he protested, "you will get hurt."

"I don't care," she replied, agitated, and she pulled on his shoulders to pull him on top of her, but he held his torso up with his arms, causing her to pull herself off from the floor. This caused him to smile at her frustration, which in turn made her release him and she fell to the floor with disappointment. "Fuck!" she said, and she rolled her head to one side.

The vision of her long locks spread on the floor and her chest which moved up high as she sighed and caused her firm small breast to press up into his face, aroused him even more. He bent down, taking care not to place too much of his weight on her, and started to kiss her while pushing his one knee in between her legs to signal that they should part. They did, and he placed both his legs in between hers, while placing his rock-hard penis on her vagina. She could feel every inch of him on top of her and her wetness in turn soaked his underpants.

This drove them both crazy and at the same time, their bodies found a rhythm that eased their arousal for a few seconds, but then frustrated them even more. Nicole found herself mumbling from underneath Mika's lips: "I want you so badly."

Mika didn't need another invitation and he swiftly lifted himself from her with his one hand while he pulled down his cotton restriction with the other and returning back in his position, with his manhood on top of her womanhood. It was warm and hard and pressed down on Nicole's clitoris, to the point of nearly hurting her, but she didn't care.

"Are you sure you want this, Nicole?" Mika said while holding it in place.

"Yes," Nicole said softly while looking him straight in the eye in an attempt to convince him.

Without a word, Mika lifted his body from hers with one hand and took his penis in the other. He couldn't see the opening to her as it was dark, and she lay with her head to the only source of light, the window, so he aimed at where he thought his target was, expecting an easy entry.

As he pushed his body forwards, he found resistance. He frowned in confusion and re-aimed and pushed a little harder. Still, the lips to her vagina wouldn't part enough for him to enter her, so he released his penis and stood up onto his knees. He reached down with both his hands, feeling for the opening and pulled its veils apart. Her lips were closed, which he hadn't felt before, but they parted with slipperiness, making it tricky to keep them open.

Then with him still holding her open, he aimed his free erection in her direction and pressed forward. He found his mark and his head slipped into her, but it couldn't freely fill her, so he kept it in the deepest position he could, affording himself time to position himself to penetrate her fully. Nicole longed for him to do so, as her deepest cavity ached.

"Just put it in," she begged softly.

"It's not that easy," Mika tried to explain and then it hit him. "You haven't done this before, have you?" he accused her.

"No," Nicole said shyly.

Still holding his position, he said: "Are you dead sure you want this?"

"Yes! Please just do it!" she begged and before she knew what was happening, he gave one hard thrust, having him end up deep in her and he held there without moving. Nicole nearly screamed as a burning sensation tore through her body. And although there was pain involved, the ache for satisfaction was greater. Nicole reached for his lips and started to kiss him softly and in response, he slowly started to move inside of her. Nicole threw her legs around him as he did this, her wetness lubricated a smooth passageway for him.

The fullness of him inside of her felt comforting and stimulating and his penis hit an extremely sensitive spot deep inside of her. It caused her body wanting him to touch it continuously. Her arms spontaneously gripped him as her legs did and without warning and with all her strength she clung to him, guiding his weight so that his body had no choice but to hit that magic spot continuously. Suddenly and without warning, she let out a scream as her body went into a spasm around his aroused passion. He lifted one of his hands, while supporting his weight on the other, and he placed it on her mouth in an attempt to muffle the sound. She in return held her breath, only making the orgasm worse. She had never felt such an intense orgasm, her vagina had a life of its own, pulsating in spasms around his penis as if it was trying to suck the life out of it. She climbed the steps of a multiple orgasm with each thrust he gently gave.

Mika had to concentrate hard not to lose control, and also to stay inside of her, as her opening was unbelievably tight and muscled and with each contraction, it threatened to push him out. With each slow thrust, Nicole dug her nails deeper into the skin on his buttocks as she tried to claw him deeper into her, and then it happened, the heightened bliss of a multiple orgasm, pulling all her muscles into a spasmodic state, where her back was arched as when he had fingered her, now only trapping his penis in a firm trap. It took all of his strength to fight back and keep himself buried deep inside her, which caused him to lose control of his semen, filling her body and letting out an unworldly grunt.

Nicole was holding her breath as to not let out another scream of satisfaction. Her ears were buzzing as she could actually hear her blood flow in her ears. Her senses were so heightened that she could take in every little detail in that capsule of time. Her ears were making a pulsating shushing sound, her heart pounded profusely in her chest, and she held her breath in fear of losing this intoxicating feeling and then everything became pitch black around her as she lost consciousness for a few seconds as a result of lack of oxygen.

Mika collapsed on top her, out of breath. His body weight pressed the little oxygen left in her lungs from its cavity. Mika's head rested in the small of her neck and she struggled to breathe, so she gathered all the strength she could muster and started to push him off her.

"I can't breathe," she whispered out of breath.

"I'm sorry," he apologised in a daze and lifted his torso off hers, but not leaving her body.

They looked at each other, both soaking in the feeling of contentment. Nicole pulled him closer with her hands behind his head and he came down to her, resting on his elbows, but taking her in an embrace, as her arms encircled his neck. They hugged each other tightly without saying a word.

"Maybe we should get back to the rest," Mika's consciousness kicked in.

Nicole could have stayed there with him for the rest of the night, but knew it wasn't possible, so she let him release her. He offered her his hand when he reached a standing position and she took it. It didn't even take any effort as he pulled her to her feet.

"Are you okay?" he checked.

"Yes," she said, confused why he would think she wouldn't be.

"Because you are bleeding," he said softly.

Only then did Nicole realise he had bloodstains on his pubic area.

"No, I am fine," she convinced him, but actually the rawness of her vagina became very apparent when she started to move. They both set about cleaning themselves and ridding the bathroom floor of any evidence of what had just happened. When they were dressed, Mika took her in his arms and kissed her on her forehead.

"Thank you! You are amazing," he said, looking down at her.

"You too," she reciprocated the feeling and then he took her hand and led her out of the bathroom, into the lit kitchen.

In the kitchen, Nicole pulled on Mika's hand which made him turn around to face her.

"What's wrong?" he asked with a frown on his forehead.

"I think I should rather go home, Mika," she said softly.

"Why?" he asked, even more confused.

"I am a bit sore," she looked to the floor, as she felt embarrassed by her disposition.

Mika released her hand and cupped her face with both his hands, lifting it up so that he could study it. He found a very vulnerable look on it.

"Nicole? Did I hurt you? I am so sorry," he said, genuinely concerned about her and he placed a soft firm kiss on her closed lips.

"No, you didn't, Mika, really, it is just sore now." She too was frowning now. "I will be fine, but I really think I should go home," she continued.

"Okay, are you sure?" Mika asked.

"Yes," she replied.

"Come," Mika said, taking her hand again and he guided her out into the yard, where the rest was already way into their meal.

"What have you two been up to?" Eugene inquired teasingly. Mika sternly glanced at Eugene as the rest of the shift broke into laughter. Mika came to a standstill behind the row of chairs, sheltering Nicole's body from the rest and then announced: "Nicole is not feeling well, so she will be going home."

"Aah no, man!" one protested.

"Nicole, come on, we will give you something to drink that would make you feel better," another teased. None of the men wanted her to leave now. It would mean they would only have Grete to keep them company.

"I am sorry, you guys," Nicole started with a smile on her face, "but I have to go." Mika didn't give the others a chance to argue any further, he started walking to the gate. Eugene followed them. At the car, Nicole and Mika hugged and he kissed her. When Eugene reached them, he too opened his arms and took Nicole from Mika's release.

"Thank you for coming," he said while still holding her tightly. "It was really nice meeting you. You are welcome to come and visit again."

"Thank you for having me. Next time, I will stay longer," Nicole replied. Eugene released her, and Mika opened her car door for her so that she could get in. Through the open window of the closed car door, Nicole said: "I will phone you tomorrow." Mika nodded and tapped the bonnet of the car in a gesture for her to drive.

"What have you done to the poor girl?" Eugene teased Mika as he threw one of his arms around Mika's shoulders, while they both watched Nicole's car disappear around the corner.

"Nothing, my dear friend, I did absolutely nothing," Mika said, and he turned to walk his friend to the back of the house where they continued to eat and drink till late that evening.

Mika was mesmerised by what had happened between the two of them and for the rest of the night and the days to follow he had constant flashbacks of their lovemaking. He was partly regretting it as he had a strict policy not to sleep with any of his girlfriends if he couldn't see a permanent future with them. And in Nicole's case, he didn't. It wasn't that Nicole wasn't good enough; in fact, she was the best thing that had ever stepped into his life, but the fact that she didn't come from a well-to-do family didn't really fit in so well with his plans for the future.

He was ambitious and adamant to make something of his future and to move away from his life in Milnerton. He wasn't prepared to live the simple life his father and mother did. He was now torn in two. Nicole was addictive, someone you wouldn't easily get out of your system, and after tonight, it was clearer to him than ever.

Nicole finally stopped in front of their house in Table View. Suddenly, the three-bedroomed duplex seemed enormous, and she felt so small. She sat there listening to her Depeche Mode CDs, unable to leave the warm security of the car and the soothing music. In her mind's eye, she played back every delicious second of her union with Mika. She sat there for about an hour without moving, she wanted her cocoon of bliss to last, but nothing ever does.

As she sat there in her own web of thoughts, her mother opened the front door, indicating to Nicole to come in. Irritated by the disturbance, Nicole reluctantly sighed as she switched the radio off. As slow as she could, she walked the few steps to the door, where her mother was waiting for her.

"What are you doing?" Hazel said, agitated. "You have been sitting there for an hour already."

"I know…" Nicole replied, preoccupied by her thoughts.

"Do you want to eat something?" Hazel went on.

"No, it's okay, I ate at Mika's," she lied, as food was the last thing on her mind. "I am going to take a bath now," she said as she planted a kiss on her mother's turned cheek. "Sleep tight," she said, not giving Hazel a chance to reply, she skipped up steps as she fled up the staircase to her room. Only when she finally sat in the bath and she had washed away all the evidence of the night's occurrences, did she realise how irresponsible she was.

"Shit, he came inside of me!" she panicked. Until now, she hadn't needed to use any form of birth control.

What the hell am I going to do? she thought to herself and then she remembered how the girls in the college had once spoken about the morning after pill. "That's exactly what I'll do," she said out loud.

Chapter 11

The next morning, she slept in. She only woke after twelve, only to find the house cloaked in silence. This was odd, as it was Saturday and her mother hardly ever went out.

Maybe she went to the shops, she thought, not really worrying about it. It actually suited her just fine. It gave her freedom to set the pace for the day. She hoped that her mother wouldn't make too much of a fuss of her being there, as she wanted to cram as much into the week as possible. For one, she was dying to see Ava and Ben. She hadn't spoken to them since before she went to College. In a very short time, she had become so close to them that they now substituted her feeling of loss for not having siblings.

Funnily enough, her discomfort of the previous night had dissipated, and she was again able to move swiftly as she set about finding the house phone and phoning Ava. Ava was excited to hear from Nicole and invited her to come visit her and Ben, as she had moved into Ben's place when Nicole was away.

"So when did this happen?" Nicole laughed from sheer joy.

"Come visit me and I'll tell you everything," Ava replied. They discussed their plans for the night. Ava and Ben were going to have a barbeque for only the three of them, and Mika if he could make it. Nicole was to be there at seven. After Nicole put the phone down, she immediately phoned Mika's house, but there was no answer. She then phoned the station where he worked, and they informed her that he was only working in the evening. Nicole asked the Charge Officer to give Mika a message that she was looking for him, as soon as he came in for night shift. Disappointed, she placed the phone down and sighed.

Well then, it is only the three of us, she thought to herself.

Nicole needed to get to the pharmacy for the morning after pill and thought it a good idea to spend the rest of the afternoon on a bit of shopping, as she needed some new underwear. She only had practical panties and bras and then that one lacy G-string, but now things had changed; she needed to be prepared, since her relationship with Mika had taken on a whole new level.

And I should probably get birth control while I am at it, she reminded herself as she ran her to-do list through her mind. Luckily, the shops were walking distance from where they stayed so she didn't need her mother's transport for the day. The morning after pill was quite easy to get. The pharmacist didn't even look judgmental about her asking for it and explained quite matter-of-factly how to use it, as if it were headache pills. She thought to herself: *He obviously gets a lot of girls asking for it*. And in her naivety, it was strange to her. She even felt alone, as if it only happened to her. This was a sure curse of being an only child. The pharmacist also recommended a birth control pill, before she could ask for it, and continued to explain to her how it worked.

"You should also consider using condoms," he said before he turned his attention to the next customer. Nicole felt a little embarrassed when she turned to go pay as the elderly woman behind her looked totally annoyed with her and her promiscuity.

Nicole stopped for a cold drink at one of the coffee shops so that she could swallow two of the pills the pharmacist had given her. Then she moved on to buy herself three sets of underwear and finally, on the spur of the moment, she decided to look for a summer's dress, as it was ridiculously hot. Nicole found a powder blue floral cotton dress in one of the shops. It hugged her body softly; it had spaghetti straps running over the shoulders, showing off the delicateness of her bone structure and tanned skin. Satisfied with the image reflected in the fitting room's mirror, she bought it and walked home. When Nicole arrived back home, there was still no sign of her mother.

I probably missed her, she thought. Nicole set about getting herself ready for the barbeque that evening. She couldn't resist trying on one of the new sets of underwear she had just bought, and she liked it so much that she decided to keep it on. It too was powder blue. When she had finished, her mother had still not returned and she phoned Ava to explain that she had no way of getting there until her mother came back.

Nicole was getting worried as her mother didn't leave a note. Nicole decided to be the responsible one when Ava sent Ben to come pick her up. Nicole left a note on the kitchen counter, explaining that she was going to visit Ava and Ben and that Hazel shouldn't wait up for her, before she left the house. Ben was happy to see her and he hugged the breath from her lungs before she climbed into his car. They made small talk in his car on their way to his house. He drove an old Mercedes that he had lined out with fur. Little bobblehead animals paraded in the back of the car window.

Ben was a character. He was six foot two and weighed 130kg. He was overweight, but not wobbly, he was firm and strong. He looked like an oversized Kewpie Doll, only with a reddish-brown beard. His head was always shaved. A golden hooped earing dangled from his left ear, lending him the appearance of a pirate. His arms were huge and flaunted backyard tattoos, but contrary to his hardened exterior, he had a heart of gold. His eyes reflected this, as he had the longest eyelashes Nicole had ever seen on a man.

Ben lived in the same house his parents had and before them his grandparents. Both his parents and grandparents only had one son each as they weren't well off. Their house was in the bad part of Brooklyn. This didn't bother Nicole at all. She loved visiting them there. The neighbours still cared about each other. Everyone knew each other. It was a very small and intimate community. Something she wasn't used to as where she stayed, hardly anyone greeted each other or took the time to even get to know each other. If you were in trouble or needed something, it was your problem. Here, where Ben stayed, there was always someone offering to help. She loved it.

When they reached their house, Ben's Rottweiler welcomed them from behind the high wall in front of the house. This wall unfortunately was also part of living in Brooklyn, as gangs ruled the streets at night. Ben's house was never targeted though. Ben was a gentle soul when it came to the people he loved and cared for, but could be viciously cruel if needed be.

"I will put Brute away; he has been grumpy the last few days," Ben said as he climbed out of his car with effort. Nicole waited in front of the front gate until Ben reappeared to fetch her. When Ben returned, Ava joined him.

"Nicole!" she exclaimed when she saw her and took her in her arms, hugging her the way a mother would when she hadn't seen her child for a month. The warmth of the welcome was comforting to Nicole and she gave in to the hug, letting her head rest on Ava's chest.

"You cannot believe how much I missed you, Ava," Nicole said, feeling all emotional.

What's wrong with you? Nicole reprimanded herself internally and she quickly let go of Ava, who had picked up weight in the month that had passed. Ava had always been on the bigger side, but now she was even bigger than usual.

Nicole put it down to the fact that she had moved in with Ben, as he loved eating. Preparing food in his house was like a social get-together. As soon as the smell of food filled the air, his neighbours would pop in to say hello in the hope of getting a free meal, which Ben was too glad to share, as he always made too much food and he thrived on the compliments he got.

He considered himself quite the connoisseur, but in fact his food was nothing more than tasty, home-cooked meals. His kitchen was small, but he managed to cram a small four-man table into the entrance to the kitchen. It was shifted up against the wall and cabinets, so only two people could sit at it. And this was exactly where they headed.

Ben had been busy spicing the meat in the kitchen before and returned to doing so. Ben and Ava didn't really worry about green salads, they much rather preferred starch and therefore, Ava was making potato salad. Nicole took a seat at the kitchen table and lit a cigarette. They fell into discussion as if there hadn't been a lapse of absence; Nicole giving them a full account of her experiences and them in return reminiscing about their days in the College.

Soon enough the preparation work was done and they moved to the living room, which looked out on the barbeque area in front of the house. Mark set about lighting the fire in the fireplace which consisted of a metal drum that was cut in half, with four legs welded on to it. It was getting dark now and Ava took Ben a beer, while she poured herself and Nicole a glass of cheap red wine. They settled on the oversized couches they had managed to fit into their lounge. It was upholstered with a black velvety material, with maroon, purple, blue, white and golden fine lines in all directions on it.

The lounge set had DIY shelves on the walls, which was decorated with an assortment of bric-a-brac. The most prominent, a Buddha statue, a newly acquired hubbly pipe and Ben's glass container of tobacco and his little wooden box with his utensils and paper for rolling his own cigarettes. Next to it was a wooden stand for his three pipes, of which one was carved out of ivory and his prized possession, as it had belonged to his father, who committed suicide in their backyard when Ben was still a young boy. Under this particular shelf, Ben placed the only chair that came with the lounge suit. This was his chair where he spent most of his free time. As his weight made it an effort to move, he preferred not to spend too much energy. So, after the fire was lit, he came inside to sit in it.

"Ah, that is better," he spoke to himself out loud and then he uncomfortably reached up to light his pipe. They chatted about an hour away before the first person, smelling the barbeque fire, arrived. It was Ben and Ava's neighbour from next door.

He was a thirty-two-year-old bachelor. He was of average height and very well built as he spent hours in the gym. His body was his pride and joy as he loved the single life and the chase and conquering of women. It was his claim to self-value. Unfortunately he thought the more time you spent in the sun or under the lights of sunbeds, the more alluring your toned body are to woman. As a result, his skin had aged beyond its thirty-two years.

He had the whole surfer image although he didn't even own a wet suit. He did own a second-hand surfboard he had found at a pawn shop in the main road. And although it accompanied him to the beach, when he went to tan and impress the desperately attention seeking older woman of Clifton, it spent its time stuck in the sand where he placed it on arrival. If he wasn't dressed in a T-shirt and shorts he opted to bare his chest and wrap a sarong around his waist, mostly going bare underneath as well. Dale had shoulder length curly blonde hair. How natural the blond locks or the curls were, is debatable, but nobody dared ask, as he had a fragile soul.

That evening, he had just returned from the beach and therefore had his sarong on. As he unloaded his surfboard from his car, he saw the smoke coming from Ben's house. Smoke meant a barbeque and free food. Dale did odd construction jobs, so he didn't have a consistent income. His parents had left him, the only child, their house and their pension on passing. He wisely clung to it, as he knew it had to last him a life time and it wasn't much to begin with, but from the interest he received from investing it, he could manage to afford his car and pay the normal cost of living.

"Hi Ben," Dale called into the house as he entered the front door.

"Dale, we are in the lounge, come through," Ben called back. Ava pulled a face at Nicole and rolled her eyes. Although Ava felt sorry for him and tolerated him mostly, she didn't particularly approve of his lifestyle, as she had been married to a womaniser who slept around as if it was going out of season, leaving her to look after his small children. She didn't really talk about her life before her divorce, but Dale reminded her of that time. Nicole found her friend's pulled face humorous and she grinned at Ava. Ava enjoyed the limelight, so she put on a whole display when Dale's face appeared around the corner.

"Hi Dale, how are you," Ava said in a patronising tone only recognisable to Nicole.

"Hi Ava, how are you," he said tenderly as he took the few steps to where she was sitting on the couch, placed against the wall to the entrance of the room. Nicole was sitting on the couch adjacent to Ava and to the right of the door. Ben's chair was against the wall opposite the door, so Nicole was hidden from his sight, except if he turned his head to the right, which he didn't. He was focussed on Ava, and he bent down to kiss her on her cheek and gave her a hug. Then he stepped forward to take Ben's huge hand in his to greet him properly.

"Hello, big fellow," he said as he shook Ben's hand.

"Don't start," Ben said, aiming a playful punch in Dale's direction, causing Dale to jump out of the way and turning to sit on the couch opposite Ben. As he turned around, he was startled by Nicole's presence.

"Fuck me," he exclaimed and immediately apologised. "I am so sorry for my language and bad manners, you gave me a fright," he said in an inappropriately charming and gentle voice. It took him one stretched step to reach Nicole and without warning, he picked Nicole's right hand up and stroked it gently while he spoke to her.

"Hi, I am Dale," he introduced himself. Nicole pulled her hand away and reoffered it to shake it. He took it but instead of a firm shake, he held her hand softly.

"Hi, I am Nicole," she replied. Nicole studied his body, as it was hard not to. He stood in front of her a few seconds longer than was necessary, affording her the time to study him as he did her. His body was rock hard. He had good muscle tone, but his muscles weren't stretched beyond the point of looking natural, which Nicole liked. There wasn't a gram of fat on his torso and with every movement his muscles moved under his skin. He wasn't hairy at all and only displayed a few hairs under his navel running down under his sarong. He had a broad and defined jaw, green eyes and a well-set nose. Proportionately, he was perfect.

He was attractive, and Nicole's body responded to him instinctively. In that moment, they both felt the physical attraction nature had implanted in all of us.

Dale took a seat hopelessly too close to Nicole and flung his arms open and over the headrest of the couch, while sitting with his knees wide apart so that his knee closest to Nicole slightly touched her. Nicole looked beautiful and sophisticated, the way he liked his women, and one of the reasons he went to

Clifton. Clifton Beach was where all the who's who hung around. It is a pristine beach with white sand surrounded by rounded boulders and clear blue waters. It is surrounded by bungalows and villas that only the rich could afford. Most, who spent their summer days here, had nothing else to do and they took care to eat right and exercise, so they could flaunt their superiority to the man on the street.

"So, what do you do?" Dale asked, thinking initially that she must be from a wealthy family, because the girls in their vicinity didn't look like this.

"I am a police student and I am busy with my training," Nicole replied sweetly. "And you?"

"I am a building contractor," he tried to sound important.

This was his standard reply to all, even Ava and Ben thought this to be true.

"Come Nicole," Ava protectively invited as she didn't like the fact that Dale was trying to impress Nicole. Nicole followed Ava outside where they took a seat around the fire, while they left the men inside to talk. When their drinks were finished, Ava disappeared into the house to refill their glasses. At that precise time, Dale came outside to join them at the fire. Ben was firmly stuck in his chair and would only move when it was time to barbeque the meat. Dale and Nicole were thus left on their own.

Nicole sat in silence, not having much to say to Dale, nor finding it important to make small talk as she already had someone in her life. Dale took a stance at the fire, stretching his hands out as to warm his hands in the heat of the flames, but he was actually studying Nicole's long legs that were stretched out in front of her. It aroused him. Nicole looked at him in amazement as his arousal made itself clear from under his sarong. It was an orange dip-dyed one and the light from the fire caused it to become slightly transparent, affording her to see his erection slowly rising to the point where the light material pressed it against his body and hugging it so tightly that it bulged over the outline of it.

Nicole wondered if she should look away, but it was difficult to do so. His erection was impressive, it was definitely bigger than Mika's. Nicole wondered what one should do with it as Mika's was already more than she could handle, but it still strangely intrigued her. She kept staring at it, not realising that he now was looking straight at her face and enjoying the fact that she couldn't take her eyes off it.

He actually stood a little more erect as to show off more of his pride. Suddenly, Nicole was shaken from her trance as Dale let loose a scream: "Holy fuck!" It rang in her ears. Nicole was bewildered as she tried to figure out what was going on. She witnessed him flung around and shouting, "Damn it Brute, what the hell!"

Then Nicole saw blood slowly soaking through the material of the sarong, as Dale's back was turned to her. It didn't even take Ben five seconds to spring into action and reach Brute, grabbing him by his collar and placing a fierce punch straight on his nose.

"No," he reprimanded the dog. It took all his strength to pull the dog back and he dragged Brute through the house and to the back of the house. Nicole heard how Ben was shouting at Ava for letting the dog slip past her when she had opened the back door to do something outside. Dale was now turned with his head as far back as possible to assess the damaged to his behind.

"Damn dog!" he said as he saw the blood seep through his sarong.

"Are you okay?" Nicole said, trying not to laugh from shock.

"Yes, but anyway," Dale said embarrassed, "I have to go in any case." He didn't make a lot of sense, but Nicole put it down to him feeling embarrassed by the situation and to save face.

"It was nice meeting you!" Nicole said.

"Yes, likewise," he said hastily as he fled out of the yard and back to the safety of his house where he could lick his wounds and tend to his ego.

When Ben returned, he asked Nicole where Dale had gone.

"He went home," Nicole explained. "He said he had things to do."

Ben bellowed out a monstrous laugh, "Yeah right! Good one, Brute." And he laughed again. "He just wants attention, now he got it!" Nicole now laughed with Ben.

Ava joined them outside and she too seemed pleased with the fact that Dale had gone. Ben started to tend to the meat on the barbeque and Ava and Nicole kept themselves warm with one glass of red wine after the other, but pacing themselves, as to not get to the point where they were so intoxicated that they couldn't enjoy themselves. There was a cool breeze blowing in from the sea. Brooklyn was so close to the ocean that you could sometimes smell the saltiness in the air.

Nicole loved the peacefulness of spending time with Ava and Ben. They would discuss life, philosophise and joke. When Ben had finished with the meat, he took the metal dish in and Ava followed him to help. Nicole didn't move as she was content in the spot and mindset she was in and didn't want to leave the feeling. She stared into the light of the smouldering coals as her mind drifted back to the previous night.

The fire warmed her face and skin from the front and the chilly wind-swept coolness over her back, causing her to hit out in goose bumps and she shivered. At that moment, she felt two huge warm hands softly stroking her shoulders down to her arms and back up. "Are you cold?" a very deep and gentle voice, which Nicole didn't recognise, asked.

Nicole flung around and startled by his presence looked up in to the face of the tower of a man that dwarfed her. She immediately stood up and turned to him, to lessen the difference in height as not to feel so intimidated by the stranger's enormity, but it only emphasised how tall this man was and towered over her by nearly a head and shoulders. He was well built and extremely attractive. He had dark brown hair, brown eyes, an olive skin and full lips. Nicole felt her heart racing as her whole being was intimidated and attracted to him at the same time.

"Uhm, who are you?" she stumbled over her words as she couldn't gather her thoughts.

"I am sorry, did I startle you?" he said, ignoring her question. "It looked like you were cold."

"Uhm, yes a little," she admitted. He made her feel like a little girl and it annoyed her.

"Why are you sitting here on your own?" he kept on questioning her.

"No, Ben and Ava went in to…" she tried to explain that she wasn't a sorry sight, but then Ben came out to call her.

"Oh, I see you made it," he said as he saw his friend with Nicole. "You are just in time," Ben continued. Nicole was confused and irritated that Ben had not warned her about his friend being invited. Not that something like this would normally irritate her, but now she got the distinct feeling she was being set up by Ben to meet his friend.

"Nicole, this is one of my dearest friends, Ian," Ben said with a gloating smile proudly displayed on his face, as he saw the reaction Nicole had to Ian. Ian was still standing right in front of Nicole, where she stood glued to the ground underneath her. Ian offered her a hand, an enormous hand, which she took softly, and his hand swallowed hers with a firm but gentle grip.

"This is Nicole," Ben continued.

"I have heard a lot about you," Ian said while not letting his stare part with hers, "but Ben's description of you didn't do you justice," he continued. Nicole pulled her hand from his and broke eye contact.

"Thank you," she said softly and then fled inside. As she passed Ben, she bit down on her lower lip, frowning at him and then she aimed a playful punch to his upper arm.

Ben started laughing.

"Come, let us join them," Ben invited Ian into the house and they set about dishing up food and eating in the lounge. Ben and Ian mostly talked and Nicole, from their discussions, had the opportunity to summarise Ian. He was truly a gentle soul. He had his own car repair business. He had another older brother. Only his mother was still alive and he looked after her. His older brother was engaged and he was single.

He was very involved in his community and although he could have already bought and lived in a much better area, he felt a loyalty to his community and therefore opted to stay there. He was a good prospective partner for any girl looking for a down-to-earth, well-mannered and loyal partner. And then the best part was that his appearance was a true testimonial of how right nature could create human beings to perfection, when all circumstances came together.

He was beyond attractive. When they had finished eating and had their last drinks for the night, Ian excused himself as he had to get up early to open his business. They said their goodbyes, but when he reached Nicole, instead of shaking her hand, he took her in his arms to hug her, picking her up from her feet in doing so and softly put her down again. Nicole didn't know what to do, so she clung to his shoulders.

"It was really nice meeting you. I hope I will see a lot more of you," he said gently, smiling down at her and she smiled back.

"I am sure you will," she said. Ben didn't waste any time in taking her home, as he too was tired and wanted to go to bed.

The next morning, Nicole woke to a silent house and assumed that her mother was already sleeping the previous night when she got home, and was still sleeping. She couldn't wait to see her mother and hear where she was the previous day. With a lightness to her step, she jumped out of bed and tip-toed down the steps to make herself some coffee. When she reached the kitchen, she found her note still lying on the counter. She frowned as she thought her mother would have thrown it away after she had read it, as her mother was meticulously neat.

She decided to make her mother coffee as well, so that she could wake her and get to the bottom of what was going on. When she had finished the coffee, she went up to her mother's room and knocked on the closed door. Her mother's door was always closed. There was no answer, so she slowly pushed it open, only to find her mother's bed untouched. Nobody had slept in it.

"Mother?" Nicole called, but she got no answer. Nicole ran down the steps in search of her mother, but she was nowhere, not even outside. Nicole went to the garage, expecting to find it empty, since if she wasn't home she would have taken the car, but to her amazement she found it standing in its place.

By now, Nicole was worried about her mother. This wasn't at all like her mother. Nicole took her coffee and went to sit in the tiny garden. She was confused by her mother's disappearance and disappointed that Mika hadn't returned her call or called her out of his own. She was trying to figure out her next move when the phone rang.

It was Mika, he wanted to know if he could see her that night as a group of his friends and their girlfriends were going out to dance. She was so relieved that he finally phoned that she didn't even bother to ask him what he had been up to. He arranged with her that he would come pick her up that evening at seven and then said goodbye.

Nicole decided that it wouldn't help pondering about where her mother was as it wouldn't bring her back and decided that if she wasn't back by that evening, she would phone her father as he would know what to do. She decided that as she had nothing planned until that evening, she might as well go to the police station and visit her old shift as they were working afternoon shift. Everyone was very excited to see her. They did warn her though that when you finished your training, it wasn't a guarantee that you would be placed at your own station.

A student normally got placed where he or she was needed. This meant that you could even be placed in a different town or province for that matter. Nicole hadn't realised this and became a little worried. Her life was here. Although where you stayed played a part in your placing and they tried to place you as close as possible to home, sometimes it was inevitable, as some areas had a shortage of officers. At this particular time in South Africa, in the early nineties and still in the Apartheid era, there was a new shift towards democracy.

Most South Africans were tired of the injustices that were going on and as such the government needed to enlarge their police force in preparation for the referendum that would be held in 1993.South Africa had seen countless violent riots and unrest in the past and didn't know what to expect when South Africa would finally join the rest of the democracies. The intention of the government was not only political but also to join international sports, entertainment and the global financial market. Not really about the noble cause of it.

This shortage of police members made it possible for a lot of new recruits to finish their training in the shortened time of three months, instead of six. There was a lot of mixed feelings about the changes that would follow if the country would finally become a democratic country. Mostly the true racist whites, which were the smaller portion of the new youths, were terrified by the untruths they had been fed over the years by the government and their own parents. There were whole new breeds of white youngsters who craved democracy and welcomed the thought of it.

Nicole was one of them. Her parents were liberal and had always had a problem with the way the government excluded certain races from benefiting from the spoils of their flourishing country.

With her placing after College on her mind, Nicole returned home at about four o'clock. When she opened the door, to her relief, her mother was seated at the kitchen counter drinking coffee and sorting out some paperwork.

"Thank God!" Nicole exclaimed. "I thought you went missing."

Nicole's mother looked up, confused by her concern.

"Sorry Nicole, I thought you were going to do your own thing, so I didn't think it necessary to bother you," Hazel said matter-of-factly, returning her attention to her work.

"You would never just leave without telling me, what is going on, and where have you been? You didn't sleep here last night," she accused Hazel.

"Why are you stressing so much?" Hazel said as she put her cup down and looked up at Nicole to study her face. "We are both adults and we don't have to report to one another."

"Well, I was worried. You never leave like this without warning. You could have left a note," Nicole argued.

"Fine, next time I will do so, but while we are talking, I need to discuss something with you," Hazel said calmly and in an instant, she relived the feeling she had when her parents told her they had to discuss something with her and then went on to pull the carpet from under her feet, by announcing their intention to divorce.

"Should I sit down?" Nicole asked with a sickening feeling in her stomach.

"If you want to," Hazel said plainly. Nicole chose to sit down on the lounge suite close to the kitchen and Hazel came to join her.

"It's nothing serious," Hazel started, but Nicole didn't trust Hazel.

"I met someone," Hazel announced without any sign of excitement.

Nicole couldn't believe it. *Where did she find the time and where did she meet him?* she thought to herself.

"I have been going to AA meetings," Hazel said as if Nicole had known about it all along. Nicole should have known, the signs were there, but she had chosen to ignore it. Now she sat there on the couch, unable to speak. She was too scared to say anything that she would regret, and she was trying to make sense of this new information.

Hazel continued to tell her about this man she had met there, how he was addicted to painkillers, since he had been in a terrible accident that had left him emotionally needing to numb himself to cope with his broken body. Hazel had gotten engaged to him while Nicole had been away and successfully applied for a job in Gauteng. She was planning on moving there in two months' time and was going to rent her house out, so Nicole had to find a place to stay for when she got back. This was if she was stationed there.

"See, I gathered since you are financially independent now, you would be able to rent a place of your own," she explained.

"Yes," Nicole said slowly, not agreeing with her mother, but not being able to show her true feelings. She was so shocked that her mother hadn't warned her about such a big decision in her life, which affected Nicole's life in such a drastic manner as to leave her without a place to stay and this while she only had been a week here. There was also no way of her being sure that she would be placed at her old station, so she couldn't exactly look for something until she was sure of where she was going. Nicole couldn't believe her mother would even let a person with an addiction become close to her, let alone her confessing to having one of her own.

"I need to get ready for tonight, Mika is taking me out," Nicole said in a daze, wanting to flee the room.

"Well, you guys must enjoy it," Hazel said, and Nicole felt like a stranger in her own home. Her mother had morphed into a stranger to her; someone she only shared a house with. She felt so sad and alone in that moment that she couldn't stop the tears from running down her cheeks as she slowly dragged her feet up the stairs and into her room. She went to sit on her bed with her head in her hands, not making a sound. She sat there motionless and as soon as she realised she would never make sense of this point in her life, she shook her head in an attempt to gather herself.

"I will not pity myself!" she said sternly out loud.

Come on, this is a good thing! You have to cope on your own at some point and at least she has someone who will be there for her. Nicole wiped the tears from her face and set about getting ready for the night. She opted for jeans and a white spaghetti strap fitted t-shirt. She pushed her feet into black pumps, lightly dabbed a little make-up on her cheeks and eyes and accentuated her beautiful eyes with mascara. She had no will to make an effort tonight. Nicole looked beautiful when she was dressed fashionably, but one could only truly appreciate her beauty when she opted for a natural look.

It wasn't long before the doorbell rang. Nicole grabbed her purse and ran down the steps. She rushed to open the door and called to her mother before disappearing through the door: "See you tomorrow." She didn't even give Hazel time to reply and slammed the door behind her and turned the key to lock it.

Mika was looking particularly smart that evening. He was wearing a light blue Polo golf shirt, weathered bleached jeans and brown leather shoes. He added a small amount of gel to his fringe, making it stand cheekily in the air. The shirt fitted his upper arms snugly, accentuating his well-developed biceps.

"You look nice," he said hesitantly, and Nicole immediately regretted not having made more of an effort.

"You too," she replied as they hugged. He walked her to his car and opened the back door, because the front seat was taken up by Eugene. In the backseat, Grete sat smiling friendly at her and in the middle sat a pretty blonde-haired girl.

"Nicole, this is my friend Natasha," Grete said as Nicole seated herself next to the girl.

Nicole smiled at the girl and studied her. She had fine blonde hair, blue eyes; she was petite and had a perfect set of teeth. She was dressed in a black mini dress and golden silk blouse, both showing off her perfectly formed legs and breasts.

"Hi, I am Nicole, pleased to meet you," she said methodically. The girl only smiled back at her and Nicole couldn't place what it meant, but she didn't care, as she was more interested in getting out of the house than having fun or meeting pretty girls. Nicole tried to catch Mika's eye in the mirror, but he didn't look at her at all. He was very quiet all the way to the club they went to.

There were a few spots they used to go to, but one of the favourites among the young, and old, police members was Sound Wave. This dance place was set up in an industrial area in Bellville. Here they played all types of disco and slow dance music. Tables circled the dance floor. People could bring their own drinks or buy it from a cash bar at the entrance.

Normally, Nicole loved coming here, as she loved to dance and was quite good at it. There was never a shortage of willing suitors to sweep her off to the dance floor. Although Nicole didn't want any attention, her height, slender build and her luscious auburn locks drew the attention of men and women inside. She didn't even notice, where normally this would give her a boost of confidence, placing her in a good mood and willing to dance with most of the men that came to ask her.

Nicole opted to take a seat in the farthest corner from the dance floor in the hopes of being ignored. Mika came to sit next to her and he and Eugene packed out their brandy and Coke they brought with. Grete and Eugene sat opposite Nicole and Mika and then Natasha took a seat next to Mika and closest to the dance floor. Nicole stared at the dance floor, which was already filled with people dancing to the music. The venue was dark and only dimly lit by coloured lights. Mika offered them all a drink and Grete and Natasha declined.

"We are going to drink some champagne tonight," Grete said and stood up to go buy a bottle at the bar. Natasha stood up and followed them.

"Nicole?" Mika said.

"Uhm…yes," Nicole said, not knowing what Mika had asked while Mika thought Nicole meant she wanted a drink of brandy and Coke. Mika poured Nicole the same drink as he had, which was quite strong. Nicole hadn't had the drink before, but it was sweet and tasted a lot like a cool drink. Nicole finished her drink long before the others, while Natasha and Grete sipped on their champagne like true ladies.

Soon, the first man appeared and asked Mika if he could steal Nicole for a dance. Mika didn't protest and Nicole reluctantly stood up and followed him to the dance floor. As soon as she started dancing, she remembered how dancing made her feel free and how she could escape her troubles for the time she did so, so she asked the young man if he wanted to keep on dancing the next two songs as well. At the table, the other four were deep in discussion and the few times she did make eye contact with Mika, he smiled at her and returned his attentions to the discussion.

At a point Nicole became worried that Mika would feel she wasn't giving him enough attention, so she went back to the table, where a drink was waiting for her. To her disappointment, he didn't even miss her. Mika seemed more interested in talking to the other four than her. She sat back in her chair trying to follow the conversation, but her mind kept moving back to her discussion with her mother. Nicole didn't realise how fast her drink was disappearing down her throat nor how soon it was filled when she put her empty glass on the table. Although Grete and Eugene did leave the table a few times to dance, Mika didn't seem interested in dancing at all.

He was too busy with his discussions with Natasha. All too soon, Niccole's head started spinning. She couldn't concentrate on Mika's face as it too moved. With a lot of effort, she managed to utter her words: "Mika I don't feel so good." For the first time that evening, Nicole had Mika's full attention.

"Do you want to go home?" Mika said, genuinely concerned.

"I think it would be better," Nicole said.

"Okay, mmmmm, it is still very early, Nicole," he said to Nicole.

"I don't think Eugene and Grete would want to leave now. Maybe I should take you back and come fetch them?" He debated with himself out loud. Nicole felt very dizzy.

"Do what you must, but I have to go home now," she said in an urgent voice while it looked like she was going to gag. Mika helped Nicole to her feet and Natasha mimicked his movements by standing up opposite him. She looked concerned as well, Nicole thought, as her attention was drawn to her as she moved.

"Okay, don't worry, I will take you home," he said

"Should I go with you?" Natasha said in a sweet and caring voice. "I will go and tell Eugene and Grete that we are taking her home," she offered.

"Yes, that would be great," Mika said thankfully. "Will you get her handbag?" Mika asked as Nicole's arms and legs were useless. He had to throw her one arm around his shoulder to support her weight as her own legs didn't have the strength.

"Yes, of course," Natasha said with a smile and set off to find the other two to let them know they would be gone for a few minutes.

At the car Natasha opened the back door for Mika and he helped Nicole into the back where she immediately fell asleep. Natasha took the front seat and they drove Nicole home. Nicole slept the whole way home and only when Mika finally pulled her upright to get her out of the car, did she open her eyes again. Her head still spun and in her confusion, she apologised: "I am so sorry," whispering in Mika's ear while she clung to his neck. Mika saw that she wouldn't be able to walk all the way, so he easily lifted her in his arms.

"Will you knock on the door for me?" Mika asked.

"Yes, of course," Natasha replied sweetly while holding Nicole's bag. Hazel was surprised and annoyed by the disturbance, but she let Mika and Natasha in.

"Do you mind taking her to her room?" Hazel asked Mika.

She took Nicole's handbag from Natasha.

"Thank you, you may stay here," Hazel ordered Natasha as Natasha tried to follow Mika up the stairs.

Mika carried Nicole up the stairs and placed her on her bed softly. Nicole opened her eyes and realised that he had done so.

"Thank you, Mika, I don't know what happened," she tried to apologise for her poor state.

"Shhh, just sleep it off, we can talk tomorrow," Mika said and pulled her blankets over her. Nicole gave in to her intoxicated state and drifted off into a black abyss. Mika pulled the door closed behind him and darted down the stairs to where Natasha waited.

"Thank you, Mika," Hazel said sternly while she was holding the front door open in a gesture for them to leave.

"It's my pleasure," Mika said and left with Natasha following him.

The next morning, Nicole woke up to her first meeting with a hangover. Her head was heavy and throbbed so much that she struggled to lift it. As soon as she stood up, everything spun around her and she had to sit down again. As if she was on a sea vessel, her stomach turned and the sickening feeling made her call to Hazel.

"Mom!" she called pathetically. Hazel's face appeared from behind Nicole's bedroom door.

"Yes Nicole?" she replied in an annoyed manner.

"I don't feel very well," Nicole complained while holding her head and trying to keep her eyes open.

"And so you shouldn't!" Hazel said sternly, and slammed Nicole's door closed.

The nerve, Nicole thought to herself as her mother's attitude angered her. *She is the last one to judge me.*

Her anger gave her enough determination to get up from her bed and although her head felt as if it was going to burst at any given moment, she cleaned her room. She took a shower, dressed and made her way to the kitchen. Hazel was once again at the kitchen counter, busy with paperwork.

"Do you want some coffee?" Nicole asked.

"That would be nice," Hazel said in a friendly voice. "I am sorry for my reaction earlier. I just don't want you to develop a problem."

"I won't, mom," Nicole tried to appease her mother. "This was the first time and definitely the last time. I didn't even realise I had too much until it was too late," Nicole continued.

"I am sure," Hazel replied and laughed at Nicole's state. "I would suggest that you don't drink coffee now. Rather drink a lot of water, take some painkillers and make yourself a greasy breakfast."

"I will puke if I have to eat anything greasy now," Nicole pulled her face at the thought.

"It's your choice, but I really think you should reconsider," Hazel said.

"I wouldn't even be able to make it, Mom, that's how bad I feel," Nicole moaned.

"Fine, you go sit down, I will make it," Hazel said, taking pity on Nicole.

Nicole ate the whole breakfast that Hazel brought her. It went down slowly and although she gagged a couple of times, it stayed down. After she had drunk the water and tablets her mother had left on the coffee table, Nicole lay down on the couch and fell asleep again. It was only late that afternoon when she woke up again. Once again, Nicole was on her own, as Hazel had left. The house was uncomfortably silent. Nicole sighed as she sat up straight on the couch. It took her a few minutes to muster the will to stand up and move to the kitchen where she found a note saying: "Nicole, I left food in the fridge. I won't be back until tomorrow. I went to see Pete. Remember to lock up if you go out. You are welcome to borrow the car. Lots of love. Mom."

Nicole frowned at the thought that her mother's boyfriend had come to fetch Hazel while Nicole was there and still her mother didn't introduce them. It seemed odd to her that her mother wouldn't want to have them meet. Then the phone rang. It was Mika.

"Hi Nicole," he said without any detectable emotion.

"Hi Mika," Nicole replied cautiously.

"Listen, I won't be able to see you for the rest of the week as I will be working and I need to help my mother with a few chores in my off time," he said matter-of-factly.

"Are you cross with me?" she asked disappointedly.

"No, why should I be. You are a grown woman," he said plainly.

"But..." Nicole tried to keep him on the line as it seemed as he was in a rush to say his say and then say goodbye. "I thought I would see more of you. You know I only have until Sunday evening," she protested.

"I know," Mika said. Nicole was stunned and confused by his lack of compassion or interest in her longing for him. There was an awkward silence.

"I will see what I can do," he said with a hint of pity in his voice.

"No, it's fine, if you cannot you cannot," she replied stubbornly. "I actually have a few things of my own to do," she lied.

"Okay..." Mika said, confused by her attitude. He was used to women flinging themselves at him or needing him. He didn't know what to make of it now that Nicole didn't seemed fazed about the fact that he was offish.

"So, I will phone you later in the week?" he asked in a gentle voice.

"Whatever suits you," Nicole said, now properly angered by him not wanting to see more of her, especially after they had shared such an intimate experience together. They said their goodbyes and put the phone down. Nicole was properly disappointed, she expected someone who cared for someone else not being able to stay away from that person and to make an effort to make it possible to see each other. She still felt drained from the previous night, so she decided to eat and spend the rest of the day in front of the television to catch up on some of the local meaningless soap operas.

The following two days, Nicole spent at home, searching the local newspapers for apartments she could rent and to get an idea of what she could expect to pay if she did so, but she didn't find any, so by the second day she threw the newspaper on the counter, deciding to take one day at a time and worry about housing when she had finished with College. She did her washing, cleaned the house and organised her room, all in attempt to keep busy. She did walk down to the beach a couple of times and just sat there with her feet in the soft warm sand, far away in thought.

As unsure as her future was, she wasn't worried about it anymore, she had surrendered to the unpredictability of it. She realised that you couldn't fight the inevitable and her best bet on survival was to ride the waves of life as the came rolling in. It was in these quiet times of surrendering that she found peace with herself, her situation and her disappointments. By not expecting anything, she could minimalize her disappointments to the bare minimum. And so, as she walked home on the second day after sitting and watching the sunset at the beach, she was at peace.

The next morning, she stood up with a smile. She decided she had spent enough time moping about and felt ready to make good use of her last day before she had to leave for College. She made herself and Hazel a breakfast which she served on the patio. She even made an effort to make small talk with Hazel. The weather was a little overcast, but it was welcoming after the hot summer's days that had preceded it. There where they sat, Nicole could smell the saltiness in the moisture blown in by a soft sea breeze.

What a great day, she thought as she sat back in her chair after she had finished her breakfast. Her mother was in a pleasant mood as well and they both actually enjoyed their time together.

"So, what are you up to today?" Hazel enquired.

"I haven't decided yet," Nicole replied thoughtfully as she was trying to figure out what she would do with this day. "Maybe I will hit the shops, as I won't be seeing shops soon," she smiled at Hazel.

"You can always join me?' she suggested to Hazel."

"I am sorry, Nicole, but I will be going out today. I have already made plans," Hazel apologised, but when she saw the disappointment on Nicole's face, she felt bad.

"Do you want me to cancel?" Hazel asked, but not really expecting Nicole to say yes and Nicole picked up on it.

"No, don't worry, I will be fine," Nicole said, trying not to look disappointed. She had enjoyed their morning together and wanted to make a day of it, but also didn't want her mother to feel obliged to spend time with her.

While Nicole was busy dressing for her day out, she heard her mother call to her from the opened front door: "Okay Nicole, I will see you later, don't wait up!" Nicole frantically grabbed her dress from its hanger in an attempt to dress herself fast enough to run down stairs, so she could see the man who had come to pick her mother up, but before she could pull it over her head, she heard the door slam closed and the key turn in the lock. She didn't get discouraged by it and chased them down, only to reach the parking bays in front of their duplex after Hazel and Pete had already left. She stamped her right foot on the tar, bruising it a bit.

"Damn it!" she said out loud. She retraced her steps back to her bedroom. She pulled her dress straight and continued her beautifying ritual. While she was still busy applying her make-up, the phone rang.

"Hello, Nicole speaking," she answered in a cheerful voice.

"Good morning, Nicole," Mika's familiar voice echoed in her ear.

"Good morning," she said friendly, "how have you been?"

"Fine," he said plainly, once again not giving a hint to his emotional state.

"So, why are you phoning?" she asked him petulantly.

"I wondered how you were," he explained, "and I thought we could see each other today?"

"Yes, that would be nice," Nicole said, taking care not to hint at her excitement.

"Okay, I will see you in a bit then?" he asked.

"Of course, whenever you're ready," Nicole replied sweetly.

An hour passed before she heard the doorbell ring. She couldn't reach the door fast enough and smiled at Mika as she opened the door. Nicole was wearing a black dress with a floral pattern on it. It showed off her long limbs. The neckline came down in a low V, affording the rounding of her breast to peep out slightly from the hem. Her hair caressed her shoulders. Mika was once again taken aback by her beauty. He smiled back at her and stepped forward to greet her. Nicole spontaneously opened her arms for him and he slipped his arms around her waist, hugging her tightly. As she pulled away after the hug, he leant forward holding her tightly and planted his slightly parted lips on hers.

"Hey," he said as he pulled away.

"Hey," she mimicked him.

"Come, I want to show you a special place today, this is the perfect weather to go there," he said mysteriously.

"Okay," she said, "let me quickly get my jersey."

"No, it won't be necessary, I will keep you warm," he offered.

"Fine," Nicole smiled at him with a little frown pulling at her forehead, as she couldn't figure out his mood.

Mika drove in the direction of Cape Town and then took the last entrance to the City. He kept straight on, driving up Table Mountain, past the turn off to the cable car on Table Mountain, along Kloofnek Road. As they reached the top Nicole saw the Atlantic Ocean displayed in all its glory. The intense blue-grey waters unsettled, foaming as it hit the distinctive boulders that mark the coastline of Camps Bay. The sky was overcast, and brush strokes of different shades of grey clouds flowed into an endless soft backdrop. The soft breeze had now turned into a cheeky wind, sweeping through the palm trees lining the street.

It painted a beautiful picture and if it wasn't for Mika's presence next to her, it could easily have been interpreted as sombre, Nicole thought. Mika pulled off at a parking spot at Bakoven and climbed out of the car to open Nicole's door for her. Nicole shivered as the cold air hit her. Mika took her in his arms and gave her a bear hug.

"Maybe I should get my jacket for you," he said, concerned at the sight of her discomfort.

"Wait here," he said caringly and went to the back of the car to fetch his denim jacket for Nicole. He held it behind Nicole so that she could stick her arms into the sleeves. It was way too big for her small frame. She hugged it as she revelled in the warmth of it. It smelled like Mika and she closed her eyes as the smell of him and the fresh sea air filled her nostrils. Mika took her hand and led her down the embankment in front of them to a secluded spot at the water's edge, where, when it was warm, people sunbathed naked.

Nicole didn't know this as she had never been here before or knew that one could climb down to this jewel of nature. Grey boulders surrounded them and Mika encouraged her to follow suit, climbing onto one of these boulders, where Mika opened his arm for Nicole to come and sit under the protection of it.

"Is this what you wanted to show me?" Nicole asked as her eyes swept over the picturesque surroundings. Mika stared into the horizon, which merged with the dark see into an undistinguished greyness. He didn't answer as his mind was far away.

"Mika?" Nicole asked to draw his attention.

"Sorry, yes?" he replied without looking at Nicole.

"Is this the place you wanted to show me?" she asked gently.

"Yes," Mika replied, still far away in thought.

Nicole stared in the same direction as Mika.

"It is truly beautiful," she whispered. They both sat there with the wind blowing them closer together and Nicole placed her head on his shoulder as they sat in silence, listening to nature's soft swooshing sounds. A faint mist started to kiss their skins and the coolness of it was soothing.

"Nicole…I have to tell you something," Mika broke the silence while he still sat motionless.

"Yes?" Nicole asked cautiously; she became extremely worried, as he looked very serious. He normally did, but this was intense. He paused for a long while before he spoke again.

"I…" he said, and Nicole could see how he was trying to figure out how he was going to say what he was struggling with. He looked at Nicole and he saw her worried expression. He had deep feelings for her and didn't want to hurt her.

"I love you," his courage gave way. Nicole let out her breath, as she was holding it and took a deep breath. Relieved and not wanting him to get a chance to change his mind about what he wanted to say, she leant forward and placed her lips on his. She found willing lips and they continued to kiss patiently, with wet droplets running down their faces and mingling with the wetness of their mouths.

Frustrated by his cowardliness, Mika gave in to his strong physical arousal for Nicole and his penis became hard and erect, wanting to feel her warmness not only on his lips, but also wanting, longing, and needing to own her whole body. Mika placed his one hand on the cold rock behind Nicole and pressed her body slowly back next to him, leaning over her upper body, kissing her softly and then more intensely, sweeping waves of emotion through her soul and body. The hard rock made it impossible for Nicole to give in totally to her need for him, so she pushed him back on his back and pulled away from him to look at him. He lay there out of breath, looking back at her.

Nicole needed to be sure that he wanted what she wanted to give to him so badly, so without thought she slipped her slender fingers over his groin, feeling for his erection and finding the hard warmness of it captured underneath his trousers. Her hand kept on rubbing over it harder and harder, while their gazes were fixed, until he groaned with frustration. Nicole took both her hands and opened his trousers and pulled his penis from where it waited for her. She worked gently with his manhood, as this was the first time she saw a penis in full view and it was the first time she had handled one. The softness of its exterior amazed her and she looked down at it to study it.

It was longer in length than the palm of her hand and she slowly and instinctively moved her hand softly up and down his shaft, pulling the skin covering its head back every time she moved her hand down. This fascinated her. Instinctively, she wanted to lick and taste it, but had to fight the urge, because she was brought up to believe that such things were scandalous. While she was transfixed by the sight in front of her, unbeknownst to her, it made Mika have to pull on all his willpower not to explode in her delicate hands. Nicole spotted a wet droplet right on the tip of his penis and she frowned as she looked at it, as it didn't move like the water droplets on her hands and his erection. She released her one hand and with her index finger, she touched it and it stuck to her fingertip. She rubbed it between her fingers to feel the consistency of his natural lubricant.

Once again, she had to stop herself from putting it to her tongue and tasting it. This frustrated Mika to the point where he needed to be satisfied urgently, so he wanted to come up from where he lay, but as he moved, Nicole said: "No," and she pushed him back down. Mika listened and lay back down, looking up at the grey skies filled with a mist of droplets. Nicole stood up and then placed her legs on either side of his legs, standing over him. Her dress was now clinging to her legs and he could appreciate her frame as a result.

Nicole didn't stop there, she bent forward and slipped her hands underneath her dress and pulled her white cotton panties off, letting it linger at her ankles. Nicole bent forward and stood on her knees, while positioning her vagina over his erection. Mika grabbed the sides of his trousers while groaning in anticipation, as Nicole took his penis in her one hand to hold it in place and then she swallowed him whole with her wet and swollen womanhood, resulting in him grabbing her by her buttocks and pulling her down hard on him. She let out a squeal as it went in deep and hard and the sting of it pleasured her.

Mika thrust against her furiously, holding her so that she couldn't move. Mika groaned louder as his passion built inside of him and Nicole's soft protests only spurred him on more until he cleansed his loins of its built up sperm, while giving a final hard thrust. They were emerged in wetness and Nicole fell forward onto his body, lying there out of breath. When she had gathered her breath, she pulled away from him, leaving him on his back, still motionless. His eyes were closed and only his chest moved heavily in search of oxygen.

Nicole pulled up her panties. She curled up in his arms there on the rock. They lay there for what seemed forever. Then Mika slowly pushed Nicole up and tucked his limp penis back into his trousers.

"Thank you," he said and pulled Nicole closer and kissed her passionately. Nicole didn't know what to say, so she kept quiet.

"We should get back, don't you think?" he suggested.

"Yes, it is probably best," Nicole agreed and on their way home they were both silent. Mika made an effort to hold Nicole's hand, rubbing it softly, every time he didn't need it to shift the gears. When they reached Nicole's house, Mika said that he probably should get home when he kissed her goodbye in front of their front door.

"I will phone you in the week. I hope you travel safely and thank you again for today," Mika said as he turned to walk away from her. Nicole was left with mixed emotions. She liked Mika deeply; maybe even loved him and he awoke feelings in her that were addictive. She wanted him, but he was constantly serious, which worried her. It felt to her as if he was keeping a distance and she didn't like it. Luckily, she had her morning-after pills that she had already taken, so she believed she would be sorted, and she didn't have to worry about that as well.

The next day was uneventful. Nicole packed her bags and lounged around the house counting the minutes until her mother came home to take her to the airport. She and Hazel greeted politely and Nicole finally relaxed when she saw the familiar faces of Tanya and the other girls, who were going to the College with her, as she took her seat on the airplane.

Chapter 12

Nicole welcomed the routine of College life, as it afforded her the opportunity to focus on nothing else. The only drawback was facing Melanie daily in her room. Melanie's annoying know-it-all attitude had really become a problem for Nicole, and although Nicole wasn't the type of person who normally entered into a dispute, she was worried that she would reach boiling point and say something that she would regret later. When Nicole entered the familiar surroundings of her dormitory, she decided to make a stop-off in Tanya's room first to avoid Melanie. When she entered her room, she saw another young woman on her bed with her back turned to Nicole. They were deep in discussion, with Tanya reporting to the young woman all she had been up to on her leave. They were so busy talking they didn't even notice Nicole entering the door. For a moment, Nicole's heart skipped a beat; the short-haired girl had a small Gemini tattoo on her right shoulder, peering out from underneath her sleeveless t-shirt she was wearing. Her head was positioned exactly where it was the previous time Nicole saw these two together in the showers, although they were fully clothed and not nearly as close together, but from where Nicole stood, the picture in front of her took her back to that uncomfortable morning.

I should rather leave them alone, Nicole thought to herself, but curiosity got the better of her, she needed to see the face that could convince a straight girl into giving in to such forbidden pleasures.

"Okay, so you say we cannot see each other during training?" Nicole overheard Tanya asking the girl on the bed.

"No, things are difficult as it is. I am sorry, Tanya," the girl said softly in a caring voice and Nicole could swear she could recognise it. Her mind was running through all the voices she could remember of the young women she knew in the College, but struggled to match it to this voice.

"It's a pity though; I really loved our get-togethers, Lisl," Tanya said, disappointed.

"Oh Nicole," Tanya said excitedly as she saw Nicole in the doorway. "Come in," she invited Nicole as Tanya made her way past Lisl, who flung around as Tanya spoke to Nicole. Nicole stared straight into Sergeant Dietrich's face and it took all Nicole's acting skills not to show how shocked she was to see her there.

"Oh, Sergeant Dietrich," Nicole tried to hide the fact that she felt uncomfortable with the knowledge of what these two have been up to and the fact that she had overheard part of their conversation. "I didn't mean to interrupt," she apologised. Sergeant Dietrich wasn't Tanya's Sergeant and furthermore, students and platoon sergeants weren't allowed to mingle socially, so it would be difficult to explain her presence in Tanya's room.

"Nicole," Sergeant Dietrich said, a little flustered, but also happy to see Nicole. "I was just leaving," she said as she stood up, facing Nicole in the doorway.

"Thank you for bringing me the message, Sergeant," Tanya said in a very formal voice, in an attempt to cover for Lisl.

"Next time tell your parents I am not a messenger," Lisl turned her head to Tanya when she spoke in a fake annoyed tone and Nicole couldn't see the expression on her face, but saw Tanya's downcast eyes and she felt a pinch of pity for her friend. As Sergeant Dietrich passed Nicole, she looked up into her face while smiling mischievously.

"Hope you had a great leave?" she asked Nicole.

"Yes Sergeant!" Nicole called out while looking straight in front of her.

"I am down here," Sergeant Dietrich replied teasingly. Nicole, armoured with the knowledge of what she had found out, felt daring and looked down straight into Lisl's face.

"Yes, I know," she teased back while only one corner of her mouth pulled into a smile, hinting at her knowing their little secret. Lisl nodded in recognition and she was forced to squeeze past Nicole as Nicole didn't make way for her to leave the room.

"So," Tanya turned her attentions to Nicole, while she returned to unpacking her suitcase, "what juicy news do you bear?"

Nicole laughed out loud: "You mean, what juicy stories you have to bear?" Tanya threw her head back as she laughed. "Oh, you don't want to know," she said ominously.

"So, did you have sex?" Tanya teased, knowing that Nicole was still a virgin and that she was so excited to see her beau.

"Actually, I did," Nicole said proudly and laughed at Tanya's shocked expression.

"What? You must tell me everything," she said, leaving everything and taking a seat opposite Nicole on Tanya's bed, where Nicole had made herself comfortable. Nicole told her everything and how she now thought they had a deep and lasting bond. Tanya gave Nicole a hug after she relived the events of the past week.

"I am so happy for you," Tanya said. "I am so proud! You are now officially a woman," she teased Nicole in a motherly voice, "and a potential drunk." They both burst out laughing.

With a smile on her face, Nicole greeted Tanya and walked over to her room to face Melanie, where she found her sitting on her bed. Her suitcase already neatly unpacked, her side of the room in perfect order and her in the middle of her bed, legs together, hands on either side of them on the edge of the bed, while her arms were stretched as she leant forward, as if she tried to carry her weight on them. Her head was bent forward deep in thought. She sat there in silence as if she was waiting for something.

Nicole felt sorry for her as for the first time Nicole realised just how isolated Melanie felt. Her mother's efforts to give Melanie the perfect upbringing, kept her from experiencing life in its entire glorious splendour. Even now as a grown woman of almost twenty-three, with a degree, enough financial backing from her parents behind her, she was so used to doing everything perfectly and the way her parents wanted her, that she was afraid of living.

It was then, as Nicole stared at the sorry sight that she decided to make an effort, to look past Melanie's annoying habits and show her that life doesn't have to be so serious.

"Melanie!" she called out in a fake excited voice. Melanie looked up in bewilderment.

"What?" she asked worried, not used to people wanting to talk to her, especially Nicole.

"How was your leave?" Nicole asked and hopped onto her own bed opposite Melanie's, letting her suitcase plunk down on the floor in front of them.

"It was nice, and yours?" Melanie replied.

"No man, I mean, what did you do?" Nicole asked, frustrated.

"Oh well, I was mostly home. My mom made me some new suits, do you want to see?" she said excitedly.

"Yes, of course," Nicole said, genuinely interested in seeing what her mother had managed to create for her. There was no denying it, her mother was brilliant at following a pattern to the tee, and her workmanship was something mentionable. And although these suits her mother had made for her, consisting of skirts and jackets, were perfect for work, they were plain and proper.

"Your mom is really talented," Nicole said impressed, which caused Melanie to glow with pride. Before they knew it, they had managed to have a full and lengthy conversation and although Nicole had to initiate most of it, once you got Melanie going, she seemed unable to stop. Nicole realised that Melanie also only wanted to be accepted and her way trying to do so, was by trying to be perfect. Nicole felt guilty and silently vowed that night to include Melanie more in the social circle she hung out in, in the hope that she wouldn't be so lonely.

The following morning, Nicole woke up to find a very friendly Melanie. They both divided up their work of cleaning the room before inspection, as opposed to their normal way of each one of them only doing their own half. This turned out to be beneficial to both of them as the work went much faster than usual and Nicole was able to be ready faster than usual, with time to spare to make a phone call before she had to line up for inspection. She ran to the phone booth at the end of the hall. Luckily, everyone was still busy preparing for inspection, so she found the booth open. She dialled Mika's home number and his mother answered in an annoyed tone: "Yes."

"I am sorry to bother you, but may I quickly speak to Mika? This is Nicole speaking," Nicole said as friendly as she could muster.

"No, I am sorry, he is busy. I will ask him to phone you later tonight when he has time," she said emotionless and put the phone down before Nicole could say anything. Stunned, Nicole looked at the handpiece she still held in her hand.

What on earth? she thought to herself. She knew his mother wasn't the friendliest person, but this was plain rude. There wasn't too much time to ponder on it as their day was about to begin, so she ran back to her room to double check her bed and cupboard before she heard: "Platoon! On the ready!" Nicole ran to the door and came to a standstill next to the opening; she glanced at Melanie who smiled at her while they stood in a resting position with their feet spread and their hands held together behind their backs.

"Platoon, attention!" the call came again and in unison, both platoons on either side of the hall came to attention.

This morning, Sergeant Dietrich did inspection. She was particularly lenient and hardly pulled bedding this morning. At Nicole's room, she stepped on Nicole's toes, as was her custom, but she didn't look at Nicole as she walked into the room, made a quick turn and walked out.

"Well done, you two," she said as she came out and moved on to the next room. Nicole and Melanie looked at each other and smiled. This was the first time the Sergeant did not find fault with anything in their room.

The day flew past for Nicole, without her thinking about Mika and before she knew it, she and Melanie found themselves in their room after study with time to relax. Now conversations naturally began without one of them having to make an effort to initiate it. Suddenly, Nicole heard someone call her from the hallway.

"Nicole!" She heard the girl call.

"Nicole! Come on, man, we don't have the whole fucking day, there are a lot of people waiting for the phone," she shouted, agitated. Nicole rushed to the phone, panting as she took the handset from the girl's hands and pulling the door to the phone booth closed behind her.

"Hi, this is Nicole speaking," she said.

"Nicole, this is Mika," she heard his voice over the phone.

"How are you? I tried to phone you this morning, but your mother wouldn't call you to the phone, she said you were busy," Nicole said.

"I know, she told me," he said. "Nicole..." he said, but didn't finish his sentence.

"Yes?" Nicole asked cautiously as she sensed his sombre mood. "Is something wrong?"

"No, not really. There is no easy way to say this, so I will just say it," he argued with himself out loud.

"I cannot see you anymore. It isn't working for me," he said, rushing his words, making it hard for Nicole to understand what he was saying.

Not sure if she had heard right, she repeated his words: "You cannot see me anymore?" with a heavy feeling in her stomach as her words rang in her ears.

"Don't you mean you don't want to see me?" she accused him and she had to bite down hard on her lip to control the urge to cry.

"No, I cannot see you anymore," he said softly. "I am really sorry, but there isn't much to discuss." Nicole was so shocked that she couldn't gather her thoughts enough to argue with him and then her shock turned to anger.

"Well then, goodbye," she said, slamming the phone down, not allowing him to answer her.

"Fuck you! You are a bloody idiot!" she screamed at the top of her lungs at the phone. "Fuck you!" When Nicole walked past the girl next in line that had called her to the phone, she pressed her chest to the girl's and pointed her index finger, as she poked her the chest and she screamed at her too: "Fuck you too!" And then she walked to her room, tears streaming down her cheeks.

Her thoughts were running between possible explanations for their breakup. As always, she first looked at what she could have done wrong and the only thing she could think of was that she was drunk when they went out, but that was normal for their age, so it was probably not the reason. Then she thought it was his mother's doing, as she was sure the woman didn't like her one bit and she decided it probably would be the most probable explanation.

"Bloody mommy's boy!" she said deep in thought, out loud as she entered her room.

"What the hell happened?" Melanie asked.

"Mika just broke up with me, without an explanation. Saying he cannot see me anymore! I am sure his mother set him up to this," Nicole said sadly as she went to sit on her bed, facing Melanie. She was unable to stop the tears from appearing in her eyes. The tears were more out of frustration and anger than mourning the loss of a true love.

"I hope you didn't have sex with him," Melanie said, worried. Nicole looked up at Melanie, shocked that she even knew what sex was, as she was so naïve, or so Nicole had perceived her.

"Yes, I did," Nicole said as she stopped crying and frowned at Melanie.

"What does that have to do with anything?" she asked annoyed. Melanie explained to her how she had had an affair with one of her lecturers at university and how sweet he was. He had been quite a bit older than her, but he treated her with so much respect. The affair went on for nearly a year when she finally felt she wanted to give herself to him, as she had believed they shared the same love for each other. The night was very romantic and she thought she had found the perfect soul mate, only to realise the next day he didn't want anything more to do with her. After some detective work from her side, she came to learn that he had a wife and two children, and that she wasn't the first student, or the only one, he had seduced in this manner.

"So, you see, you shouldn't have given in to him, most men are out to use girls," Melanie said seriously, believing the conclusion she had made.

"I don't agree with you and although I regret having given him the pleasure, I don't think it has anything to do with it. I was the one who initiated sex, not him," Nicole said.

"It was a natural thing, something I didn't give thought to, unlike you, who was constantly pushing for it. Although you said no, and he respected it, he still left you wondering about it and you made a decision based upon the fact, that when you had said no, he didn't push you further, believing he respected you," Nicole explained.

"I disagree, all men are the same, they love the chase and when they have had their fill, they move on," Melanie said adamantly.

"Well, think what you may, I believe his mother is behind this, but if he wants to be such a coward, then I will have to show him what his cowardliness has lost him," Nicole said adamantly, not knowing how she would do this, but vowing to herself that if she ever got the chance, she would. It had become a defensive tool to cut pain or discomfort out of her life as quickly as possible, as Nicole was in search of contentment and as such she needed to cut all thoughts of Mika out for now. What this did mean though, was that she could now hang out with the rest of the young men in College.

"Whichever way....you know what this means, don't you?" Nicole asked Melanie.

"You are rid of him?" Melanie looked confused.

"No silly, we can go to the dance they are holding for the College in a week's time," Nicole said with a smile on her face as she wiped the evidence of wetness on her cheeks away.

"Yes, you are right!" Melanie, who hadn't planned on going, said excitedly, since she had now been invited to do something with Nicole. Freed from any responsibilities outside College, Nicole could now throw herself into College life. Not taking anything too seriously, she glided through her courses and nearly got the highest marks of all the students, finally ending up in the top ten.

She also went to the dance and enjoyed it thoroughly and although there were a few suitors, she wasn't interested in getting involved with anyone. She was finally free of all commitments, except her commitment to the police force, but to her this one commitment was beneficial to both parties. Before they knew it, all the platoons started to practice for their graduation. This was to be held at Loftus Versveld Rugby Stadium in Pretoria. Nicole couldn't wait for this day and there was a feeling of excitement amongst all the students, causing them to give their all at practices.

They first had a prize giving ceremony on the College grounds. This was held on the athletics fields, so that they could accommodate all the students. The students were dressed in their formal summer uniform. This, for the women, consisted of a light blue skirt and jacket with lapels on the shoulders. The buttons were gold with the police emblem on it. The lapels were fitted with the emblem as well and only when you received a rank above constable, did you receive stripes or stars, according to the rank you held.

The entire group of women had to wear a blue police hat and their hair had to be neatly tied into a ponytail or bun at the back of their heads, if they had long hair, to accommodate the hat. All the girls were encouraged to wear make-up as they had to portray a well-groomed image of the Force. Jewellery was allowed so long as it was complimentary to the uniform and not ostentatious. Nicole's platoon stood to the back when they took their place in the parade. This made it difficult to see the podium where all the officers stood.

Since it was summer in Pretoria, it was very hot. Nicole was grateful when they received the order to stand at ease, as this meant she could move her feet a little, seeing that standing in the attention position in Pretoria's heat could make the strongest men faint. It felt like an eternity that they had to stand still, with their heads facing forward and she didn't take in a word that was said, as it took all her energy just to stand still. Just before Nicole couldn't take anymore, the order came for them to stand on attention and they were marched off the grounds to their dormitories.

"Urgh! That was tiring!" Nicole sighed as she flopped onto her bed.

"You could say that again!" Melanie agreed as she too copied Nicole's actions. Melanie was a little disappointed about not getting the best student award, as she firmly believed no one would have been able to beat her overall score of ninety-three percent, but unfortunately, one of the male students got ninety-four percent.

"Are you disappointed for not having the highest marks?" Nicole asked as she stared at the roof.

"Yes, a little…" Melanie said softly.

"Well, you did brilliantly nonetheless, so don't worry about it," Nicole tried to make her feel better.

"I am so tired," Melanie said.

"Then sleep," Nicole looked over to Melanie and smiled at her.

"What are you going to do?" Melanie asked.

"Ah, I will go sit in Tanya's room," Nicole said, wondering what she would do to past the time, since they had their last classes the day before and would graduate the next day. Most of the students were packing their belongings and polishing their shoes for the big day. They were to wear their full winter's uniform, with their dark blue long-sleeved blazers, greyish-blue skirts and hats. Nicole's uniform had been hanging ready in her cupboard since the start of that week, as she couldn't wait to finish with the College, so she had nothing to do.

Nicole changed into a pair of sweatpants and a t-shirt before she left the room to find Tanya. Tanya wasn't in her room and most of the girls were sitting outside in the garden, trying to find a cool breeze. Nicole went to the end of the hall to look through the windows at the stairs if she could spot Tanya outside, but she wasn't to be found. Nicole then checked the rooms one by one, only to find one or two lost souls still packing and not knowing where Tanya was, when she asked them. When Nicole reached the end of their passage where the two Sergeants' quarters were, she saw Sergeant Dietrich's door standing slightly ajar. She heard two voices coming from it; one being Sergeant Dietrich's and the other, she could swear, was Tanya's.

Oh, so that is where she is, Nicole thought to herself as she turned disappointedly to join the others outside. As she started to walk away, she heard Sergeant Dietrich's voice: "Nicole!"

Nicole flung around and stood on attention. "Yes Sergeant!"

"I need to talk to you," Sergeant Dietrich said tenderly as Tanya came out of her room and passed her. Tanya smiled at Nicole knowingly, without saying a word, and disappeared into her room. Nicole walked slowly to the Sergeant's quarters and came to a standstill in front of the door.

"Yes Sergeant?" Nicole asked in a gentle voice while looking down at Sergeant Dietrich.

"You don't have to call me Sergeant Dietrich, call me Lisl," she said in a friendly voice while looking at Nicole and smiling.

"Yes Sergeant," Nicole said and started laughing at herself for not being able to do so. "I mean, okay, Lisl." They both laughed.

"Would you like to come in, I have some fresh coffee made if you want some?" Lisl asked Nicole.

"Yes!" Nicole accepted as she hadn't had a decent coffee in about two months. "That would be nice." Nicole entered Lisl's room as she held the door open for Nicole. When Nicole was inside Lisl closed the door behind her. Lisl's room was neat and practically furnished. Everything was perfectly spaced and everything was in its place. Her bed was neater than Nicole could ever make her own bed. On it were two teddy bears though, which Nicole found odd. She didn't think Lisl to be one to hold herself up with meaningless trivia such as soft toys.

The room she entered was separated into two areas; a small seating area and a bedroom area and on the one wall was a built-in cupboard and at the entrance was a small kitchenette. Lisl had her own fully fitted en-suite bathroom.

"Come, sit," Lisl invited Nicole as she got them both a cup of coffee. Nicole took a seat, while roaming the room with her eyes in an attempt to find something to hint at what type of person she was. Nicole already knew she had a mysterious side to her, she could see that she was organised, but there was little to assess her personality by.

"You like my room?" Lisl asked as she handed Nicole her cup.

"Yes, I do. I wouldn't mind a room like this," Nicole said teasingly whilst imagining how she would have decorated it if it was hers.

"So tomorrow you go home…" Lisl started.

"Yes, I am very excited!" Nicole smiled.

"You know…" Lisl struggled to gather her words. Nicole waited for her to finish, but she stopped and looked down into her cup of coffee, looking for words.

"What is it?" Nicole asked.

"I know that I seem very difficult as a Sergeant, but I am actually just a normal human being. I can also be fun," Lisl said as if she was trying to convince Nicole while still looking down at her cup.

"I know," Nicole said, not really knowing, but sensing Lisl's vulnerability.

"So, what are you going to do now that College is finished for the year? Will you be going home? There must be someone waiting for you?" Nicole encouraged Lisl to talk about herself.

"No…" Lisl said softly and she seemed a little sad.

"No?" Nicole asked as she frowned, puzzled at Lisl's obvious sadness.

"No Nicole, I won't be going home, nor do I have someone waiting for me. This is my home," Lisl said as she looked at Nicole.

"Why?" Nicole asked in disbelief.

"My parents died when I was still in high school," she started and continued to explain to Nicole how her aunt took her in, but how she always felt as if she was a burden to her aunt. How she joined the police force in order to find some stability and for financial security, so that she could look after herself and not have to ever feel like a burden again.

Nicole could relate to her situation, but pitied her for not having anyone to emotionally support her. Lisl continued to explain that her aunt didn't make an effort to see her or talk to her, as she was always worried that Lisl would want something from her and that that was the main reason she had decided to take the post as a platoon sergeant when she got the chance. This afforded her free lodgings, since she was prepared to stay in during holidays to help look after the College.

Her food was for free and there was enough personnel to keep her company. She had full use of the College transport and since the College was in the heart of Pretoria, she had everything conveniently close to her. All her basic needs were covered. This lifestyle also afforded her the opportunity to study for free and to save as much of her money as she wanted to.

"I see…" Nicole said as she digested the information.

"I like it here, Nicole," Lisl said as she saw Nicole taking pity on her.

"Doesn't it get lonely?" Nicole asked.

"No, not really, I have friends I can visit and remember, I am not a student, so when classes are out, I am free to do as I please, except for when I am on duty," she explained.

"But enough about me, tell me about yourself," Sergeant Dietrich encouraged Nicole to open up to her. "Do you have a boyfriend?" Lisl continued.

"I had one, but the asshole broke up with me, so no." Nicole said, agitated and still upset that Mika could be as callous as to break up with her without an explanation and this right after she had given herself to him.

"And you?" Nicole returned the question, already knowing that she probably didn't have one.

"Yes, I do," Lisl said as she smiled at Nicole's confused expression.

"But…" Nicole started without being prepared to finish her sentence as she then had to let out her secret of how she saw her and Tanya in the showers.

"Uhm...I thought you said you had nobody?" Nicole quickly explained herself. For some reason, Nicole's heart was racing in her chest as it had that morning when she saw the two of them. She couldn't help but relive the sight she saw that morning and she felt nervous, as if Lisl might catch on to what she was thinking about. Not only did she feel guilty for thinking back to that morning, but she strangely felt aroused by the sounds and images that were engraved into her memory.

Nicole started to shift herself in her seat as her seat suddenly felt uncomfortable underneath her, as the thought triggered her juices to flow and her flesh to swell from the blood that rushed through her veins.

"Yes, I have someone to go to, my boyfriend is Sergeant Verster," Lisl informed her.

Lisl sat confidently back into her chair as she watched Nicole with amusement.

"The one here at College?" Nicole asked in shock.

"Yes, the one that works in the main building. We have been dating for a year now. He also stays on the College grounds." Lisl smiled at Nicole. Nicole was totally confused now. She was sure it was Sergeant Dietrich she had seen with Tanya, except if someone else in the College had exactly the same tattoo as Lisl, for which the chances were slim.

"But..." Nicole shook her head, she gave up, there was no way she could ask all the questions running through her head without spilling the beans on what she had seen.

"Yes Nicole?" Lisl smiled, amused. "What do you want to ask me?"

"No, it is nothing," Nicole said as she shifted again.

"Are you uncomfortable?" Lisl asked with slightly squinted eyes to assess Nicole's behaviour.

"Uhm...no?" Nicole stalled. "Can I use your bathroom?" Nicole asked as controlled as her voice would let her.

"Of course, you know where it is," Lisl said as she pointed to it in any case.

"Thank you," Nicole sighed, relieved to get a chance to gather herself.

Why are you so bloody nervous? You are being ridiculous, Nicole reprimanded herself silently as she took a seat on the toilet to relieve herself, not only from her full bladder, but from the tension building up inside of her. As Nicole wiped herself, the slimy evidence of arousal glistened in the light of the bathroom on the piece of toilet paper she was holding. Nicole looked at it for a few seconds, mesmerised by the instinctive functioning of her body.

Nicole took another piece of paper and although it wasn't necessary, she wiped herself hard in an attempt to wipe herself dry, wanting her body to stop producing fluids, just as much as she wanted her brain to stop thinking about that morning. Nicole finally returned to Lisl where she was now lying on her bed, busy looking through a couple of CDs'.

"Do you like music?" Lisl asked without looking up at Nicole and very comfortably as if they had been friends for years.

"Shouldn't I be going?" Nicole asked, worried that she could get in trouble for being there.

"No man, you are going home tomorrow and you're practically not a student anymore," Lisl dismissed her concerns, still looking at the CDs in front of her.

"If you want to go, that is another case, then you may go, but you are welcome to stay. I like your company," Lisl said and looked up at Nicole where she was standing in front of the bed.

"No, it's fine, I have nowhere to go," Nicole smiled down at Lisl. She was in conflict with herself, she knew she should probably just leave, but for some reason she was curious to find out more about Lisl. Lisl intrigued her. The thought of a woman, not only wanting to have sex with men, but also having a need to do so with women, had never crossed her mind. The possibility of having a normal life, but engaging in something so sinful, and what seemed to be so deliciously physically pleasing at the same time, blew her mind.

Nicole had never even thought about a woman in that way, but after seeing Lisl and Tanya together in the shower, it seemed clean and strangely beautiful.

"Then sit," said Lisl while tapping with her one hand on the bed to indicate to Nicole to take a seat next to her, invited. Nicole went to sit on the end of the bed, with Lisl facing her as she lay on her stomach with her knees bent and her feet in the air near the headboard.

"So what music do you like?" Lisl asked as she returned her attentions to the CDs in front of her. She had an array of eighties music spread out in front of her, from Sting to Depeche Mode.

Nicole was a big Depeche Mode fan as she was a teenager in the early to late eighties, so she chose one of their CDs.

"Mmmmmm…mood music! I like it!" Lisl said, and she lifted herself from the bed in a swift movement so that she could put the CD into the CD player. It was getting darker now and the room was dimmed in shades of grey.

"With mood music, we need candles and wine?" Lisl suggested.

"We will get into trouble," Nicole protested since they weren't allowed to use alcohol when on duty, or on College grounds.

"That rule only applies to you. Since we live here, we are allowed a drink after work. So long as you don't tell on yourself, I won't." Lisl laughed out loud. Nicole was faced with yet another inner struggle. Lisl sensed Nicole's hesitation. "Come now, you aren't seriously scared of a glass of wine?" she laughed.

"No…oh, what the hell, that would be nice." Nicole smiled at Lisl and Lisl walked over to the kitchenette to take two glasses out, as well as a bottle of Tokara Shiraz. Lisl filled the glasses and left them on the counter to lock the door to her quarters.

"Let me rather lock the door, I don't want to get you in trouble unnecessarily by someone walking in accidently," she explained to Nicole as she picked up the glasses and walked over to Nicole, where Nicole was waiting on the bed. The Shiraz glided down Nicole's throat as she took the first sip and the warmth of it comforted her. With every sip she took and no one showing up at the door to catch them out, Nicole became less worried that anyone would show up and so she relaxed. They discussed music, menial topics about where they grew up and so forth and before they knew it they were both sitting propped up against the headboard, laughing and chatting like two close friends.

"This is fun," Nicole admitted as she looked at Lisl in admiration of her ability to separate her personal life from her day job. Nicole thought her to be very professional, as she never would have guessed her to be such a fun person to spend time with.

"Yes, it is. We should have done this way sooner," Lisl said.

"But we couldn't," Nicole laughed as the thought was suddenly hilarious to her and she doubled over, with her glass still held up in one hand, as a laughing fit took hold of her.

Lisl looked at Nicole and her silliness triggered her to join in the laughing fit. They both couldn't breathe from laughing so much.

"Shuuuut!" Nicole tried to stop herself from laughing as she held her index finger in front of her pouting lips.

Lisl mimicked Nicole and put her finger on her own lips "Shuuuut!" she said and they both once again burst out laughing. Finally they got control of their laughter and wiped the tears from their faces. Silence filled the room as seriousness came over Lisl. Nicole and Lisl stared at each other. Lisl put her glass on the dresser next to her bed and turned back to face Nicole. Then she took Nicole's glass from her hand and placed it next to hers. Nicole frowned, confused by what was going on.

"Nicole..." Lisl said seriously, but didn't finish.

"Yes?" Nicole encouraged her softly to speak. In the background, Depeche Mode's *Strange Love* rhythmically pulsed away.

"I want you," Lisl blurted it out. Nicole found it strange that she didn't find the situation awkward. She was happy in the moment. She liked Lisl and felt comfortable in the moment.

"I saw you and Tanya..." Nicole said before she could stop herself.

Lisl smiled. "Yes, I know. I saw you when you ran out of the bathroom," Lisl confessed.

"I am sorry, I didn't mean to watch. I didn't know you two were busy..." Nicole didn't know how to label what they were doing.

"I don't mind," Lisl said softly, too scared to move as to frighten Nicole, but in fact Nicole wasn't uncomfortable at all, she was overpowered by a curiosity she couldn't or didn't want to control.

"I don't know how..." Nicole stopped halfway, careful not to offend Lisl.

"Do you want to?" Lisl asked Nicole as she looked up at Nicole in a deer-like fashion.

"I don't know..." Nicole said softly, cutting herself short to bend forward and with her right hand, she took the back of Lisl's dainty neck and placed her lips on Lisl's. Lisl's lips were extremely soft and warm. Her skin felt like silk and she smelled like a fresh bouquet of flowers mixed with the musky aroma of the Shiraz they were drinking. Lisl kept her lips softly closed together, careful not to be too forward, as she knew Nicole was new to this. In the background, *It's no good* from Depeche Mode was playing.

Do we have to wait till our worlds collide? the lyrics rang in Nicole's ears, sweeping her into a state of lust.

*I am going to take my time, I have all the time in the world, to make you mine, it is written in the stars above...*the lyrics encouraged her in her intoxicated state to give in to this longing to satisfy her lust for Lisl and her sinful body. Nicole pressed her tongue through Lisl's lips and they parted all too willingly and Lisl grabbed Nicole, devouring her mouth with a passion that was suppressed for months now. Seconds merged into minutes and finally Lisl pulled away, out of breath.

Nicole could see her nipples standing invitingly erect through her t-shirt. It was obvious she had no bra on. The image of her nipple in Nicole's mouth flashed through Nicole's mind's eye and the mere thought of it made her loins fill with liquid. Nicole longed to taste the forbidden taste and reached for the hem of Lisl's t-shirt, lifting it over her head swiftly, while Lisl instinctively helped her by lifting up her arms. Nicole sat back, still holding Lisl's t-shirt in her hands. Lisl sat still with her arms next to her body, her chest moving breathlessly up and down, forcing her small firm breasts forward with each breath she took. Goose bumps decorated her skin and her nipples stood on attention for Nicole. Nicole held back as long as she could to take in the beauty of the well-proportioned body in front of her. Nicole wanted to taste Lisl, she needed to taste her.

Lisl read Nicole's need and sat backwards, resting her weight back onto her hand that she placed behind her back on the bed. Lisl pushed her breasts forward, affording the soft yellow light of the candles to paint her body a magical gold. Lisl threw her head back and closed her eyes as she waited in frustrating anticipation for Nicole's next move. Lisl sat silently cross-legged while breathing heavily. The music, light and result of drinking silky smooth wine harmoniously blended into a lusciously thick atmosphere.

"God, you are pretty," Nicole heard herself say before she bent over to take Lisl's one breast into her hand. Instinctively, Nicole slid her hand slowly over Lisl's breast, cupping it and then softly squeezing it. Nicole's body reacted to the touch of soft warm skin in a lustrous manner she hadn't experienced before. Deep inside, her womb contracted with longing for something to fill her. Nicole took Lisl's other breast in her other hand and squeezed it in the same manner. She started to massage both of Lisl's breasts, taking Lisl's nipples between her fingers periodically and pulling them softly, only to return to massaging them.

Lisl sighed with frustration and Nicole, wanting to satisfy her, bent forward and softly took as much of Lisl's one breast into her mouth as was physically possible and she started sucking on it hard, nibbling at her taut nipple as she pulled away. Lisl groaned and looked down at Nicole who still had Lisl's nipple in her mouth. Nicole could see her lust for Lisl reflected in Lisl's eyes.

"Fuck me," Lisl said in a low demanding voice. Not precisely sure how to do this, Nicole let go of Lisl's nipple and sat up straight, but before she could figure out what to do next, Lisl pressed Nicole backwards into a lying position and lifted herself to place her body in a kneeling position over Nicole. Lisl pulled at Nicole's sweatpants, pulling her panties along with it and baring her bushy womanhood. Lisl continued to pull it all the way off her legs, leaving Nicole feeling way too exposed and vulnerable. She felt nervous and for a split-second contemplated stopping Lisl before she could do the unthinkable of touching her there, but before Nicole could react, Lisl had forced Nicole's legs apart and had sunk two of her small fingers into Nicole's vagina. \Nicole gasped and grabbed Lisl's wrist in an attempt to stop her from going any further, but Lisl had surprising strength and kept her hand there until Nicole relaxed a little. With her hand still on Lisl's wrist, Nicole felt Lisl's fingers slip in and out of her slippery warmness, stimulating her need for something thick and manly in between her loins to take the ache of her passion away. Lisl was now positioned between Nicole's legs. Nicole groaned out of frustration and closed her eyes. Her frustration grew with each movement of Lisl's fingers and suddenly, Lisl pulled her wet fingers from Nicole and in a practiced movement placed her lips on Nicole, instinctively putting her right hand on Nicole's torso, as she was expecting Nicole to protest out of shock.

Nicole gasped for air as the warmth of Lisl's lips pressed down on her vaginal lips. Nicole half-heartedly tried to lift herself into an upright position to protest, but gave into the warm feeling of pleasure Lisl's softly sucking lips produced, as it merged with her own wetness. Nicole placed both her hands on Lisl's shoulders, in an attempt to push her away, but did so without much determination, as she was torn in two between wanting this so badly, but knowing that it went against all she had been taught.

Lisl didn't give way and kept softly sucking on Nicole until Nicole's hand fell from her shoulders and Nicole's body started moving with Lisl's passionate kiss. Nicole was aching inside, moaning from wanting to climax, and then, as her body started to tense up, Lisl moved her attentions further up to her most sensitive part. She stretched Nicole's labia open to reveal the smallest of rosebuds and she softly took it in between her lips and sucked rhythmically on it until Nicole let out a deep long-lasting grunt from exertion as she climaxed.

As the climax subsided, Nicole took Lisl's chin in her hands and lifted her head as she looked down at her. They were silent and Lisl looked vulnerable.

Nicole wanted to please Lisl, as she had her, but couldn't muster the courage to do the same to Lisl as she had done to her.

So, as Lisl lay back in the hope that Nicole would return the favour, Nicole hesitated, struggling to decide how she was going to approach this. By no means was she prepared to kiss another woman's private parts; to her it just seemed wrong and she felt guilty for letting Lisl do it to her and enjoying it as much as she did, but she felt she would have taken advantage of Lisl if she didn't finish what she had started, so she decided to try something different. Nicole kneeled over Lisl, with her legs on both sides of Lisl and her hands placed on the bed on either side of Lisl's torso. Nicole enjoyed sucking on Lisl's breast and decided to do so again.

She bent down over Lisl's naked upper body and started sucking on her breasts, taking turns to tantalise and tease them with her tongue and sucking on it. While she did this, she reached down into Lisl's pants with a skilled hand. Nicole was experienced at pleasuring herself and knew exactly how to pleasure Lisl in this manner, so she let her long middle finger find Lisl's clitoris and then ran her finger in a slow and stimulating manner over her clitoris, in-between Lisl's labia, down into the deeper folds, while curving it into her vagina as it disappeared into its wet and swollen folds. Nicole stroked her continuously like this until Lisl couldn't take the frustration anymore and grabbed Nicole's wrist with both hand as she tried to force Nicole's finger deeper inside of her.

At this, Nicole succumbed and satisfied her by taking three of her fingers, while holding them together, and forcing them as deep into Lisl as was physically possible and then quickly pulling them out halfway, while Lisl still held her wrist, afraid that she might stop. Nicole stopped sucking Lisl's breast so that she could give full attention to Lisl's pleasure and she thrust her fingers continuously and hard into Lisl.

Lisl came slightly upright as if she was doing a stomach crunch as her stomach muscles pulled together from the built-up tension preparing her for a climax, while she held Nicole's wrist in position and thrusting herself as if she was riding Nicole's hand, until she let out a scream as her muscles contracted around Nicole's fingers. Nicole pushed her fingers in so deep that she thought Lisl would get hurt. She held it there until the pulsing subsided and Lisl let go of her wrist and collapsed breathlessly back onto the bed.

Nicole felt relieved and shocked at the same time. Relieved she didn't have to have oral sex with Lisl and shocked at the raw intensity of their lovemaking.

Then she felt a sudden feeling of disappointment as she realised she had stepped over a line she wouldn't be able to retrace and she knew that she would be guilt-ridden for quite some time thereafter.

"Thank you, Nicole! You are amazing!" Lisl sighed softly as she still lay on her bed with her eyes closed. Nicole was already busy pulling up her pants as she wanted to hide her nakedness. Nicole hated her body for betraying her by making her succumb to such sinful pleasures and taking away all her will for self-control.

"I have to go," Nicole said seriously. "It is getting late and the others are going to wonder where I am," she explained. Lisl pushed herself onto her elbows as she looked at Nicole.

"Are you okay?" Lisl asked as she frowned at Nicole's sudden haste.

"Yes," Nicole lied, "it's just that I have to get back before Melanie starts looking for me," Nicole explained.

"You are right," Lisl said as she sat up to pull her t-shirt over her head.

"Thank you for everything," Nicole said as she made her way to the door and unlocked it.

"No. Thank you, Nicole," Lisl said while she still sat on the bed.

Nicole opened the door slightly to peer through the opening to check if there was anyone in the passage way who would witness her leaving Lisl's room, but luckily there was no one, so she quickly opened the door and closed it behind her. Nicole walked as composed as she could to her room but on her way realised how uncomfortably wet her underwear felt.

I need to shower, she thought to herself as she walked into her room, where Melanie was lying on her own bed.

"Nicole!" Melanie said, relieved to see Nicole. "I wondered where you were. It is nearly lights-out," Melanie continued.

"So, where were you?" she asked, intrigued by her friend's disappearance.

"Uh...uh..." Nicole struggled to find an explanation. "I went for a walk," she mumbled.

"You know we aren't allowed off the dormitory's grounds without permission," Melanie reprimanded her.

"Yes, I know," Nicole said softly, not looking at Melanie, scared that she would smell the odour of wine lingering on her breath.

"I am going to shower," Nicole said as she took her towel and toiletries bag and walked out of the room before Melanie could probe her any further.

In the shower, the warm water was welcoming, washing the sweat and all evidence from the night's sins away. Nicole lathered her body with soap as she closed her eyes and let the warm water and steam surround her. Nicole took particular care to wash her labia clean with soap. While she did this, she couldn't help but to think back to what had happened and although she felt guilty she still found it erotic, but she vowed to herself to never let herself do such a thing again.

She preferred men and that became apparent when she was faced with the option of having oral sex with Lisl. She just couldn't go so far, nor did she really enjoy fingering Lisl. She loved being pleasured by Lisl's mouth though, she thought to herself, but thought that any man could pleasure her in that manner and that she would feel more comfortable with that. She actually now felt a little compelled to have sex with a man, to reassure her body that she in fact did prefer having sex with men. She shook her head to clear it from thoughts of what she preferred and what not.

"Stop it! You are being ridiculous," she reprimanded herself as she rinsed the last soap from her body.

"You need to relax!" she said to herself out loud as she took the towel from the rail opposite the shower. Nicole tied the towel around her body and took a stance in front of the wash basin and used more toothpaste than usual to scrub her teeth as if she wanted to rid her mouth of them. As she looked in the mirror, she decided to place the matter behind her and focus on the next day when they would be graduating, finding out where they were placed and return home, for a short leave, before they would have to report for duty at their new stations. When Nicole returned to her room, the lights were already out and Melanie was asleep. Nicole climbed into her bed, feeling calm, and fell into a deep sleep.

After what seemed like a few minutes, Nicole's alarm went off.

"Melanie!" she called out to Melanie. "Wake up!" She was excited since this was the day they were graduating and going home for a short break before they started their careers as new constables.

"Yes, I am up!" Melanie groaned and turned away from the light, which Nicole had just switched on.

"Come on! You don't want to be late," Nicole said urgently.

Normally, Nicole was the one taking her time, but not today. Nicole couldn't wait to get back home. She had had enough of College. Nicole got dressed, took her bedding from her bed and packed it in her tog bag. Before Melanie, Nicole's suitcases and belongings were standing in a neat row on her bare mattress on her bed. She was smartly dressed in her formal uniform. Her hair was plated at the back of her head and her make-up was perfectly applied. When there was nothing more for her to do, she ran to Tanya's room for a quick chat before breakfast.

The platoons didn't have inspection of their rooms that morning, but there was an announcement that everyone had to remember to take all their belongings when they got back, since it would be handled as discarded if left behind and thrown out. After breakfast, they were allowed a quick visit to the bathrooms and then they were marched to the train station where they caught a train into town and to Loftus Versveld Sports Stadium.

There was a train station right by the stadium, allowing the platoons to get off the train and march straight into the stadium. There were two entrances to the middle of the stadium where the students were to enter. The whole group was evenly split in two smaller groups and would march into the stadium from both sides to form the formation they had practiced for the past few weeks. There were approximately one thousand five hundred students there that day. The platoons consisted of about forty men or women in a platoon. When in formation, they would form four rows of ten in each row. The platoons gathered in formation behind the stadium and when the signal was given, they were marched in unison onto the sports ground from both sides, meeting in the middle and the platoons spacing themselves two metres apart.

The bigger formation started in the middle of the field with platoons lining up at the back on both sides of the middle and then three platoons lined up in front of it so that there were four blocks consisting of forty students in a block. The final formation consisted of six blocks with four platoons lined up behind each other in one block. The precision at which they formed their formation was astonishing, considering the amount of people that had to march like one person and come to a halt at the same time. You could hear every so often orders being shouted to turn, or come to a halt.

Nicole made herself ready for a long stand as she knew the speeches would be long-lasting and dramatic and she would probably not take in a word that was going to be uttered. They stood on attention facing forward to a temporary erected podium. One again adorned with Officers and the Mayor of Pretoria. From where Nicole stood she could hardly see what was going on in front as her view was blocked by the two platoons in front of her. Suddenly, the stadium started vibrating with a thunderous roar as three fighter jets flew low over the stadium and Nicole had to fight the urge to look up at the wondrous sight. Finally, the ceremony started with prayer and the order for the students to come to a rest position.

Nicole actually wished that she was sitting in the pavilion, where most of the students' parents were sitting to watch them graduate. She was sure her father would be somewhere there in between the hundreds of faces. She tried to spot him by running her eyes over the rows of faces, but they were little dots to her as they were too far away for her to make out their faces. Nicole wiggled her toes and shifted her weight from one foot to the other without moving, in the manner they were taught, in order to avoid fainting from standing still for too long in the heat.

This helped pass the two hours of speeches that followed, Nicole even dosed off in her standing position for a few minutes, another skill acquired by many students in the event of them standing on attention for long periods of time. Then finally, coloured smoke flares were lit as they were marched past the podium and out of the arena. Relieved that it was over, Nicole took her seat on the train. To her it was a bit of an anti-climax. She didn't know what to expect in the first place, but had hoped for more. Most of the male students were proud and diligent, discussing excitedly how great the event was, but Nicole stared out of her window at the surroundings merging into a blur as the train sped back to the College.

At the College, the students were lined up on the parade area and everyone was handed an envelope which they were to open as soon as they were dismissed. The Head Sergeant made a little speech congratulating them on their graduation and then he gave the order: "Platoon, Dismissed! Hup two three, hup two three!" and as the platoons followed the order and fell out of formation, when they had dismissed all of them, they in unison reached for their hats and threw it high up in the air, as they shouted and whistled with pure elation.

Nicole's envelope burnt her fingers and she couldn't tear it open soon enough and then she slowed down as she took the folded piece of paper from it. She took a deep breath as she slowly opened it. "Table View" was the only word she noticed and she let out a scream of joy.

"Melanie! I am placed at Table View!" she shouted.

Melanie ran to her and grabbed her around her neck. "I am so glad for you."

"Where are you placed?" Nicole came to a standstill to focus on Melanie.

"In Pretoria, at the Head Office," she said with a smile on her face and Nicole couldn't gather if she was happy about it or not.

"Are you happy?" she asked carefully before she reacted.

"Yes!" Melanie smiled and grabbed her again and they hugged as they laughed. As they hugged, Nicole recognised her father's face where he waited for her under a tree nearby and she let Melanie slip from her grasp and ran to him, never to see Melanie again.

Nicole grabbed Johan and hugged him tightly.

"Congratulations, my girl! It was a beautiful ceremony," Johan said proudly to Nicole.

"You were there!" she said gratefully.

"I wouldn't miss it for the world. I am so proud of you. Now go get your suitcases so that we can get out of here," he encouraged her. Nicole spent the night with her father because she could only catch a flight the next morning back to Cape Town and she wanted to spend some time with her father, since she knew she wouldn't see him soon after she had returned to Cape Town.

Chapter 13

Nicole's mother was waiting at the airport as they had arranged beforehand, to pick her up. Hazel was in a chirpy mood, asking Nicole how her graduation went and making small talk. Nicole was taken aback by the warm welcome she received, wondering how long it would last or what her mother was hiding from her, as this was normally the case when she was so talkative. The drive home with Hazel babbling away until Nicole couldn't take it anymore.

"What are you hiding?" Nicole accused.

"Nothing!" Hazel said, offended by the accusation and she fell silent.

"No, there is something you aren't telling me, I know you too well." Nicole kept on trying to figure out what Hazel was keeping from her.

"I don't know what you are talking about," Hazel defended herself. "I do have to talk to you though."

"Aha! I knew there was something." Nicole accused her of hiding something.

"Oh, please Nicole, you are pissing me off now. Here I am being decent and all you can do is to throw accusations around," Hazel said as she stared at the road ahead.

"I am sorry," Nicole said, regretting being so hostile in her approach, "it's just that I can sense something is bothering you when you talk so much. So, what is it?" Nicole softened her approach.

"I didn't want to talk to you here in the car," Hazel said, subdued.

"You might as well talk to me about it now," Nicole suggested.

"Okay if you insist, but for the record I wanted to wait until we got home and you were settled in," Hazel said, still staring in front of her.

"So?" Nicole encouraged her.

"Well, Pete and I have found a wonderful apartment and for a reasonable price. We also found a tenant for my house who wants to move into the house on Monday, so we have only this weekend to find you a place to stay in." Hazel let the news hang in the air for Nicole to absorb. Nicole's mind started spinning, not being able to make sense of the information and how her mother could be so callous to only inform her of this now.

There surely was a point where she knew this would be a possibility and could have warned me sooner, she thought to herself.

"So you mean I have tomorrow to find a flat, since the day after is Sunday and it would be impossible to find a place to stay?" Nicole said, stunned. "Well, welcome my child, now fuck off?" Nicole said out loud without thinking what she was doing.

Hazel's whole body stiffened and she clenched her teeth in order not to say something she might regret. It took all her willpower not to explode and when she had gathered her composure, she replied, "Now that was uncalled for. I didn't know until yesterday that the woman was going to take the apartment for certain."

"But you knew there was a possibility and you didn't inform me. Thank you so much," Nicole said sarcastically and they both fell silent while Nicole turned her head to her window and she felt a wetness of disappointment welling up in her eyes.

When they reached the house, Nicole walked into a warzone of packed boxes and belongings ready to be packed in taped up boxes. She felt sick to her stomach as the tension of her reality hit her. Talk about being thrown into the real world. She always imagined a subtle letting-go process when a child leaves the house, but she was being kicked out into adulthood and she wasn't' sure she was ready for it. What made matters worse was the fact that she had nowhere to go and had the practically impossible task of finding some place to stay in one morning.

Nicole knew she wouldn't be able to stay with Ava and Ben as they only had a two-bedroom house and Ben's mother stayed with them. Nicole wouldn't dare ask anyone else as she was too proud. Nicole was so disappointed that she didn't even speak to Hazel when they got home and Hazel had so much to do that she didn't even notice, nor did she care, as she had a new life waiting for her and she knew Nicole was financially independent and therefore would somehow cope, although she might not like it.

So she got stuck into packing the rest of her belongings while Nicole went upstairs to take a bath and climb into bed. Sleep had become one way for Nicole of escaping her worries, when she felt unable to sort them out.

"Nicole?" Nicole heard someone calling her in her sleep.

"Yes," Nicole answered with her eyes still shut and irritated by the disturbance as she had only fallen asleep a few minutes ago.

"Nicole…" a gentle woman's voice spoke to her.

"Yes?" Nicole opened her eyes, not sure if she was dreaming and through slits, she saw Hazel holding a cup of steaming coffee out to her and the room was brightly lit by daylight.

"What? How late is it?" Nicole said confused.

"It is nine o'clock already; you should wake up and dress if you want to find a place today. I will help you," Hazel offered as she had enough time during her long hours of packing the previous night to realise how daunting the task would be for Nicole, as this would be the first time she would have to look for a place to stay. She knew that Nicole probably would not know where to begin and although she thought Nicole old enough to sort her own problems out, she took pity on her and felt a little bit guilty for placing her in this predicament.

"Oh shit!" Nicole said as she jumped out of bed. "Are you serious? That would be so kind of you," Nicole said relieved as she knew she needed some guidance and wasn't going to be stubborn in taking help from Hazel.

After Nicole pulled on a dress and pulled her hair into a ponytail, she got into the car with Hazel in search of a place for her to stay. Hazel suggested that they should probably stop at the local estate agents and hear if they had rental apartments available at short notice and that was exactly what they did. At the first estate agent, the agent had one one-bedroomed apartment available. It was on the main road and walking distance from the police station, which would be perfect for Nicole as she didn't have her own transport. The best news was that the apartment was available immediately. Nicole felt hopeful as the estate agent spoke to Hazel about the apartment and suggested they went to have a look.

The apartment was quite large for a one-bedroom flat. The front door was situated in an entrance hall with a double bedroom leading off to the left, with a full en-suite bathroom. The passage opened up into an open-plan living and kitchen area. The kitchen was quite large for that sized apartment and the living room was enormous. The living room window faced the sea and Nicole could see the blue of it glistening in the morning sun.

"This is perfect!" Nicole said out loud.

"Yes, I think it can work," Hazel agreed with Nicole's opinion. "How much is the rent?"

"It is R900 and a month's rent in advance as deposit," the estate agent said dryly.

Nicole nearly swallowed her tongue as the words were uttered.

How the hell am I going to afford this? she thought to herself as she made the simple sum. As a constable in the police force, in the early nineties, she would only earn about R1200 a month and with deductions, she only got out a little more than R900. Nicole felt devastated.

"Do you have anything cheaper?" Nicole asked.

"No, this is the cheapest. You might be able to find a cheaper place in a cheaper area," the agent suggested, but Nicole knew that would not be a feasible solution as she didn't have transport. Hazel stood in silence and Nicole felt like screaming at her, "Now what?" but she didn't.

"What am I going to do?" she asked Hazel softly as the estate agent gave them some space to think it through. Hazel ignored Nicole and walked to the estate agent.

"We will take it," Hazel said, and Nicole looked at her mother, stunned.

Nicole didn't have furniture or a deposit and she felt helpless. Not afforded much of a choice, she sheepishly followed her mother and the estate agent to the car and drove with them to the agent's office where she methodically signed the rental contract for six months, as Hazel had asked them if they could rent for six months instead of the normal year so that Nicole could move if the apartment didn't work for her.

Hazel knew that Nicole didn't have much of a choice, but to take the flat, she needed a place to stay and as long as she had a roof over her head and she could get to work, chances were good that she would be alright. Nicole knew this too and therefore gave in to the circumstances. Nicole for the first time felt utterly helpless; everything happened so fast. Within an hour, her mother had produced a deposit, which she was grateful for, she had to empty her account to pay the first month's rent in advance, and she was handed a key to her new, empty apartment.

Only when they drove home could Nicole, humbled by her situation, muster the courage to thank her mother.

"Thank you," she said simply and softly.

"It is the least I could do," Hazel replied emotionless.

Nicole felt like crying, as everything felt overwhelming. She was broke, but had a roof over her head.

"Can I take my bed?" Nicole asked cautiously.

"Of course, your bedroom furniture is yours," Hazel said more enthusiastically.

"You know what? I would have had to store most of my big furniture pieces, so maybe if you like, you can use it and then I don't have to pay storage for it?" Hazel suggested.

"Really?" Nicole felt a wave of relief wash over her.

"Yes. Why not? It will help both of us, and Pete has his own furniture he wants to move up. I don't want to get rid of mine, so you might just as well use it. Then you will have a fully furnished flat!' Hazel said excitedly as this was not only a way to soothe her guilty conscience, but it would favour her as well since she wouldn't have to worry about storage on such short notice.

"Thank you so much," Nicole said and hugged her mother while her mother was still driving, and Hazel actually smiled, relieved that her daughter was sorted.

That afternoon, Pete and Hazel moved the furniture to Nicole's flat while Nicole went to report to her station. Everyone was very happy to hear that she had been placed back at their station as most of them were very fond of her. When she returned to their house, Hazel had bought Nicole groceries for her first month and drove her and her clothing to her new apartment so that she could get settled in. Nicole spent most of the evening unpacking and moving the furniture so that it suited her. When she had finished, her flat was furnished in a modern way and she had everything she needed.

She finally went to sit on the large couch she had placed underneath the big window overlooking the sea and she appreciated her surroundings and her hard work. The full moon shone an ominous yellow. It made a reflection on the black sea water. Nicole sat in silence appreciating the beauty of the view from her living room and she smiled, satisfied and filled with excitement by the thought that she had her own place. She felt independent and all grown up and relieved that she was so fortunate to find an apartment so quickly. She decided that this spot in front of the window would probably become her favourite hangout spot, from where she could watch what was going on outside and ogle the moon and sea.

Nicole didn't realise it yet, but soon she would prefer to sleep on the couch with the lights off and the windows open so that the moonlight filled her living room with its soft glow. Everything seemed possible.

The next day Hazel came to say goodbye to Nicole and promised to contact her as soon as they had settled into their new surroundings. Nicole had slept well and was in a good mood, so she didn't procrastinate too much about how her mother leaving the province would affect her. Nicole seemed confident enough, to Hazel's relief, about the new circumstances, when she came to greet her daughter. She was worried that Nicole might not handle the move so well when it finally came to that, as her daughter had seemed quite emotional over the months following her and Johan's divorce.

"I am just a phone call away," Hazel reminded Nicole, while thinking back to when she herself had to leave home more than twenty years ago and about how disillusioned she was when she realised that being on your own wasn't as glamorous as one had imagined. She felt a deep compassion for her daughter for wanting to be so independent and she felt proud of her daughter for taking charge of her life in this manner. As she hugged Nicole, she whispered: "I am so proud of you." And when she pulled away, she planted a kiss on Nicole's head like she used to when Nicole was a little girl.

Nicole spent the rest of the week sorting her cupboards, washing her uniform and doing day to day chores. She took long walks down to the beach and along the beachfront. Since she didn't have a phone line yet and wouldn't be able to afford one in the near future, she had no way of phoning Ava and Ben to come and fetch her so that she could visit them for some company. Nor was she able to let them know that she was staying on her own now, or where she was staying.

She decided to wait until she was back at work to let them know. She decided to make the most of the few rest days that she had and spent her hours lazing about, since when she would return to work, she would be a police officer and there would be no excuses for mishaps.

The week flew past and all too soon she was dressed and ready for her first day as a police officer. Nicole opened her front door to let herself out. She felt awkward in her uniform, although it had become part of her the last three months, but in the College, it had been different; there she had been surrounded by hundreds of fellow students dressed exactly like her. As a student, working at the station, she worked in civilian clothes, but now as she stepped out of her flat, she was the only one in the visible vicinity in uniform and it felt out of place. For the first time, she felt distinguishably different from the men and women walking and driving along the street. She had entered in a separate world functioning inside of the real world, a union of like-minded individuals, driven by a need to uphold law and order.

Although she felt conscious of the fact that she was standing out like a sore thumb, she felt proud and she gathered herself as she started walking in the direction of the police station. She looked as good as one could possibly look in a police uniform. The high-waist pencil skirt fitted her perfectly and showed off her perfect proportions. Nicole's hair was tied back into a long ponytail that hung to the middle of her back. Her well-toned calves pulled tight as she walked in her high-heeled police-issue shoes and it didn't take long for the first car to pull up beside her and ask if they could offer her a lift.

Police officers were respected in the old South Africa (during the Apartheid Era) and as such, people would blindly trust anyone in blue uniform. Women in the police force in the old South Africa were mostly only seen in the Charge Office or behind the desks in the offices. They were seldom posted on the vehicles patrolling the streets and mostly worked outside when they were needed when women were arrested, or with rape charges.

Things were slowly changing though, and the chauvinist attitude of the men were slowly making way for a new breed of police officers who treated women in the Force with a little more respect and equality. For this reason, it was not often that you would see woman in police uniform, let alone a pretty young one, walking down the street, swaying her hips, as if she should have been on a runway instead of being dressed in a uniform on her way to work, police work.

Nicole smiled at the sight of the young man offering her a lift as he grinned at her. She had to decline the offer, as they weren't allowed to hitch hike. She watched as the young man drove away disappointedly. This would become a regular occurrence as she walked to work. Except for the lifts she was offered, she also realised how intrigued children and other women were at the sight of her. As if she was a wondrous creature from another world, or a lower life form, people would sometimes stare and point and discuss her. She couldn't always gauge their intentions.

Mostly, it looked like they respected her position, but she did however know that her peers, who were fortunate to study at university, regarded themselves superior to those who had chosen to join the police force, army or navy. They thought these individuals to be of lesser intelligence and that they lacked ambition and they weren't afraid to mention this. Before she decided to join the Force out of circumstance, she as well fell prey to this perception, but after her hard, physical training and the amount of work they had to study, she had a different opinion of this all together and she felt proud of the fact that she had survived the College and that she was chosen to wear the uniform.

As Nicole entered the station, she felt nervous and excited, the way she did when she was still at school after each December holiday. It was as if her whole being instinctively knew this was the beginning of a future altering learning curve. There was no turning back and she would now finally be afforded the opportunity to experience the full meaning of being a police officer. She wouldn't be protected and kept from anything. She was now one of the groups and as such had just as much responsibility towards her peers as they had to her.

This made her feel secure and she smiled as she entered the doorway to the Charge Office. The Charge Office was swarming with men as they were taking over from the previous shift. Nicole expected to see her old shift in the Charge Office, but instead, she saw faces she didn't know and she felt disappointed. For some naïve reason, she thought she would be placed on her old shift, but in fact shifts are shuffled at times and due to her leave ending on a day that her old shift was off, she had to start on a new shift.

There were a lot of young men in the office, which was unusual; she could remember the shifts she had to deal with as being of middle aged and suddenly as the men stopped to look at the pretty new girl in uniform, she felt utterly out of place. There wasn't even one fellow Police woman in sight. She looked down in order to avoid their stares and she came to a halt in front of the Charge Office Commander.

Although he was looking down, there were no mistaking who this man was, it was Sergeant Swart. The overweight and sweaty man she managed to ignore when she first came to the station. His black hair had thinned out since she had left and his skin seemed paler than before. She stared at his fingers as they moved over the page and they still reminded her of stuffed sausages.

"Good afternoon," Nicole said polite. "I have to report for duty."

Sergeant Swart looked up and managed to smile at her. She wondered how it was even possible as his cheeks were so fat that it looked as if his mouth shouldn't be able to open. His black moustache rimmed his lusty smile and his teeth looked unbelievably small for such a big man.

"Hi Nicole, it is so nice to have you back," he said excitedly as he stood up and offered a sweaty hand for Nicole to shake. Nicole took it cautiously and shook it. His hands were soft and his grip even softer. Her insides turned as she was uncontrollably filled with disgust by his touch. Something about him was totally off-putting and it wasn't only his appearance.

"You are on our shift," he continued and she became despondent by the thought of having to deal with him, but optimistic now that she was going to be on her old shift. The young men in the office ogled her wide-eyed as they finished packing their belongings and Nicole realised they were the shift from which her new shift was taking over.

Why couldn't I be on their shift? she thought to herself.

The young men took longer than was necessary so Sergeant Swart reprimanded them. "There is nothing here to see, you may go now, and you are taking up too much space," he said, annoyed by their behaviour. Nicole looked at them as they made their way to the door; at the back, there was one very attractive Sergeant. He had a thick bush of black hair, cut into a crew cut. He had a dark skin and mysterious brown eyes. He was about half a head taller than Nicole and he had an amazing body. He was naturally muscled and she couldn't help but notice how his well-rounded muscles moved in his rear end as he walked, so she smiled as she looked at the sight of it, but then he turned and looked her straight in the eye, smiling knowingly back at her.

"You can wait here with me," Sergeant Swart suggested.

"Where is the rest of our shift?" Nicole asked. She couldn't wait to see her old shift again and hoped to see Ava's face.

"They are standing inspection. They will be here soon," he said as he sat back down again and leaned over to pull the chair next to him out for Nicole.

"Come. Sit!" he ordered and Nicole reluctantly took the seat while she clung to her police-issue handbag on her lap. She could hear an older man's voice coming from the holding cell where they took fingerprints. The voice sounded familiar, but she couldn't figure out who it was as there were soft murmurs from other deep voices also traveling her way.

"Shouldn't I go to them?" Nicole asked.

"No!" Sergeant Swart barked at her.

So Nicole sat in silence for the ten minutes it took to finish inspection and then one after another, policemen appeared from behind the wall parting the Charge Office and the holding cell. They were all new to her and with a heavy heart, she braced herself that she was not placed on her old shift and that Sergeant Swart had somehow managed to end up on her new shift as well. Although Nicole had seen all of the men before, she didn't know one of them and she felt gutted. She estimated the youngest member of their shift to be about thirty-four and she was by far the youngest at nineteen.

"Are we ready?" she heard the familiar voice again from the holding cell and then Sergeant Mostert made his appearance. He was still talking when he looked up into Nicole's face and they both smiled with joy.

"My dear child…" he said as he stretched his steps to reach Nicole and took her in his arms while hugging her tightly. In that moment, Nicole relaxed and felt so thankful for him being there on her shift. He was by far the oldest on their shift.

"Are you the shift commander?" she asked, hopeful.

"Yes," he grinned at her.

"I am so glad," she said as she grinned back at him.

"We will talk after the shift has received their orders. You can go to the Station Commander's office. There are a few papers you have to sign and then when you come back, I will explain your duties to you," he said charmingly and so Nicole went to the Station Commander's office.

As Nicole walked down the corridor, the office personnel came to greet her. Nicole finally made it to the Station Commander's office. She noticed that the plaque on it has changed and read it out loud: "Captain Liebenberg."

"Yes," an answer came from within the office, "come in." Taken off guard, Nicole hesitantly entered the office. In the one corner in the light of the morning sun was a chair and in it sat a young Constable with curly blond hair and blue eyes. He sat motionless and looked straight at Nicole as she entered and then smiled approvingly while he nodded. Nicole saw a Captain behind the desk in the office and without acknowledging the Constable, focussed her attentions on the officer.

Nicole saluted her senior and stood on attention as the man in front of her appraised her. She didn't make eye contact and waited for him to order her to stand at ease, but he took longer than she had anticipated. The young man in the chair stayed in his chair watching them silently and his presence started to annoy her as she could feel his eyes on her.

"At ease," the order finally came and the Captain in front of her offered her his hand.

"Good morning, Captain Liebenberg, I am Nicole Burger," she introduced herself as she shook his hand and made solid eye contact with him. He was still in his early thirties. The Captain was quite attractive except for the black furry moustache on his upper lip. It made him look like the old mentality police officers, who acted all diligently, but were chauvinists who still thought that women in the police force should work in the office and had no place in the field.

He had a full head of black hair, he was neatly built and Nicole could see he took meticulous care with his grooming as every hair was perfectly styled. He had steely blue eyes that looked cold and calculated and although his face seemed emotionless, the rounding's of his cheeks lent a softness to it that suggested he had a sensitive side. He pulled away and took a seat, not offering Nicole one to sit on.

"Good morning, Constable," he said plainly and turned his attentions to the paperwork in front of him.

"This is formality," he continued while turning the papers to face her and pointed at them as he continued to explain that they were for her pension fund, medical aid, etc. "You can sign at the bottom," he said, not looking up at her. Nicole stepped forward and bent over the table and signed each paper as he showed her where to sign, not reading anything she signed, as she trusted it was all a formality.

"That's it," he announced as she finished signing the last paperwork. "Welcome and I hope you enjoy working here." All Nicole could think about was where their previous Station Commander was and why they had a new one.

"You may go now," the Captain said, agitated as Nicole still stood there in deep thought.

"Oh yes, that's right," Nicole said as she saluted him again and walked out.

In the corridor, Nicole turned around and looked back to where the Constable sat still in his chair. He was looking back at her while a skew smile appeared on his face. Nicole quickly turned around as she heard Captain Liebenberg's voice.

"So, my dear cousin, how is that sister of mine?" Captain Liebenberg started, and Nicole turned her attentions away from the two occupants in the office behind her. For a moment, she wondered how they could be cousins with the one being light-blond and the other with such black hair, but she could see the similarities in their demeanour, their pale skin and their build. While she stood still in the corridor, she tried to gather her thoughts; she was disappointed at the fact that this was now her Commanding Officer, she had liked the previous one so much more, and then a voice startled her.

"Nicole!" Sergeant Muller greeted her; he was the first face she met when she came to the station and here he was, to her relief, as she needed answers.

"Where is the Captain?" she asked. Sergeant Muller explained to her that he was promoted to Major and therefore was transferred to Head Office as his rank was too high for such a small police station, thus the new Captain.

"Aah, I see…" Nicole said disappointedly, as the original Captain had a much friendlier and approachable demeanour.

"Well, I'll see you, I have tons of paperwork to do; I have been transferred to office hours," he said gratefully. A lot of policemen wanted to work office hours as they would see more of their families. Nicole preferred the shifts as she wasn't stuck in an office doing paperwork all day and she enjoyed being off in the middle of a week, as the shops weren't as busy as on weekends when civilians took over.

Nicole made her way back to the Charge Office only to discover the shift had already been assigned to their posts. As she wasn't assigned to one of the patrol vehicles, she was placed in the Charge Office with Sergeant Swart as Charge Office commander. "Urgh!" she sighed as she took the seat next to her sweaty Charge Office Commander. This would be her destiny for the following weeks, as the men preferred working on the patrol vehicles, as the work in the Charge Office meant dealing with the office personnel and a lot of paperwork, keeping the incidence register up to date, receiving and booking out of prisoners, taking complaints from civilians, writing up dockets as charges were laid and registering them in registers so that they could be sent to the detectives.

So not only were you stuck in an office all day, you were quite busy, depending on the shift you were assigned in the Charge Office. Night shifts weren't as busy though, but depending on the shift members, it could get busy, especially if the members working outside were lazy. It was customary for the officers at times of menial call outs to find some lame excuse for not being able to open a docket on the scene and referring the complainant to the Charge Office so that the staff there should take the statements and open the dockets.

Nicole discovered this all too soon, as she was fluent in English and Afrikaans. Most of the Afrikaans Police Officers, of which there were many, weren't as fluent and struggled to write a proper statement and therefore quickly picked up on Nicole's capabilities and loaded her with the task of taking statements and opening dockets. Nicole didn't mind this as she liked listening to the people's stories and it kept her busy, busy enough not to have to deal with Sergeant Swart who was also kept busy.

He hardly ever got assigned to a police vehicle. Which was probably down to the fact that he was overweight, Nicole thought. The shifts passed quickly and before Nicole knew it, she had been working as a constable for about a month.

After a few weeks, Nicole's food supplies were running low, as the end of the month drew closer. On her off days, she used her time to clean her apartment, do washing by hand in her bathtub, as she didn't own a washing machine, jogging and sleeping. She didn't see much of Ava and Ben as their shifts didn't allow it and although she had the company of the police station staff, the meaningful conversations she had were few and short-lived as work kept all of them busy, so after a month she started feeling a bit lonely.

Nicole felt relieved when she finally got her first pay slip since she needed some toiletries. When she opened it, she felt panic and disappointment taking hold of her stomach and wrenching at it in such a nauseating way that she had to sit down. Instead of the excitement she had felt when handed her pay slip, she just stared at it in disbelief.

How on earth am I going to survive? she thought to herself as she ran her eyes over and over the numbers on it to make sure she wasn't imagining it. After all her deductions, she was left with little more than the money to pay her rent. There was no way she would be able to buy decent groceries with the amount left. That evening, she ran her head through possible solutions of how to deal with this predicament and finally fell asleep, only to wake up the next morning with the same sickening feeling in her stomach. Nicole decided to pay her rent first and then worry about what she was to do the rest of the month.

After she did so, she went to the local grocery store and wandered around in it, too scared to spend the little money she had but decided to buy the absolute necessities, which to her was toothpaste, soap, shampoo, washing powder and a razor. After she had placed these items in her basket, she looked longingly at the foods displayed on the shelves and she felt like a little girl in a candy shop not being allowed to take some. Her eyes skimmed the fruits and vegetables and her eyes fell on a special offer they were advertising on their potatoes. There were huge 10kg bags of potatoes.

Why not? she thought excitedly as her mother had once lived on a diet of potatoes when she was on one of her fad diets, trying to lose some weight. Nicole smiled, relieved as she would have money left for a tin of coffee and a packet of sugar.

"It's not ideal, but it's food," Nicole consoled herself, proud of being able to make a plan with so little money. And that was how it would be for the remainder of her stay in the apartment. She would have one packet of potatoes and black coffee and sugar as a treat, which she used sparingly. Nicole made her suppers as interesting as possible by making different dishes with her potatoes. She made mashed potatoes, chips, pocket potatoes and potato bake. Nicole hardly ate during the day except for when someone at work would offer her something.

Luckily, coffee, sugar and milk was free at work, so she didn't suffer the lack of such a luxury. This very low kilojoule diet and Nicole's running to keep busy and fit caused her to lose weight and within a month, she had the body of a model. She was too focussed on surviving to be able to enjoy the perks of her new appearance. Nicole did however phone her father once a month to ask him for enough money for cigarettes, as these helped her suppress her appetite enough so that the lack of food didn't feel like torture.

Soon Nicole was set into her ways and the routine became comfortable; even Sergeant Swart didn't bother her too much. He sometimes did get under her skin when he tried to discuss his personal life with her. Nicole tried to avoid personal conversations with him as he made her feel very uncomfortable, until one day. Nicole felt sorry for him that day as he entered the office in a very sombre mood.

Where he was usually very confident, loud and even somewhat rude, this day he was somewhat subdued. He greeted her very softly as he took his place behind the Incidence Register where he was normally stationed, but this morning Sergeant Mostert also noticed Sergeant Swart's sombre mood and said: "Swart, I think you and Burger need some fresh air. I will take charge of the Charge Office today." And he handed Sergeant Swart the keys to one of the patrol vehicles. Nicole couldn't believe her ears. She was actually posted on a vehicle and the excitement built up inside of her as she started wondering what the day may hold.

"Thank you, Sergeant," Sergeant Swart said gratefully in his usual loud voice.

Only later would Nicole realise that men were hardly ever Charge Office Commander for the period that Sergeant Swart was, but that the men on her shift in fact didn't like working with him as he was socially awkward and that was the reason they had placed him in the Charge Office. Nicole, being the youngest and the most junior in rank, was therefore posted with him. Now that he was posted on a vehicle, it made a lot of sense to give Nicole the chance to see what it was like to work outside and Sergeant Mostert argued that since it was a Sunday, there wouldn't be much going on as well, so it wouldn't do harm to place Nicole on the patrol vehicle as well. This way, everyone would be happy. Nicole didn't care that she had to patrol with Swart, as she just wanted to get out of the office.

When they reached the vehicle, Sergeant Swart continued to do inspection of his vehicle. Their station was one of the few that had a petrol pump on their premises and as such, surrounding stations had to fill up their tanks at Table View. Sergeant Swart filled the tank, filled out the petrol register, while showing Nicole how it was done and then booked out the vehicle in another register, again showing Nicole exactly what had to be done. When they climbed into the vehicle, of which Nicole was the passenger as she didn't have authorisation, Sergeant Swart showed her how to answer the radio when called by Radio-control or any of the other patrol vehicles in the vicinity, as she would be in charge of the radio while he was driving.

Nicole felt a little nervous and excited at the same time. She was somewhat naïve still in her idea of what it was like working in the field. She thought it to be exciting and adventurous. Soon enough, she was to discover it wasn't so, as the first two hours passed without them having to attend one complaint. The driving around in the afternoon sun in a vehicle with no air conditioning and little conversation, as Sergeant Swart hardly said anything to her, other than explaining to her how to keep her pocketbook up to date, made her feel very lazy and she had to draw on all her energy to stay awake.

Nicole made a lot more entries in her pocketbook than was necessary, but it kept her awake. Normally, they would report their arrival time at the station in the little police-issue pocketbook, with the time and date and an entry stating: "Report for duty and inspected by", where their Sergeant in charge of the shift would sign. Sometimes it was a Warrant Officer in charge of shifts, but hardly ever a higher rank at such a small station. They would then continue to note all assurances and patrols in their books. Written warnings would also be done in the little books, where they would then let the perpetrator sign in acknowledgement.

These little books were their protection as it was testimony of their actions and whereabouts when faced with civilian complaints. These books were to be handed in at the station when they were full. Unfortunately, not all policemen were honest and these books were sometimes used to protect them from prosecution when they misbehaved, by making false entries. Nicole at this stage couldn't even imagine that policemen would be dishonest, as she wasn't and still measured other people according to her own conduct, the way a lot of young people do because of their lack of experience with people. She also still believed that those who chose the police as a career did so as they had a strong set of morals and wanted to uphold these in the community. This was soon to be changed.

Sergeant Swart was hungry and to Nicole's relief decided to make a pit stop at the station. Nicole lazily dragged herself out of the vehicle and into the coolness of the Charge Office. Sergeant Mostert smiled at her as he recognised the look of utter boredom from working outside on a Sunday afternoon. Nicole didn't know that in time, most of the policemen did "privates" (civilian duties with their police time and vehicles) on quiet days.

"Having fun?" Mostert asked teasingly, knowing the answer.

"I am tired!" Nicole dragged her words out and hung her shoulders, like a little girl complaining to her father. Sergeant Mostert started to laugh.

"Not all you thought it would be?" he asked with a smile still lingering on his mouth's corners.

"It's just quiet outside. I know Sundays are quiet, but this is brutal," she complained again.

"Then maybe you should be posted outside more, you will soon enough prefer working inside," he said, convinced that she wouldn't be able to handle some of the conditions outside and that she needed protection.

"Really?" Nicole said and her whole body straightened at the thought of the adventure of it.

"Let's see," he agreed to consider it. Nicole went to the kitchen, got herself a cup of coffee and returned to the Charge Office to catch up on Sergeant Mostert's doings the past week. Sergeant Mostert was an avid punter at the Milnerton Race Course. He had made quite a bit of money in this way in the past, once predicting the Pick-Six and winning R300,000. With this, he had paid off his bond and had enough left to invest in a secure pension fund apart from the one provided by the police force. He was thus financially well off and one of the most stress-free people Nicole had come across in the police force. She loved listening to his stories. Although he didn't share his good fortune with his fellow members, he and Nicole had become really close and he trusted her and cared for her like his own child.

"Come Nicole," Sergeant Swart interrupted their conversation abruptly.

"Do we have to go?" Nicole whinged.

"Yes," he replied in a stern voice. So Nicole reluctantly stood up from her chair and rolled her eyes at Sergeant Mostert who could only smile at her annoyance. Nicole followed Sergeant Swart and as they climbed into the patrol vehicle, she saw something reflected in his eyes. A dark side, a side to a human being she wasn't familiar with and therefore couldn't recognise. She shuddered at the sight as it made her feel uneasy. He wasn't looking at her, but it was there, underneath the surface, for those sensitive to detail, to discover.

Where Nicole before didn't want to spend time alone with Sergeant Swart, she now wanted to run, but couldn't. She thought that she would talk as little as possible and hope the shift's end would reach them sooner than later.

Sergeant Swart started driving in the direction of the beach and continued along the beach road in the direction of Melkbosch Strand, their neighbouring area. There was not much to patrol on this road as it exited the town and wound all along the unscathed beach front, with its white sand dunes and indigenous Fynbos. Nicole couldn't understand why they were leaving their area and driving such a long distance as they were supposed to patrol their area and report to Charge Office if they were leaving it and even worse had to ask permission to do so, which he didn't. Nicole felt uneasy in her seat, not really knowing what she should do. Her first instinct was to let Charge Office know what they were up to, but she didn't want to agitate Sergeant Swart as he was her senior.

"Should I let Sergeant Mostert know that we are leaving the area?" Nicole asked as sweetly as she could possibly muster, while she bent forward to pick the radio piece up.

"No," Sergeant Swart said sternly and placed his clammy hand on her wrist, stopping her from bringing it to her mouth. Nicole, with her arm still trapped, looked straight into his dark brown eyes, shocked by the firm touch. His pupils somehow seemed to disappear in the darkness of his mood and she struggled to keep eye contact and looked down submissively while pulling her wrist free from his soft fingers.

"I-I thought I could show you our area and our neighbouring station. We don't need to announce it over the radio. Radio Control is full of shit with these things. There is nothing going on anyway and since we have time and it is only a few minutes away, I thought I might just as well introduce you to your surroundings?" He checked himself as he recognised the look of fear in Nicole's eyes.

"Oh…" Nicole said carefully, "so won't we get into trouble?"

"No man, you have a lot to learn," he said as he laughed inappropriately loud. "This is not the first time someone has left the area without asking permission and it won't be the last." He nearly choked as he continued to laugh. Nicole felt embarrassed and annoyed, so she stared out of the window to avoid eye contact with Sergeant Swart.

"Oh, come on…" Sergeant Swart started at her. He was suddenly in a very talkative mood and she could hear that another laughing fit was hiding in his voice.

Dare to laugh, you bastard! she cursed him in her mind as she tried to ignore him.

"Come on, Nicole…don't be so stubborn," he pleaded in a gentle voice. "I didn't mean to laugh at you; it's just that you are still so innocent. I didn't mean to upset you."

Nicole could swear he was genuinely trying to be nice, so she decided to act normal. *This is better than driving in circles around Table View*, she thought to herself.

"So where are you taking me?" she changed the subject, hoping that he would do the same and he did, relieved that she wasn't going to put up a fuss about him wanting to take her for a drive.

"I want to show you Melkbosch Strand's police station. It is tiny and they have practically no crime. I wish I worked there. Imagine it…a life where you go to work and have to do practically nothing and get paid for it?" he said as he visualised it. Nicole couldn't see the fun in that.

Spending the rest of my life the way I have had to do today? she thought to herself. *No thank you.*

"Then why don't you ask for a transfer?" she asked, hoping that he would actually consider it.

"My wife won't move here and I cannot afford to work so far from home," he started explaining. And although Nicole normally wouldn't encourage a conversation with him, she was puzzled by the fact that he was married. She couldn't understand why anyone would want to spend time with him, let alone marry him. The thought of a woman having to kiss him disgusted her, so her curiosity got the better of her.

"So, you are married?" she asked and looked at him as he drove along the long road at a snail's pace and looking dead ahead of him. Suddenly, his face became serious again.

"Yes I am. She is such a wonderful woman and so pretty," he said as he smiled at the thought. He freed his one hand from the steering wheel and took his wallet from his shirt pocket and handed it to Nicole.

"Open it!" he ordered. Nicole did so without protesting. Inside of the weathered leather wallet was a picture of a pale-faced dark-haired girl with green eyes. She looked frail as she was really skinny, but somehow, through the plainness of her dress sense and lack of make-up, she was appealing to the eye.

She is pretty, Nicole said in thought. "How old is she?" Nicole asked before she could check herself.

"She is twenty-five," he replied smiling. Nicole watched his face carefully as the tone of his voice, his expressions and the words coming from his mouth all said something different. This confused her.

"How old are you, if I may ask?" Nicole asked, now extremely curious to understand Sergeant Swart better.

"I am thirty-two," he said and he looked a little saddened by the fact.

"Nicole…you can ask me anything you want," he said after a pause and turned to her as he said it, placing his left hand on her knee for a second and then lifting it to take hold of the steering wheel again. Nicole felt freaked out by his touch and shifted her body as close to the passenger door as possible. She tried to figure out how a woman like the one in the picture could even consider marrying Sergeant Swart. The girl could easily have found a better suitor she thought. Nicole wasn't prepared to take her eyes off Sergeant Swart as she was adamant to slap his hand if it dared enter her personal space again. Sergeant Swart suddenly looked very sad and deep in thought.

Nicole sensed that something was troubling him and had to ask as she held his wallet for him to take. As he took it from her, he looked her straight in the face and pulling his lower lip the way a child would before they start crying and she could swear he was about to cry, but he turned away before she could make sure that the wetness in his eyes were the start of tears and not that of normal moisture. Nicole felt somewhat sorry for him. He was obviously tormented by something.

"What is wrong?" she asked, needing to know, but expecting him not to disclose the reason as it clearly was a very private matter.

"I don't know how to start," he said quite seriously and Nicole was surprised that he actually wanted to talk to her about his worries.

"Where you want to?" she suggested, not knowing what to say to him. By now they had already entered Melkbosch Strand and Sergeant Swart turned on to a gravel road on the outskirts of Melkbosch Strand; a tiny little community of artists, surfers and pensioners. The gravel road entered into a gravel parking lot between indigenous bushes. Nicole was amazed at the size of the station; she thought that their building was small for a police station.

"This is it," Sergeant Mostert said, not stopping but slowing down enough for her to take the whole building in. Nicole expected him to stop and show her inside, but instead he made a U-turn in the parking lot and exited the way they had come in.

"I didn't know you get police stations that are so small," Nicole said in amazement and she stretched her neck as far as possible to stare at the station.

"That is not the smallest; you get satellite stations that consist of caravans and two to four police officers manning them," he laughed and then turned back into the road they came with, but instead of keeping straight on in the direction they came from, he turned onto a road travelling through farm land at the first junction.

"Where are we going now?" Nicole asked, confused.

"I am going to take the N7 back to the station," Sergeant Swart explained. Nicole had never driven on the N7, a road that took you from Table View to Malmesbury and through the inner parts of the West Coast, all the way up to Namibia, thus also called the Cape Namibia route.

"Oh," Nicole said and was actually grateful that they took this peacefully scenic route.

"So…" Sergeant Swart started. He told Nicole how he had met his wife when she was seventeen and how he had waited for her to finish school. How she at first wasn't interested, but her family was very poor and how he so kindly helped her parents financially and that a love grew between them and when he finally asked her to marry him, when she was twenty, she accepted. She didn't work as he preferred it that way.

They had a small two-bedroomed townhouse in Table View and that he desperately wanted her to fall pregnant as he felt ready for the responsibilities of parenthood, but how she stubbornly refused. All of it, without a pause, and

Nicole just sat and listened until his breath finally ran out and he fell silent, again in a sombre mood.

"So that is what is bothering you?" Nicole asked.

"What? The baby thing?" he said annoyed and looked at Nicole. "No!"

"Then what is it!" she said agitatedly.

His mood swings irritated her and his bombastic blow-ups made things even worse. She didn't feel like talking to him further, but he had no inclination to stop there.

"Well, something terrible happened..." he continued in a soft, almost sad voice.

All Nicole's senses told her not to, but she had to ask: "What happened?"

"Well, last night I made us a romantic dinner..." he paused and looked at Nicole to see if she was listening and when their eyes made contact, he looked away, staring into the road ahead.

Do I really have to listen to his marital problems? Nicole thought as she sighed.

"Well, she hadn't been happy with me for a while now. You know how it goes?" he continued, but Nicole didn't know.

"I was trying to make up for what she felt I did wrong," he said leaving Nicole in the dark as to what he had done wrong, but she deduced from the seriousness of his mood and the fact that she was pissed off with him for so long, it was something really bad. Nicole sat quietly hoping he didn't expect her to participate in the discussion.

"After we had eaten, I washed the dishes," he said, in a manner suggesting that he normally didn't and that he only did it to win her favour. "She was actually in quite a pleasant mood," he continued. Then he inappropriately went on about how he told her how much she meant to him and how he kissed her and how she finally succumbed to him and they started making love.

What is he going on about? she thought, disgusted by the thought of him, naked, pounding away at such a fragile frame as his wife's.

"Nicole, you don't understand," he said. "I didn't mean to, but something terrible happened," he said looking very serious.

What terrible thing could possibly have happened? she thought.

"I turned her around to do her from behind..." he paused as he relived the previous night in his mind and Nicole's face uncontrollably distorted by the graphic visualisation of the act. "Everything was still going smoothly..." he paused again, "and as I pulled out and wanted to penetrate her again..." Nicole didn't want to hear anymore, she wanted to open the door and jump out, and seriously contemplated doing so, but she was trapped by the speed at which they were driving and by his superiority.

"As I penetrated her again, I accidentally penetrated her anally," he said and looked at her shocked face and his eyes pulled ever so slightly smaller. His stare took a little longer than necessary and Nicole, grossed out by what she had to listen to, turned her head and she could swear she saw a faint smile on his mouth.

How the hell do you penetrate someone accidentally in their anus? she tried to make sense of it as the image flashed past her. *It is impossible*, she thought. *I am no expert, but it sounds very suspicious.*

"She won't talk to me now. She has never ignored me, but no matter what I say to her, she won't talk to me," he complained.

"Did you stop though?" Nicole asked as she thought it.

"No! I told you it was an accident, I didn't know," he said not so convincingly. Repelled by the thought of him hammering away at his wife in such a violent manner as to force himself into her, she pulled a face of disgust: "You should have stopped."

Nicole didn't believe that his wife, if she was now so upset about what had happened, wouldn't have complained during the act. She wondered if he truly believed himself that he was innocent in his actions and that his wife was being harsh in her reactions, this after he had raped her in such a brutal manner. Nicole couldn't believe that he was mad enough to rape his own wife and then tell a nineteen-year-old stranger about it.

What does he want to accomplish with this? and the possibilities frightened her. Nicole for a moment didn't know how to react or what to say, they were entering Table View again, and she felt relief rush over her.

"Oh, so now I see where we come out," Nicole said, looking at the road, trying to take his mind off what he had just told her.

"What?" he said startled as he understood her wrong.

"The road, Sergeant, I didn't know where it connected back to Table View, but now I understand," she said pointing to the road in front of her.

"Oh yes, the road..." he said as his mind was drawn back to reality.

They both stayed silent until they had reached the station, as if they silently agreed there was nothing further to discuss. When they reached the station,

Nicole went to the bathroom to gather herself and decide what her plan of action would be as she wanted to avoid being alone with him on patrol at all costs.

"Ah, Sergeant Mostert, I will talk to him," she decided and she did when she returned to the Charge Office. She waited until Sergeant Swart disappeared into the corridor, when she softly whispered to Sergeant Mostert that she really didn't want to work with Sergeant Swart outside, without explaining to him why, but he seemed to understand her distress and posted her to the Charge Office for the last part of their shift.

After that, Nicole was once again mostly posted in the Charge Office, but now at least Sergeant Mostert made an effort to post Sergeant Swart on the patrol vehicle more regularly so that Nicole could get a break from his presence. The times she did have to deal with him, though, she kept to herself, avoiding conversations as much as possible, not affording him the time to discuss his personal life with her.

Chapter 14

Before long, Nicole became part of the workings at the station, with most of the women and men there taking notice of her positive attitude towards her work and her willingness to help with projects beyond her duties. This and her non-judgmental, pleasant personality made her stand out as a team player. Only a few of the older women at the station didn't take much liking to Nicole, as she stole their thunder with the younger policemen. Nicole had to deal with them complaining about petty little things, like the one afternoon when she just came in for her shift, when she was called in by the older Sergeants, who were married older women, working in the offices to inform her that she wore too much perfume and that she might give the men at the station the wrong impression.

Nicole slowly became hardened by their bitchiness and on that particular day decided that she had had enough and had to stand up for herself, by marching down to the Station Commander's office and bluntly asking him if she wore overpowering amounts of perfume in his opinion, which he smilingly dismissed as ridiculous, since he too was quite fond of Nicole. He also warned the older girls to rather focus on their work and leave Nicole alone, so after that the office girls hardly spoke to Nicole, except for one of the girls that had also started working there as a student at about the same time as Nicole. The two of them soon started chatting whenever their work allowed them.

Samantha was a short girl with blonde hair and grey eyes. She was quite serious, but could be loads of fun when not at work. She started dating one of the male shift members and like most of the young police officers, liked to go dancing at local hangouts preferred by the police officers. It didn't take her long to invite Nicole along with them to these outings. Nicole loved dancing as she was a natural athlete with rhythm and picked up on the dancing styles quickly.

Her looks made her stand out, causing her to meet a lot of other police members from different stations and soon she was a regular, never needing entrance fees nor money to buy her own drinks. There were always more than enough willing men to satisfy her every need. Nicole preferred to steer clear of the advances of policemen as she had heard the men talk on shifts about the women they had conquered and the lack of respect with which they spoke about these women they had flings with.

Nicole soon became part of the lifestyle a lot of young policemen and -women lived by, especially when they were not married, as it was a way of escaping their stresses. They worked their shifts and each free night they had, and the local club was open, they were there, drinking until the early hours of the morning, only to fall asleep for a few short hours, if they were lucky and then heading back to work.

Nicole even sometimes went two days without proper sleep, disregarding the fact that she had to be on full alert when on duty. To her, this was a way of not dealing with being alone and deprived of food and the stresses of a financially struggling young adult. This lifestyle kept her busy. Only when her body could physically not carry on the pace, did she take a day off to sleep the whole day, only to crave the night life when she was well rested.

The more she started hanging out in clubs, the more she became known and the more she became known, the more she was invited to barbeques where the policemen got drunk and adultery took place, but Nicole turned a blind eye and stayed safe from any policemen approaching her. She made it very clear that she wasn't interested in any liaisons. The men actually appreciated it as there weren't many unmarried policewomen that had some sort of moral standards and thus they slowly started to develop an appreciation for her and feeling protective over her. This made her feel safe. Nicole did however on the odd occasion meet men that she took a liking in and would have a romantic kiss in the parking lot as they walked her to her friend's car after the night's dancing.

On one such evening, she met a young student that worked on a vegetable farm outside Kraaifontein, on the N1. He was extremely attractive and unbelievably well-mannered and gentlemanly. This did appeal to Nicole, so she spent the whole evening dancing with him. They didn't talk much as the music was too loud on the dance floor and he was slightly shy. She felt him tremble when he held her. He was taller than her, he had blond streaks in his hair and his skin was golden brown from working in the sun. They tried to communicate but only got frustrated so at one point, he took her hand and pulled her from the dance floor and out the front door of the club. She followed him willingly and they ended up sitting outside on the curb next to each other.

"So, what's your name?" he asked as he studied her face openly.

"I am Nicole, and you?" she asked, intrigued by him.

"I am François," he said as he looked down at their hands where he was still holding her hand and his fingers started rubbing gently over hers. She could swear he was shy. He was trembling, but his voice was steady, like someone with a lot of confidence and he knew exactly how to make conversation as he then continued to tell her about himself.

"So, I have told you everything about myself," he said after he told her the necessary. "But what about you?" he asked.

"There is not much to know, I am a policewoman," she said, waiting for the shock to show on his face, but he was unfazed by her disclosure. Nicole frowned. "You don't seem to mind?" she said, surprised by it, as only policemen normally didn't have a problem with women who were in the police force. The young girls in the Force gave themselves a bad reputation, seeing that those who weren't proper normally didn't get married and therefore they were the ones out partying.

"Do you want me to be disappointed?" he asked jokingly and smiled a warm smile at her with his straight white teeth. Nicole smiled back, he made her feel comfortable and she could sense he was of good breeding.

"No, it's just that guys normally don't act positively when they hear you are in the police force," she said, and she unbelievingly studied his eyes to detect a hidden agenda, but she didn't.

"Your work doesn't determine who you are, your ethics does," he said plainly as he looked down into her beautiful face and with his free hand, he whipped her hair back behind her ear, exposing her beautiful eyes.

"I know you have probably heard this many times, but you are very beautiful," he said as he slowly removed his hand from her face. Nicole smiled as she was taken by surprise by the fact that he didn't attempt to kiss her.

"You are different," Nicole said as their eyes were still locked onto each other's, while they both searched each other's eyes, trying to gauge each other.

"I don't think so…" he said, and Nicole saw a gentleness reflected in his eyes as he said it. "We are all as different as we are the same, it's our needs and circumstances that predict our actions and make us seem different," he continued. He was something she needed now and she instinctively knew this. There was a physical attraction, but she was more so attracted by his composure.

"I know, but we have choices, and those choices make us different," she still looked straight into his dark green eyes and he smiled at her appreciatively.

"Yes, true, but then it comes down to the strong willed and the weak, which brings us back to circumstances, influencing not only who we are, but how we came to be that way, and how we make our choices," he said more seriously.

"Then I will rephrase my statement; you are a rarity," she smiled cheekily.

"Once again, in your circumstances and from your perspective you might think so, but from where I come from, the people in your surroundings seem to be, and I am quite out of the ordinary," he laughed as Nicole laughed with him, while shaking her head at his modesty and dry wisdom.

"Then let's agree that I appreciate your uniqueness in my world," she smiled.

"And you in your world," he smiled back at her, and then he bent forward and placed his hand behind her neck, pulling her forward to kiss her on her mouth, softly, not parting his lips. He held his lips on her lips for a few seconds and then pulled away.

"I want to see you again," he said seriously, but gently. This was what Nicole had hoped for, so Nicole gave him her address and gave him an open invite to come visit her whenever he was in the vicinity. They went back in and danced the last few dances before Samantha came to call her when they wanted to leave, only affording her the time to give him a gentle hug, not knowing if it would be the last time she would see him.

The week that followed dragged by as Nicole had hoped that François would make his appearance at her doorstep, but he didn't. She thought of all the possibilities, why he could possibly not have come to visit or had not tried to phone her yet. He knew where she worked and lived. As the days passed she decided that he had probably forgotten about her and wasn't as taken by her as she had hoped, so she put him behind her and once again focussed on staying busy with work. Nicole also cut back on the amount of time she spent out dancing since she couldn't keep up with the hectic pace of going days without proper sleep and then having to work shifts.

Not another day with this sweaty bastard! Nicole thought to herself one afternoon as she was posted in the Charge Office with Sergeant Swart, but on this day there was a difference, as she was made Charge Office Commander, because Sergeant Swart didn't feel well and asked Sergeant Mostert to do so. He was in a foul mood and hardly spoke to anybody. Nicole was excited though as this would be the first time she would be in control and not only that, it meant she had a lot to concentrate on and a lot of work to do. The prospect of being busy excited her, so she took her seat eagerly behind the Incidence Register.

Every time the patrol vehicles went out on their rounds, Sergeant Swart would disappear into the corridor and to the seating area where he would fall asleep on the couch, leaving Nicole alone in the Charge Office. She didn't mind this at all, at least she was rid of him, and as soon as the patrol vehicles pulled into the yard, he would appear as if he had only used the bathroom. Nicole didn't complain to Sergeant Mostert, as she preferred it this way. It was a Saturday and therefore the office personnel weren't there, thus his arrogance in letting her be on her own.

The only other people at the station were the detainees in the cells and the detectives on duty, but they were housed in the building behind the station. It was a quiet afternoon with not much complaints coming through. At one point, Nicole decided to go make herself a cup of coffee; she could see the Charge Office through the open door to the kitchen and could hear everything that went on inside, so she took her time making her coffee. She saw Sergeant Swart passed out on the couch behind the charge office in the corridor. He was softly snoring with his mouth half open. She took care not to wake him. Even the radio was eerily quiet that afternoon. It was as if the whole Table View had come to a standstill and fell into a deep sleep in the afternoon heat.

Nicole's back was turned to the Charge Office as she was busy with the cup in front of her on the counter top. She was deep in thought when she felt two huge hands slip around her waist, while pulling her closer to a hard, warm body, which pressed hard against her backside. It startled Nicole and as she tried to free herself and swing around to see who was molesting her body, she knocked her cup of coffee over, messing coffee all over the floor and counter.

"You don't need to be so excited to see me," the deep voice said teasingly, and Nicole looked up into Captain Liebenberg's cousin's face. It was an attractive face and his blue eyes sparkled mischievously.

"What the hell?" Nicole shouted at him, startled.

"No dear sweet one, this isn't hell, this is heaven," he continued as he found Nicole's distress arousing.

"Fuck!" Nicole said, agitated by his arrogance and audacity to talk to her in such a manner.

"I would like to," he replied while laughing at her bewilderment.

"I don't know who you are, nor do I want to know. Just keep your paws off me," she shouted at him and started to wipe the coffee from the floor and then switched the kettle on again to make herself a new cup of coffee. He didn't leave. He watched her and smiled at her distress.

"I am sorry, I was only joking," he apologised.

"What do you want?" Nicole asked irately as she rethought being rude to him, as she knew his uncle was her Station Commander. He took Nicole by her shoulders and turned her around to face him.

"Let's start over," he said as he flashed a warm smile at her. "I am Nick," he said and offered his hand.

Nicole had calmed down enough to be courteous, so she offered him her hand and replied: "I am Nicole."

"I must confess I know who you are," and he smiled a knowing smile at her. "It is difficult not to miss you," he continued.

"Well, I don't know who you are," Nicole said plainly as she lied, since she didn't want to give him the impression that she had enquired about him that first day when she had seen him in Captain Liebenberg's office. He continued to tell her that he was Captain Liebenberg's cousin as his mother was Captain Liebenberg's sister, and that he worked at the flying squad, which caused him to assist all emergency callouts all over the Peninsula. They were in the area and had stopped for petrol.

"So you decided it would be funny to terrorise me instead?" she asked sarcastically.

"No, not quite, I found the Charge Office empty and since it shouldn't be left unmanned, I thought I would give you a fright," he confessed. "You know it is dangerous to leave the Charge Office like that? Someone can attack you from behind," he said in a seemingly caring voice.

"Like you did?" she continued her sarcasm.

"Oh man!" he sighed. "You are a difficult one. No, Nicole," he said as he shook his head. "Were you posted alone?" he asked curious as to why she was alone in the Charge Office.

"No, Sergeant 'whale' over there," and she pointed to sergeant Swart who was spread out over the couch like a beached whale, "is too poorly to work today," she said as she rolled her eyes at him.

"Ah I see…" he said.

"Should I wake him?" Nicole asked Nick as he was her senior, wearing his Sergeant's rank on his shoulders.

"No, let him be, then we can be alone," he smiled teasingly at Nicole. Nicole started to walk past him in the direction of the Charge Office, as the kitchen suddenly felt really small and their bodies way too close for her comfort. Nick followed her, as did his scent. He smelled wonderfully clean and musky and she fought the urge to sniff the air. In the Charge Office, he took the petrol register and started to walk in the direction of the door.

"Okay, I am going to fill the tank," he said nonchalantly before he walked through the door. Nicole felt disappointed for some reason as he left. She couldn't understand it, as she didn't even know if she liked him, but she liked the attention and his advances and arrogance was annoyingly exciting. Nicole tried to look busy for when he came back, as she didn't want him to see that she was affected by him. She was busy in the holding cell reorganising some paperwork as he re-entered the office. The holding cell was out of vision from the Charge Office.

Nick filled in the register and signed it. He bent over the counter to try and spot Nicole. By now, Nicole was properly busy with what she was doing and had totally forgotten about him when he spotted her. He made his way to her softly as not to give his presence away. Nicole was bent forward as the pigeonholes in which the paperwork was kept were low and Nick took position right behind her, but not touching her. Nicole saw his feet behind hers and flung upright and around.

"What on earth," she said, startled by his closeness and uncomfortable by the compromising position she was in when he came to stand behind her.

"You," he said, and she frowned, not understanding. He recognised the frown and continued: "You on this earth…" and he smiled suggestively at her.

"You don't make sense," she said in a fake annoyed tone and pushed her way past him to walk to the Charge Office, but as she passed him, he grabbed her wrist.

"Don't walk away from me…" he said softly, "you know you want me." Nicole stopped with her hand locked in his grip and she looked up at him as her heart raced in her chest. She could smell him perfectly now. She looked at his strong veined hands. They were well groomed and muscled and the skin covering it was tough but silky smooth. Her breathing became deep and her chest heaved up and down underneath her light blue cotton buttoned shirt. From where he stood he could faintly make out the outline of her breast through the small openings in-between the buttons. They stood like that for a few seconds, in silence, staring at each other and wanting each other, but not letting themselves act on the animal instinct.

"No, I don't," she broke the silence, not very convincingly and she softly started tugging her arm in his grip.

"Yes, you do..." he said as he recognised the look in her eyes. "Your stubbornness only makes things worse," he said in a soft husky voice as his lust for her clouded his voice and he placed his free hand on her shoulder, gently pushing her back up against the wall behind her. Nicole didn't struggle, she felt surprisingly brave as she locked eyes with his gaze and challenged him with her own stare.

"Nick, let me go," she said in an even paced tone.

"No," he replied adamantly while he moved his gaze up and down over her body like a predator which had pinned down its prey, trying to find that perfect spot to aim his fatal blow. He too was now breathing heavily and his towering presence took the breath out of Nicole's lungs as his breath blew over her face. He wasn't a smoker and his breath smelt as fresh and clean as his body did. Nicole closed her eyes as she let her head hang forward in an attempt to avoid his gaze. She knew that what he suggested they do in the Charge Office, on duty, and in uniform, was totally forbidden, but also on a moral dilemma even more so, as he was a stranger.

Nick bent down with his head and nuzzled her chin up and as she lifted her face to protest, his mouth found hers, covering it in its warm softness and forcing her lips apart to enter her mouth with his tongue. He ate her like a starved savage, while pressing harder on her shoulder and tightening his grip on her wrist unconsciously. Nicole was taken by surprise and let his tongue linger in her mouth while she tasted the freshness of his flesh. She was still trying to make sense of what was happening and trying to will herself to stop what was happening when he took a step forward and pressed his rock-hard erection skilfully against the rounding at the union of her thighs. The size of him shocked her into action and she pushed him away as hard as possible.

With a very firm "NO!" from Nicole, Nick let go of her, looking bewildered at her reaction.

"What?" he said confused.

"I can't do this," Nicole replied as she straightened her uniform. "We are on duty," she said out of breath. Nick smiled, relieved and re-approached Nicole slowly to take her in his arms.

"NO!" Nicole said firmly, "I am not going to do this. I don't know you!" she continued and with that, she pushed him forcefully away from her and fled past him to the Charge Office, with him a few steps behind her. When she entered the Charge Office, Sergeant Swart entered the office from the kitchen's side, while rubbing the sleep from his eyes and stretching.

"So, what did I miss?" he asked lazily and for the first time, Nicole was grateful for his presence.

"Not much," Nicole said as she gave Nick a death stare and then returned her focus to Sergeant Swart. "It is really quiet today. Are you feeling any better?"

"Yes, I kind of do," he said pleased by the warm reception from Nicole. Nick walked to where he had placed his vehicle's keys on the counter and scooped it up as he walked out of the building without greeting or turning back to look at Nicole.

The nerve! she thought to herself as she watched Nick leave the Charge Office.

For the rest of the shift Nicole felt compelled to converse with Sergeant Swart and did so in as pleasant manner as possible, since he had come to her rescue. The end of their shift didn't come too soon and Nicole couldn't sign out soon enough. Before Nicole could escape the Charge Office though, Sergeant Mostert called her back: "Nicole, wait for me."

"Yes," she said and turned around and stood in the doorway, waiting for him impatiently, until he finally walked in her direction. Then she turned and started walking out of the station and to the gate.

"Nicole, don't be in such a hurry," he said in a fake pleading voice. Nicole started laughing, she loved his silliness, he reminded her of her father when she was little, who would also make fake voices at her. Nicole stopped to wait for him and as he reached her, she spontaneously threw her arms around his neck and gave him a bear hug, like she used to do to her dad when she felt especially appreciative of him. Sergeant Mostert reciprocated her sentiment and hugged her caringly.

"I do love you," she said softly and released him.

"I know, dear child, I know," he said and winked at her.

"Come, I will take you home, I have something to discuss with you, but not here," he said and she could see that he had something up his sleeve and for some reason she knew she wanted to be a part of it.

As they drove home, Sergeant Mostert explained to Nicole that policemen at times had to work special duties at different venues. These included concerts, horse races, voting stations, demonstrations and so forth. Police officers from different stations were posted at these venues as normal duties had to continue and therefore those off duty were posted on such extra duties. Sometimes they were paid overtime, but not always.

Mostly the Station Commander was in charge of posting Officers on extra duties, but sometimes he asked the men and women off duty to volunteer, as some officers had a specific interest at these different events. He continued to explain that on their next off days, there were special duties at the Milnerton Race Course and that he wanted to volunteer for obvious reasons and he wanted her to volunteer as well, as he would much rather spend the day with her there than with one of the others. Nicole smiled as she always wanted to see what the fuss was about for him, so she agreed to let the Captain know the following day.

"Thank you, Nicole. It is going to be fun and I will see you tomorrow," he greeted her when they stopped in front of her apartment block and she got out of the car.

As Nicole walked up the stairs, she smiled contentedly from knowing that she had such a gentle soul on her side, who looked out for her. Her mind started wondering about the possibilities of her maybe making a bit of money on the horses, as he was a keen and successful punter. She didn't know how they were going to be able to bet though as they were going to be in uniform and weren't allowed to do so on duty. As Nicole reached the top of the stairs to the first floor of the building, she saw the tanned bare legs of a man, sitting in the hallway, sticking out behind the corner wall of the stairs.

From the distance at which his legs were positioned, she gathered that he was sitting in front of her doorway. Nicole's heart started to beat faster as she wondered who would sit there and if she could continue forward and if she should rather call for help, since it could be a vagrant. Nicole took a deep breath and braced herself as she decided to move forward and if it was someone who meant her harm, she at least had her pistol in her handbag, so she carefully slipped her hand into her bag and took the pistol in it, but still holding it in its place, before she took a step forward and into the hallway. As she came around the corner, her heart's pace accelerated as François leapt to his feet.

"Thank God, Nicole! I thought you would never come home, and I don't have a lot of time left. I need to return to the farm soon," he rambled the words off as he took the few steps to Nicole and took her in his arms, hugging her tightly and then before she could say anything, pressing her away from his body, while holding her by her shoulders. He looked her up and down.

"My word, you look cute in uniform," he smiled at her and pulled her closer for another hug. Nicole didn't resist him; she was numb from shock as he was the last person on her mind, but also the one person she wanted to see the most. Nicole pulled her hand out of her purse and hugged him back.

"I thought you had forgotten about me," she said in disbelief.

"Well, I didn't. Now make me some coffee before I have to go home, I have been sitting here for more than an hour," he said smilingly as he released her and made way for her to pass him so that she could unlock her front door. Nicole panicked as she knew she didn't have milk and couldn't offer him anything to eat, as she only had potatoes waiting for her for dinner. Her keys were stubborn in their hiding and Nicole dug round in her bag, struggling to feel their presence.

"Can I help you?" François offered, but Nicole found them in time and stuck her front door key in the lock. Her fingers were trembling as she pushed the door open.

"Make yourself comfortable," she offered and pointed to the lounge and he moved in the direction of the couch situated underneath the window. "I will be with you in a second, I need to change," she said and closed her bedroom door behind her after she had entered it.

"Nicole..." she heard him call to her as she opened her cupboard to find something comfortable to wear.

"Yes," she called back.

"Can I put the kettle on? I am really pressed for time," he said.

Oh flip! she thought. "Yes, if you want to," she said but hoped he would rather just sit on the couch. Nicole didn't want him to discover the lack of supplies in her kitchen. But unbeknownst to her, that was exactly what happened as he wanted to treat her by making her coffee and discovered there was nothing in her cupboards. He didn't mention it and closed the doors softly so that she wouldn't catch him doing so. He only switched the kettle on and went to take a seat on the couch again.

Nicole, in her panicked state, threw aside the idea of taking her time to dress comfortably and alluring, as she just wanted to get out of the bedroom and into the kitchen to avoid a catastrophe, in her opinion. She grabbed the first things she saw, black tracksuit pants and a grey fitted t-shirt and pulled it on. With her bare feet, she entered the hall and she sighed a sigh of relief when she saw he was sitting on the couch and nothing had been touched in the kitchen, except for the kettle, which was boiling by now.

"I don't have milk. I haven't had time to go buy some," she explained.

"Don't worry, I drink my coffee black," he lied.

Nicole finished the coffee and placed the two cups in front of him, before she went to sit next to him on the couch. They drank coffee and they fell into easy conversation about their respective days since their first meeting. They both kept the conversation light. François did apologise though for not contacting her sooner. He explained that they were very busy on the farm at the moment, harvesting the vegetables and the little free time he had, he had spent on sleep.

He did confess though that he thought about her a lot, and that they would soon be less busy, affording him time to visit her more. Not once did he attempt to touch Nicole, which she found refreshingly different from the men she was used to. He promised to visit her soon and she explained to him how her shifts worked so that he could plan his next visit around her working schedule. Their conversation was pleasant and comfortable and Nicole enjoyed his company and all too soon he looked at his watch and abruptly stood up. "Shit, I am going to be late," he said as the sun started to set on the distant horizon.

"I am really sorry, Nicole, but if I don't go now, I will miss supper and I won't get enough sleep for my hectic day tomorrow. I truly wish I could stay," he apologised while he already made his way to the front door. Very disappointed, she followed him.

"It is okay, I understand, but thank you for visiting. I really enjoyed it," she said softly. When he opened the front door, he flung around and before she could register what was happening, he took her shoulders in his hands and placed a kiss on her forehead.

"Lock the door when I leave," he ordered as he walked out of the door.

"I will," she promised as she watched him leave and she closed the door and locked it as she had promised.

Nicole went to the couch and flopped down on it. She felt happy for the first time in a few months. François seemed interested in actually spending time with her, Nicole, not someone just wanting her body. She had become so accustomed to the attentions of the policemen always flirting and making comments as soon as she was in their vicinity. She chose to ignore it as much as possible, but at times it made her feel as if there weren't any men left that had more on their minds than just sex. François made her feel cared for and she was excited at the prospect of this new relationship.

The week flew by as Nicole was light hearted because of François' visit. When the weekend drew closer, Sergeant Mostert reminded Nicole that he would pick her up the Saturday for their special duties at the Race Course. Nicole was excited; not only would she get to spend a day out, but she would spend it with Sergeant Mostert. He made everything fun. He was an optimist and could make anything seem like a positive thing. So on the Saturday, she dressed in her uniform and waited in the street in front of her apartment block for him to come pick her up, and as usual he was on time, with a warm smile to welcome her.

They drove to the race track, where there were already countless cars of eager punters parked in the parking lot and many more arriving. There was a buzz of excitement as the people made their way through the gates and to the betting cubicles. Sergeant Mostert led Nicole to the meet up point of the policemen working that day. There they were given their orders. They were not allowed to place bets, had to be visible and contactable.

They received coupons for their lunch, which they could redeem at the cafeteria. Nicole was pleased by this as she hadn't eaten a decent meal that whole week and was craving meat. They were paired up and luckily, Nicole got paired up with Sergeant Mostert as they were standing next to each other. Each pair got a hand radio between them and then they were sent off to patrol the area.

Sergeant Mostert took the lead and led Nicole to all the different areas, to explain to her the workings of the race course. He took her to the starting blocks, where he showed and explained how the starting cubicles worked. There were a few jockeys on their horses trying to coax their high strung horses into their separate starting cubicles. Some were tame and didn't resist being led into the cubicles, but there were two beautiful stallions that resisted by pulling away and shaking their heads. Nicole appreciated the muscles under their skins as it moved, and she could notice their superiority by their stately postures.

Then Sergeant Mostert took her to the show ring, where the horses could be appraised by the owners and the gamblers. Here Nicole saw the jockeys up close. They were all brightly dressed and were talking to the owners of the horses. The owners were smartly dressed. After some small talk and well wishes, the jockeys got on their horses, which were held by stable boys. The horses were led by the stable boys in a circle, while an announcer announced each horse's name and number as an introduction to the crowd, as well as by who it was owned.

It amazed Nicole how small the jockeys were. Not only were they short, but they couldn't have weighed more than 55 kgs, Nicole thought as they were led past her. This part of the race course was meticulously landscaped to impress. The surroundings looked luxurious and the owners had a small V.I.P. section from where they watched and where they were offered champagne to sip on. Nicole could see herself stand there sipping on champagne, while watching her pure bread walking past and her wealthy influential husband next to her, adoring her.

Her dad always said she was born for the finer things in life, but now she was here, standing in her police uniform, she suddenly felt insignificant. This feeling was a far cry from the feeling of pride she had had when first joining the Force, when she felt important by the knowledge that she was serving a good cause and she would be able to be independent. The realisation dawned on her that there was so much more to life than the tiny cocoon she found herself in. And for the first time in months, she felt hopelessly depressed by the life she saw before her as a police officer. Nicole turned to Sergeant Mostert. "I am hungry, can we go eat?" she asked, as she wanted to flee this confrontation with reality.

"I need to make some notes," he replied, not focussing on Nicole. Nicole for the first time saw the gamblers' gaze in Sergeant Mostert's eyes, as he was so focussed on the horses, writing down feverishly what horses raced and when. He looked fixated on the horses.

"We aren't allowed to bet," Nicole reminded him softly.

"I know," he whispered back without looking at her. "Don't worry, I have my ways. If you want to put a bet in as well, I will organise for you," he whispered.

"No, it's fine," Nicole said and although she actually wished she could, because she could do with the winnings, she didn't have money to bet with.

"Okay, then you can go eat. I will join you in a few minutes," Sergeant Mostert told her.

Nicole set off to the cafeteria without Sergeant Mostert. She ordered a burger with chips and a milkshake. She savoured every single bite and afterwards, she lit a cigarette while drinking a cup of coffee, when Sergeant Mostert came to join her. He ordered his meal and then told Nicole that he had betted on the Pick-Six. This is when you predict the first six places in the main race of the day. He was so sure he was going to win and kept on chatting like an excited child. The only thing that kept running thought Nicole's head was how he was able to make a bet while in uniform. It would have been impossible.

"How were you able to make a bet?" she said when she couldn't take the curiosity any longer. He then explained that he had a friend working at the track that would bet on his behalf and if he won money, he would give him ten percent of the winnings. This made sense, but Nicole was worried about what would happen if he was found out. He explained that this was not the worst thing that one could do and that there were few policemen left with a clean slate. Their misdoings could range from drinking on duty, to money laundering, the list was endless and therefore, most turned a blind eye to others' bending of the rules, since if they came clean, there would surely be someone who would rat them out as well.

"This is why, Nicole," and he looked Nicole seriously in her eyes, "you don't trust anyone, and you keep everything to yourself. Be very selective about who you trust," he continued. Nicole could see the earnestness in his eyes and decided to take his advice to heart.

When they had finished, Nicole felt very tired. They had been walking half the day and her stomach was full. Sergeant Mostert recognised the lazy look on her face and couldn't help feeling sorry for her, so he suggested she go to the ladies bathroom and catch a quick nap to recharge her batteries.

"Are you serious?" she asked at the prospect of sleeping.

"Yes, I have done it many times. I will be in that vicinity," and he pointed to the finish line. "If you want to join me again, I will cover for you," he said with a smile on his face.

Nicole knew she should have said no, but she so desperately wanted to close her eyes for a few minutes and she thought to herself that what she wanted to do was a lot less serious than what Sergeant Mostert had already done, so she thanked him and walked to the ladies bathroom, where she entered a stall, locked it behind her and took a seat on a closed toilet. She placed her handbag behind her head and stretched her legs out in front of her and before she knew it, she fell into a deep sleep, only to wake suddenly after what felt like a few minutes. She heard knocking on the door.

"Yes," she answered in her daze.

"Are you okay in there?" she heard a young girl's voice from outside of the stall.

"Um, yes…I will be out in a minute," she said as she straightened her clothes and hair.

"Okay," the girl said, and Nicole heard her footsteps as she left the bathroom. Nicole looked at her watch and saw that it was close to four o'clock. She had nearly slept for two hours; she needed to get to Sergeant Mostert, as the main race had probably already started.

Nicole found Sergeant Mostert hanging over the rail of the track as he cheered his picked horse for first place. He hadn't even missed Nicole as he didn't even turn to acknowledge her presence as she took a place next to him. She felt relieved that she was obviously not in trouble and just then Sergeant Mostert started cursing as his horse came second. Nicole was shocked at his behaviour as he was normally so gentle and composed.

Sergeant Mostert turned away from the rails and walked away, with Nicole trailing behind him. He ripped his betting tickets to pieces and threw them in the nearest dust bin as he passed it. Nicole knew he had probably lost a lot of money for him to react this way. He didn't speak again until they had been signed out by the officer in charge and was in the patrol vehicle on their way back home.

"Are you okay?" Nicole prodded him.

"Yes, I am," he said in his usual gentle voice as he had had enough time to gather himself.

"Don't start betting, Nicole," he said simply and she nodded wide-eyed at him, as she recognised a torment in him that she didn't want to experience.

The following day, Sunday, Nicole was awakened by a knock on the door. She was still rubbing sleep from her eyes as she peeped through the peephole and saw nobody. She turned to climb back into bed when the doorbell rang again and she flung the front door open agitatedly. As she did so, François grabbed her around her waist and shouted, "Wha!"

Nicole got such a fright that she uttered a weak yelp. François nearly doubled over at the situation as he laughed.

"It's not funny!" Nicole scolded him and turned to walk into her apartment, still dressed in her very short nighty.

"Well, I think it is," he said joyfully. "Come on, you cannot possibly let this perfect day go by without walking on the sea sand," he asked while he followed her into the apartment. Nicole smiled at him, she was glad he had come to visit.

"Wait for me in the lounge, I will get dressed quickly," she said and slipped away to dress into a pair of denim shorts and a weathered tank top. She pushed her feet into a pair of flip flops and tied her hair into a knot on top of her head. Little strands of hair fell out and framed her face. She opted to only apply a little mascara to enhance her long lashes. When she entered the lounge, François was sitting in an upright position at the end of the couch as if he was anxious about something. He looked up at her as she came in and smiled appreciatively as he ogled her beautiful legs.

"Listen, I brought you something," he said uncomfortably but whilst trying to mask his uneasiness.

"Why?" Nicole said before she thought it through and she realised that it could have sounded rude, but didn't mean it that way. She just didn't understand the need for him to bring her anything.

"No, it's nothing serious!" he countered as he didn't want her to feel uncomfortable with him bringing her gifts so soon in the relationship. "I will go get it in the car quickly if you don't mind?" he said and didn't give her a chance to reply as he leapt from the couch onto his feet and walked out of the apartment.

"Okay, then I will make some coffee…" she called out to him. He didn't even take five minutes to return and as he entered, he held a huge weaved basket filled with vegetables.

Nicole started laughing; she thought him to be so sweet and caring and a typical farmer, bearing gifts of nature. She fondly remembered how her grandfather told her how he, who had also been a farmer, would pay the doctor with live chickens, eggs or vegetables.

François stopped in the doorway, not sure if she thought him ridiculous and hesitated for a second before he continued and placed the basket on the counter top. Nicole immediately swallowed her laughter as she realised he might take it up the wrong way.

"Oh, my word, how sweet you are," she said quickly before he misunderstood her. François smiled at her proudly.

"We are allowed to take some of the crop when harvesting and since I cannot possibly use it all, I wondered if you wanted some?" he explained his gift. Nicole was at his side by now and started looking through the basket. It was filled with carrots, broccoli, corn and cauliflower. There was also a two-litre plastic bottle filled with fresh milk from the dairy farm next to the farm where François farmed. Nicole noticed there were no potatoes.

"Thank you so much!" she said gratefully and turned to him while she spontaneously threw her arms around his neck and gave him a tight hug and planted a kiss on his cheek. Finally, she had more than potatoes to cook. From there on, he would once a week, bring her vegetables and milk when he came to visit. Sometimes he would also bring her fresh eggs, when there were more than they used on the farm.

They spent the day at the beach, playing beach tennis, walking along the coastline and sunbathing. They talked about their childhoods, their families and their goals for the future. While he had many, Nicole was at a loss as to what she wanted from the future, she was living her life day by day, not affording herself the luxury of thinking further than tomorrow. She felt downcast when confronted with the question of what she wanted to achieve in the future. She opted for the answer: "I will see when I get there."

Recognising her mood, he took her hand and reassured her: "One doesn't need to know exactly what one wants at the starting point, as you go along you will eventually find your heart's desire."

"I hope so…" she replied as they sat next to each other and watched the sun set.

Nicole loved his warm and down to earth and unpretentious company. She realised that she could spend a lot of time in his company without him annoying or offending her.

"Come, we must go back," he said as he stood up and pulled her to her feet, when the last red and orange tinted rays of the sun lingered on the horizon. They drove back to her apartment in silence, both of them having the whole day to contemplate their new-found friendship and the pleasure it brought to both of them. On their way back, François stopped for a pizza and a few beers. Nicole was grateful he did this as it meant he wanted to stay a little longer. She thought he would want to get back to the farm and she didn't want him to go.

"I hope you are hungry?" he said as he climbed back into the pick-up truck.

The pizza smelled delicious.

"Of course, yes," she smiled at him as he placed the pizza on the seat in-between them.

They finished the pizza while drinking beer. Nicole hadn't had as much fun in a long time. The conversation flowed easily and soon it was close to twelve o' clock. François was looking at his watch.

"Oh no, time flies when you are having fun," he said with a smile on his face, surprised by the fact that he had stayed so long without even realising it.

"Yes, you should probably go..." Nicole dragged the words out like a little girl regretting having to say goodbye.

"Except if you don't mind me sleeping over tonight?" he suggested as he didn't feel like driving back after he had had a couple of beers.

"Yes, of course, you may!" Nicole said excitedly. "I will make a bed for you on the couch," she said and went to fetch a cushion and blanket for him. She was still innocent in her thinking that he would want to sleep anywhere else but in her bed.

"Thank you," he said while he adored her enthusiasm in preparing his bed on the couch.

Nicole cleared the coffee table of the leftover pizza and beer bottles. She placed the left-over pizza in the fridge and then went to say goodnight to François, who was sitting on his temporary bed. The curtains behind him were still open and she asked him if she should close it for him.

"No! You have such a beautiful view from here, it would be sinful to hide it," he said as he turned to look at the millions of sparkling stars strewn across the dark sky.

"If you put the lights off, you can really appreciate it better," Nicole said, pleased at the fact that he too appreciated nature and her favourite place in the flat, so she walked over to the light switch and switched the lights off. Immediately the harsh synthetic light disappeared, and the soft low glow of natural light spilled into the room. They were instantly transported into a magical time of the day. Where long shadows linger and draw distorted shapes on their surroundings.

Nicole stood behind him, watching the dark sky in awe, the bright stars and the city lights, dancing in the night. Instinctively, she moved over to the window and pushed them open to let the cool sea breeze fill the room.

"How fortunate you are," François said, deep in thought, while not looking at Nicole.

Nicole stood at the window smelling the salt in the air. It took all her will to turn around and leave the room so that he could sleep. For a moment, she regretted letting him have the couch.

"Okay, goodnight François," she said as she started to move towards her room.

François grabbed her wrist in her passing and he came to his feet. Before she could say anything, he took her in his arms and placed a soft warm kiss on her lips. He pressed it down firmly on hers before he pulled away, but not letting her out of his grip.

"I really had an amazing day with you," he said while looking down into her eyes.

"Me too," she said endearingly. Then he bent forward and kissed her gently. His tongue stayed absent in the kiss. His lips softly took hers in his mouth while he carefully sucked and pulled on her lips with his. Nicole followed his lead and after he pulled away, he placed another firm kiss on her mouth, before he let her go.

"Night," he said as he pursed his lips together as if he was holding himself back from doing more.

"Night," Nicole took her cue and turned to go to her bedroom. There she closed the door behind her and poured herself a warm bath. After she had bathed, she dressed into her nighty and climbed into her cold hard bed. She suddenly felt lonely in the dark room with its tiny window, which faced the back of the building, with its washing lines, which reminded her of her responsibilities and the depressing consequences of it. Nicole stared at the few stars she could spot from her window. She would have wanted to open the window to be able to smell the fresh air at least, but since the window was facing the walkway behind her, she couldn't as anyone would be able to climb through it. Nicole tossed and turned. It seemed impossible to fall asleep. Then she remembered she had milk and she thought that drinking a warm glass of milk would help her settle down and sleep, as it had done when she was still a child in her mother's house.

Nicole took care not to wake François, so she tiptoed to the fridge. François was lying with his back to the kitchen and she gathered that he was already fast asleep. The light of the refrigerator brought light to the fact that there was actually food in her fridge and she smiled at the sight of it. She looked back at François, while still holding the door open and in that moment she felt a deep appreciation for the caring he had displayed in the short time they had known each other.

He obviously was in this for more than just the physical part, as he didn't even want to share her bed. And now, where she stood, she actually felt disappointed that he didn't ask to do so. She turned back to the fridge and took the milk from it to pour a glass.

"Can I have some too?" she heard François' voice carrying in from the lounge. Startled, Nicole squinted to look at François in the dark.

"Of course, yes," she said and took two glasses from the cupboard and poured milk into them and then warmed the milk in the microwave before she picked it up to join François in the living room. As Nicole placed the glass of milk on the table in front of François, he moved his legs under the blanket covering it, so that Nicole could sit next to him and he signalled to her to sit on the spot.

"So, you can't sleep either?" he asked her.

"No. Not really," she admitted.

They drank their milk while they stared at the stars. When they had finished, François laid back down. Nicole took it as a signal that he wanted to sleep so she stood up to take the glasses to the kitchen, but as she bent forward to pick them up, he took her wrist gently. Without saying anything, he opened his blanket with the other hand so that she could join him under its warmness and she did. He let go of her wrist and held his arm open for her to come lay in it, which she did.

Nicole felt relieved that he wanted her close to him and she snuggled into his body, smelling him while her cheek pressed against the smooth warm skin on his chest. François folded his other arm around Nicole's shoulder, cradling her, while pressing his chin against her head. They lay like that, in silence, while his breathing slowed down to a peaceful pace. Nicole felt his warm body through her nighty and she felt aroused by his hard, naked chest against her stomach. Nicole's hands spontaneously started searching the outlines of François' chest, slowly circling out to his middle.

François had already nodded off and lay perfectly still as she stroked him. Nicole's fingers kept on investigating the contours of his body and he groaned softly. Nicole took it that he enjoyed it and before she could stop herself her fingers slipped in under the elastic of his trousers. Nicole softly let her fingers slip through the hair concealed by his trousers and then pulled it back, while softly digging into his skin while doing so, before she came too close to his manhood. She did this a couple of times before François stirred and groaned harder while he slipped his own hand under the elastic of his pants, taking her hand in a firm grip, holding it still for a moment. Nicole kept her hand as still as possible, not knowing if he wanted her to stop or continue.

François arched his back slowly while he pressed his loins forward, thrusting against the air above him, then he pressed her hand down until her fingers touched the soft skin of his erection. Nicole followed his lead and encircled him with her fingers. His penis fitted perfectly in her hand with only the tip protruding from the top of her fingers. His erection was as relaxed as he was, nothing impressive.

She felt a little disappointed by the lack of substance as she started stimulating him in the hopes of it growing in size and determination, but to her disappointment it didn't. Nicole frowned and wondered why she didn't have the desired effect on him, but before she could intensify her attempts in giving him a proper erection, he pulled her hand from him and out of his pants.

"Sorry, I can't do this," he said, and he pulled her closer into his arms and gave her a hug.

"It's okay," she said although she didn't understand why he wouldn't want her to pleasure him. She was too embarrassed to press the issue further, so she lay still while he fell asleep and she wondered about the reason for his inability to be aroused by her. After a while, she too fell asleep and they slept like that until the next morning when the sharpness of the rising sun woke them both.

"I will make coffee," Nicole said as she jumped to her feet, still confused by the previous night.

"Thank you, Nicole," François said as he pulled his shirt over his head and headed for the bathroom. When he had finished washing his face and brushing his teeth, he appeared only to drink his coffee and inform Nicole that he needed to go. From that evening, Nicole didn't even try to push things in that direction again. François would come to visit her, they would chat, spend the day together, they would kiss, but nothing more and then they would sleep in each other's arms. It became a welcome and secure ritual.

At times, Nicole did wonder about the fact that he didn't want to go any further, but finally decided that he probably was really proper and didn't want to have sex until they were really serious, since that was the way they, as Christians, were brought up to believe things were done. Nicole too was brought up this way, but to her it seemed a natural progression of things, so she didn't overthink the rules of her religion, when it came to intercourse.

Now that Nicole had the companionship of a decent young man in her life, it felt as if her life had direction. As with most, Nicole now had a sense of security, and François' presence, gallantry, morality and steadfastness had a slow but deep effect on Nicole. Suddenly that which didn't bother Nicole previously, started to bother her to the point where she spent time trying to make sense of it. At first it was little things, like her realising how much her language had deteriorated, to the point where every second descriptive word was replaced by a swear word.

She first realised this when François commented on it. She had been bombarded by the way the rest of her fellow policemen spoke to such an extent that she had been desensitised, not realising how much she swore. She felt embarrassed that she had succumbed to their way of doing things. That was only the beginning of her awareness as she then realised that those that had to uphold the law, were first to break it, as the policemen didn't think it wrong to hold shift barbeques on their night shifts, where they would sometimes drink a beer or two.

She heard how the policemen would boast to each other how they had fun chasing vagrants in the bush where they slept, terrorising them and sometimes even assaulting them, in an attempt to get rid of boredom. Nicole, countless times, had to witness how police vehicles were used for private matters while the policemen were on duty, even fetching kids from school and doing shopping, while they should be patrolling their area. The worst was the crude way the men spoke of women and how the women in the police force were subjected to sexual harassment, with men grabbing their bums, making comments on the size of their boobs and discussing and guessing the size of the policewomen's nipples. And except for this, which Nicole had witnessed first-hand, Nicole heard horror stories of officers actually forcing young policewomen to touch them inappropriately or even worse, them touching the young recruits inappropriately.

The girls didn't dare complain as the men stuck together like glue. Those girls who dared complain were transferred or targeted until they decided to quit. Nicole realised that she had ignored all this, because until now the influence on her life, up to this point, had not been significant enough to overpower her need for financial independence. Now that François was part of her life, she started wondering if she too shouldn't take a stronger stand against that which she thought was wrong, but she wasn't ready yet.

She weighed the consequences of having to take a firm stand, and it didn't make sense to rock a boat, which she single-handedly couldn't fix, so she decided to turn a blind eye and only work on her swearing and try to steer clear of the misbehaviour of her fellow officers.

This survival attitude came in good stead, as she didn't make any enemies in the police force, nor did she tarnish her perfect record. She opted to make as little waves as possible and kept amicable relations with the rest of her colleges. On one such occasion, she was reminded of how necessary it was to be on friendly footing with them, when some of the local policemen where pissed off with the owner of the local club, because he dared to refuse one of them entry, as he was drunk.

Nicole had joined Samantha on an evening out. They were still dancing when one of the young men came to her and whispered in her ear to get out of the club as soon as possible and go home. Nicole didn't ask questions, but did as she was told. Luckily for her, she was warned; those who weren't suffered an attack of teargas canisters being opened into the air vents to the club, causing havoc with people trampling each other and a fire to break out in the kitchen, as the staff couldn't see what they were doing.

Nicole only heard of the incident the next day when the men were talking to each other about what they had done. This type of bullying was normal amongst the policemen, and business owners seldom complained about the terrorising, as it made them vulnerable to even more attacks. There wasn't much a Constable, like Nicole, would be able to do to change this, so Nicole didn't even try.

Naively, Nicole thought that this misbehaviour was about as bad as it got and since in her opinion it wasn't too serious, she kept to herself. She at least did her duty to the best of her ability and believed that this behaviour wasn't the norm. At least she had François, who was a separate, independent entity from the police force, who gave her a sense of normality. Work and the life in the police force was a world within a world, which she thought she could separate and that the two didn't necessarily have to influence one another. Unfortunately, this was a wish more than it was a reality; Nicole was still oblivious to this.

Chapter 15

As per usual, Nicole found herself posted in the Charge Office with Sergeant Swart one winter's afternoon. Nicole was beginning to become immune to the feeling of disappointment each time she heard the news and the fact that she had seen François the previous day made up for the fact that she had to tolerate the Sergeant today. The day started off quiet. It was a Friday and as usual after four in the afternoon, prisoners awaiting bail were brought back from court for detainment in their cells. Nicole helped the Sergeant receiving the prisoners, taking stock of their possessions, writing it up in a register and booking them into the Incidence Register.

Nicole loved the methodical process of painstakingly filling in the registers. She was one of the only policewomen, except for Ava, to do this accurately and she took pride in her work. Although it was not the most challenging work, it was a lot of paperwork, since they weren't computerised as yet. There was a certain consistency and order to it that she found comforting and reassuring. While she was helping Sergeant Swart to do the administration, he and the Officers delivering the prisoners were busy searching the prisoners for hidden sharp objects or weapons. They took their belts and shoe laces to protect them from committing suicide with it or killing one another.

One prisoner in particular was a bit cocky as he was an illegal immigrant and didn't regard the South African white-dominated society and its restrictions applicable to him. He, as a graduate of Cambridge University, couldn't understand why he was detained like an animal and even worse, treated like one. It was a very tall black man from the Republic of Congo. He was fluent in English although his native tongue was French. He had gentle, proud eyes, but Nicole sensed that he knew hardship.

This was because they have been fighting a civil war for the past thirty years, unbeknownst to Nicole, and also the reason for his presence in South Africa. As Nicole took their belongings and had to write it up in an inventory, which they had to sign, she needed to communicate with them. All the prisoners were very subdued as they were all—but one—black South Africans and were used to the brutality that they had to face, if not. The other prisoner was a white male who had committed fraud and was treated significantly better than the rest. Although he too was detained in the same holding cell, he was locked up in his own cell, while the others were cramped up in two small cells. He got a blanket while the others had four blankets between the eight of them.

And prisoners do not share, except if they were about to have intercourse and in that instance, it was more like forceful sharing. Rape was another one of prison's perks. The black prisoners were pushed around; they were sworn at, called names and overall treated with no respect. If they asked something, they could expect a slap in the face as a reply, like Sergeant Swart displayed to Nicole's surprise as one of the prisoners asked to use the loo and Sergeant Swart, who was in a very bad mood, swung around and slapped him so hard across his face that he stumbled while spitting out his words in Afrikaans: "Jou fokken dom kaffir! Met wie de fok praat jy? Ek is nie jou donnerse meit nie en jy sal my meneer noem."

With this, he swung another slap in his direction and missed him with a few centimetres. This translated to: "You fucking dumb kaffir! To whom the fuck do you think you are talking? I am not your bloody servant and you will call me mister." Nicole stood there in disbelief; it happened so fast that she didn't know what to do or say.

On the one hand, she wanted to ask Sergeant Swart what the hell he was thinking assaulting a prisoner and in front of her where she was now immediately a witness and would have to recall the events if anyone laid a charge against him. Nicole panicked in her ignorance. She felt disgusted not only by the way Sergeant Swart treated the man, but also about the fact that he had that instance made her a part of a very difficult situation, as when faced with lying to protect him, Nicole didn't know if she would be able to and she knew that not doing so would have dire consequences.

What Nicole didn't realise was that this seldom happened in the Apartheid Era and when it did, it didn't go far, as people hardly ever showed up for trail, if the legal system even let it go that far, so she actually had nothing to worry about. Nicole stared at Sergeant Swart in disbelief as he turned his back on the older man whom he had slapped to continue his work. The poor man, who was arrested for petty theft of a packet of rice, which he stole for his starving family, was in his fifties and as a result of the assault and his desperate need of a toilet, unwillingly relieved himself on the floor. As the smell of his urine filled the room, Nicole worriedly looked at the puddle; she felt desperate and wanted to help the man hide it, but she could do nothing as the old man found himself held up by his throat against the wall behind him, his feet dangling in the air.

Sergeant Swart pushed him up against the wall so hard that his wind was taken from his lungs and he struggled for air. Nicole wanted to scream, but no sound came out; she looked at the young immigrant for help as he was bigger than Sergeant Swart, but knew he probably wouldn't or couldn't do anything. What she saw in his eyes was respect, respect for her compassion, respect for her desperation and wanting to help, respect for her disregard for the rules of her society and respect that she didn't want to conform. She also saw compassion for her situation and he as a true man with honour acted, not only to protect the old man, but Nicole from having to stand up to her superior and with that Nicole's respect and compassion with the suppressed races in the country grew.

The young man took two steps forward and took the Sergeant by his shoulder, but before he could say anything Sergeant Swart went ballistic, letting the old man fall to the floor, gasping for air. Nicole didn't even see Sergeant Swart's fist making contact with the illegal immigrant's face. She was looking at the old man on the floor; all she saw was a body falling and hitting his head on the cement floor with such force that it made a sickening slapping sound and then there was silence.

The other two policemen that were there stopped Sergeant Swart as he wanted to carry on with his assault on the limp body in front of him.

"No! That is enough!" one said and it seemed to bring sense back to Sergeant Swart as he stepped back and started breathing deeply in an attempt to calm himself.

"Fuck, man! The fucking bastard!" he swore as he turned to the registers in front of him and he shook his hands and arms as if he tried to shake what had happened from his being.

"Let's get these bastards to the cells," he continued. Nicole was shaking by now where she stood, frozen. The old man looked at her in a pleading, but also judgmental manner and she felt ashamed for not having enough courage to stand up against Sergeant Swart when she needed to. Now because of her, the immigrant had been hurt. She held her breath, hoping for some sign of life from the still body lying on the floor and she could feel wetness building up in her eyes. The other two policemen saw Nicole's reaction to what had happened and with the agenda of protecting themselves from prosecution, immediately went forward to the immigrant and turned him on his back to check for any sign of life.

"Hey you!" the one said in a thick Afrikaans accent, "are you still alive?" while he softly slapped him in his face in an attempt to revive him. The man slowly came to and started to groan. He was totally disorientated when they helped him to his feet and made him sit on the floor, as he was unable to stand.

Nicole was nauseous as she instinctively knew there was something seriously wrong with the man, as where there were once intelligent eyes, bewilderment from confusion looked back at her. She bit on her lip as she knew the man who he once was had been erased in that one sick incident. Her whole being screamed, but her body refused to act on it.

Nicole excused herself as she felt her guilt and disgust wanting to burst from her insides and she rushed to the toilet where she vomited into the toilet bowl in front of her, until her stomach spasmed, but nothing came out. When she returned, the Charge Office was once again quiet. The policemen had left and Sergeant Swart was sitting behind the Incidence Register, as if nothing had happened. Nicole took her place next to him. She sat in silence for a while and then she dared ask.

"So what do I write in my pocketbook?" as she remembered that all accounts had to be documented in it.

"Nothing," he was quick to answer.

"Nothing?" she asked with tears welling up in her eyes.

"Yes. Nothing," he said and looked at her and his eyes scared her.

"I will not lie," she said softly as she looked down.

"I already made an entry that the prisoner was rowdy and that I had to use physical force to detain him. There was a struggle and he fell," he said agitated and gave Nicole a death stare. "Wasn't that what happened?" he asked in a threatening tone.

Nicole just looked at him as she wiped the tears from her cheeks. She didn't know what to do.

"You just keep quiet, it isn't your problem. The guy is fine! Believe me, the bastards have wooden heads. They don't die easily," he said as he started laughing, trying to make light of the situation. Nicole's stomach turned again as vomit found its way into her mouth, but she swallowed it. Then she looked down to the floor and stayed that way until the shift ended.

When the other officers returned from their patrols and Sergeant Swart had to give the Charge Office over to the next Charge Office Commander, they had to do inspection of the prisoners and check for any injuries as to note them in the Incidence Register. While this inspection was taking place, Nicole's heart raced in her chest and she was praying that nobody would ask her about the young man.

Luckily, everyone was tired and more focussed on getting home, than on the fact that she looked stressed and was abnormally quiet. Luckily for Sergeant Swart, who escorted the next Charge Office Commander to the cells, the young man didn't bear any visible marks on his face and when asked why he was lying so quietly, Sergeant Swart said he is probably sleeping and that he had spoken to him a few minutes back, which his colleague in good faith believed. The takeover went smoothly and Nicole got away without having to disclose anything of what had happened in the Charge Office that evening.

This didn't mean that she got away with it; she was ridden with guilt and had to write a false entry into her pocketbook of her whereabouts when the incident had happened. Nicole wrote up that she was in the toilet and thus would be able to deny that she had been present when the assault took place. This knowledge she took home with her, to digest it in the coming hours of the night and to make her disappointment in herself and the fact that she had become an accomplice to a crime, in a second of cowardness, part of her being, her burden and her mental breakdown.

She was now as much a part of the "Force" as she was forced to realise that she was no civilian anymore. She had been infected by the Force suddenly, without warning, like all who join the force are. It is like a virus, catching you unawares when you least expect it, but taking hold of your being in such a way that even if you want to get rid of it, it becomes more difficult to rid you of the pustules of guilt that come with the survival within its perimeters, than most are willing to bear.

Nicole didn't sleep much that night and the next day was the first day since she joined the police force that she didn't feel like going to work. She felt emotionally drained by the little sleep, but she gathered herself and walked to work. She dragged her feet and when she passed John who was busy in the garden watering the grass, she didn't even look up to greet him, and she didn't even notice him. Nicole entered the station; everything looked fine as everyone was busy with the changing of shifts. There was no fuss; Sergeant Swart was on his post in the Charge Office.

"Come on, Nicole, you are taking over Charge Office today," Sergeant Mostert said hastily as he was trying to organise the rest of the shift.

Nicole was taken aback by this, as she thought Sergeant Swart would be posted as Charge Office Commander, but also slightly excited at the prospect and immediately, with a new sense of purpose, she took her place behind the registers and started carrying over the registers. Sergeant Swart was posted with her in the Charge Office, but he was busy with inspection, as were the other officers.

Sergeant Mostert came to Nicole when they had finished. He was holding everyone's pocketbooks and came to ask Nicole for hers. This was normal for the Shift Commander to check the pocketbooks and sign them after inspection. Today however, after Nicole handed her book over, Sergeant Mostert went to the Station Commander's office along with the previous shift's Commander and his shift's pocketbooks.

"Continue with your duties and the rest may go home. We will return these on your next shift," Sergeant Mostert said as he lifted the pocketbooks for them to see. When Sergeant Mostert and the shift had left, Nicole leant over to Sergeant Swart's chair and asked: "What is going on?" hoping it had nothing to do with the previous night.

Sergeant Swart looked at her seriously: "One of the prisoners escaped last night."

"Oh my God! How?" she asked shocked. Nicole ran her mind through the possible ways in which the prisoner could possibly escape, but there were hardly any logical ones she could think of, as the cells were to her mind impenetrable.

"I don't know all the details, as I said it happened overnight," he said glumly and today he looked more miserable than usual, but there wasn't the usual hint of aggression, he looked depressed. Sergeant Swart didn't even look at her when he spoke, he just stared at the table in front of him and only looked up when the first complainants entered the Charge Office. He helped the civilians in a civil manner and then went to his chair and wrote up his dockets.

Soon, Nicole didn't even bother to figure his mood out, since the day was busier than usual. When Sergeant Mostert came back into the office, he looked at Swart and then at Nicole and shook his head.

"Does anyone of you know anything about what happened last night?" he asked seriously.

"I don't even know what happened," Nicole replied while she was secretly hoping he wasn't talking about the assault.

"And you?" Sergeant Mostert looked at Sergeant Swart.

"No. You are talking about the escape?" Sergeant Swart asked. "We weren't even on duty," Sergeant Swart said innocently.

"Well Nicole," Sergeant Mostert started explaining while he first continued to look at Sergeant Swart, assessing him before he turned his attention to Nicole. "Apparently, one of the prisoners went missing out of the cells between your shift and the next. You say you know nothing and the shift who took over had received all the prisoners as they signed for them, but confessed they didn't do a proper head count. When they finally did do a proper inspection, they were one prisoner short," he explained, and he looked somewhat disappointed and worried.

As Shift Commander, it was his responsibility to be aware of all that took place on the shift and would be held partially responsible for anything going wrong on his shift, except if it was proven he had no way of knowing or had a part in it.

"As far as I know, all the prisoners were in the cells when we signed over. This is so weird," Nicole said confused. "Did he break out?"

"No Nicole, nobody broke out, it is impossible that the prisoner had just disappeared, and the weirdest part is he was only in as an illegal immigrant, so I cannot understand why he would try to escape. He wasn't a hardened criminal," Sergeant Mostert said with a frown on his forehead as he tried to figure it out. Nicole felt her heart sink into her shoes as she heard who had disappeared and she looked at Sergeant Swart. Sergeant Swart was looking back at her.

"What?" he asked, annoyed at Nicole for drawing attention to him.

"Nothing," Nicole said softly and she looked at the table in front of her. Nicole was properly pissed off with Sergeant Swart as she knew he had something to do with it.

"Well, there will be an investigation, as someone wasn't doing their job," Sergeant Mostert said as he turned to join the men outside.

When Nicole and Sergeant Swart were alone, she questioned him about it. He convincingly explained to Nicole that he really did place the prisoner in the cell and had nothing to do with the man's disappearance. Nicole believed him, but wondered why or how he disappeared. Sergeant Swart told her that no matter what, they were free of blame as the shift that took over had signed that all prisoners were in their cells and unharmed. So if anything had happened to the prisoner, it would be that shift's problem and therefore, she should relax.

Nicole decided not to ponder on it too much and she continued working as if nothing had happened. The day couldn't end soon enough and their rest days were a great relief as work wasn't that much fun anymore. Sergeant's Swart's presence had now become more problematic, than it was up until this point. He was unpredictable and he scared her.

Nicole fell into a deep sleep after their last night shift before their off days, only to wake from a knock on the door after six the evening. She had been so tired that she had slept the whole day. Disorientated, she jumped out of her bed, not realising she only had a t-shirt and panties on. As she unlocked the front door she realised her predicament and hid behind the door as she peeped around the edge of the door to see who it was. François' friendly face was looking at her with amusement as the top part of her thigh peeped out as well.

"Mmmmmm," he said, pressing his lips together and pulling them into a smile.

"I am sorry, I will go get dressed," she apologised and fled to her room to pull some sweatpants on. She forgot to think of putting a bra on as well and much to François' amusement, greeted him with her nipples protruding through the thin material of her T-shirt.

"Mmmmm...." he teased her as she pulled away from the hug she gave him and he looked down to where the tiny outlines of her nipples proudly displayed themselves.

"Oh shit!" she said as she folded her arms over her chest. "Wait here!" she said as she went back into her bedroom to find a bra. When she returned a warm cup of coffee was waiting for her on the coffee table.

"Thank you," she said as she gratefully flopped down on the sofa into his opened arm he held for her. She snuggled into the warm safety of his caring.

"So...are you going to join me for the next two days? I am going to Worcester to visit my aunt. I told them about you and she said you are more than welcome to come with. They would like to meet you," he explained.

"You know what? I would love to get away for a few days," she smiled up at him. "When are we going?"

"As soon as you are packed…" he smiled back at her and kissed her on her forehead, releasing her as she jumped to her feet.

"Well then, I will get packing," she said excitedly and did so.

The drive to Worcester was peaceful, as they drove through the Hottentots Holland mountain range. The whole valley was dipped in shades of green as the winter rains had filled the whole landscape with life. The Hugo's River curved alongside the N1 and Nicole watched mounts of white foam dance on the water as it raced down the river bed alongside them. It was slightly overcast, and misty banks swallowed the tops of the mountains on either side of them until they finally opened up to the flat plain behind it.

The road was lined with fields and soon they were in Worcester. It wasn't a very large town and François' aunt lived in the better part of the town. Although it was the more privileged area, her house looked quite plain. It was a four-bedroomed home with an outside cottage, where her parents lived. As François pulled into the yard, his aunt came out to greet them. She was obviously waiting for his arrival. She was a large woman with short blond hair, tanned skin and a friendly smile. She looked like she should have been living on a farm and not in town. She had slacks on and a buttoned-up blouse with sandals. The fact that she looked so friendly and relaxed made Nicole feel relaxed about meeting her. Two Jack Russells were jumping at her ankles for some attention as she showed François where to park his car.

"Welcome, welcome!" she said as she zoomed in on Nicole, as Nicole climbed out of the car and before Nicole knew what had hit her, she was stuck in a firm embrace. Nicole welcomed it as it made her feel at home and she tried to free her hands enough to reciprocate the hug, but the woman let her loose before she managed to do so.

"I am Mara," she said, "and you must be Nicole. You have done well, François!" she said as she turned her attentions to François, not giving Nicole a chance to say a single word.

All Nicole could do was smile, she was quite a jovial character and Nicole knew that she would be the entertainment of the visit, so she picked up her bags and followed François and Mara into the house. They followed Mara into the passage where she stopped at the first room and said: "This will be your room," assuming they were sleeping together.

Nicole looked at François, confused. He smiled at her. "Come on, you heard Aunt Mara!" he said as he gently pushed her in the small of her back to enter the room, which she reluctantly did.

"I will leave you two to settle in and then I will meet you in the kitchen," Mara informed them. The room was extremely neat, with white linen on the bed, towels laid out on it, and fresh flowers in a vase on the dressing table. There was only one bed, a double bed, in the middle of the room and Nicole looked at François. Nicole couldn't understand that Mara offered them a bed to share, as it was frowned upon for a young unmarried couple to share a bed.

"Are we sharing this room?" Nicole asked François in disbelief.

"Yes, I hope you don't mind," he said as he walked over to where Nicole stood and where she dropped her belongings.

"No, it's fine," she said. He smiled at her and took her in his arms as he looked into her face.

"You know, I think Mara likes you," he smiled.

"Well, I like her," Nicole replied and then François kissed her tenderly. As they hadn't been very physical in their relationship, this took her off guard and she gave in to the kiss. His kiss was warm and steady and although it wasn't the most passionate kiss she had had before, the surprise of it managed to arouse her enough to lean into him and kiss him back gently. She followed his lead, not wanting to do something to spoil the mood. He placed his hands firmly in the middle of her back and pushed her into his hard body.

Nicole felt the comfort of his tenderness enfold her and she closed her eyes as her heart started quickening its pace and then, as suddenly as it happened, it was over as he pulled away from her. She opened her eyes and studied his face, looking down at her out of breath and holding her by her shoulders as if he was afraid she would come closer. Nicole saw something in his eyes. If he wasn't so in control, she would have sworn it was the reflection of a passion wanting to be unleashed, but his composure made her unsure. She opted to stay still and let him take the lead in everything, since she sensed that he was able and used to closing up in an instant if he didn't feel in control. Nicole looked at him, hoping he would continue to kiss her.

He in return was taken by surprise by the passion he had felt when kissing Nicole, there was only one person before Nicole that could make his blood boil the way it did with Nicole and she was part of the reason he didn't even pursue a girl up until now. The girl was out of bounds for him and he thought he would forever be trapped in the grip of his child hood crush. The girl with whom he had grown up with and had his first kiss, his first everything with. He was until this kiss trapped in the web of their passion for each other.

Nicole's presence was slowly breaking down the walls that had kept him in his obsession with the one he wasn't even to think about. François felt strangely saddened that his obsession wasn't as strong as he had thought it was, but also elated that he had found someone that could stir the same emotions in him and for this he was grateful to her, as he now looked at her slightly blushed lips, from his kiss. He smiled at her as he realised he could love her.

"Come, let's go get some coffee, before they miss us," he said with a mysterious smile on his face and took Nicole's hand and pulled her to the kitchen.

In the kitchen, Mara and her mother was sitting at the kitchen table. They both looked up at the two entering the kitchen. François took a seat opposite the two women and pulled a chair out for Nicole so that she could join him. The two older women were grinning at Nicole, waiting anxiously that she would say something. There were four cups of coffee on the table and some home baked biscuits. Mara and her mother were already sipping on their coffee and after each sip they would hold it and grin at Nicole. Nicole felt under pressure to say something.

"Hi, I am Nicole," she said in the direction of the older woman and stretched over the table to shake the woman's hand.

"It doesn't work that way," the old woman said, smiling at Nicole. "Come here," she said, indicating to Nicole to come to her. "Here, we hug." Nicole laughed and jumped to her feet to give François' grandmother a firm hug. His gran held her for longer than was necessary, but Nicole didn't mind.

"Nicole, you can call me Nanna," she said as she let go. When Nicole took her seat, she was drawn into a pleasant conversation with the two women who were asking her about herself. They sat around the table for nearly two hours. Nicole loved François' family, they were down to earth and welcoming. François, although he took part in the conversation, gave the women the space to bond properly.

Soon enough, Mara stood up to start preparing supper as it was getting dark outside.

"Come, you must see this!" François said excitedly and pulled Nicole to her feet by her arm. Nicole followed him outside onto the porch. Mara's house was situated on a hill and close to the highway from where they could see the stretched-out landscape. The whole landscape was painted orange with long grey shadows reaching out over the ground as the sun was slowly moving to the west. It was beautiful and Nicole filled her lungs with the fresh air of the country. She was used to the salty moist evening air of Table View, but here the air was crispy dry with a hint of dust mixed into it, but fresh and unspoiled.

Table View was slowly being swallowed by Cape Town's suburbs, which were rapidly expanding with new developments. This saddened Nicole as she missed the unscathed coastline with its white sandy dunes and indigenous plants. Unfortunately in the name of tourism and town beautifying, the coastline was developed as well and where there were once dunes, they were landscaped and replanted, with wooden walk ways periodically spaced so that visitors wouldn't walk over the newly planted greenery. It's ironic how nature takes its own course, as the plants struggled to take root and the sand banks that were created were being blown away by nature's breath.

Nicole smiled at the thought and looked at the miles of untouched land. She knew it would only be a matter of time, before this landscape would also be populated by the ever-hungry entrepreneur. As she was mesmerised by the view, she heard François call: "My God, Lieke, what are you doing here?" and he jumped off the porch to lift Lieke from her feet and swing her in circles before placing her on the ground. Nicole felt jealous as she watched the obvious closeness of the two.

The girl was short, but naturally beautiful. She had no make-up on and if she had applied any, she would have spoilt her amazingly perfect complexion. Nicole seldom felt intimidated by another girl, but this one made her feel inadequate. Not only did she have a body to die for, with all the right curves in the right places, she had the most voluptuous breasts wobbling underneath the white cotton blouse she was wearing and Nicole looked down at her own smaller firm breasts and sighed. Nicole watched how the two stood and grinned at each other for a few seconds longer than she would have liked.

"Nicole, come here," François remembered her. "This is Lieke." Nicole came to stand next to François and looked down into an annoyingly perfect friendly face.

"Hi, I am Nicole," Nicole introduced herself and offered a hand.

"Hi, I have heard so much about you," and before Nicole could stop her, the pretty girl's arms flew around Nicole's neck and she stood quite cutely on her tippy toes to reach.

Oh, how perfect, Nicole thought to herself as she sighed. Lieke released Nicole and Nicole decided that she wouldn't let François see her discomfort with their apparent closeness.

"This is my cousin," François continued. "We grew up together and are more like brother and sister," he explained their bond to Nicole.

Nicole relaxed a bit when she heard this. Still, she felt inadequate.

"So, what are you doing here?" François asked Lieke.

"I heard you were visiting, and since I haven't seen you in such a long time I couldn't resist coming to visit as well. I thought I would surprise you," she smiled sweetly.

"Oh Nicole, Lieke is studying her LLB at Stellenbosch University. She is second year now and doing really well. We haven't seen each other in what?" he said only for Lieke to continue.

"I think it's been nearly three years. Am I right?" she asked.

"It feels longer," he said, unable to take his eyes off his cousin.

"You look great!" he said as he appreciated Lieke's appearance.

"You don't look too bad yourself!" she said teasingly and playfully punched him in his stomach, to which he grabbed her from behind and captured her arms with his one arm and tickled her with the other. Nicole didn't like the physical contact between the two although they were family, as she knew all about cousins. She too had a cousin that liked her way more than was appropriate. The difference was that when she was a young girl she didn't lead his advances on. These two were way too comfortable with each other for her liking.

"Supper is ready!" they heard Mara's deep voice from the kitchen. Relieved to have an excuse to turn her back on them Nicole turned away without saying anything and walked into the house without waiting to see if they were following. She headed to the kitchen where she took a seat at the kitchen table next to Nanna where she kept Mara company as she was busy taking the last dishes to the dining room. Nanna placed her one hand on Nicole's arm, which was resting on the table in front of Nicole.

"Everything alright?" she asked softly as if she sensed Nicole's mood.

"Yes," Nicole smiled at her and placed her free hand on Nanna's hand and squeezed it.

François and Lieke had entered the house, but got stuck in conversation in the living room. Nicole felt left out, but reprimanded herself, arguing that they were just very close and that she was being unnecessarily jealous. Nanna, Nicole and Mara took their places at the table before François realised they were waiting for them.

"It's nice to have you both here for a change," Mara said dryly as she started dishing up for everyone. Nicole mostly kept quite at supper, letting the family catch up, as they obviously had lots to catch up on. What Nicole did gather from the conversation though was that Mara's husband had died a few years back and that Lieke didn't visit her mother that often. There was unresolved tension between the two of them, but she couldn't figure out from what it sprouted.

When they had finished Nicole helped clear the table and offered to wash the dishes.

"That is so kind of you," Mara said as she welcomed the help. François and Lieke went to sit on the porch where Lieke lit a cigarette and they continued their conversation. Nicole went to the kitchen to help Mara. Nanna took her usual place at the kitchen table to fill out crossword puzzles.

"They are very close?" Nicole said out loud before she could stop herself.

"Yes," Mara said and didn't elaborate.

"I am really glad François met you," Mara said after a few minutes of silence while drying the dishes that Nicole had washed.

"I am glad I met him," Nicole replied. "He seems like a good guy."

"He is…" Mara said but didn't finish her sentence.

"Your daughter also seems nice," Nicole prodded Mara for clues.

"Yes," Mara said. "Well, that's me, I am tired. If you need anything, François knows where everything is," she said and walked out before Nicole could continue their conversation.

"Goodnight!" Nicole called after her and she replied with a "Night!"

"Make us some coffee?" Nanna's voice brought Nicole back to reality.

"Yes sure," Nicole replied and made coffee while Nanna spontaneously offered to explain what she saw Nicole was wondering about.

"Mara's husband was abusive and Lieke blames her for not divorcing him and thereby sparing her the hardship of it. François was her rock while they were growing up. It's difficult for Mara to see Lieke and likewise for Lieke to see Mara, but I am sure they will find peace someday. They just need to talk," Nanna said.

"Oh," Nicole said innocently as if she wasn't wondering about the dynamics of the family.

"After Lieke's dad died, there was nothing that kept her here, so she moved out," Nanna continued. Nicole drank her coffee while listening to Nanna drift off from her story to her own parents and how she had had her own tiffs with them, but how they sorted it out in the end, but Nicole didn't concentrate on what she was saying as she heard François and Lieke's voices carried in from the living room, where they had made themselves comfortable and she thought to herself it was strange that François didn't include her in the conversation.

"There was an abortion," she heard Nanna say and she looked at the old woman.

"Sorry, what did you say?" Nicole asked.

"Lieke had to have an abortion," Nanna continued with her story.

"From whom? Her father?" Nicole said shocked.

"No silly! You weren't listening," Nanna started laughing.

"Who was the father?" Nicole asked.

"We still don't know," Nanna said as she shook her head. "She wouldn't tell us when she fell pregnant. Lieke is stubborn that way," she said deep in thought. "But you don't want to hear the family gossip; do you want a biscuit?" Nanna offered.

"No, it's getting late, I should probably head off to bed," Nicole excused herself.

"Well, enjoy it, this old woman struggles to sleep," Nanna said as she smiled at Nicole.

"I will, goodnight," Nicole said and planted a kiss on the old woman's forehead.

As Nicole passed the living room, François' back was facing her and Lieke was facing Nicole as she was sitting opposite François. Lieke was sitting cross-legged on the couch and her blouse was unbuttoned way lower than Nicole liked, while the soft rounding of her breasts were playfully moving in the opening as she shifted her weight.

Nicole was going to say good night to the two of them, but as she came into Lieke's view, Lieke kept on talking to François, while looking straight into Nicole's eyes and then back to François as if she hadn't notice Nicole. Nicole stood still in the doorway for a few seconds, waiting for Lieke to acknowledge her presence and invite her in, but although Lieke once again looked at Nicole, while taking care not to alert François, she continued talking to François as if Nicole wasn't there.

It was clear she wasn't welcome, so she turned and walked to the bedroom where she put on her nighty and climbed under the crisp white linen and wondered if her feet wouldn't dirty the bedding, but decided she didn't care. She just wanted the visit to be over. Nicole wanted to spend time with François, not his aunt and if this was the way the visit was going, she could just as well go home. Nicole drifted off to sleep, still annoyed, but the fresh air made it difficult not to fall into a deep sleep.

Nicole's sleep was disturbed by François' warm body climbing into the bed next to her. She was relaxed as she was still very much in a sleepy state. She turned her back on him in order to continue sleeping, but François snuggled closer to her and pushed his one arm in under her head and the other he wrapped around her waist and pulled her closer to his body, as to cup it with his.

Nicole loved the feel of his warm chest against her back and she pulled the blankets closer to her chin, giving in to the comfort of François' presence and the softness of the bedding covering them. François breath was warm as it blew into Nicole's neck with every breath he took. Slowly his breathing slowed to a deep and rhythmic pace and Nicole drifted off to the peacefulness of sleep, only to be disturbed by François pulling Nicole even closer into him and pressing himself against her. Nicole took a deep breath as his body's warmth made her very aware of the chemistry between them.

François continued to let his free hand stroke the contours of her body, finally letting it glide over her hips and over the rounding of her buttocks, until his hand reached the seam of her nightdress. Here, he hesitated for a moment before he continued to lift it to above her waist so that he could continue his exploration of her body. Nicole sighed aloud from the pleasure it gave her and she kept her eyes closed although it was too dark to see anything.

The darkness only heightened their senses as they had to rely on it for them to visualise what they were feeling. Nicole turned on her back so that he had better access to her front and François stroked her stomach. His hand intensified its stroking and at times he squeezed her flesh hard as he bit down on his teeth to contain the urge to take her. When he couldn't control it anymore he lifted onto his elbow and bent down to kiss Nicole. It was a slow, tender and very controlled kiss. While he kissed her, his hand slipped in under the elastic of her panties and he stroked her hair before he wandered further, but she caught his hand before he could enter her.

He paused his kiss for a second and then continued more passionately and then pulled his hand from Nicole's while he pulled her panties down, without resistance from Nicole. Nicole gave in to him, placing her arms around his muscled neck and stroking his back. François positioned himself between her legs, while still continuing to kiss her mouth, not giving her much time to breathe. Nicole had to push him lightly away to take a breath only for him to take that time to pull his penis from his boxers and direct it in her direction and as he came in to continue to kiss her, she felt him entering her with one swift thrust.

He kept himself deeply buried inside of her, while kissing her and then started slowly thrusting into her. With each thrust, the force and speed with which he did so intensified until he collapsed on top of Nicole. Nicole, with the thought of an abortion lingering in her mind, pushed his upper body off her.

"I am not using birth control!" she whispered in shock.

"Don't worry, I used a condom," he whispered back and hugged her, while she gave a sigh of relief. Then François climbed off Nicole and excused himself to go take a shower. When he came back, Nicole had pulled on her panties and was lying in a bundle under the blankets in the dark. She was waiting for him, confused by what had happened, but François was in no mood to talk; he climbed into bed, took her in his arms and kissed her on the back of her head.

"Thank you," he said as if she had done him a favour. Nicole frowned at this and kept quiet. She finally fell asleep in his arms.

The next morning, Nicole woke before François and the rest of the house, so she took a shower and packed her bag, deciding to ask François to take her home. Although she loved spending time with him and he gave some sort of normality to her life, she instinctively knew she would never be able to trust him, nor did she find the intimacy between them intimate. To her, it was more a physical release to his needs and an offering of comfort on her part. Nicole was wasting her time in investing in a relationship with François; they were nothing more than friends and as she realised this, she decided to inform him as soon as they returned home.

When the rest of the house finally woke, they had breakfast. Lieke was nowhere to be seen and Mara informed them that Lieke had decided the previous night to return to Stellenbosch.

"Well, we should probably be getting back as well," Nicole replied to the news.

"Why? I thought you two were staying longer?" Mara looked disappointed.

"No," François came to Nicole's defence. "We were only visiting for the night. Nicole's shifts start in a day's time, she still has a lot of errands to run." To which Nicole smiled at François. He was in a good mood and was very gentle and caring, carrying Nicole's bag for her, opening the car door for her when they got in and trying to make conversation with her. Nicole wasn't used to this behaviour from him. When they finally greeted his aunt and grandmother and were alone in the car on their way home, he opened up to her.

"Nicole, I love you. I thought I would never find someone like you. I think you are perfect for me," he confessed his love for her. Nicole didn't know what to say, she was about to break up with him and now he was confessing his love.

"Oh…" she replied at a loss for words.

"Is that all you have to say? Are you shocked?" he asked teasingly.

"No, I just don't know what to say…" she continued while trying to buy time so that she didn't have to break the news to him in the car with the long road home still ahead of them.

"Well then, when you do, you can say something," he smiled at her and placed his hand on her thigh.

"I will do that!" Nicole smiled back at him. "Would you mind if I sleep? I am still a bit tired," Nicole asked as she wanted to avoid being pulled into a conversation about feelings, when she knew she had none for him.

"Of course!" he said and offered Nicole his jacket as a pillow, so she made herself comfortable and let the sound of the tires on the tar sing her to sleep.

In Table View, François softly woke her by shaking her shoulder gently.

"Nicole, we are here," he said softly and she wiped the sleep from her eyes while she tried to focus on where they were. They were only a few kilometres from her apartment when she found her focus and then she panicked. She didn't want him to come up into her apartment and spend more time with her. She didn't want to give him false hope, so she needed to act quickly, so when they pulled into the parking area of her block of flats she turned to him.

"François, I have to tell you something," she said softly. François was anticipating a confession of love just as he had given her an hour back.

"Yes," he said as he switched the engine off and turned his attention to her.

"I don't love you the way I should for us to have a proper relationship. I think you are the sweetest guy, but it just doesn't work for me," she rushed it out, scared that her nerve would fail her. François just sat in shock and looked at her. Then he shook his head while he looked in front of him.

"Why now?" was all he got out.

"I only realised this last night," she said softly as she looked at her hands that she was fiddling with in her lap.

"Why, am I that bad?" he asked sarcastically, hurt by her rejection.

"No, it has nothing to do with that," she nearly whispered. "I am really sorry."

"Then what, is it Lieke?" he asked with a frown on his forehead.

"No, why would she have anything to do with this?" but Nicole didn't want an answer on that question. "I just don't love you the way I should. You are a dear friend to me. That is unfortunately all." François had a very determined look on his face and the muscles in his cheeks were taut.

"Well then, so be it," he said without looking at Nicole. François climbed out of the car and unpacked Nicole's belongings and offered to help her carry it to her door, but she declined as she didn't want to torture him. He looked as if he was trying his best to control his emotions. Nicole waved at him as he drove off, but he didn't acknowledge the gesture.

The stairs leading to Nicole's flat felt steeper than usual and the two bags she carried seemed to weigh more than when she had packed them. They fell with a thud to the floor as Nicole released her baggage. She needed to unpack right away, to empty them of their contents and sort her washing and pack away that which she needed to. She knew if she didn't, it would bother her until she did. Nicole didn't like clutter, nor did she like postponing organising that needed to be done. It didn't even take her ten minutes to unpack and finally tossed her travel bag into her cupboard.

The next day, Nicole went for a run as soon as she woke up. The fresh morning air burned the passageways of her nose as she breathed it in with every pace she took. Her feet rhythmically announced her determination to finish the path she had chosen this morning to finish. She tired within the first five minutes, but pushed through, finding strength and comfort in the burning of her muscles. When she climbed the stairs to her apartment, her legs were lame from the exertion, but her being was empowered by the small accomplishment of being able to push through her own mental barriers.

She ran herself a warm bath and with a calm mind she lay in it, soaking up the soothing of it. As per usual this was the time when her mind seemed to place things in perspective as it was quite enough for her to make sense of things. And then it came to her: Since she had nothing to do on her last day off, she might as well check in at the police station to see if there was anything she could help with. It was customary for the policemen and -women to, on their off days, help with things such as tending to the gardening, to do some filing or help with painting, or whatever project the PRO of each station was busy with, to promote the image of the station and police force.

Why hadn't I thought of it sooner? she thought to herself. It would be a great way to keep herself busy on her off days when she had nothing to do and no one to talk to and it would look good on her record if she was actively involved in helping out at the station, above and beyond her normal duties.

With a new-found enthusiasm, she pulled on jeans, t-shirt and sneakers and made her way to the Charge Office to find out if there was anything she could help with. To her disappointment, the PRO of the station was off sick that particular day and the office personnel suggested she came back the next day, so Nicole went to the Charge Office where her old shift was working. On her way past the Station Commander's office, Nicole caught a glimpse of Captain Liebenberg who noticed her as well and called her into his office.

"What are you doing here?" he asked politely.

"Moring Captain, I thought I might be of assistance to the PRO. But I see he is off today," she explained. Captain Liebenberg looked impressed by her eagerness to help as he smiled at her.

"Well, I am sure he would be grateful for the help seeing that we are busy upgrading the grounds. We need all the help we can find. We were thinking of building a fish pond at the side of the building and maybe keeping a few ducks on the grounds. So if you are free next Saturday, you are more than welcome to join us," he said.

"I will do that, thank you," Nicole smiled back at him and walked out of his office.

In the Charge Office, her old shift was happy to see her and asked her to stay and drink a coffee before she took off, so she did. Ava was on her post as Charge Office Commander and Nicole pulled up a chair close to Ava. Ava always made her feel wanted and today was no different as she immediately lit a cigarette for the both of them. Nicole gratefully filled her lungs with the warm smoke and relaxed into her chair as the two of them started talking. Ava even gave Nicole some chores to do, as she used to, when they were working together in the Charge Office.

"I miss this," Nicole confessed to her.

"We miss you just as much. I hate that our shifts are making it so difficult to get together. We never see you anymore," Ava complained.

"Can I ask for a transfer to another shift?" Nicole wondered out loud.

"You can try, but the Captain is full of his own ideas," Ava said sceptically. "But before you do, you might be wasting your time, as Ben and I have applied for a transfer to Milnerton police station as it is closer to his house," she continued.

Nicole looked at Ava shocked. "No! I understand why, but no. So you are leaving us?" she complained.

"No, we are not leaving you. It is just easier for me and Ben. You will still see us on your off days. With luck, our shifts might correlate in such a manner that our off days fall together," she consoled Nicole.

"Yes, hopefully," Nicole said, disappointed.

"Talking about seeing you, we must make a plan to see each other again. We have so much catching up to do. Ben is finally pushing to get married. I thought he would never get to this point," Ava continued.

"That is great news," Nicole said excitedly and hugged Ava tightly. "I am so happy for you," she said, truly happy for her friend.

"Why are you so happy?" Both women looked up at the man who interrupted their conversation. It was Nick, Captain Liebenberg's cousin.

"We weren't talking to you!" Ava said, agitated by the interruption.

"I am sorry, I am just happy to hear that Nicole is happy," he said teasingly and winked at Nicole as she looked up at him. Nick was also dressed in civilian clothes. He was dressed in a t-shirt, jeans and sneakers. His t-shirt was light blue and fitted, allowing the perfect form of his well-proportioned body to show through it and the blue brought out the intense blueness of his eyes against his tanned skin. Although Nicole wasn't in any way attracted to him, he looked quite handsome where he stood towering over the two of them. He looked like a naughty boy and she couldn't help but to smile at him. Somehow she knew she had to be careful of him, but strangely she thought she might be wrong about him.

"Why are you in civilian clothes?" he continued as if he was oblivious to having interrupted a discussion between the two women.

"I am off today," she said trying to look uninterested. "I just came to say hello to my old shift."

"Well, what a coincidence? Me too and I came to say hello to my uncle," he said smilingly, and Nicole didn't know what to make of it.

"Mmmmm…might be you are following me?" Nicole teased.

"You will never know, would you?" he replied with a grin and by now Ava was properly pissed off by the young man.

"Don't run away, Nicole, I am not finished with you. When I come back, we will continue this; first, I have to see my uncle. Is he in?" he asked Ava.

"Yes!" she replied abruptly. "Why don't you go through?" she asked sarcastically while indicating with her hands in the direction of the Captain's office and so Nick followed.

"I don't like that arrogant little bastard one bit. He is trouble," Ava said softly.

"I don't know, Ava, he seems quite friendly," Nicole tried to defend him.

"Too friendly if you ask me," Ava replied, not impressed by the young man. They continued talking about the probability of a wedding between Ava and Ben and Ava asked Nicole if she would consider being her bridesmaid. Nicole accepted the challenge and asked Ava to keep her up to date on when and where they were planning to have it.

When Nick returned, he came to sit on the Charge Office table opposite Nicole. This angered Ava.

"Why don't you two go outside, we are working here?" Ava suggested as she was not in a mood to tolerate the young man's advances on Nicole.

"Okay," Nicole replied and gave Ava a hug and kiss as she came to her feet. "I will see you soon. Enjoy the rest of your shift," she said and walked out of the Charge Office with Nick following her.

"Wait Nicole, you keep on running away from me," Nick said as he caught up with Nicole, who was walking with determination. Nick grabbed her by her wrist and pulled her closer to him. Nicole plucked her wrist from his grip.

"Don't do that," Nicole said, alarmed.

"What?" he asked, confused.

"Don't touch me," Nicole said sternly.

"I won't hurt you. I am sorry if I frighten you, Nicole. It's just there is something about you that I cannot resist. I will behave, I promise," he said sincerely, making Nicole feel as if she had overreacted, but she was too stubborn to admit it and kept her pose.

"As long as we understand each other," she said firmly.

"Yes, we do. Now, on a different note, what are you doing today?" Nick asked gently.

"Not much, why?" Nicole asked.

"No, I thought we might do something together, seeing that I have nothing to do as well and tomorrow my shifts start," he complained.

"Mine too," Nicole admitted. "Yes, why not?" she said pleased by the fact that she didn't have to spend the rest of the day on her own. She welcomed the company and she thought to herself: *How harmful could it be to trust him, as his uncle is our Station Commander. There is no way he would do something to embarrass his uncle.* They walked over to his car and he opened the door for her.

"I know! Why don't we go for a picnic?" he suggested as he climbed into the car.

"Isn't the weather a bit overcast for that?" Nicole asked as the grey mist drew over the beach front.

"Yes maybe, well then, why don't you come drink coffee at my house?" Nick suggested.

"Yes, that would be nice," Nicole agreed, hoping to meet the rest of his family in order to get a clearer picture of who he was. Although he was friendly and open, he didn't give away a lot about himself. Normally she could deduce a person's character in an instant, but with him, except for the art of manipulation and being well educated, she couldn't gather much more. They drove in the direction of Durbanville, a well-to-do suburb of Cape Town.

This made Nicole feel a bit more comfortable and soon they stopped in front of a large split-level house in a quiet tree filled street. The house was quite attractive from the outside and the splendour of it made her feel at ease, as she was used to these types of surroundings from her own childhood. She smiled at him without saying anything and he smiled back.

"Well, here we are," he announced and he got out and opened the door for Nicole to get out, which she did.

Nicole followed Nick down the paved walkway into the house. The house on the inside wasn't at all what Nicole had expected. The house was sparsely furnished with old furnishings. The curtains were dusty and drawn partially closed. The whole house was filled with the darkened hues of sun trying to shine through the thick curtains. It was apparent that whoever lived here didn't have money to decorate the house up to standard to compliment the beauty of the architecture.

"It's dark in here, can we open the curtains?" Nicole asked Nick, but then a voice from a dark corner behind her answered: "No! I don't like the light!"

"Shit!" Nicole exclaimed as she flung around to see who was behind her. Nicole had to squint to make out the large figure seated in the corner on an old weathered leather lounger. The man's t-shirt was a few sizes too small for him and his stomach protruded from underneath the material. He had black sweatpants on and his feet were bare. There was unkempt curly brown hair on his head and his untamed beard framed the little that was visible of his face. Nick came to Nicole's rescue and took her by the small of her back and steered her away from the man in the direction of the stairs.

"Ignore him, he is my roommate. We are renting this house, he has the bottom part of the house and I live upstairs. It's much better there anyway; come, let me show you," he said in a calming voice.

Nicole followed him up the stairs to the first upper level where the windows had no curtains, but instead were dressed in blinds that were pulled back for the light to enter the rooms. The building had big windows and from where Nicole stood, she could see Table Mountain in its blue glory in the distance. The view was breath-taking as the view was un-spoilt by tall buildings and the house was situated in Durbanville Hills.

"Wow! The view is amazing," Nicole mentioned as Nick came to stand next to her to admire the view.

"Yes, but if you like this, you should see what it looks like from the roof!" he said.

"Will you show me?" Nicole asked sweetly.

"Yes, but first, let me make you some coffee?" he asked while he turned to switch the kettle on where it stood on the kitchen table, which was situated in the middle of the upper level.

"That sounds great!" Nicole said as she took a seat at the table while Nick made coffee and started a conversation about where he grew up and other facts about his childhood. To Nicole, he seemed surprisingly pleasant and he didn't display the arrogant attitude that he had when they were in front of other people.

"I might have misjudged you," Nicole said when she got a chance.

"Oh, did you?" he asked teasingly. "So, how did you judge me?"

"I thought you were arrogant, self-absorbed and a bit of a prick," she confessed as she smiled shyly.

"Well, I might be confident, but that's a bit harsh!" he said as he smiled at her. "I am actually not that bad, Nicole; if you would give me half a chance, I would be happy to show you how gentle I am," he said more seriously.

"I am sorry, it's just that you come across that way. And seriously now, I think you seem nice, but I have just broken up with my boyfriend, so I am not interested in finding another one, just yet," she explained.

"It doesn't matter, I can wait. Especially for you…" and he winked at Nicole as he said it.

"Yes, I am sure…" Nicole said teasingly, not taking him too seriously.

"Come," he said, "let me show you the view before it gets dark." Nicole followed him up another set of stairs that opened up onto a deck on the roof, from where they could view the neighbourhood.

They stood there for some time watching the cars drive past and Nick showed her where the racecourse was and to where the boundaries of Durbanville stretched. Nicole was about to turn to Nick to tell him how beautiful it all was, when he simultaneously turned to her and their faces were a few centimetres from each other.

He spontaneously continued to come closer until his lips met hers, before she knew what was happening. He started kissing her gently but with passion and pulled her closer with his hands on her waist until their bodies were pressed against one another. Instinctively, Nicole's lips parted, letting him explore the softness of her mouth. She closed her eyes from the pleasantness of his kiss and leant in against him. His body was rock hard, his hands were huge on her waist and he was tall enough to intimidate her by his size.

If only he had a different personality… she thought as his kiss became urgent and then Captain Liebenberg's face flashed before her. With that thought in her mind's eye, she suddenly pushed Nick away from her.

"Sorry Nick! I can't, I don't feel that way," she said while her hands were still on his chest and he was still holding her by her waist.

"Why?" he asked, disappointed and leant forward to continue kissing her.

"NO!" she said, firmly pushing him off her. "I cannot do this. I don't want this."

Nicole turned her back on him and looked at the countless houses in front of her.

"Just give me a chance?" he pleaded.

"No, you know what, I think you should take me home," she said firmly and she started down the stairs and made her way to the front door. When Nicole reached the front door, Nick had caught up with her, where he grabbed her by her wrist.

"Wait Nicole, I didn't mean to put you off, I didn't mean to…" but before Nick could utter another word a voice came from the shadows: "Not another one Nick," and then a horse bellow of a laughter followed, which annoyed Nicole enough for her to pull her wrist from his grip and flee into the open air outside the house.

Nick didn't even attempt to get Nicole to stay longer, he sensed that he had to let her set her boundaries in order for him to ever have a hope of getting close to her, as she was the type of girl that, if she was pushed too hard, would cut herself off totally. He thus walked to the car, opened her door for her and closed it after her without saying a word. Nicole got in and when Nick got in, he started the car and started driving her home. Only when they got close to the station did Nicole soften up a bit and try to appease his wounded ego.

"I am sorry!" she said, opting not to look at him, as she felt guilty for kissing him back before she stopped. She felt as if she had led him on and felt partially guilty for his persistence in perusing her.

"No, I am," he said sincerely.

"Let's not think about this. You are a good guy, I am just not up for a relationship," she tried to make an excuse for not feeling attracted to him.

"Yes, let's forget about this, I won't bother you again," he said bitterly and then stopped in front of the police station, where he let her out and said a civil goodbye before he climbed in his car and left her to walk home to her apartment.

Nicole felt relieved to be rid of him. For now, the freedom, of not having to take anyone but herself into consideration, was much more appealing than the occasional short-lived satisfaction of having sensual physical contact with a male partner. She could sort herself out perfectly well for now. Nicole's sense of relief was short-lived though for when she returned to the police station for her next shift, Captain Liebenberg's attitude changed drastically towards her.

Where he once seemed pleasant and pleased to see her, he now in passing didn't even greet or acknowledge her presence. Nicole was puzzled by this.

Surely he couldn't be disappointed to such an extent, that Nicole and Nick didn't hit it off, that he held a grudge against her. She put it down to just a bad mood and that it had nothing to do with her. Unfortunately, Nicole's sixth sense was seldom wrong and when she got to the Charge Office, Sergeant Mostert was waiting for her anxiously.

"Nicole, I don't know what the hell is going on, but Captain Liebenberg was asking a lot of questions about you and your conduct during working hours, even about your off time," he said seriously. Nicole frowned as she realised that her first suspicions might have been right.

"Are you serious? But…I didn't do anything wrong, did I?" she asked and as she did this, she remembered the pending internal investigation of Sergeant Swart.

Oh my God! she thought to herself in a state of inner panic. *I hope it's not that!*

"Did he say anything about why he wanted to know all these things?" she continued, bombarding Sergeant Mostert with her questioning.

"No. I was wondering if you knew what was going on," Sergeant Mostert asked, very concerned and wanting to help Nicole if it was in his power.

"I honestly have no clue, except… No, it won't be…" she stopped in midsentence as she didn't want to discuss anything in front of Sergeant Swart or the other police officers.

"Well, I think it is time you are on patrol duty," Sergeant Mostert said to Nicole's relief. "You will work with me today," he informed her. As Nicole walked to the door with her hand bag and her pistol, which she was loading and placing in it, since she hadn't ordered a holster for it yet, she caught Sergeant Swart's eye. His stare pierced through her being like an ice-pick would through soft snow and the sight sent chills down her spine.

In the patrol vehicle, Sergeant Mostert gave Nicole her pocketbook, which had been inspected by the Captain. Nicole's conscience was driving her mad and she didn't realise that it was showing on her face. It was a masterful art of many in the Force to lie without flinching and to hold their composure, even though they were worried. Nicole however hadn't mastered this skill and like a selected few, wouldn't ever master it totally.

"What's up, Nicole?" Sergeant Mostert started at her as he saw the worried expression on her face. "What is chasing you?" he asked honestly concerned.

Nicole shook her head. "It's nothing…" she said, trying to sound convincingly while trying to figure out what she would say to him if he cornered her. She felt that she couldn't possibly confess to him what had happened that night. In doing so she would place him in the unnecessary position of having to choose to convey it to the Captain, or even worse, he would have to be stand trial with her and Sergeant Mostert for his negligence in not picking up that one of the prisoners was injured.

"Come on, Nicole, I know you well enough by now to know something is bothering you, and if there is anyone who can help you, it's me. So, out with it!" he said in a stern voice like her father used to use on her.

"It's nothing really. Captain Liebenberg's cousin wanted to take me out yesterday…I thought it couldn't do any harm…" she started, hoping to disguise her true worries from him.

"Did he hurt you?" Sergeant Mostert asked, alarmed.

"No, no…it's nothing like that. He did try to kiss me though and I didn't want to, so he got upset, but he didn't do anything wrong. I am thinking that the Captain might be upset with me for rejecting his cousin…I don't know…" Nicole said as she looked at her hands that she was clenching in her lap.

"Oh, I see…" he said and gave a deep sigh as he thought on how to approach the situation.

"You know," he said as he placed his warm bony hand on both her hands, still knotted in her lap. "Even if he is upset with you about rejecting his cousin, which I doubt, he will get over it, but I truly think he is just on edge, since there is an internal investigation pending on the missing prisoner. He is just as accountable for the disappearance, as I am, as the rest of our shift and the shift that worked after us is," he said dryly as the relevance of what he was saying hit him fully. He gathered himself and continued: "You don't have to worry, Nicole, you did the right thing by turning him down. I don't like the young man's arrogance and his lack of respect for his fellow officers. That family is a little full of it; they come from a long line of officers and as such think they have a lot of pull in the Force. They might have, but they are not as powerful as they think they are. I have a few connections of my own, so if he bothers you again or the Captain becomes a problem, you can talk to me, okay?" he asked and patted her hands before placing it on the steering wheel again and smiled at Nicole who was looking up at him now.

They didn't speak of it again; they attended complaints and patrolled the area. At lunchtime, they stopped off at the Charge Office to have something to eat and while Sergeant Mostert was eating in the kitchen, Nicole found an opportunity to speak to Sergeant Swart. He hadn't really spoken much to anyone and he was in such a foul mood, that nobody dared speak to him, but she needed to and there wasn't a lot of time to do so, so she had to be swift and make every second count. Nicole's heart pounded in her chest when she approached him, while he was busy tending the registers.

"Sergeant Swart?" she approached him slowly and softly.

"Yes Nicole?" he said in an abrupt manner.

"Can I ask you something?" she whispered.

"What?" he replied, even more abruptly and Nicole nearly didn't bother to continue, but needed to know what was going on.

"What happened to the prisoner? Are we in trouble? I am really scared…" she whispered, and her eyes glistened from the moisture filling her eyes.

Sergeant Swart took pity on Nicole.

"No Nicole, you are not in trouble. No one is at this stage…" he said softly so that no one could hear but her. "It is compulsory to investigate a disappearance."

"But, what about the other shift that took over from you? Are they in trouble? Do you know what happened?" she whispered even softer.

"Yes, so don't worry! I took care of the situation and since they don't know on which shift it happened, they cannot pin it on us if you keep your mouth shut," he continued in a serious voice, nearly spitting the words out.

"What do you mean; you took care of the situation? He was fine, wasn't he?" Nicole asked, shocked and nauseated all at the same time, as she knew deep within he couldn't have been.

"Nicole. Dammit! I don't want to discuss this with you! Let's just say the prisoner wasn't okay, so I took care of it. Do you really want the details?" he said in a threatening tone and Nicole pulled back instinctively. Her survival instincts kicked in and she immediately knew she had to ignore the whole situation and hope nothing came of it.

"Nicole!" Sergeant Swart softly called to her as she wasn't facing him anymore.

"Yes?" she said deliberately sweetly in a controlled even toned voice.

"Look at me! If any of this comes out, I am taking you down!" he said fiercely as if he already had the urge to attack Nicole.

"Yes, I understand," Nicole agreed, stripped from her bravado. He was right, she didn't want to know the details of what had happened or how he was able to take a fully-grown man from the cells without her noticing, or even hiding it from the shift that took over from them. And although she thought she could leave it there, the thought of her not being able to help the man, or that Sergeant Swart was probably getting away with murder and she was forcibly helping him, left a mark.

That night when she went home, she phoned Samantha and asked her to come pick her up if they were going out to the local club, which they did. That night she accepted every single shot and drink that was offered to her by willing suitors and as a thank you, danced with them, but nothing else, until the lights merged with the music into a pleasant trance, where she could forget about everything.

For those few blissful hours, she escaped into the dark shadows of the night, which were decorated by the bright and beautiful colours of the night. Her inner being numbed by the intoxicating liquid offered to her, floated on the dance floor, back home and into her bed, where she fell into the blissful darkness of sleep.

This would become her fix, her addiction, not the alcohol, not the socialising, not the transfixing music, but the escape from the daily stresses and the guilt with which she was slowly filling her soul. Within that following weeks Ava and Ben's transfer came through and they left the station.

Ava was right, it is a good thing, Nicole thought. *There is something seriously wrong with this station.* So Nicole decided to follow Ava and Ben and apply for a transfer. Unfortunately, when she had finally gathered the nerve to approach the Captain about it, she was greeted by an uninterested wall. The Captain didn't even want to listen to her reasoning for this decision.

"We cannot afford to let you go, Constable, now I have work to tend to," he dismissed her when she bothered him with her plea.

A week after Nicole wanted to apply for a transfer, she was relieved from her worries by a fortunate turn of events. Someone on the other shift that was involved in the disappearance of the prisoner voiced their concern about Sergeant Swart's conduct that night.

Unbeknownst to Nicole, as well as the rest of the station, the Charge Office Commander that took over from Sergeant Swart confessed that he didn't do a proper head count and that he didn't wake one of the prisoners that was sleeping when he looked into the cell. This made the internal affairs investigator interrogate Sergeant Swart, who admitted to assaulting him, but not that he had something to do with the disappearance of the prisoner.

To spare the Force unnecessary embarrassment, it was found that the prisoner had escaped by breaking through the roof of the cell and Sergeant Swart was boarded for stress, a regular occurrence in the police force. It would also be too difficult to prove that Sergeant Swart had something to do with it, as there were no witnesses and there was the situation of the other Charge Officer, a good man, who would have to be charged with negligence for not doing his work properly.

Very conveniently to all concerned, he got a slap on the wrist and Sergeant Swart got a golden ticket out of the Force. This meant that effective immediately, Sergeant Swart received his full pension and didn't have any misconduct charges on his record. A fair deal for Sergeant Swart, but not so fair to the poor man, who was no more.

When Nicole heard the news of the Sergeant being boarded for stress and that the prisoner had escaped, although she knew the truth, she let out a sigh of relief. She could finally put this whole episode to rest and although she knew she would for the rest of her life wonder about what really happened to the prisoner, she knew there was nothing she could do to make things right by him.

Chapter 16

Finally, now that Nicole had no more worries forcing her into hiding, and now that Ava and Ben had been transferred, it gave Nicole the opportunity to visit them more regularly and even their shifts coincided so that their off days overlapped. Nicole was grateful for this, as she was starting to feel the burden of living alone, with no support structure. Seeing that her mother and father were caught up in their own world, where they were trying to build a new life with new life partners, Nicole's needs didn't seem to feature in their lives as much.

This disappointed Nicole, since the need for support from a child never really seemed to cease to exist, although it was more for spiritual support. And like they used to, when she was still a student, Ava and Ben took her under their wing, letting her spend as much time with them as she needed to.

Soon enough, Nicole was again invited to spend her off days with them. Nicole was in good spirits when she finally finished her last evening shift and was dropped off at Ava and Ben's house. The door was open when she arrived at about seven in the morning. It was a chilly morning and the mist blown in from the sea banks of Milnerton hung in the Brooklyn air, but Nicole felt warm, she knew she would be able to take a warm bath, have a warm hearty breakfast and crawl into a warm bed, only to wake later to the company of her best friends and now her family.

She dropped her bags in the spare room and made her way to the bathroom to run a warm bath. Then she made herself a cup of coffee before she closed the bathroom door behind her. The steam filled the room and she wiped the mist from the mirror to study her reflection. She wasn't looking like the eighteen-year-old girl she was when she had started at Table View police station. Instead, the reflection of a nineteen-year-old nearing her twenties was staring back, and although the changes might not be visible to others, she could see them clearly reflected. Her eyes, where they had once seemed deer-like, seemed more intense and her mouth, which was doll-like in its soft pouty shape, now seemed more spread out in shape and her lips full and sensual. There were no wrinkles, but where she used to go bare-skinned, she had now perfected the art of make-up, which she wore every day and as she started clearing her face, she seemed dull without it. She frowned at the changes. *How could my face have changed so much in the nearly two years?* she thought and then, as she relaxed her frown to study her face, she realised that it was the shape of her features that had changed, it was the muscles in her face she used, that changed.

Her eyes were now pulled tight by scepticism and her mouth wasn't relaxed enough to take on its doll like shape. It was pulled slightly back by the tautness of the muscles surrounding it. Somehow saddened by the reflection, she also loved the new look as she stood back and looked at it from a distance. Her long hair was resting on her slender bare shoulders, her soft creamy white skin looked flawless as it draped her delicate frame. Her breasts seemed to have changed as well, her nipples had darkened a little from the near transparent colour they had as a child. Her hips have slightly filled out to emphasise her narrow waist.

Seeing her reflection like that, she realised how beautiful a woman she had become and although it filled her with pride and confidence, she felt disappointed in not having someone to share it with. She shrugged her shoulders as she tied her hair into a bun and climbed into the bath to soak her work stresses from her body. When she had finished, she took her cup to the kitchen and went straight to bed, pulling the door closed behind her, as she knew the rest of the house would soon be starting to rise. Nicole cuddled up in a bundle under the warm blankets and fell into a deep sleep.

"Nicole?" a voice cut through the silence of Nicole's dream.

"Nicole? It is nearly five o'clock in the afternoon! Come on, girl, you have been sleeping the whole day…" Nicole heard Ava's voice again and she opened her eyes to find Ava hovering over her with a cup of coffee in her one hand.

Nicole came upright and took the cup from Ava.

"Thank you!" she said gratefully as her throat was dry from sleeping.

Ava made herself comfortable on the bed next to Nicole.

"I am so glad we get to spend time together again," Ava said. "I really have missed our conversations," Ava continued.

"So did I," Nicole said while redoing her ponytail.

They continued to catch up on time lost before Ava finally stood up and took Nicole's empty cup from her to take to the kitchen.

"Well, get dressed, we are having a barbeque tonight. Ben has gone to get some wood and meat," Ava said before she left the room. Nicole pulled the blankets over her head as she lay down again, she wasn't feeling like getting out of the bed. If it was up to her, she would easily stay in bed, sleeping for another couple of hours, but unfortunately, she was a guest and thus had to gather herself and get dressed.

She threw the covers off and jumped out of bed. It took her a few minutes to make her bed and dress in a pair of jeans and a t-shirt and a pair of leather sandals. She looked in the mirror at the ponytail she had readjusted earlier and decided that the slightly messiness looked perfect, as little strands of hair fell from it, framing her face. She joined Ava in the kitchen, where Ava was cooking potatoes for a salad and busy making a green salad for the evening. She had hardly entered the kitchen when she got her first order: "Will you prepare the snacks? I have placed everything on the table?"

"With pleasure!" Nicole replied happily and got to work, preparing biscuits with cheese, peppadews and figs on them. She also filled a bowl with nuts and another with sliced biltong (dried meat). Then she took them to the lounge overlooking the patio. For some reason, even if it was only the three of them, it always felt like a special occasion when they were barbequing. Ava opened a beer for them as Nicole returned to the kitchen, where Ava had finished with her preparation work. Then they retired to the lounge where they waited for Ben to return.

They were already busy with their second beer when Ben returned, and the sun was busy setting on the horizon. In this house, everything and everyone ticked to Ben's clock, and he took things very easy. Ava was used to this and although she was a bit more organised and diligent than Ben, she had become accustomed and grown to love his relaxed attitude towards life.

"Where did you stop off?" Ava teased knowingly.

"I ran into Ian at the shops. He said he might pop in later," he said with a mischievous smile pulling at his mouth, as he nodded his head in the direction of Nicole at Ava as to indicate that she was the reason he wanted to do so. Nicole shook her head. Although he was attractive, she wasn't in any way intending in entertaining the idea of them having a romantic relationship. For now, men were disappointing and she just wanted to do her own thing.

"Ben, you are full of shit!" Nicole said as Ben started laughing from his stomach and went to the kitchen to open his first beer and spice the meat after which he lit the fire. Nicole loved staring at the flames as it turned the darkness into an orange hue. Little sparks flew up into the night sky as the wood made little explosions from the heat. Hypnotised by the flames, music and conversation Nicole drank quite a few beers and soon enough she was feeling the warmth of the alcohol filling her veins.

Although Nicole nibbled on the snacks, she wasn't particularly hungry, she revelled in the feeling of escape as her mood soared with the intoxication that took over her body and soul. She had become so accustomed to the feeling and gave into it. She felt happy, without a care and so she chatted away on a wave of light spirits.

After Ben had finished barbequing his lamb chops, they dished up and ate. Nicole didn't eat much, she was still drinking, not curbing the volumes she consumed and soon, her mood of light-hearted bliss turned on her like a whirlwind. When she took her seat in the living room where Ben and Ava were still filling their huge guts with food, Nicole stared at the carpet in front of her, underneath her feet.

"Nicole, are you okay?" she heard Ava ask, concerned.

When Nicole looked up, Ben was nowhere to be seen, it was only her and Ava sitting in the living room. Nicole felt a little bewildered as she hadn't realised that so much time had passed as she glanced up at the watch hanging on the wall. It was one o' clock in the morning and the last time she had looked, it was still ten o' clock. Her beer was still hanging from her hand that hung over the armrest of the couch.

Oh my God! Did I fall asleep? she thought, but she instinctively knew she had her eyes open.

"Nicole? Are you alright?" Ava asked again.

"Oh yes! Sorry, I was just deep in thought. Where is Ben?" Nicole asked.

"He went to bed. What is bothering you?" Ava prodded.

"I don't know…" Nicole started.

"You do, just spit it out," Ava encouraged Nicole to tell her what was chasing her mind.

Nicole had to think what it was that made her feel so sombre. And then it all came flooding into her consciousness, she had tried not to think about her circumstances, but it was difficult to ignore, and although she wanted to escape her worries by climbing on the wave of intoxication, she wasn't able to do so.

"Where do I begin?" Nicole said seriously as she lit a cigarette and without really thinking too hard about, it the words spilled out of her without barriers. Nicole confessed to Ava that she felt continuously alone, she felt isolated from the world, her family and even of Ben and Ava, as they were focussed on planning a life together. She confessed her financial situation and that she was mostly starving. Also, that she was mostly dependent on the kindness of others for food, when and if invited to dinner.

She confessed that she felt confused about her career in the police force and that if she had the choice over again, she wouldn't have gone this rout. The tears were now flowing as fast as the words. Ava silently listened while Nicole let everything spill from her being and when she was spent, Ava stood up and came to sit next to Nicole.

"Nicole, now listen to me. This is probably not the career choice most of us would have made if we had a better choice, but it pays the bills and you at least have medical aid. There are so many cheaper options open to you for lodgings; you don't need to rent a flat. So many of the policemen and -women take in flatmates and I know you only have a one bedroom flat, but we can always ask if someone needs a flatmate.

"We can even try the Barracks in Sea Point. I stayed there, and it is not only cheap, but you have the company of the other girls living there." Ava tried to console Nicole. Nicole hadn't even thought further; she didn't have the necessary guidance and she felt inadequate for not thinking further than her circumstances to try and find cheaper lodgings.

"The only problem is that I have signed a lease for a year and if I don't stay on, until then, then I lose my deposit," Nicole explained while she wiped the tears from her eyes.

"Well, when is the lease period over?" Ava asked caringly.

"In three months' time," Nicole replied.

"Okay, then we have enough time to find you a place to stay. In the meantime, I have a suggestion for you in connection with your financial situation," Ava said calmly.

"What, there is not much I can do about it," Nicole said curiously and now she had stopped sobbing.

"Well, it is up to you, but if you feel up to it, I can arrange that you date some of the officers at head office?" Ava said as if it made perfect sense.

"How is that going to help me?" Nicole asked, annoyed at the fact that Ava wanted to pair her up with someone. She was feeling lonely, but didn't feel up to a relationship.

"I don't think you understand. I am not talking about the policemen, I am talking about the officers. There are some officers that date young policewomen. They are prepared to help financially for your companionship…" she dragged the words out, as to give Nicole time to understand.

"Do you mean, you get paid to date them?" Nicole asked, shocked.

"Well, if you want to put it that way, but it's more of a mutual understanding. You befriend an officer, he takes you out and then he looks after you financially. It's more like a token of appreciation. You don't have to sleep with them if you don't want to, but if you do, you can make up to R300 a night," Ava continued. Nicole's head was making the sums, that would be one third of her monthly salary, and a lot of money for one night, and more importantly the cure to her financial distress, but she had to offer something greater in return. She wasn't sure if she would be able to do so. And then it puzzled her how such an exclusive club could exist in the police and how Ava knew about it.

"How do you know about this?" Nicole asked as she looked at Ava, searching for the truth.

"I did it when I was younger," she said matter-of-factly, without a hint of regret.

Nicole was shocked beyond belief. She couldn't imagine that Ava who was always so in control, could have been so desperate, like she was now, to do such a thing.

"I didn't know I was doing it, Nicole…" she started to explain. "An officer befriended me, and one thing led to another and we started dating. He was married, but I didn't know it and after the first evening we had slept together, he left money on my vanity table. At first, I felt disgusted that he had left money, but then I realised he wanted to help. After that, a few other officers approached me, but I declined. Only then did I realise what was going on.

"I kept seeing the one officer until I financially didn't need him anymore and then I stopped it. I know how to get you into that if you need to," Ava said as if she was talking about the weather.

"No! I wouldn't be able to do that!" Nicole said as the thought of her having to sleep with officers twice her age for money, was just not something she felt comfortable with. She knew that if she did it, she was admitting that there was no hope, and she wasn't about to be defeated so easily.

"No, I think that I will just hang in there until I can find a cheaper place to stay. Thank you for the thought anyway," Nicole declined Ava's offer.

"It is not as bad as it sounds, Nicole," Ava explained. "Even Ben did a similar thing by sorting out some of the divorcees in Table View, while on duty, and they would reward him afterwards. It was a beneficial understanding that helped him get through a tough time. A lot of young policemen do it, but you cannot talk about this!" she warned Nicole.

"I won't," Nicole assured her. "It's just that I can't do it. I don't judge, I understand the extent of desperation one has to deal with, believe me." And tears welled up again in her eyes.

Ava felt for Nicole, so she squeezed her shoulders and smiled at her, "Well then, we just have to find you a place to stay," she said enthusiastically.

As Ava had promised, she helped Nicole apply to move into the Barracks at Sea Point police station. They were full, but had placed Nicole's name on the waiting list so that as soon as there was a place available, Nicole could move in. There, she would pay a total of R350 a month, which would include her washing being done for her, three meals a day and water and electricity included. She would get a furnished room of her own and the best part would be that there would be girls around her in the same position.

This gave Nicole hope, and with this hope, she was able to continue living her life of poverty as she knew it wouldn't be permanent. Ironically, as she was deep down still hoping that Mika would one day come back to her, she found out, on her return to work, that he was now engaged to the girl he had cheated with. Nicole was very disappointed and angered by this. She hadn't had the chance to get over the incident, and somehow, she thought he would have moved on from the girl and that would have given her some form of relief, but now they were engaged to be married.

"If I ever get the chance, I swear I will get back at them both," she swore silently when faced with the news, but she was also freed from him, as the news cut the emotional ties she still felt for him. Ava and Ben were happy about the news that Mika was now taken, as they didn't think he would be a suitable partner for Nicole. He was just one of those men who would cheat on his partner, no matter how much he loved her, as he loved himself more. Ben wanted Ian to befriend Nicole, since he was his best friend and he was also single and wanted to find someone decent to settle down with.

"If only Nicole wouldn't be so stubborn," Ben complained to Ava.

"You cannot force her, Ben," Ava warned Ben, when he confessed his plans to get the two of them together.

Before Ben could concentrate on his matchmaking scheme, there was the more important issue of his wedding to Ava. It was time they made it official and over the following weeks, the two of them set about to plan their wedding. They asked Nicole to be the bridesmaid and Ian to be the best man. Nicole felt honoured to be part of this special occasion. It was after all a fairy tale come true.

Therefore, she set about helping Ava to make arrangements for flowers, booking the venue, and making handmade gifts for the guests, as well as making the invitations and thank you cards for after the wedding. Ava and Ben had a very limited budget, so they were going to have the reception, as well as the wedding ceremony, at a local town hall. It wasn't a big or fancy venue, but it was big enough for their fifty odd guests and since neither Ben nor Ava was very religious, they had no need for a church ceremony.

Ava opted to wear a shop-bought dress of pink silk and Nicole would wear something out of her own cupboard to save costs. One of the policemen at Milnerton Police station offered to DJ for them and Ava organised a cash bar for the guests so that she didn't have to pay for everyone's drinks. Although it was a very basic wedding, everyone was excited about it. It was an opportunity to dress up and party, not that anyone needed an excuse to do so.

The day before the wedding, Nicole set about arranging the tables in the hall, decorating them and the hall with colourful flowers. She placed candles on the tables, which were placed on both sides of the rectangular-shaped hall. In the middle of the room, at the back, the head table was positioned so that the guests had a clear view of the bridal couple. Ava had ordered a huge bouquet for this table and asked that only the bride, groom, best man and bridesmaid were to be seated at it, as only Ben's mother was still alive, and Ava didn't want to be reminded of both of their losses. It took Nicole the whole day and way into the night to finish, but it was satisfying and that night she slept peacefully from the exhaustion.

As soon as Nicole woke up the next morning, she made her way to Ava's room as she was too excited to sleep late.

"No, come on, Nicole!" Ava complained when Nicole climbed into the bed next to Ava, like she normally did. "It's too early!"

"I can't sleep! You are getting married today, Ava!" Nicole nearly screamed from excitement.

"I know… Okay, fine then, why don't you start breakfast for us?" Ava gave in to Nicole's excitement. Nicole jumped out of the bed and headed for the kitchen. She was filled with energy and started making breakfast for her and Ava. Ben had decided to spend the night with his best man at his place to give Ava and Nicole the space to ready themselves for this important event in their lives. Both Ava and Ben were single children and therefore they had no family present that day, except for Ben's mother who was still asleep in her room. She was nearly eighty, but still very energetic and healthy.

Ava had booked a manicure and pedicure for them. It would be the first time Nicole would go for such luxuries, so she was looking forward to it. Ava had also booked a local hairdresser to come do their hair at her house later the afternoon. They decided to do their own make-up, as Ava didn't like too much of it.

When breakfast was finished, they both dressed in tracksuits. As they got to the car, a grey pick-up truck pulled up next to the car. It was Ian, he had quickly popped in to come fetch Ben's razor which he had forgotten to pack. He was very pleased to see Nicole in her grey tight-fitting tracksuit and ponytail tied high up behind her head. He didn't even look at Ava when he talked to her to find out where he needed to go look for the razor. Nicole looked fresh and natural. Her beauty mesmerised him, and he didn't hide it from her as he stared at her.

"I will see you tonight," he tried to start a conversation with Nicole, who just looked at him while smiling at his clumsy handling of the situation. "You will save a dance for me, won't you?" he asked as he stopped midway entering his pick-up.

"Yes Ian, I probably will," Nicole said, in control, as she wasn't even entertaining the thought of getting involved with him. With a huge grin on his face, he climbed into his car and left, as did Ava and Nicole.

After their nails were done, they returned home to find the hairdresser already waiting for them. Nicole set about making a light salad for both of them while Ava's hair was being done. Ava was very plain, so she opted to have her hair done up in a soft bun, with fine strands of hair rimming her face. The hairdresser managed to convince her though, to put some flowers in her hair.

Nicole loved her long locks and wanted it run down her back, so she opted for soft curls that gave volume to her already thick hair.

Then Nicole managed to convince Ava to let her do her make-up, as she normally wore very light make-up. When Ava was finished, she looked beautiful. Nicole was amazed at what subtle make-up could do. Ava was transformed from plain to polished and when she had finished dressing into the pink gown she had bought, her large frame even seemed delicate. Nicole wore a simple black pencil skirt and jacket, with a light pink blouse Ava had lent her. Nicole wore a pair of black heels, keeping her legs bare. They had hardly finished when they heard a deep voice calling from the foyer.

"Girls…are you ready?" Ian called cautiously, not wanting to enter and find someone half-dressed running around in the house.

"Yes!" Ava called back.

Outside, Ava and Ben's old blue Mercedes was polished and decorated with ribbons to announce the big occasion. Ian was dressed in a black suit, white shirt and pink tie. He looked ridiculously handsome in a suit. His hair was styled in a modern style with gel, and for the first time Nicole thought he looked appealing. She had only seen him in his working clothes, which were normally covered in grease. She smiled at him as he glided his eyes over her long bare legs and nodded in appreciation.

"You look quite handsome," Nicole said, as she climbed into the car and he held the door open for her.

"And what can I say? You look great as always," he replied while winking at her.

As they drove to the venue, passing cars hooted in recognition of the big day and Nicole turned to Ava to find her with her hands clenched in her lap.

"Are you okay, Ava?" she asked, concerned.

"Yes! Just a little bit nervous. The last time I did this, I agreed to a very abusive relationship. It just takes me back, that's all," she said as she stared out of the window.

Nicole placed her hand on Ava's.

"Just remember, Ben isn't like that! You have nothing to worry about," Nicole tried to settle her nerves.

"I know!" Ava said, still staring at the road ahead. Then they pulled up onto the lawn in front of the hall, where Ben was waiting, dressed in a black suit, pink shirt and pink silk tie.

"Oh my goodness, look at Ben!" Nicole said as she noticed him. Ava looked at Ben and both the woman giggled at his obvious discomfort at being forced into a suit. He was readjusting his tie as it bothered him, but as soon as he spotted the car, he let go and pulled at the ends of his jacket to pull himself together. He looked a little nervous, but extremely proud as he opened the door for Ava. He only had eyes for Ava as she stepped into the afternoon sun.

"You look beautiful," he said as he kissed Ava's hand, which he held to help her get out of the car.

"Thank you, Ben, and you look very smart," she replied, smiling at him. The love between the two was clearly visible and Nicole felt a little envious of their bond, but happy for her friend that she had found someone who felt as strongly about her as she did about him.

The actual wedding ceremony was over way to soon, with them ending it by exchanging rings and a kiss. They had written their own vows which had all the girls in the room wipe a tear and during the entire ceremony Nicole was painfully aware of Ian constantly glancing over at her. It seemed as if there was something magical in the air. Couples were hugging each other, holding hands and looking deep into each other's eyes as Ava and Ben declared their love for each other. And when the minister, who married them, announced: "I give to you mister and missus Baardenhorst," Ben turned to the cheering crowd and with a thundering voice announced: "Let's party!"

Soon enough, the music was harmoniously setting the mood of the evening and everybody was eating and drinking happily, with people coming over to the main table to convey their well wishes to the couple. Nicole silently sat next to Ava, whilst eating her meal. Ian was still sitting next to Ben, but kept leaning forward and looking at Nicole as if he wanted to say something to her. Ava saw this and squeezed Nicole's hand while she knowingly looked at Nicole.

"You know he really likes you?" she whispered at Nicole.

"Yes, I gathered as much, but he is so much older than me," Nicole said unsure.

The age difference made her nervous. Although she was nearing twenty, he was nearing thirty, and she was still feeling like a child deep inside. Not only did his age intimidate her, but his sheer size as well. He was close to two meters tall.

"He is such a good guy, he will take things at your pace, Nicole," Ava tried to still Nicole's fears.

"I don't know," Nicole said as she looked at his smiling face, and for a moment she felt tempted to throw all caution to the wind, as he looked really attractive.

"Promise me you will at least get to know him?" Ava asked sweetly.

"Okay, I will try," Nicole said, unsure and as if he had heard their conversation, he came to his feet and walked around the front of the table and came to stand right in front of Nicole.

"Nicole, can I get you a drink?" he asked in a gentle voice.

"Yes, that would be nice," she forced herself to say, and she looked at Ava who smiled at her appreciatively.

"Why don't you walk with me to the bar?" he asked, encouraged by the positive response.

Nicole hesitated for a second and then remembered her promise.

"Okay," she smiled at him as he held a hand for her as she stood up. As they walked away Nicole glanced back at Ava who was looking at them and Ava winked at Nicole in encouragement.

Ian and Nicole got a glass of wine and decided to stay in the bar where they had space to have a conversation. At first it was a little strained, but the more they spoke, the easier it became, and soon they were both engrossed in a pleasant conversation about life, their likes and dislikes and then even started flirting a little. Nicole actually started enjoying his company and soon as her legs grew tired and she was looking for a chair to sit on, he pulled her onto his lap, as he found the only available chair in the bar.

His huge frame so close to her made her slightly nervous, which in return aroused her, and she knew that if he approached her, she would have kissed him eagerly, but true to his gentlemanly ways, he didn't. Nicole was still laughing at a joke he had made, while facing him, when she felt a hand on her shoulder.

"Nicole," a familiar voice sounded in her ears.

Nicole turned around, still laughing, to find Dale standing in front of the two of them. His face seemed strained. Nicole hadn't even noticed him there until then.

"Oh, hi Dale, I didn't realise you were here," she said while still smiling from laughing so much.

"Yes, I was late," Dale said as he stared at Ian holding Nicole on his lap.

"At least you made it," Nicole said light-heartedly, as she returned her attention to Ian, who was looking sternly at Dale and she found the way they stared at each other comical.

"Come dance with me," Dale continued. There was a nice song playing and Nicole loved dancing.

"Would you mind if I do?" Nicole asked Ian.

"I am not your keeper," he said, and she knew that he didn't want her to go with Dale, but she wanted to dance. The wine had put her in a pleasant mood and she was in her usual party mood. She wanted to climb on the wave of intoxication and ride it into the abyss of no worry, so she jumped off Ian's lap, kissed him on his cheek and suggestively whispered into his ear, "I'll be back." This seemed to appease Ian as he smiled at her and stood up to find Ava and Ben.

Dale had a lot of rhythm and the two of them fluently took over the dance floor, gliding over it as if they had been a pair for years. Nicole enjoyed his dancing skills so much that she continued to dance with him for a couple of songs, since he didn't show any intention of stopping. He was actually pleasant company on the dance floor, making jokes and small talk. His social skills were well developed, and Nicole could imagine how he would be able to woo most women. Even she liked his subtle pursuit and knew that if he was so skilled at chasing, he sure as hell would be skilled physically as well. This thought was extremely tempting to her as a young woman, only just becoming comfortable in her skin as a sexual being.

Where emotional ties don't bind one, one obviously cannot get hurt, she thought.

So when he finally stopped at the end of a song with them both out of breath and he suggested they step outside to cool off and catch some fresh air, Nicole accepted. They walked outside where it was already dark. There were dull streetlamps lighting the garden around the venue and a walkway tunnelling through it.

"Let's walk? I want to show you the garden," he suggested as they fell into silence.

"Sure," Nicole replied and let him take her hand and lead her into the dark corners of the garden.

"I really enjoy your company, Nicole," Dale started as he led her, apparently knowing the garden well.

"I must admit you are fun too," she smiled and started wondering where he was taking her.

"I am glad you feel that way," he said as he glanced back at her before focussing on where they were going.

"Watch out for the branches," he warned as he bent to duck underneath a big tree standing in front of what seemed like a cottage.

The building was small and couldn't have been more than twenty-eight square meters in size. In front of the little two-windowed brick building, there was a covered patio. The misty sea air had now evolved into a gentle drizzle and they took shelter underneath the roof.

"What is this place?" Nicole asked.

"Storage, I suppose," Dale said as he shrugged his shoulders. It was so dark here, Nicole could hardly make out Dale's frame. The huge tree in front of the building blocked the little light that was able to reach the front of the building with a dark shadow. Dale wasn't holding Nicole's hand anymore. There were three steps up to the level of the patio. Nicole was still standing on the top step when she heard Dale's voice near her feet.

"Come, sit," he invited. Startled by his presence at her feet, she sank to his level and the cement floor was cold underneath the thin material of her skirt, which caused her skin to hit out in gooseflesh.

"Are you cold?" Dale anticipated.

"A little bit," Nicole said as she tried to wrap herself in her own arms. Dale took his jacket off and draped it around Nicole's shoulders. Grateful for the warmth of it, she hugged it tight to her body. Nicole could only faintly make out the outlines of him, and in the dark he actually seemed like a stranger as the shadows transformed him into an unrecognisable man. She could conjure up any stranger in her imagination if she wanted to, as she had only a frame as reference. She did notice though, how well rounded the outlines of his torso was underneath the tight-fitting shirt he had on.

He was extremely well-defined and she wished to see what he looked like without his shirt on. Here in their silence, she felt the electricity of her longing for him and his longing for her. Never in her wildest dreams would she under normal circumstances have thought of wanting him, but here in the darkness, she was wrapped by the comfort of the unknown and the excitement of exploration. So, she leant forward to feel for his face and instinctively found it as she placed her palm on his jawline, cupping it.

"Sorry, but I can't see you, so I have to feel for your face," she said pretending to have done so innocently.

"I have no problem with that," he said in a husky voice and placed his hands on her face.

"And now I know where you are," he said teasingly and pulled her closer and ever so gently placed his lips on hers. They held it there softly for a few seconds, as if they needed to get comfortable with the feeling of it. Nicole heard Dale's breathing was deep and constant. He smelt lovely, his hands were hard and large on her soft cheeks, but his lips were incredibly soft, full and warm. In the shadows, Dale's frame looked much younger than he did in the light and Nicole could imagine that he had been quite handsome when he was younger.

As if he sensed her mind wandering, he slowly started to kiss Nicole, parting her lips to intrude her mouth with his thick tongue. Nicole parted them willingly and let him roam freely inside of her, reciprocating the passion building up from the wetness of his kiss. With every drop of saliva produced by her mouth, her loins echoed it and soon she was slippery and wet from wanting and anticipating more. Nicole couldn't take the teasing any longer, frustrated by his unwillingness to let his hands wonder over her body, so she tugged at his shirt. Without stopping his passionate lingering on her mouth, he skilfully undid his buttons and pulled his shirt from his torso and pressed his skin against her body, offering the feel of it proudly to her slender fingers.

Nicole couldn't get enough. Her hands frantically ran over every inch of his muscled stomach, his large arms and his narrow middle. She lingered at the zip of his trousers, taking in the sheer size of his erection, and it excited her. The hardness of it aroused a primitive urge in her and she groaned as she squeezed her nails into his flesh. He grunted back at her as he pushed her to the floor behind her back and she willingly let him.

Finally, he had the permission he wanted, and slid his hands underneath her skirt, pulling her panties to her knees and then placed his one hand under her head, supporting it as to have her be as comfortable as possible while he took full advantage of this offering. Dale kept kissing Nicole, while she closed her eyes as she gave into the wanting. With his free hand, Dale started massaging Nicole's bare inner thigh, kneading it forcefully, but not coming close to where she was now aching for him. His rough hard hands on her soft fleshy thigh made the blood in her body rush to her most intimate parts in anticipation of him.

When he finally reached her, she was swollen and slippery and his fingers glided over and through the slimy lips of her opening. He kneaded her flesh until she groaned out loud from frustration and then he inserted two of his fingers deep into her to satisfy her aching being and she rode his fingers until she was about to climax on his thick coarse fingers.

"Dale!" Nicole heard Ava's agitated voice and with the sound breaking through the darkness, Nicole's pleasure was plucked from her loins.

"Dale! Is that you?" Ava asked again as she came closer and Nicole pulled her panties to cover her shame.

"Fuck!" Dale said softly as he pulled his shirt on and pulled Nicole to her feet.

"Yes Ava!" he called back and as Ava reached them, he stuck his wet fingers in his pocket while still rubbing the slipperiness of it between his thumb and fingers. If it was possible, he would have smelled it.

"What are you two doing here?" Ava asked, very angered by their disappearance.

"We came for a walk and we were wondering what was in this building, so we came to have a look," he skilfully lied in an even tone. Nicole kept quiet as she knew she wouldn't have control over her voice, as her breathing was still racing and she was painfully aware of the uncomfortable slipperiness between her legs, as if Ava could notice.

"We are going to cut the cake. You have to come inside," Ava said sternly as she turned to walk back to the main building and like children that had been caught out, they followed. Nicole passed Dale to take her place next to Ava.

"Are you okay?" Ava asked Nicole softly as they walked.

"Yes," Nicole answered back.

"Are you sure?" Ava continued, not convinced by Nicole's answer.

"Yes Ava, I am sure," she appeased her friend.

With that, they reached the main building and Dale disappeared. Ian was nowhere to be found when they wanted to cut the cake.

"He probably went home," Ben explained, giving Nicole a death stare when Ava asked about his whereabouts. Then the cake was cut, the guests ate the cake, photos were taken, and all Nicole could do was run her mind over the lusciousness of the pleasure Dale's fingers had given her. And that night, when they finally reached home and she crept into her bed, she finished off what Dale had started.

Ben and Ava couldn't afford to go away for their honeymoon, but at least took a week off from work to spend some quality time together. Since they were living in the suburbs of Cape Town, they really didn't have to go anywhere as they were right in the middle of one of the most picturesque cities in the world and there were so many things to do. So, they made time for romantic dinners, long walks on the beach and visited some of the holiday destinations they normally didn't get a chance to visit, while working the long hours they did.

Being the social beings that they were though, this kept them busy for the first three days before they felt deprived of social interaction from their friends, so they once again asked Nicole over for a barbeque, as well as some of their other friends, and of course Nicole wasn't passing the opportunity to visit with them.

The usual crowd of friends arrived for the festivities. Eugene and Grete took care of the music and soon everyone was happily chatting away around the fire, with alcohol flowing freely. Nicole wasn't in the mood for drinking like she usually was. She was feeling somewhat withdrawn as she looked at the couples that shared a special bond. Although the men and woman were separated into two groups, she noticed that the couples every so often made eye contact or walked over to check on one another.

Nicole longed for that connection. Someone who had her back, a partner in life who would look out for her as much as she would him, but for some reason she had no luck in this department and she tried to figure out what it was that kept her from such happiness. Maybe she was too picky she thought and then she started hoping that Dale would also come over, as he at least wanted her attention. Dale was banned from Ava and Ben's house though, without Nicole knowing about it, after the incident at their wedding.

"Nicole, are you alright?" Ben came over to her where she sat next to the fire, on her own, away from the conversation.

"Yes. I am enjoying the warmth of the fire," she explained, but didn't face Ben, since she knew he would see she was lying.

"Man, have another beer!" he encouraged as he didn't know how to deal with the emotional dynamics of women. Nicole smiled up at him, appreciating his clumsy attempt at cheering her up and she took the beer he held out to her and placed it next to the full one standing at her feet.

"Thank you, Ben," she said softly as she smiled at him and he proudly walked away believing he had made her feel better. For the rest of the evening, Nicole faked feeling chilled, talking friendly to whoever came to sit next to her for a chat. When everyone had dished themselves something to eat, Nicole took a piece of chicken from the dish and without dishing it into a plate, ate it next to the fire and threw the bone into the fire when she had finished. Even the small piece of flesh seemed to be too much of an effort to finish.

I should have stayed home, Nicole thought to herself as she watched the bone blacken from the heat of the fire. *I could have rather slept.* And then she regretted agreeing to sleep over at Ben and Ava.

Finally, the rest of the crowd left and Nicole helped Ava clean up after the guests. Ben took a seat in the living room and when the women had finished, they went to join him.

"I don't understand why Ian didn't come?" Ava said as she fell back onto the sofa.

"He was probably working late again," Ben replied. Nicole didn't even know that he was invited, and knew that he was probably invited for her sake. She wished they wouldn't push so hard to get them together, but also started wondering if she shouldn't just give in and date him, since there was no one that really excited her. Nicole didn't want to settle for just anything, she wanted someone that challenged her on all levels.

If she wanted a friend to sleep with, there were plenty available, but she knew that would ultimately bore her and she would rather be alone and want someone, than sit with someone that limited her possibilities of experiencing life and all it had to offer to the full. While Nicole was still busy contemplating this, Ben took his pipe and tobacco jar from the shelf behind him and started filling his pipe.

"Nicole, are you smoking with me tonight?" he smiled at Nicole and held the pipe up to her so that she could see what he meant, as if she didn't know. Nicole loved the smell of Ben's pipe and the tobacco. The sweet smell seemed to soothe her.

"Yes. Why not?" she replied, and Ben returned to filling the pipe, while she watched attentively. When he had finished, he lit the top with his lighter and pulled hard on the end until thick fumes of smoke escaped his mouth and floated up to the roof. Then he took one draw on it for enjoyment and passed it over to Nicole for her to take a puff.

Tonight, the smoke tasted somewhat sweeter than normal and she pulled hard on the pipe, fascinated by the red glow the leaves of the tobacco made as she pulled on it. The burn of it filled her lungs as she pulled the smoke deep into her lung cavities and taken aback by the strength of its burn, she started coughing.

"Slow down there!" Ben warned as he laughed at Nicole's distress.

"What is in that?" Nicole asked. "It doesn't taste like your normal tobacco."

"I mixed two tobaccos," Ben explained without saying what types. "Thought I would give it a try. Do you like it?"

"Yes, it's nice, but strong," Nicole said while Ben was puffing away at his pipe. Nicole took the pipe from him each time he offered it to her and then she filled her lungs with the strangely soothing burn of it.

Soon Nicole felt very relaxed, her muscles became lame and she flopped over onto the couch she was sitting on. Nicole had felt intoxicated a lot of times, but this was not the same, she had never felt such calmness fill her body. It was as if she was floating on air in her reality, but on another level or dimension. She could hear everything going on crystal clear, she could feel everything, but she was numbed by an eerily pleasing calmness of soul and body, rendering her motionless, she was trapped in this state.

She didn't really want to come out of it as well and as she lay on the couch giving in to the pleasure of it, she started giggling at the sensation of not feeling anything, but also feeling everything at once. Nicole didn't notice that Ava had left their company to retire to her bed. Time seemed to pass at a different pace and when Ben picked her up and laid her down on the floor in a sleeping bag with a pillow propped under her head, she happily smiled at him as he shook his head and smiled at her.

When he left, he switched the lights off, except for the lava lamp in the corner of the room and unable to move a muscle, Nicole was transfixed by the luminous colours and shadows it cast on the walls. Nicole heard the front door open, two male voices, one laughing, probably Ben. She looked at the purple hues, she heard footsteps, she looked at the yellow balls of oil bubbling up in the lamp, she heard Ian ask her if she was okay and she could feel her lips say yes, but her soul seemed to be disconnected from her body as her soul was floating loosely in her skin.

Then she felt Ian climb into her sleeping bag and starting to caress her, and while she closed her eyes and gave into the sensation, she could see everything clearly without being able to stop, nor wanting to stop it. Seconds, minutes, she couldn't register, but soon, her pants were undone, and Ian slowly filled her insides with a hardness and length she hadn't felt before. His body seemed to ride the waves of her soul as his shaft stimulated her insides to the point where her loins spontaneously wanted to spasm around him. He was very gentle with her and she so wanted to reciprocate his passion, but she couldn't move or will her body to.

Suddenly, she became panic-stricken as she realised she was not in control and there was something seriously wrong with the picture. Her senses slowly came flooding back into her from the shock of the realisation that she was drugged. Ian seemed to recognise the panic in her face as he suddenly withdrew from her.

"I am so sorry!" he said equally shocked. "I didn't know."

"No!" she managed to say. "Please help me." Ian pulled her to her feet and walked her to the bathroom so that she could wash her face with cold water in the hope of sobering her up, but it wasn't the water that did the trick. By this time the effects of the magical smoke she had so pleasantly inhaled had worn off, and body and soul were making connection again. He held her hair as she washed her face. As she came upright, he held a towel for her and wiped her face.

"Are you okay?" he asked.

"Yes, I think so," Nicole said, unsure. Ian looked ashamed and as if he wanted to flee, but he first took Nicole back to where her bed was made for her in the living room on the floor, before he kissed her on her head and then left. The floor didn't seem as soft as a cloud anymore, it was hard and cold, but luckily, sleep came over Nicole just as quickly as the fog did and she slept soundly.

The next morning, she was the first to awake. As she lay there on the floor her mind wondered back to what had happened the night before, and she realised Ben had drugged her. She was pissed off with him for doing such a thing to her, as he was supposed to be her friend. She knew he had an odd sense of humour, but he had taken it too far this time. She didn't want to think that he had orchestrated such an elaborate plan as to drug her so that Ian could fuck her, nor that men could be so callous as to plan such a thing together.

No, that seemed too farfetched and she decided that it was just a weird accumulation of events that panned out to look like it was planned that way. Still, the fact that Ben had given her some form of drugs without letting her decide if she wanted to take or not was unacceptable. She also now had to deal with the fact that Ben was obviously using drugs, and she wasn't really comfortable with this knowledge, as she had promised herself years ago, she would never go there.

And now, without a choice, she had. Nicole realised that if she was sober the previous night, she would have slept with Ian in all probability, but would have been able to enjoy it and not feel so embarrassed by the state she was in when he came to her.

"Fuck Ben! You're and idiot!" she said out loud as she got up to pull herself together.

She didn't mention anything to Ava, who was blissfully unaware of what had taken place. She didn't want to upset her friend, nor did she want to put herself up for disappointment in discovering that Ava actually did know about Ben's drug use. It was safer for her to believe her dearest friend was innocent in this all and decided that she would just be more vigilant in not trusting Ben and his pranks.

Chapter 17

Nicole returned to work and to the motions of Charge Office work. Nicole felt somewhat sombre, since all the men she was interested in had left her or disappointed her expectations and it became more apparent that there weren't too many options left for her to choose from. She started wondering if there was someone out there that would suit her, appreciate her and acknowledge the qualities in her that she valued as important. Although she preferred being alone to being stuck with someone that didn't enhance her life, she still longed for the companionship of a soul-mate, but was doubting that it really existed, since most of the relationships around her seemed to be a compromise between two parties with a mutual goal. She thus opted to ignore her loneliness and focus her energy on her work.

Nicole was busy in the Charge Office, still running her head over her decision to let life just happen naturally and not to procrastinate too much on what the outcome of her path into the future holds, when she heard someone enter the office. As if nature was taunting her, she looked up into the face of the young stranger that held the door for her at the psychiatric evaluation when she had applied at the police force.

Nicole nearly swallowed her tongue as he flashed a confident smile at her in recognition. He had looked handsome that day when she first laid eyes on him, but here, now, he took her breath away. He had become even more muscular from his physical training, his dark skin was even darker from days spent exposed to the sun and his hair was cut neatly in a crew cut, which suited his broad jawline. Nicole wanted to speak to him, she needed to know who he was, but her will failed her and she could merely stare at him.

It was clear that he wasn't there for business, as he confidently walked through the Charge Office, smiled at Nicole without saying a word and then continued out of sight down the hallway, only to appear a few minutes later. Once again Nicole got a smile, but also a cheeky wink and then he disappeared.

Oh my God, Nicole thought to herself. *He is certainly by far the most gorgeous man I have ever seen.* Nicole turned to Sergeant Mostert who was drinking his coffee in the Charge Office.

"Who is that?" she asked out of breath. Sergeant Mostert didn't look too pleased by her reaction towards the young man's presence.

"That is Sergeant Griffin, he works at SANAB," he said lazily.

"Oh my word, he is attractive," she blurted it out as she thought it without checking herself.

"Be careful of that one," Sargent Mostert warned her. "He has a reputation of being a lady's man and he is engaged to the new girl in the office."

Nicole felt disappointed and sank back into her chair. "The skinny blonde one?" Nicole asked, hoping it wasn't her, but knowing it was the only new girl on the station.

"Yes," Sergeant Mostert said and with that, all Nicole's hopes were set aside, as she was not prepared to meddle in other people's happiness and she felt inadequate compared to the slim and beautifully groomed blonde that worked down the hall.

"What is SANAB though?" she asked her Sergeant.

"It is the narcotics bureau," he answered her, annoyed by her interest in the attractive young man and then he stood up to take up his duties on the patrol vehicle outside.

Nicole was left with the image of the young man and his beautiful smile lingering in her mind's eye, while continuing her daily tasks. After that he would often pop in to visit his fiancé, always making a point of showing Nicole that he noticed her with a big welcoming smile, but also always with a deeper meaning of appreciating her more than a promised man should. This flattered Nicole, but also confirmed Sergeant Mostert's assessment of his character, so Nicole never attempted to start a conversation with him. She did however revel in the attention and the pleasure of staring at his beautiful body and face when he made his appearance.

Although Nicole was settled in her routine of working at Table View police station, she still longed to work with Ava and Ben at Milnerton. The station had a young and fun vibe, whereas Table View was more strewn with older officers, set in their ways and sticking to work and focussing on their families, which wasn't a bad thing, but for a young woman without family, it became boring.

She missed the fun she had with Ben and Ava and also she felt a distinct change of attitude towards her from Lieutenant Liebenberg. She now knew it was because of her not wanting to date his cousin, but since she wasn't prepared to go there, she wanted to transfer badly, so badly that she mustered the courage to once again apply for a transfer to Milnerton. She was met by a surprisingly positive approval of her application, as there was a senior Sergeant from Milnerton wanting to transfer to Table View. Nicole couldn't believe how quickly a transfer could take place, since she was ordered to report to duty on her next shift. Lieutenant Liebenberg looked all too eager to get rid of her and said they would put the paperwork through, but there was no need to prolong the exchange as the other officer desperately needed to work closer to home.

The transfer couldn't have come at a better time as well, as Nicole's lease contract on the apartment was about to expire, and she was looking forward to finding cheaper lodgings. Ava had told Nicole about the Barracks in Sea Point where single policewomen could rent a room for next to nothing, where your meals were cooked, your washing done and offered the companionship of other single girls in the same situation.

In this situation, it sounded like paradise and Nicole thought it the best time to apply for a room as soon as one opened up. Ava helped her with the application, as that she too had to make use of the barracks when she started out in the police and she still knew a few people at the station. To both of the women's surprise, there was a room available and Nicole could move in at the end of the month, which meant that not only for the first time since she had started working as a police officer, would she have enough money and food, but she would get the deposit back she had to put down on her apartment.

Her mother had told her that she could reuse it in any way she saw fit when it became free, as she had felt bad for placing Nicole in such an awkward position when she came back from the College—to find an apartment over a weekend. Finally, it felt as if things were turning around for Nicole, and with a new enthusiasm for life, Nicole set off on her task of packing up her apartment well in advance.

She organised storage for the furniture she wouldn't be able to take with her, as she was only offered a room, which was already furnished. She actually preferred it this way as she could make a new start, without her mother's possessions. And although she had none of her own, she would now have the opportunity to collect her own if she wanted to.

When Nicole arrived for her first shift at Milnerton, she was absolutely overwhelmed by the excitement of a new start. Everything seemed to fall perfectly into place. Everyone embraced her arrival with open arms and she was made to feel welcome, so much so, that she felt as if she knew the people for years instead of only a few hours. Nicole was placed with a young shift consisting of four men, all Sergeants, and a girl the same age as her. The girl was full-figured, blonde, with blue eyes and a bubbly personality. Nicole immediately knew they were going to get on well and she couldn't believe her luck when she met her new shift.

"Hi Nicole, I am Andrea!" the girl said, not offering a hand but taking Nicole into an embrace. Nicole smiled at the shift as they stood closer to introduce themselves and she couldn't believe how young her new shift was, with the oldest being about thirty-two and married, while the rest were still unmarried.

"Hi, I am Sergeant Laing and the shift commander," a tall slightly plump Sergeant introduced himself as he took her hand and shook it longer than she expected.

"Hi, I am Sergeant Duvenhage," the oldest of the Sergeants introduced himself and he had a sincere and kind smile. Nicole immediately knew they were going to get on well, as his eyes were kind and gentle. He had an olive skin tone, with chocolate brown hair and he had acne scars. Although he wasn't attractive, his personality made him attractive.

Sergeant Wetzel was as tall as Nicole and Nicole sensed a refinedness to him that belonged comfortably in the gay community, but she could see his gentle soul and immediately felt drawn to him as she took his hand in greeting him. Nicole soon enough discovered that he shared a home with a very gay male friend, but Sergeant Wetzel preferred to stay in the closet, as there was still discrimination against their community, not only in society during that time, but also in the police force.

For that matter, racial discrimination was only one of the aspects of Apartheid, the word encompassed so much more than race, and only if you lived in South Africa and amongst its people would you understand the depth of it. Since the racial issue was highlighted by the unrest and riots that took place in a plea to change things, there were discrimination of sex and sexual orientations, also of language, the English-speaking South Africans regarding themselves superior to their Afrikaans speaking country men and vice versa.

And although it wasn't focussed on, there was the enlightened majority, from all stands of life, slowly making their voices heard about their disapproval of the situation. Nicole, as one of this young liberated group, immediately felt empathy for his troubled life and the restrictions hung around his shoulders by society.

The last Sergeant was an extremely attractive dark-haired young man called Sergeant Basson. He looked very business-like and not much fun. He did smile friendly though when he shook Nicole's hand and she noticed a ring on his finger and she thought he was married, until later, when Andrea told her otherwise. He wore a ring from his fiancée to let every girl in his vicinity know about it, as she was paranoid about losing him.

Falling into her new routine came easily as her shift was a pleasant bunch, taking life lightly and in their stride as young people tend to. This attitude soon rubbed off on Nicole as it was infectious. Nicole was hoping to run into Mika at some point, but to her disappointment she had to find out from Andrea that Mika had been transferred to the detective's branch in Bothasig, so the chances of that happening wouldn't be too great, as even if they came to Milnerton, they would probably only go to the detective's offices, which had a separate entrance at the back. Nicole wondered how it was going with him and his new fiancé, and if they were happy. More to the point, if he was happy, but accepted that it had nothing to do with her anymore.

Within that first month of working at her new station, Nicole, helped by Ava and Ben, moved into her new lodgings at Sea Point Barracks. Since all the girls living there worked different shifts, she didn't really have the chance to befriend them. Her off days were spent with Ava and Ben and in between shifts she made up for lost sleep or took long jogs down the coastline to keep her mind and body fit. The food was plentiful, the cleaning ladies did her washing and ironing for her and her room was comfortable and cosy. Nicole dared to settle into a content pace of life, where she was afforded enough money to be able to spend some of it on herself.

She invested in some designer wear, proper make-up and had her nails done. Finally, she felt as if she fitted into her surroundings, amongst all the trendy Capetonians. Sometimes she would walk the streets of Cape Town browsing through the pavement stalls or have a bite to eat at local restaurants. The buzz of the city and its colourful people excited her and at times, she couldn't help to feel that she was too liberal for the restrictions of the Police mentality and her then Apartheid South African boundaries.

Not much out of the ordinary took place in the first few months of them working together as a shift and Nicole settled into the notion that she was amongst a group of like-minded police officers, who on a professional level upheld their vow to enforce the law as it was meant to be done. Except for Sergeant Laing, who shamelessly flirted with Nicole, whilst being engaged, there was nothing else that really bothered her about her shift.

Nicole and Andrea also started hanging out in their free time, which meant she had a girlfriend as companion, which in turn meant that the fact that her love life was non-existent didn't bother her as much anymore. What she did discover though was her new friend's love for men. Andrea was committed to her fiancé, a banker, but as such, he was constantly working and she had way too much free time on her hands. She had a light-hearted approach to men and their advances, not at all as intense as Nicole, who took everything seriously and overthought every little detail of everything.

Although Nicole could curb this drawback of her personality, her strive for perfection left her disappointed regularly. Andrea was thus a fresh breath of air and Nicole found balance in their relationship, realising through her friend that all sexual encounters did not need to be an emotional one as well, and that spontaneous sex had its place in the bigger picture.

Andrea was very open-minded on this aspect of life. She had many flirtatious relationships with men, but only one man owned her heart. Seeing that Nicole didn't have sisters with whom she could discuss these matters, or use as a sound board to find her own comfort with her sexuality, she fed from her friendship with Andrea, taking on and testing these new found realisations. Most of which was testing her flirting abilities shamelessly on the men present at their station.

The more Nicole became comfortable with her newfound sexual powers, the more relaxed Andrea became with Nicole and with disclosing her innermost secrets of liaisons. Soon enough the two were inseparable and one afternoon as they finished their morning shift and were preparing to go home, Andrea came up to Nicole.

"Do you have to go back to your place or do you feel like coming to my house? I stay very close to the station," Andrea offered.

"I suppose I can come to you," Nicole said apprehensively, as she knew she should rather go home and get some sleep, as they were working double shift that day and she wouldn't be able to keep her eyes open on night shift if she didn't.

"Don't worry, I will ask the Sergeant to post us in the Charge Office, then we can take turns to sleep," she set Nicole's mind at ease, as she knew what was bothering Nicole.

"Okay, sure, why not?" Nicole said, convincing herself that there would be no harm in doing so. Nicole loved the night shifts with her new shift seeing that night shifts were normally slightly quieter than during the day, which meant that they had time to hang around and chat and sometimes so much time that they got up to mischief.

Andrea's house was just a few blocks away from the station so they walked to her house. When they reached it, Nicole deduced that her parents, with who she was still staying, were strict and perfectionists, as the house was painfully neat. The house was modest, but there was nothing out of place or broken. It was painted white, the fascia boards were perfectly kept, as was the garden. And when they walked into the lounge, she could see why, as her father was a Major in the police force.

There was a large framed picture of him in full uniform hanging on the wall, as well as all his diplomas that he had accumulated over the years by studying through the police force. Nicole noted that he was one of the male members of society that didn't have the opportunity to study at university and therefore joined the Force, but took it seriously and made a life for him and his family by approaching it determinately and with ambition. She also thought to herself that Andrea obviously didn't have the same drive as her father and smiled at herself as she thought it.

"Yes, I know, he looks funny, doesn't he?" Andrea said as she noticed the smile on Nicole's mouth as she was looking at the picture.

"No, that wasn't what I was thinking," Nicole protested.

"Oh please, leave the old man be. I really don't feel like talking about him. Do you want something to drink?" Andrea offered.

"Yes, that would be nice," Nicole said whilst still looking at the diplomas and wondering if she shouldn't perhaps start to study as Andrea's dad had, but pushed the idea aside as she heard Andrea speak.

"What would you like?" Andrea hovered in the doorway to the kitchen.

"Surprise me," Nicole said, not wanting to ask for something they might not have in their house, but hoping for something cold as she was hot from walking in the sun. Andrea disappeared for a few minutes and then returned with two glasses of orange juice for them. She gave one to Nicole and then held it for Nicole so that they could clink glasses.

As the two girls brought their glasses together, Andrea said: "Cheers!" Seeing that they were drinking fruit juice, this seemed strange, but Nicole followed Andrea's direction. As Nicole gratefully downed half a glass of the cold fluid, she heard Andrea's protest in unison with her recognition of the taste of alcohol.

"What are you doing?" Andrea started laughing as Nicole's eyes widened with shock at the strength of the drink she had been handed.

"Shit, Andrea! I thought you gave me orange juice! What the hell?" she said as she too started laughing. Andrea could hardly get a word out as the tears streamed down her face as a result of her laughing fit.

"It is vodka and orange juice!" she managed to utter before she gave into another fit of laughter.

"Oh my God, we can't drink, Andrea, we have to work in a few hours," Nicole said amused by her friend's state, but also concerned.

"Oh, live a little!" Andrea stopped laughing and shook her head.

"We are going to get into so much trouble if we smell like alcohol!" Nicole said as she smiled at Andrea, tempted by the freedom of Andrea's carelessness in enjoying the moment. She envied her.

"No one will know, I have done this many times, I promise," Andrea encouraged Nicole.

Nicole shrugged her shoulders and took another sip.

"There you go!" Andrea praised her and she started walking to her room and indicated to Nicole to follow her, which she did.

The two girls chatted while Andrea got dressed into tights and an oversized top of her fiancé. They smoked and drank another vodka and orange juice.

"Why are you still living with your parents when you have a fiancé?" Nicole wondered.

"I prefer it this way. He is nearly ten years my senior and I want to marry him, but don't feel ready yet. He understands it that way. He is looking after his mother as well, so his hands are full as it is. There is plenty of time, don't worry," Andrea explained their arrangement to Nicole.

The idea that people could have arrangements when it came to marriage, which gave both parties the freedom they needed to keep their lifestyle, and still be committed to a loving relationship, made more sense to Nicole than the

Calvinistic way of thinking she was brought up with, where nothing was questioned and one set of rules was forced on everyone. The idea of a unique relationship excited her, since she was tutored by her parents that only a strictly monogamous relationship, where both parties stay together, sleep together, did everything together, made for a healthy relationship.

She knew that this mentality was flawed as her parents' relationship failed as a result of their restricted ideas. She loved the idea that where two individuals want to make a relationship work, they should be able to make their own rules for their specific needs, for them to be able to stay together, while giving room for each individual to keep their individuality.

There are too many differences in people to have only one type of relationship to fit everybody, she thought. And now, while talking to Andrea, her assumptions were confirmed. The magnetic pull of love will bring two like-minded individuals together as they recognise similarities and allow for differences, but the odds of them meeting are slim and therefore she understood why Andrea and her fiancé went to great lengths to make their unique relationship work. Nicole gathered some hope from the conversation, that there just might be someone out there that would fit her.

Then the doorbell rang.

"Nicole, will you go get that please?" Andrea asked as she was busy tying her hair into a knot on top of her head.

"Yes. Are you expecting someone?" Nicole asked, confused.

"Yes, I have invited one of my friends over, I hope you don't mind?" Andrea explained.

Nicole opened the door to find two attractive young men at of the door, in their blue uniforms. Nicole hadn't seen them before and gathered that they were from a different station.

"Hi," the taller of the two, who was standing in front, greeted Nicole. "Is Andrea here?"

"Yes, come in, she will be out in a second," Nicole said as she indicated for them to enter the house.

They both walked in and took a seat in the lounge as Andrea made her appearance and the tall policeman jumped to his feet and scooped Andrea into his arms and hugged her tightly while she squealed with pleasure. When he had put her down, he introduced her to his friend Dean and they shook hands as he came to his feet. Then Andrea turned to Nicole.

"This is Nicole," Andrea introduced Nicole and both men looked at Nicole appreciatively and then came to shake her hand.

"Hi, I am Henry and this is Dean," Andrea's tall, dark and handsome friend introduced himself and his slender pale, but attractive friend.

"Did you bring the movie?" Andrea asked Henry.

"Of course, I did," he said with a grin on his face that Nicole couldn't quite place.

Andrea took Nicole's glass from her hand on her way to the kitchen. Nicole took a seat and felt a little awkward in the presence of the two strangers, but they quickly made a point of questioning her about herself to keep her occupied and also to make small talk. Nicole answered their questions without letting them know too much personal information as she didn't intend to get to know them better. She decided to be polite, but was actually annoyed with Andrea for not telling her that she had invited friends over for a movie.

If she had, Nicole would have probably have gone home to get some sleep before their night shift started. Just then, Andrea returned with a tray on which four glasses were balanced. They were filled with brandy and coke this time and Nicole automatically took a glass without putting up a fuss. She knew it would actually take more effort to explain why she didn't feel like drinking, than to just drink it. She sank back into her seat and decided that she would then sleep in her chair while the movie was playing and the others' attention was fixed on the screen in front of them.

As Andrea drew the curtains to darken the room, Nicole lit a cigarette while sipping on her brandy and coke. The two young men were filled with energy and bantering continuously with each other and Andrea, while trying to pull Nicole into the fun, but she stubbornly smiled politely while making it clear with her body language that she was only a presence and not a participant. While Nicole was caught up in her own thoughts and about to finish her cigarette, Andrea took a seat next to Henry on the large couch opposite the television set.

Dean sat on the couch opposite Nicole and kept looking at her in anticipation, as if he wanted her to join him on his couch, but Nicole seemed oblivious. Even when he gave her compliments on her hair and eyes, she ignored it. Nicole snuggled into a cosy position as the screen of the television flickered into life so that she could make an easy exit into dreamland. Andrea snuggled into Henry's arm. This seemed strange to Nicole as she knew Andrea was engaged, but didn't make a fuss as she closed her eyes to take a nap, while the others were looking at the movie that was about to start. From where Nicole sat, she couldn't see the television screen clearly, she was looking at an angle. This suited her as silence fell and she heard the soft murmurs of human voices as the movie started. The sound quality was awful and she could hardly make out what was said.

Nicole shook her head to herself as she put her empty glass down after the last sip and turned her head into the softness of the cushion behind her. Soft moans filled her ears as she closed her eyes and then a slapping sound, followed by a deep groan. Nicole's eyes flew open as she sat upright to look at the screen to see what they were watching.

She couldn't believe her eyes; right there in front of her, an attractive dark-haired athletic man was thrusting his enormous dick into the hairy pussy of a slender older woman with drooping boobs. He approached the deed with so much force that the woman must have gotten hurt, but to Nicole's amazement, she threw her head back and moaned in a trancelike manner while she held her labia open with her two hands so that he could have easy access to her. Then slowly, he pulled his never-ending snake from its hole while it spat glistening white fluid over the poor woman's genitals. She didn't seem to mind as she rubbed the thick wet fluid into her crevices, as he joined her with his spilling manhood.

Nicole was, needless to say, shocked into a very attentive state and pulled her chair into a position where she could see the television screen clearly. She didn't even notice the other three in the room. She watched in amazement how one after the other act of pure lust played itself out in front of her. She couldn't stop herself from watching and with each scene that took place in front of her and with each detailed close shot, her own lust built up inside of her to the point where her loins felt warm, wet and swollen.

Then at one point Andrea and Henry excused themselves and went to Andrea's room, closing the door behind them. Nicole stood up and put the video recorder off. She felt slightly panic-stricken and guilty, firstly for being left alone with a young man who clearly felt equally aroused as she did, and secondly for watching an erotic movie, as it was still illegal to do so in South Africa. As she moved back to her seat in silence, not knowing how to handle the situation, the wetness between her legs became unbearable and she excused herself.

"Dean, I am sorry, I have to get ready for work, I am going to have to take a bath. It was nice meeting you," she said awkwardly and fled down the passageway to the first bathroom, where she ran herself a bath to rid her body of the slimy feeling between her legs.

Dean didn't even respond to her, he sat quietly and nodded as she excused herself. It was his first time in such a scenario and as such didn't know quite what was expected of him, but the burning sensation in his scrotum made sitting really uncomfortable, and he was relieved when Nicole left the room and he was left alone to adjust himself. As he saw her disappear behind the bathroom door, he unzipped his pants and pulled his warm erection out into his hand and slowly moved it up and down his shaft a few times.

He leaned into it as if his body was thrusting into an imaginary vagina. His frustration made him put it back into his pants and without thought he followed Nicole down the passage. The bathroom door wasn't a solid wooden door, it was a concertina door and was poorly fit so that the door couldn't close properly, leaving enough of an opening for him to peep through and afford him a view of the whole bathroom. He peered in and saw the naked skin of Nicole's perfectly formed bottom and the dark forbidden pleasure hidden in the opening at the top of her legs, as she was bent forward to rid herself of her panties. Once again his erection was so painful, he had to release it and took it from his pants, while slowly stroking it as he watched Nicole come upright.

She threw her long tresses back onto her soft cream silky skin. She had the most amazing shape, with curves in all the right places, but still her frame seemed delicate. The top of his head became wet in anticipation. He was struggling with himself not to enter the bathroom. Nicole bent forward again to check the water and as she did so, Dean sighed from frustration as she flashed her closed womanhood at him. She wasn't shaven. The sight of her soft curly pubic hair made her seem untouched, something that made the situation even worse for Dean.

Dean watched in awe as Nicole climbed into the bath and he marvelled at the sight of her perfectly small rounded breasts. She had light pink nipples that stood erect from the contact with the warm water against her cold skin. Dean was about to force himself away from the door out of guilt, when he saw Nicole's one hand slide down her stomach in-between her legs. He gasped at the sight. There, right in front of him, he saw how one of the most beautiful girls he had ever seen was not only naked, but was pleasuring herself with her delicate fingers.

He was transfixed and as her body spasmed into a climax, he lost control of all reasoning and pushed the door open with force, while starting to rid himself of all his clothes. When he reached the bath, he was naked and looking down at Nicole, who was dizzily, from climaxing, opening her eyes. They didn't speak a word as he climbed into the bath, in between her legs and felt for her opening. She was so slippery that he could hardly keep it open long enough to enter her.

As Nicole opened her eyes, she saw Dean towering over her. She had no time to think as he climbed into the bath with her. Every single muscle on his body was drawn hard from wanting her. She was surprised by the beauty of his pale white body. She was still enveloped in the aftermath of her intense climax and was waiting for her body to recuperate so that she could pleasure it again, but before she could make sense of what was happening, Dean filled her with his hardness. He was hard as he held himself in position.

He placed both his hands on the rim of the bath on either side of her, while she was still lying in the bath with her legs separated. As if he was doing push-ups, he kept his weight up with his arms, while he started moving inside her. She couldn't keep herself from moving against him as his hardness calmed the aching deep inside her. His thrusts became faster and more intense very quickly and before she could even respond properly to him, he pulled himself from her and sat on his knees between her legs, while white fluid ran over his hands, as he held his dick in his hand.

"Aaaaaahhh," he moaned from pleasure or frustration, Nicole wasn't quite sure, but she pulled herself into a sitting position. Dean climbed out of the bathtub. He was slightly embarrassed by what had happened, as this wasn't normal behaviour for him. Nicole was a stranger as well and as such he didn't know what to say to her. Nicole too was at a loss for words, so she washed herself, hoping that he would leave, which he luckily did.

"I…I will leave you to finish," he excused himself awkwardly.

As Nicole got out and started drying herself, she heard Andrea call from the bedroom.

"Nicole, come help! Please Nicole, come quickly!" Andrea sounded in distress, so Nicole didn't even bother putting on clothes as it would take too long, so she only tied the towel around her and ran to the room. When she reached the room, she found Andrea at the door, stricken with panic and Nicole imagined something terrible had happened. As she entered the room, she found a naked Henry sitting on the edge of Andrea's upturned bed, holding his penis in his one hand and his other hand cupping the head of it. He made for a sorry sight as he worriedly looked down at it, as if it was about to fall off and he was trying to hold it in position. Nicole nearly broke out in laughter, both from nervousness of what she might discover underneath his hands, and because of the expression on his face as he looked up at her for guidance on what to do next. Nicole tried to keep a straight face as she neared him.

"What happened?" she asked Andrea, who didn't want to be close to the damage she obviously had done.

Andrea just shook her head as she wasn't prepared to go into the details of her brutal handling of his private parts. Nicole looked at Henry, who was still cupping his penis. Nicole couldn't help gliding her eyes over the impressive contours of Henry's toned body and then her eyes fixed on the muscled veiny hand that held his manhood. Nicole had to force herself to focus on his distress.

She cleared her throat and asked, very business-like: "So what happened?"

Henry looked slightly flushed as he answered: "I am not exactly sure, but it is bleeding."

Nicole bit her lip as he looked like a small boy caught out by his mother, so she took on the role.

"Let me see?" she asked and slowly pulled his hand cupping his penis away, so that she could look at the damage. He let Nicole take his limp warm flesh from his hand so that she could examine it. Droplets of blood were rimming the bottom part of his head and she saw a small tear in the skin that covered it, and as she held it, it grew in her hand and the tear became more visible. Nicole smiled up at him.

"Oh I see…" she said. "It is nothing serious." She set his mind at ease.

"Andrea, will you go get some ice?" she asked with a smile on her face as she wondered what the two were up to.

Andrea did as she was told and went to fetch some ice, while Nicole was still holding Henry firmly in her hand. She looked up into his handsome face and smiled at him. He looked a lot calmer and smiled down at her. Before Nicole had the chance to ask him what had really happened, Andrea returned and Nicole took the ice from her and pressed it down on the tiny tear. Slowly, the piece of flesh she held started losing its volume and the blood dissipated.

"I think you can take over from here," Nicole said with a mysterious smile as she handed him back his penis.

"Thank you," he said shyly, which didn't fit his character, and made the situation even funnier to Nicole. Nicole had to compose herself properly, so she quickly made her way to the bathroom where she dressed and then she went to the living room where she found Dean, who too looked quite sheepish.

Nicole by now was totally sober from all the excitement. She and Dean looked at each other but neither one knew where to begin to start up a conversation, so they both stayed silent. After a few minutes, Andrea and Henry appeared from the bedroom. Henry was fully dressed and looked pressed for time as he restlessly stood at the front door while Andrea asked politely: "Don't you guys want to stay for another drink?"

It was clear Andrea hadn't had enough fun for one day, while poor Henry looked like he wanted to flee the harsh hands of Andrea. Dean sat firmly in his seat as he was still coming to terms with the unworldly pleasure the beautiful stranger opposite him just afforded him.

"I would like that," he answered Andrea eagerly, as he kept his gaze fixed on Nicole. Nicole smiled at him and shook her head.

"No!" Henry said firmly from where he stood in front of the door. "I have to get back to work," he explained quickly as he tried to disguise his need to get out of the house.

"Fine," Andrea said reluctantly and walked over to the door to unlock it for Henry. "I am sorry," she whispered loud enough for Nicole to hear and they hugged.

"It's fine. I will phone you in the week," Henry said as he waved at Nicole over Andrea's shoulder and Nicole nodded at him in acknowledgement.

"Come on, Dean!" Henry called from outside the door, as Dean was still lingering in the living room.

"I am coming," he shouted back, annoyed that he had to leave.

Dean walked over to Nicole and without her offering, he took her one hand and pulled her to her feet and pulled her into a tender embrace. He looked down at her shocked, but amused face.

"Thank you," he said slowly and before she could reply, he planted a firm kiss on her lips before he released her and walked out. He turned at the door for a second to wink at her and then bent over to plant a kiss on Andrea's cheek, where she was standing to hold the door open for him.

"And thank you too," he said with a huge smile on his face. Then Andrea closed the door and a dark shadow covered the place where the sun had just thrown a warm happy hue onto the carpet in the entrance.

Andrea went to sit opposite Nicole in silence and then they spontaneously burst out laughing as they looked at one another.

"What on earth happened in that room?" Nicole asked as their laughter died down.

"Seriously? You don't want to know," Andrea answered before Nicole could.

And she was right, Nicole had had way more excitement than she had bargained for. Andrea stood up and poured herself another drink.

"Andrea, you should probably get dressed, we have to get to work," Nicole said as she looked down at her watch. Nicole was neatly ready to go to work, but Andrea on the other hand, was dressed in an oversized shirt. Andrea was also clearly still intoxicated, but that didn't stop her from downing the drink she had in her hand.

"Fine, now I am ready, I will get dressed," she said as she made her way to her room, but when she reappeared, she wasn't ready at all. Instead of her normal uniform, consisting of blue skirt, button shirt, stockings and blue shoes, she had her dad's oversized field dress on, consisting of pocketed pants, boots and shirt. At that stage in the police, only the men were allowed to where this, except for the women working at special units.

"You cannot go like that," Nicole said, shocked.

"Why not? It is about time we are allowed to wear pants to work," Andrea said feistily.

Nicole wasn't about to pick a fight with Andrea in her condition.

"Maybe you should phone in and book off sick?" Nicole suggested sweetly.

"No, I am fine, let's go," Andrea said and started walking out of the door, leaving Nicole to check that the door was properly locked. The two of them had a good laugh though as they walked to the station and they reflected on the afternoon's excitement.

When they reached the station, Nicole could clearly see how sceptical the rest of the shift was looking at them. Sergeant Laing came in from outside and immediately walked up to Andrea without greeting her and said in a very angry tone: "Andrea, what on earth were you thinking? You are clearly drunk! Go home."

Andrea still wanted to argue, but was overcome with nausea, so she passively let one of the shift members lead her to the patrol vehicle and take her home. Sergeant Laing bent over Nicole and he sniffed her close to her neck and then came up straight.

"I will deal with you later," he said as he took a step back and looked down at her disappointedly. "You will be Charge Office commander tonight and since your colleague couldn't make it to work, you will be alone in the Charge Office."

Nicole obediently took over the Charge Office. Luckily, she hadn't had as much to drink as Andrea, and except for fatigue, could focus enough to do her work properly. Where normally, during night shift, the other members of the shift would constantly make pit stops at the station, this night they purposefully stayed away. As the hours stretched past, the silence of the Charge Office cradled Nicole to sleep. And soon enough Nicole was sound asleep, doubled over on her arms on top of the Incidence Register, with saliva dripping from her open mouth.

"Nicole Burger!" Nicole flew erect as the slamming sound of someone's hand hitting the table right in front of her sounded in her ears, together with the loud deep voice of Sergeant Laing.

"Sleeping on duty, I see?" Sergeant Laing said matter-of-factly.

"Uhm… Uhm…" Nicole hovered, still disorientated from her deep sleep.

"It is okay, I won't tell on you, but your register will…" he said in a snotty voice as he pointed at the smeared ink stains in the Incidence Register, as he started laughing at her.

"Shit!" Nicole blurted out as she hastily looked for a tissue to try and fix the smear she had caused, but nothing could repair the damage, so she was forced to carry on around the smear as best she could. As if the night couldn't get any worse, it did. After the men had left in their vehicles to patrol the area and she was left with her thoughts alone in the charge office, an unmarked police car pulled up to the front of the station. Nicole knew that it would be detectives.

Goddammit! Not now, she thought as she didn't want to explain the mark in the register if the detectives asked about it, since they had to sign it if they brought her a prisoner. Nicole looked down at the mark, while trying to cover it with her one arm so that they might not see it. She was still looking down when a familiar voice spoke to her.

"Hello, I brought something I need to place in the safe," the man said, not really paying much attention to her as he was looking back at his vehicle to check if he had closed his door properly and as he turned back and she looked up, they looked at each other precisely at the same time. They both stared at each other as recognition and shock set in.

Nicole was first to compose herself, although she had no control over the wild beating of her confused heart as she answered: "Mika! Yes, what did you want to book into the safe?" she said as casual as her voice would let her.

"My God, Nicole! Look at you! I mean, what are you doing here?" he composed himself and smiled charmingly at her.

"I asked for a transfer," she said, slightly annoyed by being confronted by his presence and by feeling excited by it.

"You're looking good," he said sincerely.

"What is it you want put in the safe?" She stuck to business as she didn't want to give away how he still made her feel.

"Oh yes, you are right, I brought a firearm. Here," he handed it to her and she took the docket and weapon and wrote it up in the necessary registers before she locked it away in the safe and turned the Incidence Register towards him so that he could sign it. They didn't speak, both of them not knowing where to begin, not wanting to say anything they might regret.

"My word! What happened to the Incidence Register?" Mika asked shocked.

Nicole went bright pink as she remembered what had happened.

"I fell asleep on it," she explained. "I tried to fix it, but I couldn't…" she said softly and he immediately took pity on her.

"Don't worry too much, the Station Commander is a fair guy. When he asks about it, just be honest and say you fell asleep. He will be upset but will understand. Don't try and make too many excuses, he hates that," Mika offered her some advice.

"Are you sure?" she asked, looking vulnerable as she looked up at him.

"Yes, I am," he said as he wanted to hold her, but he knew he couldn't as he was engaged to another and had to keep his distance from her, as she still awakened feelings in him that no other woman could.

"Well, I have to go now, it was nice seeing you again," he said and turned to leave.

"You too…" she said softly and watched him climb into his car and drive away.

The end of the shift couldn't come too soon, and relieved and slightly worried, Nicole made her way home.

The next day, Nicole and Andrea were called into the Station Commander's office. Nicole was extremely nervous, but Andrea seemed to be oblivious to the trouble they found themselves in. There were enough grounds against them for them to be dismissed if found guilty and Nicole couldn't afford it. So as soon as they took their stance in front of the Commander and he asked if they were drunk the previous day when they came to work, Andrea denied it and Nicole admitted drinking before she came to work. Expecting the worst, Nicole hung her head in shame and apologised for her foolishness.

"Nicole, I am very disappointed as this behaviour seems out of character for you, but I respect your honesty. This can never happen again, do you understand me?" he said very firmly.

Nicole looked up at him and made eye contact while she promised to never be so stupid again, and she meant it.

"Then you may leave," he continued. "You, on the other hand, can stay, I haven't finished with you," he said sternly as he addressed Andrea. Nicole left, but was worried about Andrea and what would happen to her. They were both lucky to get off with a slap on the wrist. What Nicole didn't know was that the Station Commander warned Andrea not to pull Nicole into other offences as he knew she was mostly to blame for initiating the previous day's mischief. That wouldn't be the end of it though, as she just couldn't stay out of trouble, but from there on, Nicole didn't participate as much as she liked to witness her colleague's actions.

Andrea, for instance, one evening on night shift in her state of boredom, came up with a game in which Nicole and Andrea were supposed to identify their fellow male colleagues by feeling their genitals while blindfolded. And if it wasn't for Nicole protesting that this would be inappropriate, the game would have taken place as the men were already lined up and ready to participate. On another occasion, when Nicole and Andrea had to book marijuana into the safe, Andrea kept a small amount back, without Nicole noticing, and when she went to the bathroom she emptied her cigarettes and filled it with the marijuana. Needless to say, in her naivety, Nicole didn't suspect anything funny when Andrea asked her to join her for a cigarette in the toilets. Nicole was oblivious to what she was smoking as she hadn't had Andrea's cigarettes before. When they returned to the Charge Office, Nicole was overcome with an inexplicable sense of happiness and later, when two detectives came in to book criminals into their cells, Nicole and Andrea were in hysterics, laughing at everything they said.

Nicole wasn't impressed by her friend though when she came forward with what had happened, knowing that if they were caught out, it would have been difficult, near impossible, to explain that she was innocent in the theft and use of not only narcotics, but the theft of police property and evidence in a criminal case. Andrea's behaviour became not only dangerous to Nicole, but it compromised her image amongst the men on the station, seeing her as equally mischievous as Andrea, and although she loved to have good clean fun, she wasn't at all as wild as her friend.

Their Station Commander did recognise the problem though and asked their shift Sergeant, Sergeant Laing, to post them separately so that Andrea couldn't cause as much trouble. Sergeant Laing, who took a liking to Nicole, didn't mind this at all, as it gave him an excuse to post Nicole with him so that he could keep an eye on her, without his fiancée suspecting anything.

Chapter 18

Although Nicole enjoyed working at Milnerton, she couldn't ignore her gradual realisation that her working environment was all but perfect. When she had asked for her transfer to Milnerton she believed that the corrupt Police Officers were few and far between, but she came to realise that even the supposedly innocent, fell into this category at times, seeing that their attempts at entertaining themselves when they were bored regularly overstepped the boundaries between accepted behaviour and criminal.

Andrea was only one case in point, and although she was seemingly harmless, she had become so desensitised that not only did she do as she pleased, she thought herself above prosecution, since she mistakenly believed she had her comrades protecting her. While this was mostly true, due to the fact that everyone had something on their fellow officers, Nicole would soon enough discover that this attitude also failed to protect one in circumstances when justice needed to be served and no one would be brave enough to take a stance.

Apart from this, there were mentalities in the police force with which she didn't agree. She couldn't understand why black, coloured or Indian races weren't allowed to join the Force as officers, enjoying the medical and pension perks as such, but they were allowed to work with fully fledged officers, serving just as hard and in exactly the same dangerous circumstances as the white-skinned police. It didn't seem fair that the government exploited them in this manner.

She had become quite close to some of the Special Officers and always treated them with the same respect she did all human beings. She even dared to reprimand policemen if they became unnecessarily personal when dealing with "Specials" (the term used for them), which didn't make her too popular amongst most of the true racists in the Force, but she didn't care.

This, of course, earned her a lot of respect amongst the Special Police Officers and when there were special duties to be performed, like visiting the elderly in their vicinity, Nicole was asked to be in charge.

On one such occasion, a few months before the Referendum in 1993, when she was asked to help with visiting the elderly in an informative operation in preparation to the big day, Nicole was faced with a lot of people refusing her companion, a Special Officer of coloured race, entrance to their homes. With each and every one of these people, Nicole refused to set foot in their homes, taking a stance against the ridiculousness of their beliefs.

At first, the "Special" she was working with tried to convince her softly to rather enter the house, as she was supposed to inform the occupants of what the day would entail and also to gather information for the government about the people living in their surroundings. Nicole stubbornly told the owners of these homes: "If my colleague isn't welcome in your home, neither am I."

With which she would turn her back on them, leaving them uninformed and with her silently hoping that they would not vote in the Referendum, as she believed this would make the odds of things changing in South Africa that much stronger. The man who worked with her that day, Jantjies, didn't tell on her; he had gained too much respect for her. He took care not to let her fellow officers know of what had happened that day, but the word spread amongst the rest of the "Specials".

Nicole was later fortunate to work during the Referendum at the voting station at Milnerton Town Hall. The outcome was positive, with the majority voting for an opportunity for all citizens, irrespective of race, to vote for a democratic South Africa. Nicole was excited as this was an opportunity for injustices to be set right. She didn't realise at that point how deep set the hatred had grown amongst the suppressed and how difficult it would be in future for them to forgive and build positively towards a peaceful co-existence.

In her mind, the fact that so many South Africans came together to bring about change during this oppression, should have been proof enough that the racist mentality was in the minority and that change was welcomed. Nicole, who as a result of Apartheid, was isolated from different races, also didn't understand the cultural differences that would lead to reverse racism, under the torch of Affirmative Action from the new governing majority. Most of these new policies, which were to be incorporated into the new legislature, was a positive move towards setting things right, but would be held in place long after the newborns, born to a democratic government, were adults and as such didn't participate in Apartheid, but had to be excluded from work, sport and other opportunities because of their skin colour. Thus, even this excitement of Nicole that things in the police would change for the better would be as short-lived as the first time she heard of young men and women in the minority overlooked for overdue promotions.

During this time of change and before the election of 27 April 1994, which would end so-called Apartheid in South Africa and make it a democratic government, there were other injustices and irregularities in the police force that started to make Nicole doubt if she had made the right choice in joining. On the one hand, she was happy living in Sea Point where she stayed in the Barracks, she was financially independent, she had good friends and she got on with her colleagues. She even enjoyed her work as a police officer, but on the other hand it became apparent how many police officers were corrupt, and the politics involved in the police made it difficult to keep respect for the noble intentions on which the Force was built, but were not being upheld.

As the months drew past, she witnessed how Andrea stole clothes, when she and Andrea had to book the recovered evidence, after a robbery at a local clothing store, into the safe, with Andrea picking out what she wanted and even offering Nicole: "Take what you want, they won't know what has been recovered." And when Nicole didn't want to participate, she was frowned upon by the rest of her shift present in the police office, as if she would compromise their wrongdoing.

Not long after this, she had to witness how the policemen raided a local bottle store. The store was damaged by a fire and the men argued that the store would be insured and as such would be able to claim for damages. Nicole was amazed by their audacity and that they didn't see it as theft, but more so, she was disappointed and disillusioned by their behaviour. Once again, she was faced with coming up with excuses for their behaviour. It was difficult for her to comprehend the extent of wrongdoing that could take place in the police force as she was bound by her morality to innocence and by her naivety to believe they were clueless of the extent of their wrongdoing.

As time progressed, the excuses were more difficult to find as she witnessed unnecessary beatings, colleagues that failed to help protect their fellow policemen in instances of danger, opting to rather save themselves, and prisoners being humiliated without reason. The worst was when Nicole was being humiliated together with a young girl that they had to search for drugs.

It happened on a night shift when Nicole and Sergeant Laing was asked to come to Salt River police station, as they had arrested two youngsters for possible possession of drugs. There were marijuana pips found in their car and seeing that the policemen couldn't find drugs during the car search, they took the young man and his blonde girlfriend to the station. There wasn't a woman on duty that could search the girl and as Nicole was the closest policewoman in the area, they needed her to perform a search. Nicole didn't mind this, but when she came to the station, she was disgusted by the attitude of the men.

They were arrogantly making rude comments about the young pretty girl, who was dressed in jeans and a white vest. It was a chilly night and because she wasn't wearing a bra, one could clearly see her nipples pressing against the thin material of her top, much to the delight of the men. The poor girl tried to fold her arms across her breasts to hide them from the hovering men. When Nicole entered, the men fell silent for a few seconds, taken aback by her beauty.

"What have you brought with you, Laing?" one of them asked arrogantly.

"Guys, this is Constable Burger," he introduced Nicole to the men who grinned at her.

"So you say you will be able to find the drugs?" another asked and laughed robustly. It was clear to Nicole that there was hardly any place for the poor girl to hide anything with the little clothes she had on. The girl's body language also suggested that she was innocent and that she was only unfortunate to have driven with her boyfriend, who clearly had used marijuana at some point in the car. These two were hardly hardened criminals, and Nicole gathered from what was going on that the policemen were merely entertaining themselves with scaring them, as she had witnessed countless times. Nicole thus shook her head in disgust.

"Come on…" The nearest to Nicole started at her as he saw her shake her head. "It should be easy for you to find something on this skinny little body," he continued.

Nicole looked up into his face and slanted her eyes as she had to bite back not to say something to him, as she knew it would only make the situation worse. The best was to play along and get this over with as quickly as possible.

"So where do you want me to search her?" Nicole said as she took the girl's arm in her right hand, meaning that they should direct her to a room where she could body search the girl. One of the men pointed to a search room at the back of the office; Nicole attempted to walk the girl to it, but in passing, Sergeant Laing stopped her with his one monstrous hand and looked seriously down at Nicole.

"I want you to do a full body search. Do you understand?"

He said it with so much authority that Nicole felt threatened by it and she nodded. The rest of the men laughed at hearing this, some even whistled while one uttered: "Ooooooh nice…"

As Nicole turned, she saw Sergeant Laing smiling slyly at the rest of the men in the office.

I am sure you all are having fun, she thought, disgusted at how degrading they were towards her and the girl, so as she entered the dressing room and felt the trembling underneath her touch; she whispered to the girl: "Don't worry, I am not like them."

The girl cautiously smiled at Nicole, too scared to utter a word.

"Okay, I have to search you so that they think I did a proper job. Do you have any drugs on you?" she asked in a gentle voice.

"No, I swear," the girl answered honestly.

"Okay, I know it is cold, but will you please take off your clothes, but you can keep your undies on," Nicole said and the girl did as she was told. Nicole whispered to the girl, "They can see your feet through the opening at the bottom so I need to do this; turn around as if you were bending over." Once again the girl did as she was told while Nicole searched her clothes, but there was no evidence of drugs. She didn't even look at the girl or touch her. The two girls could hear the boisterous laughter as the girl turned her back to Nicole and Nicole knew they thought she was doing an internal search.

Yeah right, I would give you the pleasure, she thought to herself as she turned the girl around with her hands on her shoulders.

"You may get dressed," Nicole said in a very professional voice.

The girl looked at Nicole with a grateful gaze and whispered softly a humble: "Thank you." Nicole winked at her and took her by her arm as she marched her into the Charge Office.

"There was nothing," Nicole announced and pretended to be bored with what had happened while she turned her attention to her pocketbook as she wrote up that she did a body search and that she had found nothing. The men were still smiling though and then the Shift Commander announced that the two detainees could go. Nicole could see the relief on their faces and hated the men for toying with the youngsters' emotions like that.

Incidents like these started to take a toll on Nicole, making it more difficult for her to enjoy her work and making it more and more difficult not to hang out in nightclubs and drown her feelings of guilt and disappointment with herself for not being able to turn her back on what she disapproved of. She always believed that if you didn't do so, you were condoning that of which you were a part, and now she was the one who put up with injustices for the sake of survival. Still, she chose to find excuses not only now for her colleagues, but for herself and at times she wondered for how long she would be able to do so. Clearly, she wasn't the only one who was riding that same boat as one of the girls in the barracks one night drove to Kraaifontein, about 30 kms from Sea Point on the N1, parked her car underneath the bridge and shot herself with her service pistol.

Nicole felt as if she should have been able to prevent it if she had actually taken the time to befriend the woman in the Barracks, as the girl stayed two doors down from her and Nicole argued that if she had befriended the girl, she probably would have been able to help her somehow. So after this happened, she decided to greet whoever passed her in the hall ways and if some of the girls looked like they needed company she would start up a conversation with them.

This would prove to be her saving grace as it would in future be much easier for her to stay true to herself if she could discuss her worries with women in the same circumstances as her. As part of her decision to open herself up to the rest of the world and new opportunities, Nicole made a point of stopping off at Sea Point's Charge Office, which was situated on the ground floor of the building in which the Barracks was housed.

Here, she struck up conversations with the members on duty and soon enough she had made new acquaintances. Nicole became particularly good friends with the detectives and the office personnel. One afternoon as she stopped off for a chat before she went up to her room, no one other than Grete came walking in to the door in her civilian clothes. Nicole jumped off the counter on which she had seated herself.

"Grete!" she shrieked as she ran to greet her friend and hugged her so tightly that Grete started to squirm in-between her arms for some breathing space.

"Nicole! What are you doing here?" Grete asked, surprised to see her friend there.

"I am staying in the Barracks, and you?" Nicole asked, equally curious to know the reason for her presence.

"Me too…" Grete said with a frown on her forehead. "Why haven't I heard about this?"

"I don't know? I have only recently moved in, and you?" Nicole inquired.

"I have been staying here for more than a year, but I spend a lot of time at Eugene's place, maybe that is why I haven't run into you yet?" she smiled and hugged Nicole.

"But I am so happy that you decided to join us!" Grete shrieked at the reality of what Nicole's new living arrangements meant. "I don't really get on with the other girls, but now I have you! This is going to be so much fun," she continued without taking a breath.

"I know!" Nicole hugged Grete back as she too was overcome by excitement for having someone she liked living in such close proximity to her.

It turned out that Grete stayed four rooms down from Nicole and the two started hanging out in Grete's room every chance they got. Nicole preferred her room as she had luxuriously kitted her room out with a fluffy carpet and trinkets, which transformed her room into a luscious den of romance. There were heart-shaped jewellery boxes on her dressing table, pearls and bracelets decorated her large mirror, perfume bottles neatly stacked according to length on a mirrored tray to one side and soft transparent linen decorated her windows. She had ferns planted in pots in her window and Nicole could spend hours on her frilly bedding strewn with flowers in its design.

What fascinated Nicole most about Grete was the amount of sexy lingerie she had organised in her drawer of her dresser. Grete had a petite frame, with large firm breasts, small feet and slender fingers and although she wasn't the most beautiful, her hair was styled in a pixie cut, which not only suited her face, but gave her a doll-like appearance. Grete always groomed herself to perfection and as such created an aura of perfection, which most men couldn't resist. She had constant male visitors, which looked quite disappointed when they found Nicole hanging out in her room.

Since Nicole and Grete started hanging out, Grete's visits to Eugene became less and Nicole started to realise that he was probably just a temporary crutch for Grete, since it was true, the girls didn't like her very much. Not because of her personality, seeing that she was gentle and kind, but because men couldn't resist her and she obviously needed to entertain their affections to make her feel valued.

Nicole felt sorry for her since in her view, this was so far from the truth. Grete was an intelligent woman, with a good heart and all she needed was acceptance, since her own mother had turned her back on her when she was young and had left her to grow up in her grandparents' house.

Grete was at this point just what Nicole needed to turn her back on Andrea's influence, which Nicole tolerated only because of her humanity, which caused her to desperately cling on to her friendship with Andrea, as she was scared of feeling alone. Grete was by far a better suited friend, and although Andrea had left Nicole slightly less naïve and more balanced, Grete, out of envy and appreciation, encouraged Nicole to stay as innocent as their surroundings would let them.

Grete's grooming skills rubbed off on Nicole and before long, Nicole wore perfume to work, blow dried her hair meticulously before going out to work or play and perfected the art of wearing lipstick. Nicole already had a love of beautiful clothing and therefore dressed stylishly, but her lingerie was not up to standard and this was where Grete came in to help with the wise words: "Every day is filled with surprises and you have to be ready." Although Nicole didn't exactly understand the full extent of what she meant, she took the advice to heart and invested in lingerie that would make the strongest of men weak in the knees and beastly somewhere else.

At work, things quieted down enough for her to start enjoying going there again with her new-found perfection and the men at the station noticed. Sergeant Laing in particular subtly started flirting with her, by looking at her appreciatively and making sure she noticed, or by giving her compliments. Some of the other men were less subtle though and made crude comments and suggestions of what they would like to do to her. And although Nicole didn't appreciate the approach, she revelled in the attention. She felt powerful with the confidence that she could toy with whom she wanted if she wanted to. This also made her more appealing to the men as she unknowingly flaunted her confidence through her posture and cheeky attitude. This proved to be too much for Sergeant Laing.

One afternoon when Nicole was posted in the Charge Office, Laing couldn't stop looking at the outlines of the white lacy bra Nicole wore under her powder-blue police-issue shirt. He just sat and stared at her when he and his partner on the patrol vehicle came in to eat lunch. While Andrea was chatting to his partner and the other men were busy with their tasks, he just kept staring at Nicole's chest from where he leaned over the counter in front of her. Nicole didn't notice at first, but there is no denying, when someone stares at you so intensely, one seems to notice.

Nicole felt eyes burning on her and she looked up to see what was making her feel so self-conscious. Then she saw the trance-like gaze of the Laing and she looked down to where he was looking at. She saw that her white bra was ever so subtly shining through the blue material and she smiled, humoured by the sight of it.

"Yes, can I help you, Sergeant?" Nicole asked in a mischievous tone, making her voice melodious enough to linger in the nerve endings of his loins. To her it was all a game, a way of testing her capabilities, nothing serious, and something she felt totally in control of, while trusting that the other gender on which she was testing it was in the palm of her hand and would behave as passively as the sheep like gazes they gave her. She didn't take men's raw passion, which could turn the gentlest of men into a beastly predator if pushed too far, into account, as she hadn't witnessed it before. Laing looked deep into Nicole's eyes before he spoke, without relenting on his fierce gaze. His blue eyes seemed dark through the slants they were pulled in.

"Yes Nicole, you can…" he drew out the words as he said them, as if it took all of his will power to control his voice. Nicole smiled at him knowingly and she slanted her eyes as she analysed his mood.

"How can I help you?" she asked, seemingly innocently.

"How big are those nipples of yours?" he said, stretched out and straight-faced as if they were alone and he was asking her about the weather. Shocked by his forwardness, Nicole's eyes opened up into a deer-like state and she pressed her lips together, not trusting her body with a response. Laing found this very amusing and grinned at her.

Don't play this game with me, little vixen, he thought as he wondered how her breasts looked in its naked splendour.

Nicole, determined not to be outdone, gathered herself as cheekily as only she could, while she lifted her chin stubbornly. "Oh, wouldn't you love to know? Unfortunately for you, you will never know," she said proudly as if she had won the battle and then she turned to her work and fiddled with her pen, hoping he would leave her alone. Laing kept quiet, but vowed and accepted the challenge silently, to find out what he wanted to know.

The following day, their shift was on night shift. Nicole for some reason was once again posted in the Charge Office. She had become accustomed to being posted outside and Andrea in the Charge Office and only once in a blue moon to be posted in the Charge Office, but this was two days in a row. Then she remembered the previous day and thought that her cockiness had probably pocketed her a place in the Charge Office, and with that, she decided not to show her disappointment.

Sergeant Laing ignored Nicole totally and did his duties as he would normally. Nicole pretended not to notice and did the same. Soon she was left alone in the Charge Office with Sergeant Wetzel. She loved working with him as they discussed clothing, his poodles and his flatmate. The minutes flew past like hail pebbles and before they knew it, the shift was nearly over without the rest of the shift checking in.

"They are sleeping soundly tonight," Wetzel said sarcastically, referring to the rest of the shift, when he checked his watch and saw that it was nearly five o' clock in the morning. He stood up to make them coffee when the first patrol vehicle pulled into the yard.

"You spoke too soon…" Nicole said disappointedly.

Sergeant Laing and Andrea were pulling an unruly drunk black woman by her arms into the Charge Office. They pressed her up against the Charge Office counter as they entered the building.

"Book her! I need to wash my hands," Sergeant Laing ordered as he turned to go to the bathroom. Nicole stood up to do as she was told. Firstly, Nicole had to search the woman for any weapons and confiscate shoelaces and valuable articles for safekeeping as this would make the woman vulnerable to attacks in the prison cells. As Nicole neared the woman, the woman started to spit at Nicole.

"Stop it!" Nicole reprimanded the woman. Nicole was by no means an aggressive person and even when she was confronted with violence, she opted to avoid it rather than to retaliate. Therefore, she felt annoyed by the woman's behaviour seeing that it was really inconvenient.

"Fuck you, you stupid white cow!" the woman slurred the words as she tried to spit them out, while swinging her middle finger in Nicole's face and losing her balance in doing so.

Nicole didn't respond to this, other than to look at Andrea and smile at the woman's drunken state.

"Please calm down. We are only booking you because you are drunk so that you can sleep it off," Nicole explained to the woman.

"I am going nowhere with you, fuck you, you fucking fucked up cunt," she said as she grabbed Nicole by the ends of her warm coat. Nicole plucked her coat from the smelly and dirty woman's paws. Then the woman spat on Nicole's coat.

"For fuck sakes! If you will just stop this and give your cooperation, then you can go in for only four hours. Please don't make this difficult for yourself," she warned the woman. Nicole knew that if the woman kept on acting this way, she would have to be forcefully taken to the cells and she didn't know how the men would react when faced with this. Most of the time they would only use necessary force, but sometimes things got out of hand and Nicole had witnessed this more than once, and once was more than enough.

The woman struggled to her feet, swaying as she did so and then before Nicole knew what had hit her, one of the woman's fists did. Nicole was so shocked that she instinctively pushed the woman away from her. The woman in return, spat on her coat again, leaving a slimy green piece of snot dangling from Nicole's coat.

"Fucking stop it!" Nicole shouted at the woman. By now the men and Andrea were watching the standoff between the two women. Sergeant Laing had returned and was comfortably leaning over the counter, amused, as the others were, by the sight in front of him. They all knew that Nicole was passive and seeing her yell was entertaining. She was like a fish out of water, trying to find the right thing to do next.

"Should I help you?" Andrea offered.

"No! Leave her," Sergeant Laing ordered.

Andrea reluctantly stood back as the woman swung another shot at Nicole who was so shocked by the sight of the dangling snot that she barely had enough time to react and flinch out of its way. The woman once again lost her balance and fell to the floor while grabbing on to Nicole's coat and dragging her to the ground with her. The woman ended up on her back with Nicole on top of her in a kneeling position and the woman between her legs. As Nicole looked down at the woman, she saw the woman holding the little golden cross she had worn around her neck, in her one hand. Nicole snapped and without thinking about what she was doing, she wrapped her hands around the woman's neck as the woman shrieked: "No! No! No!" Nicole had no control over her anger as all the emotions she had bottled up during the previous years came flooding out, blinding her with fury. Now she was fighting her own demons and the helpless body dangling from her hands as she hit the woman's head against the wall and she picked her up by her neck, took the brunt of it.

"Nicole! Nicole...Nicole!" the words of Sergeant Laing voice slowly made sense in her mind as she came back to reason. When she finally came out of the darkness and registered her surroundings and her reality, she saw a passed-out woman still clutched in her hands and four men struggling to loosen her grip. The sight made her nauseous with shock and she let go of the woman's neck, letting her fall to the ground. Sergeant Laing was holding her shoulders and turned her around, looking her straight in the eyes.

"Are you okay?" he asked, concerned. Nicole felt sick from guilt and regret that she had had lost control.

"Yes, sorry," she said softly. She was shaking as the other two men crouching next to the woman on the floor brought her to her feet. Luckily, the woman was fine. Still drunk, not seriously hurt, but now slightly more cooperative when asked to walk with Nicole and Andrea to the cells.

As they reached the courtyard to the cells, with the woman between them, holding her on either side by her upper arms, Andrea turned to Nicole and smiled at her as if she was planning something.

"Don't you think this cunt needs to be taught a lesson?" Andrea looked at Nicole as she looked over the woman's head.

"I don't know?" Nicole said, unsure of what she meant. "What do you think?"

"I think she does. The fucking nerve, you were trying to be civil and she started assaulting you for no reason..." she coaxed Nicole to relive her anger.

"Fuck you too, little white-haired rat!" the woman spat her words out into Andrea's face.

"You are right, the fucking nerve!" Nicole agreed, now even more pissed off that the woman actually got her to lose control. Keeping control over her emotions was Nicole's lifeline, the boundary wall between sanity and madness, which she needed to keep intact. This woman reminded her by letting her lose control for a second of how scared she was of crossing that line. Totally in control now, she needed to give outing to this emotion.

Without warning, Andrea took the woman by her wrist and as if telepathically connected, Nicole did the same and without words being exchanged, they started running with the drunken woman, who started yelling as she was pulled off her feet. Her body was dragging behind them as they ran to the opposite wall and when they reached it, they flung her body into it, resulting in the woman screaming: "Fuck you!"

Nicole and Andrea turned and started running again to the wall behind them, crashing the woman's body into the wall. Not hard enough to hurt the woman seriously, but hard enough to cause discomfort and to serve as a reminder that they were in control of her destiny. Without them even knowing it, the aim of this was to force the woman into submission. By the third time they did this, the woman realised that this would continue until she made an effort to stop it.

"Please, I am sorry," she shouted at the two young policewomen, who were now laughing at themselves, as they found the situation extremely comical.

"No, you are not!" Andrea pulled away while Nicole wasn't ready, causing the woman's arms to be stretched.

"Sorry!" Nicole was overcome with laughter and she set off in the same direction as Andrea, while pulling the woman by her arm, but both Nicole and Andrea were now overpowered by laughter and they stopped midway, still holding the confused woman by her wrists.

"Please take me to the cells," the woman pleaded.

"Let's just take her to the cells," Nicole said in-between her laughter. "This is silly."

"I know!" Andrea, still laughing, agreed. They pulled the woman to her feet and she willingly walked in silence to her holding cell where she entered without any resistance.

"Can I still go in four hours' time?" the woman asked politely from the darkness of the cell, but Nicole and Andrea ignored her as they walked to the Charge Office.

Nicole walked away, knowing that she would under normal circumstances not have been able to watch someone being handled in the manner she had just done with the prisoner and regret and shame filled her, but she took care not to show her friend that remorse had overcome her. What she did learn though was that violence was a necessary part of keeping control in situations where your life could be at stake, but vowed she would try not to take advantage of her powers in this manner again.

As days went past and her shift became more relaxed with Nicole's presence and the knowledge that she was to be trusted, they more openly started going about their business. This included skimming small amounts of weed off evidence they gathered when making busts and even smoking it on duty. On some night shifts when things were too quiet for their liking, they openly discussed sex and the girls on the station and inappropriate games, while on duty, continued.

Nicole was becoming accustomed to the desensitised environment she was spending most of her days in and over time, she didn't even listen to the men inappropriately making comments about her body, suggesting that they would like to penetrate her, cop a feel or whatever came up in their heads in her presence. It was only Sergeant Laing who never suggested anything.

This actually worried her as she could see he had a fascination with her, as he kept staring at her during their working hours and when she caught him out he always gave her a distinct eerie smile, as if he wanted her to know that he was waiting for the right moment to take advantage of her. So Nicole steered clear of him as much as possible, but as the days passed by his stares became more intense and the tension of his longing became more apparent to Nicole, until one day on their first shift day.

"Nicole, I think it is time you get to work more in the field. I think you should be on duty with me, and then I can keep an eye on you," Sergeant Laing informed her as he finished inspection. Sergeant Laing didn't ride in a patrol vehicle, like the other members. He was fortunate enough to have use of one of the detective's service vehicles, as the one patrol vehicle was at the workshop. Nicole became nervous, knowing that she would be alone in his presence, but couldn't refuse, so she gathered her things and took her place in the passenger seat. Sergeant Laing didn't take long before he joined her.

They drove for quite a bit with him explaining their surroundings to her. Nicole felt silly for thinking he would do something to her if left alone with her, as he seemed genuinely set on doing his duty and guiding her in her duties outside of the office. In the late afternoon, as their shift was drawing to an end, he announced that he had to pick something up at his house, which was situated in the area they were patrolling. By now Nicole was comfortable in his presence, even enjoying his dry sense of humour and finding him strangely charming. So they set off to his house. His house was a modest three-bedroomed home in Bothasig. It was meticulously taken care of. The house was painted a practical white.

When they pulled into the driveway, a white pit-bull dog came running to the gate to greet them. Nicole stayed seated as she watched him climb out of the vehicle and walk towards the frightening dog that wagged his tail happily as he saw his owner. Laing bent down to rub the well-groomed dog's body and it was obvious the animal meant a great deal to him.

"Come on, Nicole, he won't bite you," Laing said teasingly as he looked back to the car where Nicole still sat in her seat.

"No, it's fine," she said loudly from the open window, "I will stay here."

Laing stood up and turned to her, forgetting about his dog for a moment and looked at her in a stern manner and then relaxed his gaze as a soft unpredictable smile cornered his mouth.

"Come on, Nicole," he insisted. "I will make you some coffee, the dog won't bite and it may take a while," he offered a list of excuses why she shouldn't stay seated in the car.

Since he seemed adamant to have her join him inside, she cautiously climbed out of the car, first standing still so that the dog could first sniff at her heels to make sure she wasn't a threat and as he turned and ran into the house, she slowly followed Laing and his dog.

The house was neatly furnished with old but well taken care of furniture. She thought that he was still very young to have been able to afford a house and all the furnishings on a Sergeant's pay, so she couldn't help herself asking.

"So I see you are well taken care of," she hinted at her curiosity.

"Yes," he said.

"Is this really your house?" she asked cautiously.

"Yes, I inherited it from my parents," he said, looking at Nicole as if he wasn't listening to a word she was saying. This made her feel somewhat uncomfortable, but she continued, trying to take his attentions off her.

"Oh, this must be your parents?" she indicated to the picture of a couple hanging on the wall.

"Yes, they died in a car accident and I am the only child, anything else?" he said, annoyed at the persistent questions about his parents.

"No, I am sorry, I didn't mean to—" Nicole tried to offer her apologies at being so intrusive, but he interrupted her.

"It is fine. It was a long time ago," he said, and she could sense his words and thoughts were not in sync.

"I am going to change into a clean shirt," he said suddenly. "You are welcome to come with if you want," he said as he turned to walk to the bedroom.

Nicole felt uncomfortable and slightly freaked out by him inviting her to his bedroom to change his clothes.

"No, it's fine, I will stay here," she declined his offer and he disappeared into the first doorway. The house fell silent, except for the soft breathing sounds of his dog and the occasional scratching sounds of the animal's nails on the wooden floors. After a short silence, she heard Laing calling her: "Nicole!"

"Yes?" she replied.

"Come here," he invited her.

"No, it's fine, I will stay here," she stood her ground.

"Don't be like this, I want to show you something," he said in a matter-of-fact voice.

Since enough time had elapsed for him to have changed his shirt, Nicole thought that he probably wanted to show her some memorabilia of some sorts, so she walked to the room where she had seen him enter previously.

The sun was warmly shining into the room. There was a neatly covered double bed in the middle of the room and as Nicole came around the corner of the doorway, she saw Laing in white underwear and his police socks in front of his open cupboard, as if he was still getting changed, but he turned to her as she entered the room. This allowed her to get a perfectly full view of his naked body. He was nearly as white as his hair and although he wasn't especially out of shape, he was sprouting a small rounded stomach from beer drinking. In that instant, Nicole turned in her tracks and excused herself.

"I am so sorry, I thought—" but she couldn't finish before he had her by her wrist in his warm grip.

"No, don't feel uncomfortable," he said calmly. "I don't mind, please stay." Nicole kept her head turned away from him and pulled her arm from his soft but firm grip, which he allowed.

"I will wait for you in the car," Nicole said adamantly, now understanding what his intentions were. She understood that he wanted to create a situation where they could be intimate if she wanted to and was grateful that he wasn't going to force her to do so.

It took a few minutes before he came to join her in the car and before he started the car, he explained: "Sorry if I made you feel uncomfortable, I just thought..." but he couldn't continue and wanted her to save him from his embarrassment and she felt sorry for him.

"It's okay, I shouldn't have walked in on you like that," she offered an explanation for the both of them and he gently smiled at her before he drove back to the station.

The following days, she was posted in the vehicle with Laing and he behaved himself, with them actually having to work quite a bit as the week turned into a busy one. On the last evening, she was posted with him again. She could sense that his infatuation with her had not watered down as his gazes were plentiful, but she chose to ignore it and acted oblivious to it. This seemed to work best, but unbeknownst to her this attitude only frustrated him more and so on the last shift, as they were working night shift, he made an unusually huge effort at being funny and charming.

For him, this didn't come naturally as his serious nature was always written on his face. He hardly ever smiled and when he did it seemed unnatural and forced, but on this night, it actually looked as if he was in a pleasant mood, with constant smiles appearing easily. Nicole was once again posted as his passenger. The whole shift passed without any particularly interesting incident. Laing patrolled the area, as they should when not attending complaints.

Although Nicole felt somewhat sleepy, she wasn't so tired that she couldn't stay awake, but when Sergeant Laing suggested that they should go park somewhere and take a short cat nap, she was grateful. They reached a stretch of unscathed beach in Milnerton, where they could park without drawing attention to them and Laing parked the car pointed in the direction of the sea. It was chilly and Nicole had her thick police coat on over her normal uniform. Nicole adjusted her seat into a lying position and made herself comfortable. Laing stayed seated and Nicole became confused as he was the one who had suggested they sleep.

"Aren't you going to sleep?" Nicole asked curiously.

"No, not yet, but you can sleep; I am going to smoke a cigarette first," he said and opened his window while he lit a cigarette.

Suit yourself, Nicole thought to herself as she lay back in her seat with her head turned to her window. Sleep overcame her quickly and soon she was breathing slowly and deeply.

Sergeant Laing was still awake and watched Nicole. She was beautiful. Little strands of silky hair were framing her face and her full lips looked soft and inviting. He imagined what it would feel like to place his mouth over it while intruding her lips with his tongue. It took all his willpower not to bend over and do just that. Then he looked at her long dark lashes, making her face look delicate and soft. He sighed and watched her breathing peacefully. Nicole looked especially serene when she slept.

Laing could see himself waking up next to this beautiful creature after a long night of passionate love-making. He longed to own her, to possess her body and fill her with his uncontrollable raw passion. His eyes glided over her torso that gently lifted and fell back as she breathed in the humid air in the car. Then he remembered the sight of her nipples standing erect in her police uniform, shining through ever so slightly, but enough to make him aware of just how perky they were. He longed to touch them and feel the warmth of the soft skin on her breasts in the palms of his hands.

As if in a trance, his hands moved forward, and he unbuttoned the large button of Nicole's overcoat. It came undone easily without Nicole even moving. Nicole's hands had dropped down next to her body, since she was now sleeping soundly. Laing saw the powder blue material of her blouse peeping through the opening invitingly and his hands slowly, taking care not to wake Nicole, softly pulled at the small buttons of her blouse. His large hands skilfully undid her buttons and quickly pulled away to make sure she didn't feel him doing what he had done.

Nicole didn't move, so Laing sighed a sigh of relief before he slowly, with one hand, lifted the edge of Nicole's blouse as far as it would shift so that he could peer in under her clothes. Laing felt the uncomfortable swelling in his pants. It was painfully hard and the tip leaked moisture. Laing shifted in a more comfortable position and as he adjusted himself, he kept looking at Nicole. At first it nearly looked as if she was bare-chested since she had a thin tan-coloured silk bra on. It took a double take before he realised that she had a bra on, but the thought of her bare chest made his arousal worse. He bent slightly over her and then he softly slid his hand into Nicole's blouse, taking care not to touch her, but as his hand disappeared into her shirt, he felt her hard nipple rub softly against the palm of his hand.

Fuck, he swore in his mind, scared that he had woken her, aroused by the touch of her flesh. Nicole gave a soft sigh after she drew in a large amount of air, forcing her breast up into the palm of his hand and pressing the warm skin of it firmly against it. Laing froze, but Nicole only moaned lightly before she fell back into a pattern of deep breathing. Laing quickly pulled his hand from Nicole's shirt, having felt what he wanted to. He now knew her breast would fill his palm and her nipples were small. He felt somewhat elated by the fact that he had managed to touch her, but also frustrated by the fact that he would probably never be able to touch those firm breasts with Nicole's permission.

He looked at her again as she lay peacefully asleep. She stirred a little, sending him into panic mode realising he would have to explain her unbuttoned blouse and coat if he didn't fix it, so as soon as she lay still, he ever so carefully buttoned her coat. He didn't even try to button up her blouse as the buttons were too small and he thought that she wouldn't find it funny if one of her blouse buttons came undone. Laing now desperately needed some sort of release and started the car to get back to the station. Nicole arose from the moving car. "Why didn't you wake me?" she asked, still groggy.

"I would have as soon as we got to the station," he explained casually, his face stiffly back to the one she was used to.

At the station, Sergeant Laing made his way to the toilets, which didn't seem strange, but he couldn't reach a cubicle fast enough to take his penis in his hand, which still tingled from touching Nicole, and he plucked at it furiously until he spilled his frustration over his hand.

Nicole on the other hand also went to the ladies rooms to freshen up and in the cubicle as she went to sit on the toilet, her coat popped open over her breast area and at first, she didn't think much of it, until she was finished and stood up. She placed her hands on the unbuttoned button only to find two buttons directly underneath the open part of her coat also undone. Instinctively, Nicole slid her hand into her blouse and realised that it wasn't coincidence that her blouse and coat had been unbuttoned. It all made sense.

The bastard! she cursed to herself as she buttoned her blouse and coat. Nicole knew there wasn't a lot she could do about it as she too wasn't supposed to have been asleep on duty and therefore decided not to confront Laing, but also vowed not to trust him in future. And once again, like so many times before, something that actually needed attention was ignored and buried in a case full of unresolved emotions of injustices. By now, without her realising it, the weight of these issues was starting to weigh her down, like so many of her colleagues. Eventually the weight would get too heavy to bear, but Nicole was surprisingly strong, and her survival instincts forced her to ignore it and push forward. It would take something seriously traumatic to get her to throw in the towel and admit defeat. So she brushed it off as something trivial.

As she came out of the lady's toilets, she passed Laing and before she could stop herself, the word left her mouth: "Happy?"

"Uhm…yes," Laing looked down into her eyes with a smile lingering at the corners of his mouth, as if he thought she was a willing participant. Nicole gave him a look of pity and then smiled at him softly, while thinking to herself: *Well, that would be the last you ever get that close to me again.*

And as if she had wished it upon him, soon enough he was taken of her shift. She wasn't sure if he had asked to be moved or if he was just placed on another shift. Nicole wasn't at all disappointed about this turn of events, because Ava and Ben were placed on her shift. Ben, as shift commander, and Ava replaced Andrea's presence. Now Nicole would not only be kept from getting into trouble with Andrea, but she would not have to deal with Laing's advances.

This didn't mean that there wouldn't be incidents where Nicole had to make difficult choices and fend for herself, as she was still surrounded by policemen and women. Nicole felt alienated and struggled to see herself as part of the family, as she had problems with simply accepting the lifestyle and taking part in it, without questioning the normality of it.

Soon after the Laing incident, she witnessed, at a shift barbeque, how a married man and Andrea disappeared into a bedroom and had sex, without anyone thinking it strange and they even joked about what was going on behind the doors. Nicole also witnessed how they lied to his wife when she phoned to check up on him, saying that he was in the toilet and that he'll get back to her. She also realised that if she didn't have such strong moral values, how she would become one of these "government mattresses" as the men described the policewomen.

She sat at the BBQ watching the men and women around her and she realised she never wanted to become like them. At first, she had thought it a wise decision to join the Force as it had the image and promise of a morally strong union of men and women wanting to uphold justice and she felt that she would be part of something great and also be taken care of financially for her commitment. But now all she saw was people so caught up in their own drama, they had created themselves, as they as the law enforcers had falsely put themselves above the law by manipulation. It was like a black hole; when you first enter its mouth, you are consumed by it and it will spit you out into an abyss of nothingness, leaving your soul empty. Everything became quite clear in that moment.

Nicole was standing on the brink of joining them in the madness of what they all had become. She wasn't prepared to take that step. Instead from that moment on she would try to distance her from the life as far as possible. She would wait for that magic moment that she would be able to leave this world behind. She had to believe that someday such an opportunity would present itself, otherwise depression would swallow her, like it already had all those who had thrown all morality overboard. Nicole placed her beer on the table close to her and excused herself and returned to the solitude of her Barracks room.

The next few days, Nicole started scoping the papers for work she would qualify for. She phoned for shop assistant work and sales rep, etc. None of these people could firstly even understand why she would want to leave the police force and secondly, not one of them could offer her the salary package she was earning. She also decided not to hang out with the rest of the policemen and women anymore, as there seemed to always be some sort of situation she had to witness and stay quiet about, while all she wanted to do was scream from the top of her lungs about how wrong it was.

Nicole managed to hide her discontent with her peers well and her wanting to leave the Force in order to pass through every day without disruption. Eventually, Nicole thought she had actually found a balance in how to deal with working as a police officer and to live a normal civilian life outside of work, by opting not to mingle with them.

Chapter 19

In distancing oneself from one's surroundings, stepping back and observing, affords' one the time to get perspective on where you're really at. This was true for Nicole in the following months since Nicole had slowly started distancing herself from her peers in order not to be confronted with her morality daily. She not only saw the men and women on her station for who they were, but realised that she had little in common with most of her colleagues. She was groomed for greater things and her upbringing lent a certain finesse to her being, which sorely stood out in her surroundings. Her need to mingle with people of her own liking became greater than the need not to be alone and as such she developed a maturity and sensitivity in noticing like-minded people it opened her up to discover new friendships beyond the borders of the police force.

One of the civilian personnel at their station had become quite close to her, since Nicole decided to distance herself from her colleagues. The woman was in her mid-thirties, divorced and also kept more to herself, as she too had seen the light. She had observed Nicole during the time she started working at Milnerton and saw similarities in Nicole that made her protective over Nicole. They regularly had contact seeing that she was one of the administrative ladies and chats at work, in passing by, quickly flourished into long conversations about life and what they wanted out of it, with Nicole confiding in her that she was extremely unhappy and lonely in the Force and that she wanted to get out.

Cookie, as the woman was called by the station personnel, soon took a supportive role in Nicole's life. And as the friendship grew, Nicole spent more time at Cookie's house. Soon enough Nicole didn't feel so lonely anymore and Nicole and Cookie (Chantelle) spent a lot of time together. Since Chantelle was also a reservist, she started working night shifts with Nicole. Nicole was actually beginning to think that she could make her situation work for her.

But unfortunately, even if and when you decide to steer clear of the wrongdoings of your peers, if you are in the middle of it, it will find a way to touch you in ways you cannot fathom. And so, on the day of Nicole's twenty-second birthday, Chantelle came to pick Nicole up for a fun-filled evening of dancing at the local dance club, where a lot of policemen also got together. Nicole was dressed in a jean and sheer blouse and sandals. She dressed comfortably, intending to dance the night away with any stranger that was willing to spin her through the night. As they reached the club, Chantelle and Nicole went to sit at the bar, where Chantelle ordered champagne so that they could toast Nicole's birthday before they hit the dance floor.

Music filled the air and the rhythms whispered soft promises of magical opportunities locked away in the misty coloured lighting that echoed the music in the darkness. Nicole looked over to the dance floor as she was mesmerised by the dancers swaying in sync with the music. This was her escape from reality, where she could feel beautiful, free of her uniform and her duties, free from her worries, free from whom she had become and here she could transform into who she wanted to be, a soul making decisions that suited her. Her being not governed by the immoral and injustice service she was serving. And although she wasn't precisely sure yet of who that was, she knew the young woman she felt most comfortable with was the one she was when she could stand up to injustice and respect her fellow men.

Here she had the chance to dance with men from all walks of life and pretend not to be in the Force. It became all the more difficult for Nicole to be honest when confronted by strangers when having to say where she worked. These outings also gave her the opportunity to enjoy the attention of men wanting more from life than a government salary and the crude behaviour of most of them had been infected with. It gave her hope of meeting someone who would literally sweep her off her feet.

"Nicole," Chantelle took her arm to get her attention.

"Oh sorry…I was daydreaming again," she laughed. When Nicole turned her attention back to the bar, the barman had placed an opened bottle of bubbly in front of her and Chantelle was holding two filled flute glasses, as was the barman.

"On the house…" he announced. "Happy birthday, dear girl," he said, winking at her as all three of them toasted Nicole's birthday. Nicole took a sip, as did Chantelle, while the barman downed the whole glass as if it was but a mere mouthful. Nicole watched in amusement as the sparkling wine flowed down his thick throat with ease.

"Come on, ladies…" he encouraged them to do the same. The two of them looked at each other and laughed. Nicole shrugged her shoulders and started downing her drink, as did Chantelle, but it took them a few gulps to do so. And as they placed their glassed back on the counter, the barman eagerly filled them up again. Chantelle was quick to take the bottle from him and her glass, while standing up.

"Let's go find somewhere to sit," she suggested before they would be ordered to down another glass.

The two of them found an open table at the back of the dance floor and they both sat down to watch the dance floor and to sip on their sparkling wine.

"I can't believe he gave us a bottle for free," Nicole said.

"I think there is a lot more he'd give you for free, if you'd let him," Chantelle said and they both burst out laughing.

"Do you mind if I butt in?" a very attractive young man interrupted their conversation, as he held his hand out to Nicole.

"Yes, of course…" Nicole nodded friendly into his face as she agreed to dance with him. As she stood up, she passed her handbag to Chantelle and Chantelle placed it underneath her chair. Nicole fell into the steps of following as if their bodies were bound by the music. The two of them didn't speak, they only flowed in unison over the floor in circles of pleasure. Faces flew by as he effortlessly spun her around and pulled her back against his hard body. For a second, she recognised one of the faces as Griffin's, but she couldn't be sure and didn't care as she gave over to his skilful lead. It was magical.

Soon enough, she excused herself as she not only wanted to check up on her friend, but needed a break from the exertion. Nicole came back to an empty table. Her glass was waiting for her so she took a seat and sipped on her glass of sparkly while watching the dancers. She had hardly placed her empty glass back on the table when another young man stood in front of her with his hand stretched out to her, a big friendly smile indicating his eagerness to dance with her. Without hesitation, she came to her feet and joined him. Once again, another skilful lead took her on a pleasurable spin around the dance floor.

It must be my lucky night… Nicole thought to herself as she danced with the young man and let him sweep her lightly over the floor. As they spun around and around, Nicole's head started turning as well. And before she could even register what was going on, a sickness overtook her body, the likes which she had never experienced before. She came to an abrupt halt while holding her hand in front of her mouth.

"I am sorry…" she managed to get out and struggled her way through the crowd to the ladies bathrooms. Nicole managed to reach the first cubicle and close the door behind her before she emptied her stomach into the toilet and then everything went black. Nicole fell into darkness, with no consciousness, feeling or thought.

When she finally found a glimpse of consciousness, she felt her limp body being carried by more than one man's hands. There was no registration of whom, where or when and she fell back into darkness only to hear: "I know her. I will take her home."

Nicole came to. She was naked. Spread out in a bathtub she didn't know. She sat up straight. The water was warm and soothing. She pulled her legs up against her chest and folded her arms around them protectively. She couldn't think. Nicole's mind felt numbed. She didn't have the capacity to question anything. Nicole barely existed. Then a dark-haired man came into the bathroom.

"How are you feeling now?" he asked.

"Where am I?" Nicole asked as she struggled to lift her heavy head to look at the stranger. The stranger wasn't so strange when she looked into the face of Griffin. He smiled at her.

"Oh my God! What am I doing here?" she asked, slightly relieved that it wasn't a total stranger and trusting that she was in safe hands.

"You passed out so I brought you to my flat and you puked on yourself, so I thought I should at least wash you before I put you to bed," he tried to set her at ease and to explain why she was naked in his bathtub. And although it all seemed quite logical in her numbed state, she couldn't focus any longer as projectile black vomit spurted from deep within her and she only just managed to turn her head to empty her stomach contents into the water in front of her. For a split second, she thought it strange that she vomited black, as she only had two glasses of sparkling wine and nothing to eat that would remotely cause her to vomit black, before her body fell limp and Griffin caught her and pulled her from the bath with his powerful body.

While he was wrapping her in the towel, she was limply lying against his body; she came to for a second and managed to say: "Thank you," before darkness fell upon her again.

Slow powerful motions brought Nicole around. It was dark and Nicole, in her confusion, looked around to assess what was going on. Nicole didn't feel her body, it was numb and she couldn't move a muscle. She was lying on her back in a double bed. The room seemed huge. Everything in the room was dark and it was difficult to make out what was going on, as there were no lights shining and the curtains were drawn. Nicole was still naked and then she realised there was a man between her legs, holding himself up with his arms.

He was moving profusely, rocking her immobile body and then collapsed on top of her, out of breath, and then she gave into the darkness. Nicole woke a second time during the night, with the same man opening her legs and penetrating her easily. Still unable to move and her need to give in to her unconsciousness; she closed her eyes and drifted away to a state of non-existence.

Nicole opened her eyes to find a bright sunny day coaxing her to get out of bed. Nicole felt peaceful and well rested as she stretched her arms out over her head while closing her eyes at the sheer enjoyment of the relaxed state she was in. The covers fell off her as she did so, to expose her perfectly formed firm breasts and she looked down at them in admiration. She cupped them while smiling, taking pleasure in being blessed with their presence. As her warm skin filled her palms, it registered: *I am naked.*

What the hell? Panic filled her as she thought to herself, while pulling the covers to her chin to cover her naked body. Nicole looked around. Then she slowly remembered bits of the previous night. She was totally confused. She was still in the same room, the curtains were only pulled open now and it was morning, or so she thought.

"Oh dear God, please let this be a dream…" she hoped, but knew it not to be true.

Then she heard footsteps coming closer. She braced herself as the person's footsteps slowed in entering the room.

"Griffin…" her brain registered as he looked at her, without a recognisable emotion on his face. They stood there staring at each other, weighing up each other and planning their next move.

Griffin was first to react; "Did you sleep well?" he asked calmly as if nothing had happened the night before. Nicole's heart raced while she tried to stay focussed on seeming as calm as he did.

"Yes, urghm..." she had to clear her throat as her voice wavered. "Yes, thank you," she said in a steady voice while forcing a smile in his direction. Relieved that she seemed not to remember the night before, Griffin turned with a sigh.

"Well, let's get some coffee in you, my dad will be here shortly to take you home. I would offer, but I have to get to work," he said and disappeared.

Nicole shook her head in disbelief as her head filled with questions. *Did I participate? How the hell did I get so sick? Where is my handbag? Oh flip, my clothes?* and as she thought this, she saw her clothes neatly folded, washed, tumble-dried and stacked on the dresser next to her. *Odd...* she thought as she got up and started dressing as fast as her body would let her. *Where did he get the time?*

When she entered the living room, a cup of coffee stood ready on the coffee table and Griffin sat in the messy blanket-strewn evidence that he had slept in the living room on his couch. *Odd...* it rang in her head. Something was amiss. *Why would he sleep there if we had sex?* She frowned. She took a cigarette from him and lit it. He didn't say a word, he just sat there and looked at her. The silence was uncomfortable, and she inhaled the smoke of the cigarette as if she was gathering courage from it. She was halfway through her cigarette when the doorbell rang.

"My father!" he exclaimed, relieved fand jumped up to open the door for Nicole as if he wanted to get rid of her. *You raped me!* The icy truth spilled over her spine and every muscle in her body pulled stiff as she realised what had happened. Nicole, still in shock and disbelief, killed her cigarette with aggravated force and followed him sheepishly as she didn't know what else to do. Her head was full of questions, resentment, anger and regret. As they neared the car waiting in the driveway in front of the block of apartments, Nicole wanted to confront him, but before she could open her mouth, a grey-haired man in uniform climbed out to open the door for her.

"This is my father, he will take you home," Griffin said grimly as his father's scornful eyes fell on him. From the tense pulled lips of his father's face, Nicole not only knew that his father was aware of what had happened, but that he was here to bail his son out. He wore the brilliantly golden buttons of a Colonel. Those tiny buttons not only meant that Nicole was doomed to silence, it also meant that she had to salute the man helping Griffin get rid of his problem—Nicole.

"Morning Colonel," Nicole saluted him as painfully proper as was expected from her for being of lesser rank.

"Morning," he said in a gentle voice. She climbed into the opened door of his car and sat silently as he drove her to the station where she worked, without her having to say where she did. When he came to a halt in front of the station and she opened the door to exit her predicament, he grabbed her wrist softly.

"Are you okay?" he asked softly, as if he truly cared.

"Yes," she frowned and pulled herself free. "Thank you for the lift," she said hastily as she turned and made her way into the station.

The hallway to Chantelle's office was way longer than she remembered and when she entered it and saw Chantelle's worried face when entering, Nicole broke down.

"Oh my God!" Chantelle said softly and embraced Nicole. "Where were you? I was so worried about you."

"I am fine," Nicole spoke spontaneously, used to the unusual being the usual and knowing that there where she found herself, in that moment, she had to be okay.

"No, something happened!" Chantelle demanded.

"Don't worry," Nicole tried to calm her friend as she pulled away and wiped the tears from her face. "I am just frustrated. It is useless…"

"What do you mean?" Chantelle demanded again, while guiding Nicole into the stability of the nearest chair.

"Oh God! Chantelle, I cannot do this anymore. I don't belong here! I just don't," Nicole said, still overwhelmed by the reality of her situation. Chantelle brought Nicole some coffee and offered her a cigarette as Nicole continued to tell her what had happened the night before. Chantelle sat perfectly still, not interrupting and when Nicole had finally finished her recalling of the previous night's events, Chantelle sighed.

"You have been raped, Nicole," she only confirmed what Nicole already knew. "And you were drugged, bloody bastard." Up until this point, Nicole never even suspected as much, but Chantelle told her about a similar situation at a party where policemen spiked her drink as well and where she was raped by four policemen. Nicole sat in disbelief. "How on earth do they find it acceptable to do this and why do they get away with this?" Nicole asked.

"Well, they stick together and four against one, the odds of anyone believing that the victim was not actually drunk and participating..." she stopped and shook her head.

"Enough of that are, you okay though?" she asked caringly. "Did you get hurt?" Chantelle asked carefully.

Well, that depends on what you mean, she thought to herself, but answered: "No, I don't think so."

"Okay," Chantelle said, relieved, and took charge of a situation Nicole clearly had no idea how to handle. "Let's get you home so that you can take a shower. I still have your purse with me. When you are calm, we can decide what needs to be done," she said in a motherly voice.

On her way home, Nicole sat silently next to Chantelle while the previous night milled over in her head. Nicole got angry, a type of anger at the injustice of her situation that she had never felt before and all the anger of her parents' choices that had forced her to make choices that placed her here in this situation. The anger of being vulnerable and having to guard against the very people she thought were trustworthy, as they were to uphold law and order. Angry that the system allowed for men to make and break as they please and still get away with it.

"I cannot do this anymore..." it came out softly, while her anger grew.

"You are just upset, Nicole, don't make hasty decisions," Chantelle said.

"Don't worry, I won't," Nicole assured her, but knew that she had already decided that she needed to get out. In that moment, she emotionally cut off from anyone associated with the Force. She didn't trust anyone and she knew it was useless to make a scene of what had happened. She would be the one that would pull on the short end of this and she wasn't prepared to place that on her shoulders too. She was going to cut her losses and move on, she only had to figure out how.

While the warm soothing water of the shower washed over her body, her mind wandered to her father. She had no choice but to allow him into her life and ask for help.

With her naked body still wrapped in a towel, she reached for the phone.

"Hello, my sweet child..." she heard the warm and gentle voice of her father. "I thought I would never hear from you..." he said in a grateful voice that his daughter had finally made contact with him.

"I am so sorry, daddy...I am so sorry for judging..." and she started crying. Nicole and her father continued to have a very open conversation about what had happened the night before and how she couldn't continue her service as a policewoman. She needed to get out.

Her father listened intently and then simply said: "Well then, you need to resign. I will take care of you."

Nicole placed the phone down and immediately started dialling the police station's number and asked to speak with the Station Commander.

"I would like to resign, effective immediately," Nicole said with the authority of her father backing her. With every attempt to convince Nicole otherwise, Nicole replied with a firm "NO" and when asked why, she simply replied: "I don't want to do this anymore."

"Fine, if I cannot convince you, I will put the paperwork through, but you will have to go to Head Office to finalise the resignation," her commander said eventually.

Formalities, but I don't have to face them again... Nicole thought as she sighed, and she turned to go pack the few belongings she had. The phone rang soon afterwards and the Station Commander informed her that she needed to see the Commanding Officer at Head office that afternoon as he was the only one who could grant her an immediate resignation. So, at three o clock that afternoon, she stood in front of his secretary in full uniform, filled with the resentment and the determined calmness of a prosecutor about to put injustice to an end.

"Constable, you may go through," the secretary ushered Nicole into the Commander's office. As Nicole entered, she was shocked to stare into the face of Griffin's father.

They stood there in silence for a minute and Nicole thought she spotted a slight glimpse of sympathy from him. Before she could say anything, he started talking.

"Nicole, I know you feel you have to resign, but you really don't have to. I can organise a transfer immediately, and then you don't have to resign. I know your father stays in Pretoria, would you like me to transfer you there?" he said in a gentle voice.

It took all of Nicole's strength to stay focussed and calm. "No, I would like to resign, I am sure of it," she said firmly and with a sigh, Griffin's father handed her the papers she needed to sign.

While she walked to the table to take her stance next to him, she realised that she had it all wrong. No one could control her destiny, nor could they be responsible for her happiness. By taking charge of her life and saying no to that which caused her emotional turmoil, she could be free, as free as her parents were by cutting the pain from their lives and choosing life.

You can, after all, only really live without shackles and, in this case, manmade rules that protect the unjust under the guise of justice. As she drew the final line on the paper, her path in the police force ended as abruptly as it had started and she felt defeated, defeated by the injustice, but knew that the justice lay within her freedom. Defeat is prolonged only as long as you choose to be defeated.

The End